AMARANTOX

Prequel to the Botanicaust Series

TAM LINSEY

A Production of
Twin Leaf

Press

Print Version

ISBN:978-0-9859013-9-4

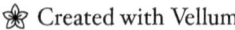 Created with Vellum

Foreword

This is the story of one woman's experience during an ecological apocalypse. In the real world, such changes would take years to occur: a slowpocalypse. For the sake of this tale, I've taken license and forced the event into a shorter timeline. Please indulge my imaginings and enjoy the story...

Part One

amaranth (noun)

1. Plants of the genus *Amaranthus*, including weeds, ornamentals, and species cultivated for their edible leaves and seeds.

2. Edible seeds from plants of the *Amaranthus* genus.

3. An imaginary flower that never fades.

Chapter One

JANUARY

The Tox didn't start with a plant. Or a seed. Or even a gene.
The Tox started with an idea.
~ THE HISTORIES

The murky gleam of a full moon reflected off the dark greenhouse roof as Jaide crept across the circle of bare earth surrounding it. Ahead of her, Trevor's shadow halted with a hand up. After a pause, he dropped to his belly against the icy ground. She mimicked the action, her heavy daypack slamming against her spine. Her heartbeat rattled against her ribs. The brim of the baseball cap she wore to hide her face from cameras blocked her view of the greenhouse, so all she could see was the gated lane. To her right, Cindy panted as though she'd just sprinted a mile, gulping and gasping for breath.

An engine rumbled from the greenhouse parking lot. Headlights winked on, casting shadows across the rocky soil.

3

She pressed her cheek against the frigid dirt and held her breath, willing herself to be one with the Earth.

The car backed up then proceeded down the lane toward Lafayette. Jaide exhaled a foggy sigh.

Once the sound of the engine had faded, Trevor rose and began his skulk toward the greenhouse again. Jaide scrambled to her feet, fingers and toes numb from lying flat against the January soil. The one-gallon can of gasoline in her pack seemed to weigh fifty pounds, but the real powerhouse for tonight lay against her thigh in the pocket of her jeans—a flash drive loaded with Trevor's computer virus.

She reached the side of the building right behind Trevor, core trembling with cold. He pulled his cordless Dremel out of his pocket. A high-pitched whine filled the air as he started to cut through the polycarbonate wall. After only a minute, he pulled a section of panel free and ducked inside.

Jaide crawled in next. Humid air, thick with the scent of soil and greenery, buffeted her face with warmth. The low drone of the circulation fans vibrated in her ears, and potted plants made shaggy shadows in the moonlight.

"I'll find the climate controls," said Trevor in a low voice. "You two look for the offices and lab equipment."

"Do you think any of these plants are dangerous?" asked Cindy, holding back against the wall.

"Nah," said Trevor. "This is only a level one bio-safety facility. Otherwise there'd be more guards. TelomerGen's probably just testing herbicide resistance so they can sell more poisons."

"So there's poison on the plants?"

"Jesus, Cindy." Trevor shoved a pair of wire cutters at her. "If you're so worried, you find the climate controls and cut the wires. I'll handle the lab equipment."

Cindy held up her gloved hands, refusing the tool. "I'm just having second thoughts about what I'm getting into."

Jaide took Cindy's hand and gave it a reassuring squeeze despite her own misgivings about this operation. But someone had to do something to stop corporations from shoving genetically modified food down humanity's throat. Soon there'd be no options left for those wanting to eat as nature intended. "This is for the future." Jaide thought of Flora, her eleven-year-old, asleep in her bed back home. "We're protecting our children's children's children."

"I don't have kids."

Many members of the Coalition never planned to add to the human population problem. At seventeen, Jaide hadn't known better. But she'd never regretted it. "Every animal and plant is one of Earth's children—one of our children—don't you think?"

Cindy nodded, and Jaide let go.

Trevor shoved the wire cutters at Cindy. "I saw some ripple vents on the exterior to the left. Go see if the controls are on the inside over there. Jaide, you search the side rooms. I'll go right and circle back toward you, okay?"

Jaide set out to find a computer terminal, sliding her feet along the concrete in the dark. Flashlights would be too easily spotted through the glass walls. She was careful to avoid touching the stainless steel tables or the Frankenstein plants on either side of her. Corporations like TelomerGen claimed they were using genetic modification to end world hunger. In reality, they were adding to it by taking away self-sufficiency; farmers weren't allowed to save their own seeds, or even worse, the modified seed would be sterile. Corporations wanted to put a patent on life.

If she could, she'd torch this entire facility. But she'd only brought enough gas to damage the computers and other hardware. The fire was to be a decoy anyway; the real damage would be done by the virus, corrupting the research so TelomerGen couldn't repeat this particular atrocity any time soon. Hopefully the infection would make it all the way to their back-up servers before their IT discovered it. Once the climate controls were out of commission, winter would take care of the plants themselves.

She reached the end of the row and squinted toward the far wall. Two doors led presumably to the offices, lab, and staff rooms. On her right, Trevor's feet scuffed against the paved floor. She tried the door on her left.

Locked.

Dropping to a squat, she fished in her pocket for the tiny flashlight she'd brought for just this event. The bulb was red, so it was less likely to be noticed by someone observing the facility. Standard doorknob, no deadlock. She retrieved her tension wrench, inserted it and the rake, then jiggled until she heard the pins drop.

Thank you, YouTube.

Twisting the handle, she pushed. The door swished open. A scent like wet pennies greeted her as she slipped inside. From large pots on the concrete, foliage reached toward the ceiling in graceful arches. Taking a chance, she shone her light upwards, curious. Atop the high stalks hung bags covering seedpods or flowers—she wasn't sure which. They reminded her of heads held upright in a hangman's noose. A shiver raced down her spine as she recognized the leaves. Amaranth, one of her go-to foods. These were freakishly tall from whatever DNA the scientists had inserted.

The need to eradicate these Frankenstein plants burned through her veins. *Not yet.* These amaranth were only prototypes. The project could be easily repeated unless she destroyed the data. Then she would come back and torch the specimens.

Moving carefully between the leaves, she looked for another door. Sweat rolled down her back beneath her hoodie in the muggy heat. At the back wall, she found two office doors. She turned the knob on the one to the right, pleased when it swung open and doubly pleased at the whir of a running computer. A wiggle of the mouse woke the screen, showing the progress of a data process. Good. She wouldn't have to hack in to upload the virus. With a few keystrokes, she aborted the program and inserted the flash drive, overriding the protocols the way Trevor had taught her. The machine hummed again as it accepted the new code.

The constant drone of the fans ceased. She smiled, but then a chirruping beep—more alert than alarm—filled the greenhouse. From the main room, Trevor shouted, "Alarm! Get out now!"

She clenched her teeth. Dammit, of course there was an alert on the climate controls. She would've thought of that if Trevor had given her a chance to plan. But they'd been out of time; tomorrow, the Coalition would be announcing a call to protest, and once that happened, the company would increase security or move the tests to a new facility. The corporation couldn't be allowed to keep its data.

Only twenty more seconds to complete the upload. She drummed her gloved fingers on the desktop. She couldn't leave the flash drive behind as evidence. Ten seconds. Another, much louder alarm joined the first—a burglar alarm. Someone must've opened the main door.

The computer screen flashed once, telling her the transfer was complete. She yanked the drive free and dashed back the way she'd come. Careening through the room with the towering plants, she underestimated a turn, and the weight of the gas can in her pack threw her off balance. She slammed into the high stalks, toppling several over. The flash drive flew from her gloved grip amid a volley of falling leaves.

She regained her balance, heart in her throat. If she stayed to search in the dark, she'd be caught for sure. On trembling legs, she bolted for the door. Her feet tangled on a fallen stalk, and she fell, landing on her outstretched palms. Fallen leaves and crushed paper bags rustled against her face as she scrambled upright and kept going.

She veered left toward the exit. Behind her, Cindy's footsteps slapped against the concrete. "Sorry. I didn't know they'd have an alarm on the climate system."

Jaide shook her head, breathing too hard to reply. Cold air blasted the sweat from her face as she burst out into the moonlight. Ahead, Trevor's form scrambled over the top of the six-foot chain-link fence. In a few more steps, she hit the cold metal and dug her toes into the gaps to hoist herself up and over, Cindy right beside her.

They caught up to Trevor as he crossed the dirt road, and together they ducked into a windbreak along the neighboring field.

"That was close," Trevor whispered. Frozen branches crackled underfoot as they crept along in the dark. At least there was no snow in which to leave tracks. They'd parked nearly a mile away and had planned their escape via Google Earth. This line of trees would lead them straight to their car on the other side. Jaide had to scramble to keep up with Trevor's long strides.

Cindy fell behind, mincing through the leaves like a timid deer. "Did you get the virus uploaded?"

"I didn't have time to hack in," said Trevor.

Jaide shot Trevor a glare he couldn't see in the dark. "I did. Barely." Her elation at finding an open computer was bittersweet. "But I lost the flash drive."

He stopped walking. "You what?"

She stopped, too, and turned back his direction. "It flew out of my hand while I was escaping. I couldn't see in the dark."

Trevor threw his hands into the air. "Well, that's just great," he hissed, steam rising from his mouth in the moonlight. Behind him, a police siren wailed. He thrust his hands back into his pockets and shoved past her. "Jesus Christ, I should've handled it all myself."

Jaide's temperature rose in spite of the icy air. "Well, the police wouldn't be arriving quite so soon if you hadn't busted through the main doors. The climate alarm would've only alerted the greenhouse manager."

Cindy caught up and slid an arm through Jaide's, hugging herself close as they walked. "They must sell tens of thousands of those drives at every outlet mall across the country, right?"

Jaide nodded. She didn't want to think about FBI cybercrimes technology at the moment. She just wanted to put the greenhouse behind her and get back to her daughter and her normal life. "Yeah, we just need to lay low."

"And destroy my computer and everything on it," Trevor added over his shoulder. "The FBI can hash the ID from every file on the drive and trace it back to the source. Thanks a lot." His anger radiated like heat through the darkness.

"You're the one who insisted we had to take the risk," said Jaide.

Trevor blew out a sharp breath and picked up his pace, leaving her and Cindy behind.

Jaide clutched Cindy tighter and stumbled through the darkness.

Chapter Two

SEPTEMBER

In the beginning days… the people wanted for nothing.
They did not search the land, but sat in one place, and
food came to them…
~ THE HISTORIES

J aide parked at the end of the cul-de-sac behind a red Subaru Forester and cut the engine. Cindy's annual Harvest Party was in full swing already, a heartbeat of music thumping through the warm evening air. In the passenger seat next to her, Flora flopped her head back against the headrest. "Do we have to go, Mom?"

Facing their friends wasn't going to be easy for either of them. They'd both bragged about their patio garden and assured everyone they'd win the upcoming Harvest Party competition for best dish. But after months of planning and cultivating, watering and pruning, a week of humid weather and cool nights had ruined the tomato crop and the chance of victory. Guilt at setting such a boastful example for her daughter weighed on Jaide's limbs. She forced a smile. "We're strong. We can do this."

"I'm going to owe Ryan five dollars."

"You'll still owe him if we skip out." In the back seat, Trigger pawed the window and whined, begging to be set free. Jaide opened her door, and the Border Collie pranced in excitement, eager for the back door to open. "Let's just go in and get this over with."

Flora scowled and flung open the squeaky passenger side. "Fine."

Jaide grabbed the minuscule bowl of salsa and a bag of chips out of the trunk while Flora released Trigger. The black-and-white dog bee-lined ahead to Cindy's zero lot-line. Jaide lifted her chin and followed, trying to set a good example for her daughter while every muscle resisted her command to move forward.

Reaching the paved walkway to Cindy's door, Jaide squelched her jealousy over the underutilized space; Cindy's half of the property had been professionally xeriscaped with native plants that required little water and fertilizer. To Jaide's eyes, the yard was ugly and useless. If she had land of her own, she'd put in a stand of corn and beans, have a few chickens for eggs, and maybe even a milk goat. Enough to be self-sufficient. But all she had were a few crowded pots on her apartment balcony. *Be proud of how much you grow in the space you have.* A few handfuls of green beans, a head of broccoli, and some cucumbers were more than most of her friends had accomplished.

Jaide reached the front door and entered without knocking, the main room already abuzz with people. Trigger headed toward the sound of men laughing in the back yard, looking for fellow canines. Flora slumped along behind. Spotting Cindy, Jaide slipped through the crowd to wrap her arms around her friend's neck. Cindy spun and hugged her back. "What took you so long? I thought you were going to help me set up."

"Flora and I ran into a few problems with the harvest." Jaide grimaced.

"Whaaat?" Cindy's high-pitched single syllable drew attention from guests in all corners of the room. "What happened?"

Heat crept over Jaide's neck and face. Better get used to explaining. She'd probably have to do it all night. "Some sort of rot set in on the tomatoes. Probably blight. It's the humidity."

Cindy looped an arm through Jaide's and led her toward the kitchen. "Well, there's always next year. And we have plenty of food." She jerked open the freezer door and pulled out a gallon bag of raspberries and a bottle of tequila. "I picked these bad boys myself out at Howler Farms. Raspberitas, everyone!"

Jaide nodded to Trevor and another woman nearby and added her pitiful thimble of salsa to the assortment of hand-spun ceramic bowls and glass casserole dishes on the island counter. Thankfully, Trevor didn't comment on her contribution. A bamboo cutting board held several types of cheese, and someone had brought a growler of what she could only assume was homemade beer. On a platter in the center, three diminutive roast birds sat in a circle, their frail leg bones jutting upward and missing heads clustered together in a huddle like a grotesque sacrificial offering.

"Who brought the chickens?" Jaide asked, stomach roiling.

"Not chicken. Squab," said Trevor, his black mustache drooping like a frown over his lips. He had a yellow stain on his button-down shirt. "Lucas raised them. Did you know he kept pigeons?"

"Lucas Harmon?" Jaide shot a look toward Cindy, who kept her gaze on the bottle of tequila she was opening. Lucas frequented the food co-op, mostly because he liked to argue with the owner about global warming.

Cindy's face reddened. "He asked about the Coalition. He's actually really smart."

A crush. Cindy had the worst taste in men.

"Oh, shudder," said a woman in a mauve wool sweater, whose name Jaide couldn't remember. "How could you eat something you'd raised?"

Lucas must've overheard from the living room, because he leaned his head around the corner into the kitchen. The setting sun in the windows behind him haloed his trim beard and curly hair with a glint of amber. "You prefer factory farmed?"

He came around the corner, barefoot and wearing wrinkled Bermuda shorts. Outwardly, he seemed to be eco-responsible, but the man was always holding a disposable coffee cup or crunching on nonorganic potato chips. And now he apparently killed pigeons.

Cindy said, "I had no idea you had pigeons. Let alone ate them."

"My newest project. I can raise them on the roof at work. They take very little space, and I get both eggs and meat."

Jaide's stomach soured at the thought of slaughtering baby birds. "No animals have to die to feed me. There are plenty of nonanimal proteins available, don't you think?"

He tilted his head and bared his teeth, pointing to a canine. "These are the teeth of an omnivore. We're designed to eat meat."

The woman who'd spoken earlier chimed in. "I've eaten quinoa and tofu for decades."

"Except nearly all the soy products are genetically modified these days," said Trevor. "The need for soy in animal feed led the GMO corn and soybean takeover."

Jaide's chest tightened. They'd agreed to stop talking about

GMOs in public after the greenhouse. Even in front of other Coalition members, they held back on the off chance police questioned members about zealots.

They kept their activities on the up-and-up these days, striving to act like good little drones who believed they could change the world through rallies and ballot measures. The incident at the greenhouse had made the news—stayed there for the better part of a month while the police investigated. But no word emerged of the flash drive or other clues. Once the news died down—no doubt dictated by the corporation—she assumed the trail had gone cold. But she still couldn't help looking over her shoulder whenever a policeman passed her on the street.

Lucas lifted his brows and nodded once. "The need to produce animal feed has spurred on GMO crops. I can't argue with that. But is genetic modification really a bad thing? We've got to do something to feed the Earth's population."

Silence as everyone stared at him.

Words clustered in Jaide's throat, too many to spit out. She thought her eyes were going to bug out of her head.

"Did you really just say that?" asked Cindy.

"Humans have been eating GMO for decades with no proven ill effects," he said.

Jaide couldn't keep quiet. "In the nineteen fifties and sixties, scientists also claimed DDT and other pesticide sprays were safe based on the fact that there was no proof they weren't."

"I have a diabetic aunt who'd be dead without insulin produced by GM bacteria," said Lucas.

Trevor's dark eyebrows drew together, creating a line that matched his mustache. "GM insulin causes type one diabetes in type two patients."

Lucas turned a stony gaze on Trevor. "Have you read that

study? Because I have, and that study had nothing to do with GM insulin versus natural insulin."

"But it hasn't been"—Trevor caught Jaide's gaze, and his face turned ashen—"proven otherwise." He finished with forced sedation and lifted his beer to make a show of drinking.

Cindy energetically pounded the bag of raspberries against the cutting board to break them up, her face pink.

Jaide decided to steer the conversation away from Trevor's anti-GMO zeal. "Don't you think corporations suppress any data they don't agree with?"

Lucas refused to be derailed. "So I'm supposed to take your word that GMO is bad over someone else's word that it's good?"

She crossed her arms. "You've obviously made up your mind already."

"Show me a case study that has undergone peer review proving the danger"—his voice rose to carry over the sound of the blender—"and I'll hop on your bandwagon."

Cindy slammed the tequila bottle against the counter top. "Enough arguing! This is supposed to be a party! Now drink up."

Instead of taking a drink, Lucas tore the hindquarter off one of the squab and took a big bite.

Jaide put Trigger on her leash and called to Flora, her voice echoing through the tiny apartment. "I'm going to the co-op. Want to come?"

Flora's voice drifted from her bedroom. "Can I buy salted caramel?"

"One." Jaide checked her faded jeans pocket for her wallet. She should have enough to splurge on one candy. She took her reusable bag from its hook near the door and folded it into her back pocket.

Flora appeared in the hallway in short shorts and a tank, the straps of her florescent yellow training bra stark against her tan.

Always concerned about damaging her daughter's self-image, Jaide schooled her face into nonjudgmental lines and asked, "You sure you want to wear that?"

Halting mid-step, Flora looked down at herself. "All the girls wear this."

"And what statement are they trying to make with it?"

Flora slumped and threw her head back to look at the ceiling. "God, Mom. Not everything has to be a statement."

Jaide gripped the leash tighter. She'd sworn to be a better parent than her own mother, but some days it took all her will not to crush Flora's independent nature. "I'm not saying you can't wear it, just that you should think about what it tells other people about you." She refrained from mentioning that some girls in this neighborhood made money by dressing that way.

"Forget it. I don't want caramel." Flora stomped back into her room.

"It's up to you. But I'm leaving now."

No answer.

Everyone said the teenage years were hardest. Flora wouldn't be thirteen until April, yet Jaide already felt constantly pelted by irrational hormones. It made her appreciate her mother a hair more, although they seldom spoke since Jaide had become a single parent. Mother insisted Flora had ruined Jaide's life. Jaide didn't want to expose Flora to that negativity. Instead, she worked on being proud of her own daughter no matter what.

Today that was going to take some extra work.

Sighing, she stepped into the grungy hallway and locked the door behind her. Someone across the corridor was playing their

TV too loud again, and the scent of frying meat polluted the air. She took the stairs down a level and exited the building. Across the street, a young girl played with a toddler on the sparse, unkempt lawn. To Jaide's right, a large-breasted woman leaned out of a peeling, second-level window and loudly berated a man standing below. Humid autumn air brought out the scent of garbage from the nearby alleyway.

Trigger pulled happily against the tether down the cracked sidewalk, stopping at the first street sign to sniff. Jaide paused to give her time to do her business. Behind them, Flora's voice called out, "Mom, wait!"

She turned to see her daughter clomping toward her in a knee-length crinkle skirt and unlaced black Converse high-tops. She still wore the bra-strap-exposing tank, but at least her bottom half wasn't on full display. Trigger pranced on the end of her leash, acting as though she hadn't seen Flora in days.

When Flora reached them, Jaide asked, "Did you lock up?"

Flora nodded and took her hand like as she had when she was little.

Jaide smiled, her heart overflowing. "I'm glad you changed your mind."

They continued walking, Flora skipping over cracks, and Trigger pausing to sniff at every signpost, corner, and tree. Their neighborhood was threadbare, but Jaide liked to think it was full of good people trying to get ahead. Like herself. Her job doing data entry from home gave her more time with Flora but didn't pay much. She saved what she could to buy a little house of her own someday.

Down a narrow alley between the dingy brick buildings, she spotted a scrawny dog gulping down a stale bun. She paused, ready to check for collar or tags, but the pooch tucked her tail and slithered underneath a wooden gate blocking the end of the alley.

Flora let go of her hand. "Want me to catch her?"

Jaide debated but thought better of intruding on private property. "Not today, love. We'll look again on the way back." She hoped the poor thing didn't get hit by a car in the meantime.

They crossed the intersection to the small co-op market and stopped beneath the awning out front. She offered the leash to Flora. "Want to stay here with Trigger, or should we tie her up?"

"I want to pick my caramel."

Jaide nodded and loosely tied the leash to the tree outside the co-op. She held a palm up toward the dog. "Trigger, sit. Stay."

Trigger lowered her hindquarters to the pavement, her brown eyes sad.

"We'll be back in a minute, silly," Flora said in a baby voice. Trigger's tail swept the sidewalk.

They entered the cool interior of the store, dim under the illumination of energy-saving bulbs. While Flora picked a hand-made caramel from the case up front, Jaide headed to the bakery at the back, mentally counting the cash in her wallet. Eating organic was expensive, but she'd save in doctor bills in the long run. She selected a loaf of day-old bread and then ventured to the produce section to look over the winter squash.

Down the aisle, she spotted Lucas in his bicycle helmet and cargo shorts, carrying his usual bleached-paper coffee cup. He grinned and walked toward her. "Great party last night."

"Yeah, Cindy goes all out." She brushed past him, hoping the niceties were over, but he took up pace beside her.

"I enjoyed talking with you last night and was wondering if you'd be interested in continuing our conversation over coffee?"

She stopped and looked up into his hazel eyes then at the cup in his hand. Her lip curled in what she hoped was a deterring fashion. "I only drink fair-trade coffee."

He lifted the cup slightly. "Me too. There's a place off Tejon that has a good selection, plus live music. We can bike there or I can pick you up later."

Great. He wasn't going to take the hint. "Listen, Lucas, I'm sure you're a great person, but we're too diametrically opposed to date each other, don't you think?"

"Keep using smart words like that and I just might want a date," he said raising an eyebrow. "I was asking you to continue our conversation from last night, not make out."

Heat flushed her face, and she dropped her gaze to the tiled floor. He hadn't asked her on a date? "Oh, well, I... I'm busy. My daughter's with me. And my dog." She swallowed, feeling stupid on multiple levels.

"Afraid I'll sway you to the dark side?"

Now it was her turn to cock an eyebrow. "Bring it on."

He grinned, but before he could reply, she added, "But seriously, not today. I really do have a dog and my kid with me. And I have a meeting tonight."

"Rain check, then. I'll see you around." He turned on his heel and sauntered away, sipping his coffee.

She watched him weave past a woman in a pink jogging suit then disappear around a corner before she realized her mouth was hanging open. What had just happened? Somehow, he'd charmed her in spite of his carnivorous, argumentative tendencies, and she'd given him an opening. Well, maybe she could teach him the error of his ways—if she ever agreed to actually meet up with him.

Chapter Three

DECEMBER

The Mothers bade us Keep the Peace.

~ THE HISTORIES

A knock on the apartment door, firm but polite, drew Jaide from her computer to peer through the peephole. A man and a woman wearing dark business suits and holding clipboards stood in the hall outside. Probably Mormons or Jehovah's Witnesses. If she ignored them, they'd move on.

She returned to the kitchen table and put her earbuds in, preparing to work the last few minutes before Flora arrived from school.

"Mom!" Flora's voice punctured the music in the earbuds. The bus must have been early. "Some people are here to see you!"

Dammit. She'd let them in.

Jaide jerked the earbuds free and rose as Flora tossed her backpack on the counter and began rifling the cupboards for a snack. The man and woman stood just inside the door. Trigger was running her nose over the man's shoes, tail wagging.

"Ms. Jaide Acosta?" the man said.

They know my name? "Uh, yeah. What can I do for you?"

He held up an open wallet with a badge and credentials. "We're with the FBI."

Jaide's heart stopped. Heat flooded her face, and the air seemed suddenly too thick to breathe. Every muscle in her body tensed, screaming for her to turn and run, turn and run, turn and run.

"Mom, can I have one of these?" Flora skipped into the room carrying one of the expensive nutrition bars Jaide reserved for their all-day rallies.

Interacting with her daughter calmed her a little. "Sure. Yes. Take Trigger with you."

Flora grinned a victory smile. "Yes! Come on, Trigger. I'll give you a cookie, too."

Jaide crossed her arms and refocused on the FBI people. "What can I do for you?"

"I'm Agent Riese, and this is Agent Bowler." The woman indicated herself and then the man. "We understand you're a member of the Coalition for Clean Food?"

Her eyes felt watery as she maintained eye contact. "Yes?"

"May we ask you some questions?"

"Of course. Come in." She turned to the living room, glad to be facing away, even if only for a moment. "Can I offer you something to drink?"

"No, thank you." Agent Riese took a seat on the edge of the afghan-covered sofa. "In January of last year, do you recall any suspicious activity among members of the Coalition?"

Her eyes glazed over as she looked out her balcony window at the snow-covered pots. Her memory overflowed with hard, frozen earth pressing her cheek, the scent of warm greenhouse soil cutting through icy air. Shaking herself, she swiveled the hard-backed rocking chair so it faced the sofa. "What do you mean?"

The man walked around the coffee table to sit at the other end of the sofa. "Secret meetings. Members breaking off from the group. Anything you might have considered odd."

Volunteer nothing. She adjusted the small rag rug that served as the rocking chair's seat cushion. "I don't think so."

"What sort of activities does the Coalition organize?"

She sat and folded her hands on her lap. *Act natural.* "Our main focus is to help farmers and land owners understand the power of organic farming, one acre at a time." That line was easy, right from the mission statement on the Coalition website. She added a shrug she hoped appeared nonchalant. "We mostly distribute educational pamphlets and maintain a website."

"What kinds of protests have the Coalition supported?"

Jaide swallowed past a lump in her throat. If they arrested her right now, what would happen to Flora? "Sometimes we hold peaceful rallies to alert the public to a local issue."

"Do you recall such a rally last January?"

She pretended a light bulb had just turned on in her head. "Oh! Is this about that greenhouse that was vandalized? We all showed up with picket signs, and the police were already there. We got a lot of press on that one." She smiled as though that was a good thing then made her eyes grow wide. "Wait, you don't think we had anything to do with that, do you?"

Agent Riese drew a pen from her pocket and poised it over her clipboard. "Can you recall who was there with you that morning?"

Jaide named everyone she could think of, including Trevor and Cindy, as they'd agreed. They'd attended the rally, bleary eyed and holding signs, to act surprised along with the rest of the Coalition members.

"Who maintains the Coalition website?" asked Bowler.

"I—I do." Her voice came out too high. Trevor had insisted that her stepping down as webmistress would be suspicious.

"How long have you had that duty?"

"I'm not sure. A long time. Three years? Four?" In the kitchen, Flora slammed a cupboard door. Trigger padded in and put her chin on Jaide's knee, tail wagging slowly.

Agent Riese leaned a little sideways and nodded toward the dining table where Jaide's laptop sat open. "You do data entry?"

Oh, God, they know, they know. Her heart pounded in time to the words in her brain. She put a trembling hand on Trigger's head, sinking her fingers into the comfort of the soft fur behind her ears. "Yes."

"Any programing experience?"

"Like writing software? No. The companies I work for have their own programs."

"What do you know about"—the woman looked down at her clipboard—"Trevor Finkman."

"Trevor?" She furrowed her brow, pretending to consider. "He's all right."

"Do you know where we can find him?" Agent Bowler asked.

"Did you try his apartment?"

"We've been unable to locate him. We hoped you might help."

Surely they already knew where he was employed. Telling them wouldn't be a betrayal. "He works at an insurance company in the IT department."

"He hasn't been to work in two days."

"He hasn't been to work?" The pit of Jaide's stomach squeezed so tight, she thought she might throw up. Had Trevor fled? What did that mean for her and Cindy? Would he leave without warning her? He made good money at his job and wasn't likely to abandon it unless he was truly panicked.

"Do you have knowledge of where he might go? Any family or recreation spots he likes to visit?"

Tiny stars pricked the edges of her vision. "Are you saying he's missing?"

"Ms. Acosta, are you all right?"

She had to breathe. Trevor had left her and Cindy to take the blame for the break-in. *Stay calm. Answer questions with questions.* That was how Trevor'd taught them. "Why are you looking for him?"

Agent Riese answered, "We want to ask him a few questions."

"Is he in trouble?"

"Not at this moment. Do you have any idea where we can find him?"

Jaide shook her head, mind spinning with how to respond. On one hand, she wanted to keep Trevor safe if they suspected him, but on the other, she didn't want to be left alone to take the blame. And she didn't want these agents to think she'd been uncooperative. "He volunteers at the food co-op sometimes."

The woman rose and held out a business card. "Thank you, Ms. Acosta. We may contact you again. In the meantime, if you hear anything from him or anything about the incident at the greenhouse, please call me."

Jaide took the card, relieved her hand didn't shake. "The Coalition would never condone vandalism," she found herself saying. She swallowed, the statement ringing more true than she liked. Why had she ever agreed to follow Trevor's plan? "Violence only begets violence, don't you think?"

"Words to live by, Ms. Acosta," said Agent Bowler at the door. "We'll talk to you again soon."

Chapter Four

JULY

No matter how deep the Hunger, the Tox will grow.

~ Mother's Proverb

The sun pounded against Jaide's scalp, penetrating her broad-brimmed hat, while rivulets of sweat trickled through her hair and ran down her neck and torso. Scattered over the hill and across the dirt road, Coalition volunteers worked in pairs to scout out and remove invasive weeds from the two-acre park outside town. At least the unseasonable heat wilted the pulled weeds so she didn't have to worry about any bits she dropped reestablishing themselves.

She looked over her shoulder in search of her daughter, who kept wandering off, distracted by butterflies or the Cooperative Extension agent's cute teenage son. "Flora, come help me."

Led by Trigger—or rather, dragged by Trigger—Flora joined her where the patch of sweet clover had taken hold among the clumps of native grass. Flora pointed to the fine-leafed seedling. "Is this one?"

"Use the card and tell me." Jaide held out the laminated color photocopy of the invasive weeds they were hunting. Sweet clover was definitely on the list, but she wanted Flora to learn to identify it herself.

"Just tell me, Mom." Her daughter tilted her head to glower at Jaide beneath her brows. "It's hot, and I want to go home." Sweat smudged her mascara—yet another battle Jaide had lost last year with the progression through middle school.

She remained silent about the smudges, refusing to turn into her critical mother. Instead, she pulled off her gloves to let the air soothe her prickling skin. "Me, too. But the weeds will keep gro—"

"I know, Mom. They grow forever and ever. We can't pull them all." Flora grabbed the plant and yanked, breaking it off at soil level. "This cause is useless."

Jaide gritted her teeth. She treasured her daughter, but Flora's heart wasn't in the work, and that made Jaide miss Cindy more than usual. After Trevor had disappeared last winter, the friends decided it would be best to see less of each other. She jabbed her pitchfork at the ground, tines bouncing against the hard soil. "We have to get the roots."

Flora hurled the weed into the orange five-gallon bucket next to them. "I'm going to get some water."

Jaide sighed and watched the gangly thirteen-year-old stomp toward the pickup where Coalition volunteers had set up a refreshment table, Trigger prancing beside her. At least someone was happy; the dog gleefully paused to greet everyone she could reach along the way.

Returning to weeding, Jaide jimmied the tines of the fork against the embedded roots, trying to free as much as she could.

"Need a hand?" The familiar voice drew her gaze as a pair of hiking boots came into view.

"Lucas?" She'd bumped into him off and on over the past year but had yet to go to coffee with him. "What are you doing here?"

He pointed to a firefighter emblem on his shirt. "Paramedic on duty. I like to keep watch over you weed whackers. Otherwise you keel over from sunstroke. Here," Lucas wrapped his fingers around the upper portion of the pitchfork handle. "I'll pry and you pull."

She released it. "You're a firefighter?"

He stomped a boot against the edge of the fork, a lock of hair falling over his eyes. Arm muscles bulging against his T-shirt sleeves, he grunted and pulled back a chunk of sod, exposing the top of the taproot. "I actually work for the hospital. I volunteer with the fire service for these kinds of projects."

Bending, she used both hands to pull. The root gave with a snap, sending her backward onto her bottom.

"You okay?" Lucas let the clod fall back into place and reached down to help her stand.

She accepted his callused hand.

"Nice tat." He grinned and rubbed a thumb over the inside of her wrist. The peace sign there had Flora's name curling through it, a celebration of Jaide's tubal ligation three years ago.

"Thanks." A sudden wave of shyness made her look away. She tossed the root into the bucket and brushed herself off. "Have you joined the Coalition? I haven't seen you at the meetings."

While Jaide still belonged to the Coalition, she'd stepped back, giving responsibility for the website to a new, eager young man. She remained in her position as secretary, at least until the next election. Stepping away too quickly might seem a little odd so soon after the visit from the FBI last November. The Coalition had buzzed with speculation for months—still buzzed

—about what had happened to Trevor and the FBI's involvement, but at least the agents hadn't come to her door again.

Lucas tamped the loose sod down with a boot. "The Coalition is a little too... emotional for my tastes. But you guys are trying to do a good thing out here."

The praise gave her courage to meet his eyes again. "We need to be passionate if we want to change the world, don't you think? One acre at a time."

"You really believe you can keep up with the weed growth?" His mouth quirked into a mocking smile.

Her good feelings wilted like the weeds in her bucket. "What do you suggest? We give up?"

"Not at all. I just don't see how a handful of idealists, no matter how passionate, can overcome the savage power of nature." He shaded his eyes with one hand and scanned the hill. "These plants are invaders, yes, but so were our ancestors when they arrived in America. And look where we are now."

"You can't compare people to plants." She grabbed the weed bucket and walked uphill toward another sweet clover. "Humans are outside of nature. We need to find a way to become a part of it again."

"By outside of nature, I assume you mean causing change to our environment?"

She set the bucket down next to the weed. "Of course. We're killing off species, polluting the watershed—even altering weather patterns across the globe."

"Are beavers outside of nature, then? They cause change to their environment—flood out fish spawning grounds and destroy existing terrestrial flora."

She scowled at him. She should've known better than to be drawn into one of his debates. "Beavers are localized. Humans do it on a global scale."

"But we evolved intellect to adapt our environment to our needs, just like beavers. Just because we're more successful, is that unnatural?"

"Yes!" She snatched the fork from him and rammed it into the soil near the weeds. "We've moved beyond nature."

Lucas rubbed his palms on the front of his jeans. "Beyond. Maybe we have."

She glanced up at him through her lashes. He stared down the other side of the hill. Was she getting through to him? "We're like parasites. Viruses. On the road to killing our host, don't you think? We have to use our intelligence to become symbiotes instead."

"Are those weeds?" Lucas pointed to the bottom of the hill near the tree line.

She shaded her eyes to see better. A tall stand of broad-leafed plants stood staunchly alone on a barren patch of earth. She pulled the laminated card from her pocket. "Let's go take a closer look."

Together they plodded through the tall grass until they reached the bottom of the hill. Shoulder-high plants with big, spear-tip leaves covered an area as large as her living room, with no other plant life growing around or between them. Lucas strode right into the big leaves.

She scuffed the naked soil near the plants. The earth was as hard packed as the rest of the hill, not tilled. "Did someone plant these?"

"What are they? Mutant poinsettias?"

Moving closer, she verified her guess with the card. "Palmer amaranth. They're native to the U.S. but not to this area. God, they're huge."

"Pull them?"

She nodded, and Lucas used the fork to free one, releasing a long root in a rain of dirt. The crushed foliage released a scent like wet pennies. A shiver of familiarity raced down Jaide's spine. What did that remind her of? Blood? She joined Lucas pulling roots. The bucket filled quickly. Straightening, she wiped her forehead with the back of her wrist. "This weed colony's too big for us alone."

"You have dirt on you." He pulled a handkerchief from his back pocket and dabbed at her forehead. A lump formed in her throat at his touch. His gaze reconnected with hers as he lowered his hand.

"Thanks," she said, pulse fluttering. She dropped her eyes to the bucket. "Let's take what we have to the pickup and show the others."

He cleared his throat. "I probably ought to be manning the first aid station."

The thought of pulling weeds alone again made her limbs feel heavy. "Did you know you can eat most weeds?" As soon as the words were out of her mouth, she felt stupid.

He cocked his head. "Is that an invitation to dinner?"

If she hadn't already been sweltering, warmth would have flooded her face. How did he always manage to put her off balance? But this time she had a quick answer. "The Coalition's having a potluck tomorrow evening, and everyone's supposed to bring a dish using weeds. Why don't you come?"

"Kid friendly?"

"You have a kid?" For some reason, she hadn't pictured Lucas as the family type.

"On the weekends I don't work, yes. She's fourteen and easily bored by her dad's lack of a life. She's at a friend's birthday party today."

"You're divorced, then?" After several dates with men who were only separated, she'd learned to be bold in her questioning. Maybe that was why Lucas had never really asked her on a date.

His face tightened. "My wife died from complications

during Suzanne's delivery. My parents keep her most of the time."

She cringed. "Oh, God, I'm sorry."

"Adrienne insisted on a home birth. Believed it was more natural." He picked up the bucket and fork and turned away.

Jaide didn't know what to say now. The death of a loved one was outside her level of experience. Even Trigger was her first pet, and she dreaded the day when she lost her. Trotting to catch up, she walked next to him in silence.

When they neared the Extension agent's pickup, Lucas handed her the tools. "I'm going to make the rounds, make sure everyone is okay. And select a few choice weeds for dinner." He winked, his usual teasing smile once again in place. "Text me the address for the potluck?"

She nodded, hoping no one minded her inviting him. He'd at least been pleasant and open to her ideas today. He sauntered through the tall grass without looking back.

To her right, a group of people talked to Grace, the Cooperative Extension liaison. Jaide picked up the bucket and carried it over. One of the men reached out to take her tools. "Let me help with that."

"Thanks." She pointed back over her shoulder. "There's a big stand of palmer amaranth around the hill. I couldn't clear them all."

Grace pulled one of the leaves free of the bucket and looked at it. "Let's bag these and go have a look."

The others joined in chopping the long stems into more manageable pieces and shoving them into sturdy contractor bags, then Jaide led the way to the remaining weeds. Grace shook her head and stared at the foliage. "It shouldn't be this tall this time of year."

A white-haired woman wearing huge glasses broke off a leaf and handed it to Grace. "At least it's not flowering yet."

"True. Let's make sure we get all the roots, everyone."

Jaide began prying out the weeds, tossing the pieces into buckets. One of the men lifted a full bucket in each hand to carry back to the pickup. "Are these the GMO weeds I've heard rumors about?"

Grace squatted near the upturned dirt, picking out bits of root and broken leaves and putting them into a small plastic zipper bag. "The rumors haven't been confirmed."

"But you're collecting samples?" He pointed to the baggie.

"Just want to be sure." Grace didn't look up.

"Why would anyone spend money to develop GMO weeds?" asked the white-haired woman.

The man said, "To force us to buy special herbicides to get rid of them, of course."

"Corporations wouldn't release weeds on purpose, would they?" Jaide asked.

"I don't trust any of them."

"It wouldn't have to be on purpose." A young woman in a yellow tank top waved a broad leaf like a fan. "Amaranth easily cross-breeds with all kinds of plants. Spread a little pollen around, or track out a few seeds, and BAM! Superweeds to beat all superweeds."

The familiar coppery scent of the crushed foliage enveloped Jaide until she no longer saw sun bleached grassland, but amaranth towering in the moonlight, seed heads covered by hangman's bags. The memory was like a physical blow, knocking the air out of her. She dropped her digging fork, putting her hands on her knees.

"You all right?" Grace asked.

Jaide stumbled away, the contents of her stomach rising. But we're miles from the test greenhouse, she thought. Could a plant travel that far in only two years? She recalled the scuff of leaves and debris falling around her when she'd fallen. The crinkle of bags under her feet when she fled. Had she tracked out the very thing she sought to protect the world from? The smell filled her nostrils, inescapable.

She doubled over and vomited, falling to her hands and knees on the rough ground.

A man yelled, "Someone find the medic."

"No, I'm fine." Swiping the back of her hand across her mouth, Jaide stumbled to her feet. She had to eradicate these Franken-weeds. She wouldn't rest until they were gone. Spinning, she grabbed a digging fork from Grace's hand and plunged it into the unyielding earth.

Chapter Five

*The fat on every people sat and wasted, and the food was
so much, it wasted. So the land replied with waste.*
~ THE HISTORIES

Jaide stared down at the pot of scorched chickweed.
What had started out as an attempt at a casserole had
turned into an inedible greenish brick. She pulled the
pot from the burner and set it aside to cool, hoping she
hadn't ruined the pan. Maybe she could claim illness and beg off
the potluck. Except she'd invited Lucas, and it would be rude to
ditch him.

Her attention hadn't been on her cooking or on Lucas today,
and it wouldn't be on the social niceties required for a party,
either. The night at the greenhouse kept replaying through her
thoughts, both dreaming and awake. Leaves tumbled around
her whenever she lay down. Fallen paper bags rattled beneath
her feet when she walked. And a damp, wet smell with a heavy
copper tang followed her like a miasma.

She opened the freezer and pulled out a baggie of blanched

garlic mustard leaves from the past spring. Her mother's chickpea curry recipe would only take a few minutes and didn't cost much to make. She chopped an onion and a tomato and tossed them into a pan of hot oil with curry powder. The sweet scent carved a hollow in her chest and made her nostalgic for home in a way she hadn't felt for years.

She dumped in the chickpeas and a can of vegetable broth and went to touch up her makeup. Lack of sleep had left dark circles beneath her eyes. She practiced a smile in the mirror. *I'll only stay long enough to be polite*, she reassured herself. And to inform Cindy of the escaped weed. Thinking about the weed turned her stomach again. She returned to the kitchen and pulled the curry off the stove. The leaves of garlic mustard were still frozen, but she emptied the baggie into the pot, stirring to thaw them.

"Flora, let's go!" she called over her shoulder. "Don't forget your swimsuit." She poured the curry into a bowl and sealed the lid. Trigger pranced to the door ahead of her, and she patted the dog's head. "Sorry, girl. We're going to Ginger's. You'll have to stay home."

Trigger lowered her hindquarters to sit, her front feet dancing in unabashed doggy hope.

From her bedroom, Flora asked, "Do I have to go?"

"You won't be alone this time. Lucas is bringing his daughter."

Flora poked her head out of her bedroom door, her brows drawn into a scowl. "How old is she? Last time you said there would be other kids, I ended up babysitting."

"But you made ten bucks. And you won't this time, because his daughter is fourteen."

The rest of Flora's body appeared in the hall, her scowl easing into a mere glower. "She better be cool."

They stopped at the gas station on the way to Ginger's and

bought eight dollars' worth of fuel. Her next paycheck was three days away, and she liked to keep a few dollars in reserve for emergencies. The lingering scent of oil on hot pavement and gasoline fumes made Jaide's head hurt.

"Why do gas prices always go up in summer?" Flora asked as Jaide climbed back into the driver's seat. "We never get to go on road trips like Angela's family."

"Gas is reformulated in the summer to reduce air pollution." Jaide unclipped her sunglasses from the car's visor and put them on before pulling into traffic.

"Why only in summer?"

"Good question. I don't know." She smiled at Flora, proud her daughter was questioning government policy. "Maybe someone at the potluck will."

Flora rolled her eyes and looked out the passenger window. Lately, she'd become less enthusiastic about Coalition members. Jaide blamed a corporate-subsidized public school system, but she couldn't afford to take time off to homeschool her daughter.

They left town toward what had once been rolling farmland, now transformed into wide acreages of manicured lawns. Jaide pulled into a long, circular driveway and parked behind a white Prius. Ginger's house looked like a modest ranch-style home from the outside, but once inside, the floor dropped a few steps down into a great room with a cathedral-style ceiling. The huge back windows and deck looked out over an acre of garden and a man-made pond surrounded by trees. Jaide ignored the view and turned right, into the kitchen. Decorative copper pots and dark marble countertops sparkled as if they'd never been used. She passed the stairway to the lower level, through the open, beveled glass double doors, and into the atrium.

A long table covered with casserole dishes ran the full length of the room. Almost all the food on the table was, expectedly, green. Had anyone cooked with the monstrous amaranth? Jaide shuddered.

Flora disappeared through the doors to the pool.

Setting her dish among the other bowls, Jaide found the side bar with the wine before joining the other guests. Ginger's husband, Price, stood outside on the patio grilling what smelled like tilapia. Ginger always provided a main course at these events, usually fish, but sometimes veggie burgers or a catered vegetarian entree. There were a few vegans among the Coalition members, but for the most part, everyone indulged in occasional seafood or eggs.

Cindy's laugh floated through the open double doors, and Jaide followed the sound to the pool deck. Standing next to a lean man Jaide hadn't seen before, Cindy held a wine glass and listened with rapt attention as he spoke. A new love interest, Jaide thought, a pang of sadness tweaking her heart. In days past, she would've already heard all about him. Instead, she put on her best smile and walked over to be introduced.

"Hi, Cin," she put an arm around her old friend's neck to hug her, but the familiar gesture felt awkward.

"Jaide!" Cindy planted a big kiss on her cheek. "I'd like you to meet Gerald. He writes for the Daily Dispatch."

"Happy to have you here." Jaide shook his hand. He was a little older than Cindy's usual choices, the hair at his temples a charismatic silver. "Are you joining the Coalition?"

"I'm actually doing a piece on the increasing use of herbicides. Cindy is teaching me a lot." He winked at Cindy.

Cindy simpered and stroked his biceps with her fingertips. "I think I'm learning more from you."

Jaide's forced smile wavered. Palmer amaranth was notoriously resistant to herbicides. Would the new weed with its genetic alterations be even more so? She turned to Cindy. "You been out with the weed warriors lately?"

"Hopefully I can find time next month." Cindy wrinkled her nose as her gaze drifted over Jaide's shoulder toward the patio doors. "Oh, God, who invited him?"

Turning her head, Jaide spotted Lucas paused just outside the double doors, a tall, thin teenager by his side. His usual wrinkled shorts had been replaced by jeans and sneakers.

"Is that his kid?" Cindy put her mouth closer to Jaide's ear as if telling a dirty secret. "I heard he has a daughter."

"I thought you liked him." Jaide had hoped to have at least one ally regarding her invitation to Lucas.

"I don't dislike him." Cindy shot a coy smile toward Gerald then looked back to Lucas. "He's just so... dominant. He argues about everything. God, I hope he didn't bring dead birds again."

Jaide couldn't help laughing. She'd missed Cindy's unfiltered comments. "He promised me he'd keep it vegetarian."

Cindy reared back and stared Jaide in the face. "You invited him?"

"He helped pull weeds yesterday. It felt like the right thing." Lucas looked over the crowded patio, meeting Jaide's eyes. He smiled, and she squeezed Cindy's hand. "I'd better make sure Flora shows his daughter around."

She excused herself and approached Lucas, who was talking to Price. The tall girl gazed with affected boredom at the empty pool. Jaide put on a smile and met the girl's eyes. "Hi, you must be Suzanne. I'm Jaide."

The girl smiled back genuinely. "Hi."

Lucas turned and grinned, raking Jaide from head to toe without trying to hide it. "You look nice. I put my food on the table. I assume that's what I was supposed to do."

"No dead birds, I hope?" Jaide teased.

Suzanne rolled her eyes toward her dad, and he shook his head. "Purely vegetarian. I looked up some recipes for wild amaranth. Did you know you can use the leaves like spinach?"

She took a sip of wine and nodded, avoiding his gaze. Of course he'd brought the weed they'd pulled together. And there was no way she would eat it—if it was genetically modified, who knew what rogue DNA the corporations had put into it? They'd created goats that made spider-silk milk and cabbages filled with scorpion venom. For all she knew, the amaranth had been engineered as a new drain cleaner. Probably not that bad, but still... She turned her attention to Lucas's daughter. "Suzanne, why don't you come with me to find my daughter, Flora. Did you bring a swimming suit?"

Suzanne nodded, and Jaide glanced around the pool to locate Flora. No sign. She was probably in the cabana, changing. Leading the way, Jaide circled the kidney-shaped pool toward the small building on the other side. Through the mullioned windows, she spotted Flora lounging on a wicker chair with a fashion magazine in her hand.

She opened the door and stepped inside. "Flora, Suzanne is here. Suzanne, this is my daughter, Flora."

Flora lowered the magazine. "Hey."

Suzanne replied, "Hey."

Lucas spoke from behind them. "If you girls use the pool, remember to be respectful of other guests." He leaned through the door and surveyed the interior of the building. "Quite the setup here."

Jaide looked around. The space was as big as her bedroom. A privacy screen toward the back of the room provided a place to change, and another door separated a toilet from the main area. Neatly folded beach towels rested in cubbies along the wall to the right. "Price is a lawyer, and Ginger works at a bank. They support the majority of the Coalition's activities."

He stepped back out of the cabana to let her pass, and together they walked back along the pool deck toward the party. "So, did you get that stand of weeds eradicated?"

She swallowed and shrugged. "Grace said the seeds can remain viable in the soil for years."

"I read an interesting article about invasives the other day. It pointed out that species have always migrated, so to call one native and another invasive is simply drawing an arbitrary line in time."

Jaide shivered, thinking of the Franken-weed stalking the land. But she didn't trust herself to talk about GMOs right now, especially with someone like Lucas. "Humans cause rapid, mechanized dispersal of species. It's no longer part of evolution. It's a revolution—against Mother Nature."

The tune "Bad Romance" suddenly blared from the speakers around the pool before someone adjusted the volume. Ginger liked to get people dancing.

Lucas said, "Oh, it's to be one of those kind of parties."

"What kind?"

"Where you have to shout over the music."

"Parties don't always have to be arenas for debate."

He put a hand to his ear, eyes twinkling playfully. "What's that you say?"

Deciding she could use a little playfulness tonight, Jaide took his hand and dragged him to the lawn, where one couple already twirled with practiced choreography. "Dance with me."

He opened his mouth as if to protest but then complied, moving in time to the beat. The song ended, and he said, "I think I'm going to need fortification for a night like this. Can I get you more wine?"

Nodding, she drained the last bit from her glass before handing it to him. She revved herself up to the next song, kicking off her shoes and swinging her arms as the sun dropped low over the trees, encasing everything in amber. Lucas returned with full glasses, and she downed almost half to keep the liquid from splashing over while she danced.

She hadn't eaten all day, too sick over the weed pulling yesterday, and the wine went quickly to her head. Losing her inhibitions felt good tonight. A slow song came from the speakers, and she drained her glass before flinging her arms around Lucas's neck. He obliged by drawing her body against his.

"I kind of like you quiet," she said, inhaling his warm, male scent.

He pursed his lips as he regarded her face. "There are other things I'd like to do with my mouth besides talk right now."

She thrust her chin upward in defiant invitation. "Like what?"

"If I tell you, I'm not silent." He lowered his face and pressed his mouth to hers.

Maybe it was the wine, but trails of molten heat flooded out from his kiss. Clinging to his neck, she was glad for the support as her knees turned to jelly.

His mouth left hers, and his wine-touched breath brushed her cheek. "The girls may see us."

Normally, the moment would have shattered because she'd have heard her mother's chiding voice overlaying the warning. But Lucas felt safe. Safe in a world filled with uncertainty, and she wanted him. She wanted to forget everything if only for a few moments of pleasure. "They're entertaining each other." She nibbled along his neck. "Let's sneak down to the koi pond. I bet no one's there."

As she pulled away to lead him there, his arms tightened, crushing her against him. "I think we'd better wait."

She relaxed and curled her fingers through the hair at the base of his neck. He smelled like spice. Cloves? "The girls are probably having so much fun they won't miss us."

He bent and brushed a kiss against her lips again, gone too soon. "For your sake as much as theirs."

Heat rose from her belly to her face. "What're you saying?"

"Did you know you're slurring?"

"I just need food." She broke away and strode toward the pool. At least she tried to stride; the ground seemed to move out from under her. Chin high, she stumbled to the atrium and searched for a plate.

"Here," his voice said behind her.

She spun to see him holding out a plastic plate. All the green food on the table smelled delicious. Then she remembered. How many of these dishes contained amaranth? For all she knew, scientists had inserted rat DNA in it to increase the protein content. The wine in her stomach sloshed and filled her throat. She dashed outside just in time to heave burgundy fluid all over the pool deck.

Chapter Six

J aide sat with her feet curled under her on Ginger's padded deck chair and stared out over the dark garden. Music pounded through the air from the pool at the other side of the house, but the deck off the living room remained clear of guests. Probably to steer clear of the woman who'd spattered their feet with vomit.

A hand holding a glass of ice water appeared over her shoulder, and she lifted her eyes. Lucas asked, "Feeling better?"

She nodded and took the glass. "Thank you." Her stomach and throat burned. "I'd really like to go home now."

He sat on the edge of the chair to her right. Light from the living area slanted through the windows to carve shadows onto his face. "I can't let you drive, but I'll take you home."

"I'm not drunk anymore." She sipped from the glass, the water hitting her stomach like a cold fist.

"Still not a good idea to get behind the wheel. Tomorrow I can bring you back for your car."

She covered her eyes with one hand. "I can't believe I threw up like that in front of everyone." Not to mention doing it yesterday at the weed pull. She was going to get a reputation.

"Food poisoning, maybe?"

"I haven't eaten anything."

"That explains it." He rose. "I'll make you a plate."

"No!" She jerked upright, sloshing water over the rim of her glass. She couldn't stomach eating that weed. For all she knew, TelomerGen had been experimenting on amaranth to create a new kind of insecticide. "I mean—I'm really picky."

"I'll bring you some of my quiche. You eat eggs, cheese, and spinach—er, amaranth, right?"

Her gut churned. "No. I mean..." How could she tell him without giving herself away? She hugged the glass against her chest, letting the condensation soak into her shirt. "The Extension Service thinks there may be a GMO weed loose."

"No kidding?" He scraped his chair around to face her and sat. "What kind of weed?"

She couldn't seem to draw a full breath. *Reveal nothing.* But she wanted him to know. She wanted everyone to know. "The Extension Agent took samples from that palmer amaranth you and I were pulling."

"So it's not confirmed?"

"The plants were freakishly tall."

He leaned back in the chair. "That doesn't mean anything. The hot spring weather made things sprout early."

She licked her lips and looked down into her water glass. "Better safe than sorry, don't you think?"

"I refuse to live a life in fear of maybes. And even if it is genetically modified, that doesn't mean it's dangerous."

In the distance, a siren wailed. She closed her eyes and pictured the patch of amaranth, the broad leaves, the bare earth around the stalks. "Something wasn't right about them. Didn't you notice how nothing else seemed to be growing nearby? Nature knows what's unnatural and avoids it."

He crossed an ankle over his other knee. "Maybe they were simply able to grow in a contaminated spot. There have been great advances in phytoremediation plants that clean up heavy metals or petrochemicals in soil. Plants like that could be a good thing, GMO or not. Although it probably isn't a good idea to eat those..."

The siren grew louder. Behind them, through the big picture windows, a small herd of people entered the living room. Jaide craned her neck to see over the back of her chair. "What's going on?"

Lucas rose. "I think the siren's in the driveway. I'll go see."

Jaide stood and followed him. Inside, people were funneling through the front door. Red light flashed against the entryway wall from the ambulance outside. Ginger spotted Jaide and rushed over, putting the back of her hand to Jaide's forehead. "Are you feeling better? Any more vomiting or pain?"

"I'm so sorry about that. I feel fine now."

"You're not the only one. Three others are sick, and one man collapsed. The ambulance is here now."

Alarmed, Jaide looked around for Flora. "Have you seen my daughter?"

But Ginger had already turned away, pushing through the crowd on the other side of the door.

Lucas took Jaide's arm. "They were in the cabana a few minutes ago."

She raced back through the atrium to the pool. A few people stood around while Price swabbed a mop through a puddle of vomit. The girls were nowhere in sight.

"Flora!" Jaide called as she ran toward the cabana.

The paned-glass door opened a crack, and Flora's face appeared. "Mom?"

"Did you eat anything?"

"Yes, I ate."

"What? What did you eat?"

Flora heaved a sigh and rolled her eyes. "Some fish and the curry you brought."

Suzanne opened the door the rest of the way and stood next to Flora. "What's wrong?"

Lucas moved to the door to put the back of his hand on Suzanne's forehead. "Some people have gotten sick, that's all. Probably food poisoning. Are you feeling all right?"

Suzanne nodded.

"Is that why you got sick?" Flora asked.

Jaide swallowed and looked at the ground. Much as she didn't want to admit being drunk to her daughter, she believed in honesty. "I drank too much too fast."

Lucas put an arm around Jaide and gave her a quick squeeze. "Your real mistake was drinking on an empty stomach. It could happen to anyone."

Her heart filled with gratitude at his attempt to defend her.

He turned to look toward the house. "Food poisonings don't usually make people sick this fast. I should help make sure everyone's okay."

Jaide and the girls followed him through the atrium and kitchen to the front door. Outside on the driveway, two ambulances sat, rear doors open and lights flashing. About thirty people clustered to watch as a man in a paramedic shirt closed the door on the lead ambulance and climbed into the driver's seat. The ambulance pulled away, waiting until it reached the end of the driveway to resume its siren wail.

Cindy elbowed through the crowd, eyes on Jaide. "They just took Gerald to the hospital."

"Oh, no!" Jaide reached out to take Cindy's hand and pull her closer. "What happened?"

"He threw up like you did. No warning. He started trembling and had to sit down. His lips turned blue—like, literally blue!"

"Oh, shit."

Cindy pointed to the other ambulance. "Other people are having the same symptoms. Betty and Hunter and Jen. Are you okay?"

"I'm fine," Jaide said, glancing back at her daughter. "Flora said she ate some of the fish. Could it be the fish?"

Cindy gasped. "What if it's tetanus or something?"

"You don't get tetanus from food." *Or could you?* That was the danger from GMO foods; no one knew for sure what the side effects might be. Disease, poison, allergies... or worse. That amaranth had to be brought under control immediately, before anyone else got sick. "Can I talk to you in private?"

"Now? I should go to the hospital to see Gerald." Cindy chewed her lip. "Can I borrow your car?"

"I really need to talk to you."

"He could be dying." Cindy squeezed Jaide's hand until the bones hurt.

Jaide bit back the desire to remind Cindy she hardly knew the guy. That was an assumption, but Cindy's track record spoke for itself. "If you take my car, how will I get home?"

Cindy cocked a brow. "You and Lucas seem pretty chummy."

Jaide shrugged, scanning the crowd. Lucas knelt next to a man who sat on the lawn, head between his knees. It seemed like a lifetime ago since she'd kissed him. "How many people are sick?"

"I'm not sure. Several. But Gerald was the worst. He said he has a heart condition. Please give me your keys."

Jaide leveled a look at her friend. "Only after you listen to me for a minute."

Cindy glowered. "Fine. What?"

"Not here." Jaide led her back inside the house and to the deck where she'd sat with Lucas only a short while ago. She shut the sliding door behind her and scanned the area to be sure no one was around. "It's about the greenhouse," she whispered.

Cindy tossed up her hands. "There's more important stuff happening right now."

"No, seriously. Yesterday while I was with the weed warriors, the Extension agent mentioned GMO amaranth. She took samples from a patch we were pulling."

"So?"

"The greenhouse was growing amaranth."

Cindy sucked in a breath. "Seriously?"

"Yes."

Silence choked the darkness.

Finally, Cindy sighed. "Figures. Is that all?"

"What do you mean, is that all?"

"There's nothing we can do about it." Cindy shrugged.

Jaide leaned closer, keeping her voice low. "We might have tracked it out that night. We could be responsible."

"Anyone working there could have tracked it out. The company should have had better safety measures in place. Isn't this why GMOs are so dangerous?"

Jaide ran a hand over the top of her hair. "It's our responsibility to do something, don't you think?"

"What do you suggest? Turn ourselves in?" Cindy put her hands on her hips. "That won't make the weeds go away."

"We should start another weed warrior group and make a point of pulling every single weekend." The plants couldn't have spread far in this amount of time. "We can rally people and eradicate it before it gets out of control."

"You won't find anyone willing to pull weeds every weekend. I know I won't."

Jaide grabbed her friend by both arms. "We can't let this spread. What if that's what's making people sick tonight?"

"Don't be silly." Cindy pulled herself free. "People have been eating GMOs for decades. Besides, the government will get it under control. It's not as big a deal as you're making it."

"You sound like Lucas." Jaide felt like crying.

"He has a point. Can I please use your car now?"

Jaide's pulse thundered in her ears. Cindy had always been fickle in her causes, joining one or another to impress a guy, but at least she'd been consistent in picking ecological issues. She knew nature was in danger. Surely she hadn't raided the greenhouse only to impress Trevor?

The door slid open, and Flora's voice drifted out. "Mom?"

"Yeah, love?"

"Can Suzanne spend the night?"

"Not a good plan tonight."

Flora cocked a hand on her hip and let her head loll to one side. "But we want to hang out."

"You can see her again next time."

"Mo-om," Flora dropped her hand from her hip and slumped forward.

"I said no!" Both hands flew to her mouth—she'd sounded just like her mother.

Flora gaped at her then withdrew, sliding the door shut with a thump.

"Where are your keys?" Cindy asked, sliding past Jaide toward the door. "In your purse?"

Before she reached it, Lucas pulled the sliding glass open from the other side. "I think this party's over. Let me drive you and Flora home."

Cindy planted a kiss on Jaide's cheek. "Sounds like your ride is covered. Chill out about the weeds, okay? I'll bring your car back tomorrow."

Jaide floundered for an excuse to stop her, but before she could think of one, Cindy was gone.

Chapter Seven

When there's nothing else, eat hope.
~ MOTHER'S PROVERB

"I'm sorry you didn't get to try my quiche," Lucas said as he pulled out of the driveway behind an SUV. "Can I take you two out to eat instead? There's a great tapas place over on State Street."

"Oh, can we, Mom? Please?" Flora begged from the back seat.

Jaide wanted to say no, but her empty stomach and the empty curry dish on her lap seemed to talk for her. "That would be lovely."

The girls squealed from the back seat. Jaide wished she could smile. "Do you think people could be sick from something besides food poisoning?"

The streetlights flashed by, strobing Lucas's face in and out of shadow. "You feeling sick again?"

"No. I mean what if—" the words stuck in her throat. "What if the amaranth made them sick?"

He laughed. "You're really dead set on the anti–GMO thing, aren't you?"

She turned to stare out the side window. She missed the old days when she could vent freely about GMOs. Talking about them now was like walking a tightrope. She had to regain her balance.

"I'm sorry," he said. "I know you're bothered by the technology. Why don't we wait to hear what the doctors say before jumping to any conclusions?"

She nodded mutely. He could be right. She felt horrible wishing for food poisoning.

"I have a confession." Lucas signaled to turn onto State Street.

A sense of dread broke over Jaide. She turned to look at him. "What?"

"I used spinach in the quiche."

Her lungs released like a deflating balloon. "Oh."

He grinned sheepishly. "The amaranth we were pulling yesterday was gone by the time I got back. You guys did a good job cleaning up."

She swallowed. Should she ask him to help? With Trevor gone and Cindy dismissive, she felt as if she'd been set afloat without a paddle atop waves and waves of toxic amaranth. "Would you want to go weed pulling again next weekend?"

"Penance for lying?"

Her lips spread in a tremulous smile. "If you like."

He stopped the car and backed into a parallel parking spot. "Let me look at my schedule. Saturday or Sunday?"

"Whichever works for you." Suddenly shy, she added, "It may be only you and me."

He put the car in park and quirked a sideways smile in her direction. The girls piled out of the car onto the sidewalk, and he pulled the keys and got out without replying. Her pulse pounded in her ears. Why did he make her so nervous? She reached for her door handle just as he opened the door from the outside. The scent of fresh bread wafted from a dingy, brick-front restaurant a few doors down.

He held out an arm to escort her. "I'll make a point to have one day off this weekend. To pull weeds with you."

"Thank you." She took his arm, amazed by the wash of gratitude that spilled over her. Pulling weeds without a partner was lonely enough when she went with the Coalition volunteers. Going completely alone was a hurdle she didn't want to leap.

Ahead, the girls entered the restaurant. Lucas held the door for her. She passed through, and her eyes widened. From the outside, she'd expected a mom-and-pop–type joint with plastic seats and paper placemats. Instead she saw mahogany woodwork, linen-draped tables, and crystal goblets. A maître d' stepped from behind his desk to greet them. "Table for four?"

She spun and whispered, "This is too expensive."

"My treat." He nodded to the maître d'. "Please."

Jaide rubbed clammy hands against the front of her jeans, thinking of the twenty-dollar bill in her purse she'd been saving for groceries between now and next payday. Letting him pay didn't feel comfortable, but neither did starving her daughter for the next four days. She watched Flora follow Suzanne to the table, shoulders back in proud imitation of her new friend. At least her daughter's dark hair had been combed after an evening in the pool, but her faded, second-hand blouse and shorts made Jaide feel even more exposed.

The waiter held out her chair, and she sat, gripping her purse against her lap with one hand. She took the menu and scanned the prices to find the least expensive items. She could get Tempura Green Beans for seven dollars, and Flora could have Loaded Potato Cakes for eight. She shut the menu.

"Something to drink?" asked the waiter.

"Just water for us," said Jaide.

Suzanne spoke up. "We want ginger spritzers."

"Make that four," said Lucas. Before Jaide could protest, he leaned close. "Ginger's good for stomach trouble."

As the waiter left, she peeked into the menu again to check the price. Four dollars a glass. All desire for food left her.

"We should share entrees," Lucas said. "I recommend the Brie and Fig Flatbread, and the Meze. Anyone have something special they want to add?"

Suzanne bounced in her seat. "I want Kobe Beef Sliders."

Jaide's mouth dropped open in horror. "Do you know what Kobe Beef is?"

"Dad says it's not real. Right?" Suzanne turned trusting eyes to Lucas.

"Not real Kobe, but it is real beef," he said.

Suzanne turned conspiratorially toward Flora. "Wait until you taste them. They're the best burgers ever."

Jaide leaned forward. "We don't eat meat."

Flora glared at her menu, face fiery red. "Speak for yourself, Mom."

Jaide's breath hitched like she'd been punched.

"I thought you ate fish?" Suzanne asked.

Lucas set his menu down. "Suz, many vegetarians don't consider fish meat."

"But fish are animals, too," Suzanne said.

Jaide couldn't stop staring at her daughter. She wanted Flora to make her own choices, but she'd taught her better. "We only eat wild-caught fish. They don't suffer a life in factory farms or require chemicals or cause soil erosion like other animals. Right, Flora?"

Flora kept her eyes on her menu.

"Let's get sliders for those who want them, and Caribbean

Tacos for those who don't." Lucas raised his brows, looking around the table for agreement.

Jaide nodded and returned to her menu without seeing it. The entire night had been one tornado after another, with no time for her to dust herself off between blows. Maybe the order would come and Flora would change her mind. She could just be trying to be cool with the older girl.

The drinks arrived in tall, thick tumblers garnished with lime wedges and mint leaves. She took a sip. The burn of ginger hit the back of her throat, and she started coughing.

"You okay?" Lucas rubbed a hand on her back. "Should've warned you about the ginger, I guess."

Her phone buzzed a text alert from her purse. Once her eyes stopped watering, she pulled it out. Cindy had sent, GERALD'S ON OXYGEN!

Jaide thumbed back, DO THEY KNOW WHAT CAUSED IT?

The first dishes arrived—what looked like a Mediterranean plate with hummus, pita bread, falafel, and tzatziki, plus the brie cheese and fruit. Saliva filled her mouth, and in spite of her previous misgivings, she set her phone beside her plate and dug in with the others. The brie melting against her tongue tasted like heaven.

Her phone buzzed again, and she read, SOMETHING I CAN'T PRONOUNCE. METHA SOMETHING OR OTHER.

She shot back, ARE THEY KEEPING HIM OVERNIGHT? HOW ARE THE OTHERS?

"Who's that?" Lucas asked.

"Cindy says Gerald's on oxygen. Metha something or other." He raised his brows. "Scary."

"Do you know what she's talking about?"

He shook his head and took another bite of hummus.

She popped a fig into her mouth. Two more dishes arrived, and Jaide picked up her drink to take a small sip, needing something to focus on besides the tiny hamburger buns bulging with glistening brown meat. Should she reassure Flora that she didn't have to eat any?

Her phone buzzed again. GERALD'S THE ONLY ONE HERE. NITRATE POISONING.

"What causes nitrate poisoning?" she asked out loud.

Lucas was eating what looked like a corn tortilla stuffed with shredded cabbage. He took a moment to swallow. "That's usually only in babies. From drinking water. Why? Is that what she's saying?"

Jaide was texting when her phone started chirping its robin-song ringtone. She answered, "Cindy?"

"The doctors say someone must've cooked with saltpeter. Have you heard of that? It sounds like a nursery rhyme."

Relief flooded Jaide's chest. It wasn't the amaranth, then. She met Lucas's eyes. "Saltpeter?"

He let out a snort of laughter. "Someone trying to cook like their grandma. It was used as a food preservative."

"Lucas says it was used for food preservation a long time ago."

Cindy said, "Ohhh, still with Lucas? How's that going?"

Warmth spread up Jaide's cheeks, and she twisted away from the table, hoping Lucas couldn't see. "He took us to dinner."

"Call me tomorrow and dish." Cindy giggled, and Jaide's cheeks grew even hotter.

"How dangerous is saltpeter? Is Gerald going to be okay?" Jaide asked.

"The doctors say he'll be fine in a few hours, once the medicine they gave him works. I bet Sam did it. She's always canning and fermenting and crap like that." Staticky voices on an intercom pierced the background. "I'd better go. Gerald will wonder where I am. Kisses."

The line went dead. Jaide returned the phone to her purse. When she turned back to the table, Flora had her mouth around one of the disgusting burgers. For the third time in two days, Jaide's stomach threatened to expel its contents. By sheer force of will, she managed to keep it down.

Chapter Eight

Looking in the bathroom mirror, Jaide twisted an elastic band around her dark hair to keep it out of her face. Lucas was picking her up any minute to go weed hunting, and she found herself unusually concerned with her appearance. Flora stood behind her in the open doorway, arms crossed. "Mom, are you mad at me?"

"Why would I be mad at you?" Jaide frowned.

"Because I eat meat." After eating out with Lucas and Suzanne the other night, Flora had confessed to occasionally consuming meat at school with her friends. Jaide was still proud of herself for not blowing up. But perhaps she had been giving Flora a bit of a cold shoulder.

"Love, I support your choices, no matter if they match mine or not." Jaide tried to view this as a rebellious phase, one Flora would outgrow. "I wasn't always a vegetarian, you know."

"I know, I know. Grandma used to force you to gag down meat when you were little."

Jaide grimaced, remembering sitting at the dinner table long after the rest of the family had been excused, eventually swallowing cold bits of animal flesh whole, just so she could get up. "Why do you think I'm mad at you?"

Flora met her eyes in the mirror. "You didn't invite me to pull weeds."

Belly fluttering with hope, Jaide spun to face her. "You want to come?"

Her daughter knit her brows in disdain. "No. I'm just used to you nagging me to come help."

The thrill in Jaide's breast flickered and died as Flora flounced out of sight. "We can always use more hands," Jaide called.

No answer. Too bad Lucas's daughter had volleyball camp this weekend, or she'd have convinced both girls to help. Jaide's heart ached that she couldn't afford extracurricular activities for Flora. Then she reminded herself that she provided other opportunities. How many little girls could say they'd carried a protest sign all by themselves as soon as they could walk? Or grew their own vegetables on a four-by-four balcony?

The thought reminded her that the veggie pots probably needed watering again. She could hardly keep up on hot days like today. She called over her shoulder, "Flora, would you water the garden for me while I'm gone?"

"Sure, Mom," Flora called back.

Jaide sighed with contentment. Flora had a good life, in touch with nature. In spite of teenage hormones and the willful consumption of meat, her daughter was healthy and happy.

A whimsical knock came from the apartment door. She smiled at herself one last time in the mirror and took a breath. She didn't know if this was a date—wasn't even sure she wanted it to be—but she'd be alone with Lucas all day, and that made her nervous.

Without looking through the peephole, she opened the apartment door and stiffened. "Trevor?"

Her missing friend screwed up his face in a chagrined smile. "Hey."

Her muscles turned to gelatin as she took in his clean-shaven lip and pallid face. He looked as though he hadn't seen the sun in weeks. Trigger brushed past her knees to investigate the visitor. Jaide put a hand against the doorframe to steady herself. "Where have you been?"

Trevor ran a hand through his hair and looked away. The slogan on his T-shirt read KISS ME I'M AN ENVIRONMENTALIST. "Yeah, about that. There's this girl..."

She waited for him to say more. When he didn't, she said, "A girl? Are you kidding? Did you know the FBI was looking for you?"

"I heard." He shoved his hands into his pockets. "Word is they've moved on."

Trigger, apparently satisfied, plodded back into the apartment and flopped into her bed with a sigh.

Jaide wasn't so easily mollified. "Moved on? How do you know that?"

"Sources." He shrugged. "You know me."

Somehow he did always seem to have connections. Like getting the layout for the greenhouse cameras. "So you're back? You've been gone for months. What about your job?"

"I don't need it. Had plenty in savings. It's cool."

Jaide blinked at him a few times. How could he be so relaxed about it? As if he hadn't been missing for over half a year? She frowned. "So who's this girl who makes you run off without a word to your friends?"

"Hippie chick. Totally on board with the movement, you know?" He stared at the floor, scuffing the toe of one shoe against a gouge in the linoleum. "We have a lead on something big."

The air around Jaide seemed to thicken, pressing about her until she could feel her pulse in every nerve ending. "A lead."

Trevor looked at her from beneath his brows. "We need a place to stay. Just a night or two."

She leaned into the hall to look in both directions then glanced over her shoulder into the apartment to make sure Flora wasn't nearby. "Are you kidding me? I thought we'd agreed to stop."

He shifted from foot to foot. "Can we talk inside?"

"There's nothing to talk about. I have a daughter to take care of. I can't be involved anymore."

"Your kid won't have a world worth living in if we don't do something about these corporations."

Nausea rolled through her stomach again. "Trevor, they're saying GMO weeds are loose." She lowered her voice. "GMO amaranth."

His face darkened, lips growing thin and pale. He pulled his hands from his pockets and balled them into fists at his sides. "This proves our point—GMO can't be contained."

"What if we tracked stuff out? Seeds? Pollen? What if it's our fault?"

"It's not. It's the corporation's. Nature shouldn't be messed with."

"We need to do something about the amaranth, don't you think? Not pursue some new and dangerous information." She pointed behind her to her bucket. "Lucas and I are going weed pulling today. Come with us."

"Lucas Harmon?" Trevor shuffled back a step. "How'd you hook up with him?"

Jaide bit her lip. Maybe bringing Trevor along wasn't a good idea, especially with the mood he was in. "He's been very helpful."

"Sure he's not a spy?"

"Of course he's not," Jaide rolled her eyes. "He's a good man."

Down the hall, the main stairway door creaked as someone opened it. Turning that direction, Trevor shoved his hands back into his pockets. "Lucas is here. I'll see you at the next meeting, huh?"

He slouched off toward the stairwell. Jaide opened her mouth to call after him but couldn't choose among all the things she wanted to say. Lucas nodded at Trevor as he passed.

Trigger bumped past Jaide's legs, tail wagging furiously in anticipation of yet another visitor.

Stopping at her door, Lucas reached down to scratch between the dog's ears. "Thought Trevor was MIA?"

Jaide still reeled from the visit. "He says he ran off with a girl."

"Know how that goes." Lucas winked at her and held up a pair of gardening gloves. "They have a way of making us men do stupid things."

She raised a brow. "I can't imagine a girl making you leave your job."

"No, but a certain girl I know does get me to pull other people's weeds."

Heat flooded her cheeks, and she turned toward the apartment to hide her face. Even if Cindy and Trevor refused to take responsibility for the amaranth, Jaide had Lucas on her side. They might not agree on everything, but differences could be good, right? Opposites attract and all that. "Flora, I'm going!"

"Bye!" Flora's voice floated from her bedroom.

Jaide grabbed Trigger's leash, the bucket, and a small hand shovel, then took Lucas's arm. She wasn't alone in this battle. That Franken-weed was doomed.

Chapter Nine

OCTOBER

Heed a Mother's words, for she will not be with you forever.

~ MOTHER'S PROVERB

J aide tied Trigger up outside the food co-op under the skeletal tree and entered the store, scanning the checkout lines and bustling aisles. The first of the month was always the busiest, and if she could have avoided it, she would have. But her paycheck arrived the same time as everyone else's, so she was stuck fighting the crowds.

She skirted past a heavy man with a full shopping cart and headed toward the coolers at the back of the store. A mom with two toddlers in a double-wide stroller chatted loudly on a cell phone while she read the label on the back of a box of cookies. Jaide reached the coolers and scowled at the sparse shelves. The co-op was usually better about keeping stocked.

An acquaintance from the Coalition opened the cooler door

next to her and added the last package of tofu to her handbasket. "Hey, Jaide."

Jaide pulled out a carton of free-range eggs. "Hi, Dee. More crowded than usual today."

"First wave of panic," said Dee, shifting her full basket to her other arm.

"Panic? For what?"

"Didn't you hear?"

Jaide shook her head. "I've had my phone off all morning."

"The EPA and USDA finally got together and confirmed that a genetically modified plant's on the loose."

Jaide's stomach dropped out from under her. She'd stalked the weed all summer, spending every free weekend with one invasive weed group or another. While the other participants agreed the amaranth was invasive and needed to be pulled, no one thought it was any worse than the other weeds, and she couldn't divulge her inside information. Now she had corroboration it wasn't normal. Yet the only words that came to her mouth were "Oh, God."

"Exactly," said Dee. "This weed's poisoning livestock."

"Poisoning?" Jaide had tried to forget the potluck, especially since Gerald was the only one hospitalized. The doctors had said his severe reaction was a complication of his heart medication. Now her suspicions resurfaced.

"I don't know the details. Bunch of sick cows or something. I'm just pissed that the first line of attack is chemicals. The state already approved pre-emergent herbicides along roadways and in public parks. Undid years of Coalition work. Buy your organic food now, because next year, everything's likely to be sprayed."

Jaide leaned against the open cooler door. Talking about the weed felt forced after all this time keeping her secret.

Forbidden. "Those plants are unnatural." While pulling weeds, she'd encountered amaranth more than forty miles away from the greenhouse. Hand pulling, even in teams, had often seemed worthless. "In the face of Franken-weeds, herbicides might not be so bad, don't you think?"

Dee gasped and then glowered at her. "Herbicide residues are the root of modern disease. Drenching the soil with toxins is not an acceptable solution."

Jaide swallowed. Maybe she'd been hanging out with Lucas too much—she was losing her values. "You're right. I've been pulling invasive weeds all summer and feel a little defeated. You want to join us on Saturday?"

"What time?"

"Eight in the morning."

Dee made a face. "I'm going to a party Friday night."

"If that's too early—"

"No. I'll be there. Just don't expect me to smile while I help repair corporate mistakes."

Dee left for the checkout line, and Jaide grabbed her last few items before heading home, anxious to scan the news feeds. Now that the GMO invasion was confirmed, she could properly rally people to join her weed brigade. *Amaranth Brigade.* She liked the sound of that.

As soon as she left the co-op, she turned on her phone. Pinging alerts for text messages and voicemail clamored for attention. Before she could begin calling people back, her robin-song ringtone chirped, and Lucas's picture lit the screen. They'd been officially dating for a few months now, but between his work schedule and carving out time for his daughter, it sometimes felt as though they were carrying on a long-distance relationship. "Hey, Lucas."

"You were right about GMO weeds. I'm eating crow."

"Ew, don't even joke. Poor birds."

He laughed. "I've spread the word here at work that you're leading a team of weed pullers. I may have a few signups for you."

"Oh, thank you! I'm renaming the movement the Amaranth Brigade. Good name, don't you think?"

"Very fitting. Wish I could make it Saturday."

"Just pull any you see while you're out on the job."

"I don't think the people I'm supposed to be saving would appreciate that. But I'll definitely make note if I see any."

He'd told her of more than a few spots over the course of the summer, even though he couldn't join her often. "Thanks, Lucas."

"Dinner tomorrow? It's the only day I have free all week."

"I have a Coalition meeting tomorrow night, and I need to rally people against this weed. You could come to that."

"Uh, I'll pass, thanks."

"Oh, come on. What do you have against the Coalition?"

"I told you. Too emotional. Most of that group would stone me to death if I brought up support for the other side."

"Then don't bring it up."

"Your friends like to talk, but they never listen."

"I listen to you. Even if you are wrong."

He laughed again. "There's hope for you yet. You sure you won't move in with me?"

He'd asked her two weeks ago, but moving would require Flora changing schools, and Jaide had made a promise to wait until high school began next year. Plus, Jaide wasn't quite sure she was ready to take that next step. "You're a pest," she joked. "I told you to ask me again this spring, when school's over."

"A guy can hope." His smile came through over the line.

She reached her apartment building and started climbing the stairs. "Call me when you have a day off, 'kay?"

After saying goodbye, Jaide put away the groceries and surfed the Internet for news on the weed. Her usual websites were pinging with wild speculations; corporations had let the weed loose so they could sell more herbicides, the plants were hallucinogenic, the government was planning to quarantine the entire state. One site even claimed the plants were actually an alien life form come to take over the world.

I caused all this, she thought, skimming article after article. Mutant weeds taking over the world happened in bad science fiction movies, not in real life. A knock at her door drew her attention. She padded to the peephole, Trigger at her heels. In the hall stood two men in dark suits.

She pulled away as if they could spot her through the peephole. Were they here to arrest her? Of course they were. The weed had been confirmed GMO. They must have proof she'd released it.

What if she simply didn't answer the door? Her lungs couldn't get enough air. Did they have a search warrant? What if they broke the door down?

The knock sounded again. Trigger cocked her head and let out a small, questioning whine.

Jaide thrust out a palm to quiet the dog and tiptoed back to the kitchen. Flora wasn't due home for another three hours. Sitting, she dropped her head between her knees. Trigger nosed up under one arm, doggy breath in Jaide's face.

Her phone started chirping from her back pocket, and she nearly wet herself. Snatching it free, she fumbled with the buttons to reject the call. *Oh, God, oh, God.* Had they heard it? Now they'd know she was inside. She sat, afraid to move, and listened. They knocked once more, then the apartment fell silent. She waited and listened. Listened and waited. Only the usual apartment sounds reached her—music somewhere in the distance, the drone of the heating ducts, traffic outside the window.

After a long while, she looked at her phone again. The little light alerted her she had another message. Her call log showed her mother as the last caller. Punching in her passcode, she listened to the recording. "Jaide, the police have been here asking questions about you. Are you in some kind of trouble? Call me as soon as you get this."

Jaide let her hands fall to her lap. It was over. The amaranth was her fault, and she had to pay the price. If only she had more time to make it right. She looked at her phone. An hour had passed. She rose and approached the door. Through the peephole, the hall was empty. Surely the FBI wouldn't give up that easily? They must have gone for a warrant.

Turning her back to lean against the door, she breathed deeply. Trigger nosed her hand, hoping they were going out again. She pushed the dog away. Did the authorities already have Cindy and Trevor? She needed to get her affairs in order and make sure Flora was protected. Striding to her daughter's bedroom, she began packing. She'd drive to her mother's and get Flora enrolled in school there.

Once all her daughter's things were packed, she dialed her mother. "Hi, Mother. It's Jaide."

"Jaide, why are the police asking questions about you?"

She forced the words past unwilling vocal cords. "I need you to take Flora."

"Are you in trouble? What's going on?"

"I can't tell you." A rushing sound filled her ears, like the pounding of a waterfall wearing away rock. "I just need you to take her."

"She doesn't even know me."

Guilt swamped Jaide. How had it come to this? Giving her

beloved daughter to the woman she'd worked so hard to avoid? "You're all the family we've got."

Her mother made a harrumphing sound. "When you had that baby, I told you she'd ruin your life."

Jaide gritted her teeth. "This has nothing to do with Flora. I just want her safe."

Silence buzzed over the line for a few moments. "For how long?"

Jaide closed her eyes, picturing her mother, hands on hips, exuding an energy that far surpassed her petite frame. "I don't know."

"Do I need to come get her?"

Jaide had planned to drive Flora herself, but if the FBI was tailing her, she wanted them as far away from Flora as possible. "Could you?"

Her mother sighed, breath hissing through the earpiece. "I knew it would eventually come to me taking in your kid. I'll be there in a few hours."

Jaide clenched her hands so tight, her nails dug into her palms. She'd sworn Flora would never be exposed to the kind of criticism her mother doled out. But what other choice did she have? Her sister had five kids of her own to raise, not that they ever talked; Alice disagreed with just about everything Jaide stood for. Jaide's Coalition friends were childless by choice. And Lucas barely had time to see his own daughter. She couldn't ask him to step in and care for Flora. Her only option was her mother. "Thank you, Mother."

They hung up, and Jaide nervously tidied the apartment while she waited for Flora. If she slowed down, she'd break down. By the time her daughter got home from school, Jaide sat at the kitchen table with a snack ready.

"Mom?" Flora approached slowly. Trigger nudged her hand in a request to be petted.

Jaide smiled, trying to remain bright. "Hi, love. I made you celery and peanut butter."

Flora dropped her backpack beside the chair and frowned down at the plate. "What's going on? Why are there suitcases by the door?"

"You're going to visit your grandmother for a while."

Flora brightened. "We get to go on a trip?"

"She's coming to pick you up in a few hours."

"Wait, you're not coming?" Flora's brow puckered. "Why?"

"Have you heard the news about the weeds?"

Flora rolled her eyes and flopped to a seat. "The teachers wouldn't shut up about it today. I felt like I was at home being lectured by you."

"I don't lecture you."

"Whatever." Flora picked up a celery stick and started crunching.

Jaide folded her hands together under the table and took a breath. Now wasn't the time to start an argument over her teaching methods. "I want you safe while this whole weed business sorts out."

"We'll be fine, Mom. We have our patio garden. And I'll eat junk food if I have to." The sly look on Flora's face was almost enough to make Jaide smile.

"Grandma Chona probably has all kinds of junk food. And your cousins live nearby. You'll have a good time."

"But you don't even like Grandma."

Jaide's gut ached as she realized the example she'd set for Flora when it came to mother–daughter relationships. "Your grandma and I don't always agree, but we love each other. She's excited to get to know you."

Flora crossed her arms and stared across the table. "What're you not telling me?"

The question hung in the air between them. This could be

goodbye. The last time Jaide saw her daughter as a free woman. She held her arms open, choking back a sob. "Give me a hug."

Flora rose and came around the table to wrap her arms around Jaide's neck in a waft of peanut butter and celery. She spoke against Jaide's shoulder. "Mommy, you're scaring me."

"I love you so much, Flora." Jaide's throat pinched around the words. "I hope you know that no matter what. Everything I do, I do for you."

"I know. I love you, too."

"I can't talk to you about things now. You have to trust me. I wouldn't send you away unless it's important."

Flora's grip loosened and her spine stiffened. "Am I switching schools?"

"Yes." Jaide clutched tighter as her daughter struggled to pull away.

"But you promised! I don't want to leave my friends." Flora jerked free and put her hands on her hips. She looked so much like Jaide's mother right now, a moment of déjà vu made Jaide dizzy.

"There is no other choice."

A red flush crept up her daughter's neck. "This isn't fair. I'm not going."

Jaide sighed. She hated to scare her, but a little fear might be warranted right now. "Would you rather be in foster care?"

All of Flora's indignation melted away. She whispered, "Are you sick? Dying?"

"No. But those are your choices."

Flora blinked and wiped one eye. "Will I get to come back?"

"Of course, love." Jaide took a deep breath and willed herself to be strong. "Think of this as a vacation. You have friends who take vacations to visit grandparents, right?"

Flora nodded and knelt to once again embrace her mother.

Jaide stroked her hair and savored the particular scent that was all Flora. "Grandma's going to spoil you rotten. You'll never want to come home."

She honestly hoped that was true.

Just after sunset, someone pummeled the door with an impatient fist. Jaide's heart lurched. What if the FBI returned before her mother arrived? She didn't know which visitor she dreaded more. She crept toward the door to look through the peephole. Her mother's dark gaze met hers as if it might bore through the door at any moment.

Steeling herself, Jaide unlatched the deadbolt and opened the door. "Hi, Mother."

"Where's that baby?" Her mother pushed past her and bee-lined for the living room, her Prada handbag swinging wildly from her forearm.

Flora hung back near the sofa, hands wrapped around a frayed purse with the last of Jaide's cash inside. Trigger hung near Flora's side, as if sensing something wrong.

Grandma Chona wrapped Flora in a hug. Her kitten-heel pumps barely brought the top of her head level with the teenager's. "Oh, how you've grown."

Flora stared wide eyed at Jaide over her grandmother's shoulder and then patted the petite woman's back. "I'm thirteen now, Grandma."

"Of course you are." She drew back, keeping her hands on Flora's shoulders to give her a once-over. "Do you have everything you need? We won't get home until past your bedtime."

Pressure in Jaide's chest welled up until her face burned. She didn't want to cry, not in front of Flora or her mother. She patted her leg and gathered Trigger's leash. Trigger trotted over, tail wagging. "I'm sending the rest of Trigger's food, but you'll need to get more soon."

Her mother turned to face her and put her hands on her hips. "Trigger?"

"The dog." Jaide's fingers grew cold around the leash. She'd neglected to mention Trigger. Growing up, Jaide and her sister had begged for pets, but her mother never even entertained the notion. Animals were dirty. How could Jaide have forgotten?

"You know how I feel about animals in the house."

"Flora never goes anywhere without her." That wasn't exactly true, but if Jaide went to jail, Flora had to take the dog. Where else could Trigger go?

"Well, it's not coming with me."

Jaide rested a hand on Trigger's head. "Please. She's part of our family."

"I'll take care of her, Grandma, I promise." Flora smiled winsomely at her. "You won't even know she's there."

Jaide's mother crossed her arms, unaffected. "I told your mom while she was growing up and I'll tell you now, my home isn't a zoo. Dander and feces and dug-up lawns. Take it to the pound if you have to."

Flora gasped and drew away. "That's cruel! I'm not going without Trigger!"

New panic reared up inside Jaide. Whatever happened, she had to get Flora to safety. "It's okay, Flora. Trigger will stay with me. Get your things."

"No! I won't go."

"Flora, we talked about this—"

Flora stomped down the hall to her bedroom and banged the door shut.

Turning to her mother, Jaide begged, "Mother, please reconsider."

"Are you going to let your daughter act like that?" Her mother's gaze cut through Jaide like lasers.

Jaide couldn't find her voice.

"If she's going to be living with us, she'd better learn to respect her elders." With that, her mother marched to the bedroom door, shoved it open, and disappeared inside. Her voice pounded through the apartment. "Get up and get your things, young lady."

Heart in her throat, Jaide skittered down the hall in time to see her mother grab the covers Flora had dragged over her head and fling them aside. The tiny woman leveled a finger at Flora. "I'll carry you out of here if I have to."

Flora sat up and stared wide eyed at her grandmother. Her gaze shifted to Jaide. "Mom?"

Jaide took a deep breath and let it out. Chona might be petite, but the woman could and would hoist Flora over a shoulder and carry her from the apartment if need be. And Jaide would let her to keep Flora safe. "Do as she says."

On stiff legs, Flora rose, clutching the purse with the cash. Dropping her chin, she followed her grandmother out of the room, but her eyes remained on Jaide as she passed.

Jaide almost relented. Her baby girl looked so lost and forlorn. Then she pictured FBI agents dragging Flora to foster care while she watched, helpless in handcuffs. She couldn't allow that to happen. Her mother might be tough, but she was family.

"I'll see you both down to the car," Jaide said, following them into the hallway. Trigger whined as Jaide shut the door, leaving the dog behind.

Downstairs, a new Impala beeped as Mother deactivated the alarm, headlights bright in the darkened street. Dad made excellent money selling real estate; Flora would be well taken care of, at least. While her mother placed the bags in the trunk, Jaide turned to Flora and opened her arms.

Her daughter flung herself against Jaide's chest. "I don't want to go."

Jaide kissed the top of Flora's head, eyes bleary with tears. "I know, love. Me either. But this is best. It really is."

From the shadows across the street, two men in business suits climbed out of a dark sedan, their eyes trained on Jaide. Her fingers hooked against Flora's back. How could she be so stupid? Of course the FBI would be waiting for her. Now Flora would see exactly what Jaide had hoped to spare her. She pushed her daughter away. "Have a great time. I love you." She looked at her mother. "Take her, Mother. Thank you."

She stepped backward toward the building, hoping to at least escape into the foyer before the men crossed the street. Flora grappled for Jaide's hands, her sweet little face creased and flushed. "No, Mom. Please let me stay."

The men reached the Impala's bumper.

She jerked her fingers from Flora's grip, heart breaking. "Go with your grandma. Now, Flora."

"Jaide Acosta?" one of the men said.

Her pulse roared through her ears. Why was her mother just standing there? "Mother, take her!"

"Ms. Acosta, I'm Agent Phillips with the FBI." The man held up a badge.

Her mother opened the car's back door. "Get in the car, Flora."

Jaide's tongue felt paralyzed. She stared at the man's credentials without seeing them.

"Mom?" Flora's voice seemed to come from far away. "What's going on?" Somewhere in the background, Jaide's mother's voice jabbed the air with familiar authoritarian fierceness.

The second man moved to flank Jaide's other side, blocking Flora from view. "We need you to come with us to answer a few questions."

Jaide kept her eyes on the badge and nodded. The second man put a hand around her elbow and guided her across the street.

"Mom! Mom!" Flora's cries were muffled as the agent sealed Jaide into the sedan's back seat.

Chapter Ten

Never carry a man past his prime.
~ MOTHER'S PROVERB

J aide stared at the clean-cut agent across the wood-veneer table. He had a raised mole on his neck that reminded her of a chocolate chip. Behind him, a mirror covered the upper portion of the small room's wall just like interrogation rooms in the movies. She kept her hands in her lap, afraid their trembling would betray her, and avoided her own terrified gaze in the mirror.

"We've been looking for Trevor Finkman." His blue eyes bored into her like sharp-edged ice. "You know Trevor."

She nodded, breathing in shallow draughts through her nose. She hadn't seen Trevor since that day he'd shown up at her apartment. Had he followed through with his big lead? She licked her lips and kept her eyes on the agent's mole.

After a moment, he folded his arms and leaned forward to rest his elbows on the table in front of him. "We have video footage of that night at the greenhouse."

She grew light-headed as the blood drained from her face. Trevor had assured her the reflective tape on their baseball caps would hide their features from the cameras. This guy had to be bluffing. "I don't know what you're talking about."

"That's not all, Ms. Acosta. We've talked to Cindy Blunt."

Her gaze flicked up to meet his eyes. Had Cindy given up their names? But they'd made a pact... She squared her shoulders. Even if Cindy had betrayed them, without any physical evidence, it would be one person's word against another. "Like I said, I have no idea what you're talking about."

"A flash drive was left at the scene. Are you sure you have nothing to say?"

Every muscle in her body tightened. That damned flash drive. Yet the man hadn't actually accused her of anything. Maybe they hadn't been able to trace it. He was trying to trick her into talking. She shook her head and remained silent.

"The U.S. Attorney seeks to charge those involved with domestic terrorism."

The room seemed to tilt and spin. "What do you mean, domestic terrorism?"

"Twenty-five years in prison, Ms. Acosta." The words hung in the air for a few seconds while the man regarded her. "Your daughter will be a grown woman in that time. Probably have kids of her own by then."

"I'm not a terrorist." Jaide's throat ached around the words. Terrorists were men with beady eyes and machine guns. How could they call breaking into a greenhouse terrorism?

"Tell us what you know about Trevor's current plans."

Jaide clenched her folded hands beneath the table and tried to breathe normally. Was she under arrest? The FBI hadn't handcuffed her. Or Mirandized her, for that matter. Did they have to read rights to suspected terrorists? Doubt flooded her system like truth serum. "Should I have a lawyer or something?"

"Should you?" The man smiled as though he'd caught her in a trap.

"I have rights."

The door opened, and a woman entered carrying a laptop. "Hello, Ms. Acosta. I'm Agent Riese. We met a few months ago at your apartment."

Jaide nodded but said nothing.

Pulling another chair to the table, Riese sat and opened the computer. She clicked a few keys then spun the screen to face Jaide. "Here's a photo from one of the greenhouse cameras that night."

A black-and-white image of a figure sprawled on the floor among broken stalks, fallen leaves, and crushed paper bags. To Jaide's relief, the reflective tape on the baseball cap created a nimbus that blotted out the figure's face—her face. Then her attention shifted to the figure's outstretched arm. The coat sleeve had pulled up to expose a bare wrist—and a tattoo of a peace sign. Under the table, Jaide clutched her opposite hand around her tattoo as if to hide it. Could they identify her on that mark alone? She looked back at the agents.

One side of the man's mouth lifted in a self-satisfied smile. "Remember the greenhouse now?"

Agent Riese clicked shut the computer. "We're placing you under arrest for acts of domestic terrorism, Ms. Acosta."

A ringing filled Jaide's ears as the agent continued with a litany of her rights. Terrorism? Twenty-five years in prison? When she'd agreed to the break-in, she'd thought she might serve a few months for vandalism. Have a blot on her permanent record. Even when the FBI had put her into the car, she'd believed she could come back to her daughter within a few days—months at most.

Then she remembered Trigger, shut in the apartment alone. "My dog!"

Agent Riese frowned. "Ms. Acosta, do you understand your rights?"

Jaide shook her head. "I need someone to take care of my dog. She's alone in my apartment."

"All right. Is there someone we can call?"

Jaide looked down at her hands, knuckles white from clenching them together. Who could she ask to take Trigger? Lucas came to mind first, but his own daughter lived with his parents because of his time-consuming job. Cindy was likely in jail alongside Jaide. Mother refused to even consider taking a pet... The word "forever" floated through Jaide's head. By the time she got out of prison, Trigger would probably be dead. Jaide closed her eyes against tears.

The man rose. "I'll call the Humane Society."

"Wait!" Jaide thrust a hand out as if she might catch the man's sleeve. Maybe Trigger could be Lucas's firehouse dog. "Let me make a phone call."

"Terrorists don't get phone calls."

Jaide's blood turned to ice. "I get a phone call."

"That's only in the movies, Ms. Acosta. Under these conditions, you're not permitted to talk to anyone but your lawyer." Agent Riese held a pen poised above the pad of paper. "If you don't have someone for the dog, we'll be forced to contact the Humane Society."

"Please. Just one quick phone call."

"Sorry."

This wasn't how she wanted Lucas to find out about her incarceration, from a stranger asking a favor on her behalf. But what else could she do? "Lucas Harmon."

Agent Riese jotted down his number. "Do you have a lawyer you'd like us to call?"

"I can't afford a lawyer." Jaide wiped her eyes with the heels of her hands.

"We'll get you a public defender, then. Please come with me."

They took her to a desk and placed her hands on a scanner to record her fingerprints. Then she stood in front of a screen for photographs. The whole process felt surreal, as if at any moment someone would jump out and tell her this was a YouTube prank.

An officer escorted her to a corridor with cells on one side and a solid cement-brick wall on the other. Dim overhead florescent lights cast cold shadows in the corners of the cells they passed. The officer stopped and opened a cell holding two cots and a toilet. Inside, a black woman in baggy jeans lay on one bed with her hands behind her head. On the other bed, a smaller woman with very short goth hair sat with her elbows on her knees. They each glared at her as the cell door clicked shut, but said nothing.

Jaide stood frozen just inside the threshold, thinking of horror stories about jail. Were these women hardened criminals? What if she said the wrong thing and got stabbed while she slept? The dark woman's eyes closed again, and the short-haired woman returned her attention to the floor between her feet. Jaide let out a quiet sigh. These were just women like her. No reason to think they might wish her harm.

She took a step into the cell toward the bed with the goth woman. The inmate's head jerked up, and her face creased into what Jaide decided was a warning. Backing up, Jaide sank to the floor in the corner against the bars. Maybe the stories weren't all hype. She leaned her head against the cell wall and stared down the corridor. From neighboring cells, women's voices echoed against the concrete. Someone snored loudly, and someone else tapped an annoying rhythm against the metal bars.

At least her cellmates were quiet. Jaide closed her eyes and tried to cleanse her mind of panic. Flora was safely away and not in some random foster home, and Lucas would care for Trigger, no matter what he thought of Jaide's predicament. After an hour, chill from the cement floor invaded her bones. Her bladder ached, and she cracked an eye toward the stainless steel toilet. To use it, she'd have to pass between the women. Maybe she could hold it until the public defender arrived. She squeezed her eyes shut again, wrapping her arms tighter around her knees.

An officer arrived and opened the cell to admit a heavy-set woman with a newly blackened eye and a nose crusted with blood. She wore only one shoe, and her shirt had a tear at the shoulder, exposing her bra strap. The sour scent of alcohol and sweat filled the cell. The woman stumbled straight to the toilet and dropped her drawers.

The sound of her peeing made Jaide tighten her thighs. How much longer would she have to wait? The guard had gone before she thought to ask. Raising her chin, she addressed the room, "Do any of you know how long it takes to get a public defender?"

The short-haired woman narrowed her eyes. "What're you in for?"

From the other bed, Baggy Pants said, "It's the fucking middle of the night. Public defender ain't gonna show up 'til business hours tomorrow."

"Sometimes it takes a couple of days." Short-hair shrugged. "Depends on what you did."

Black-eye pulled her pants up and slurred, "Or the bastards told him to take his time. You rot in a cell a few days thinking the public defender don't have time for you, and you crack."

"Oh," said Jaide. A few days? The knot in her stomach twisted tighter, unanswered questions jabbing at her insides like rough-edged boulders.

Black-eye turned to Short-hair. "Move over."

Short-hair curled her lip in a silent snarl but complied. Black-eye sat on the bed and scooted back into the corner, drawing her bare foot up onto the mattress.

If Jaide was going to be here a few days, she'd have to use the toilet some time. She rose and approached the toilet. Baggy Pants's eyes popped open, and the other two turned their heads to watch as she passed.

"I'm just going pee," Jaide said.

"So go," said Baggy Pants, and closed her eyes.

Short-hair sneered but at least turned her face away, toward the cell bars. Black-eye leaned back against the wall and closed her eyes.

Completely self-conscious, Jaide did her business. There was no toilet paper and no sink to wash her hands. But at least her bladder was no longer under threat of rupture. She stood at the toilet and eyed the other bed. Baggy Pants still sprawled on her back, taking up the entire space.

"Excuse me," Jaide said, facing the bed.

Baggy Pants didn't open her eyes.

"Could you move over so I can sit?"

Still no response. Short-hair let out a tiny snort of laughter behind her.

Back of her neck prickling, Jaide resumed her seat in the corner. She could do one night on the floor. Maybe Baggy Pants's lawyer would show up first thing, and she'd vacate the bed. Jaide couldn't sleep right now, anyway. Her mind kept running over and over the image on the video. Was she the only one they'd identified? She pressed her cheek to the cold metal bars. If only she could talk to Cindy and Trevor.

What if the FBI was trying to scare a confession out of her with a night in jail? There had to be other people in the world with a peace-sign tattoo on their left wrist. The video was flimsy evidence at best. As long as she kept her mouth shut, she had a chance. Her lawyer would probably tell her they didn't even have a case against her.

She wasn't giving up on freedom yet.

Chapter Eleven

J aide startled awake to the cell door clanging open. The guard left it ajar and continued down the corridor. For a moment, she thought she was being set free, but Baggy Pants and Short-hair rose and filed out without any show of excitement. Jaide stumbled upright on stiff legs to follow along, tailbone on fire from sitting on the concrete all night. Along the corridor, prisoners filed out of the cells and toward the exit.

She merged into line as guards directed them to a cafeteria filled by rows of fold-up tables with built-in benches. Two hair-netted women stood behind a counter, handing out orange trays. The familiar scent of cooked oatmeal made Jaide's stomach rumble. At the counter, she accepted the bowl of gray, overcooked porridge with gratitude. She couldn't even remember the last time she'd eaten or drunk. She thought back to yesterday—how could it only have been yesterday?—when she'd sent Flora off to school with a cheese sandwich, an apple, and a baggie of carrot sticks. She vaguely remembered nibbling on a slice of cheese before sitting down at her computer with a cup of tea.

Tea would be nice, she thought, looking ahead toward the beverage station where women picked up plastic cups of artificial fruit punch. No sign of tea or coffee. When she reached the stop, she opted for water instead of the chemical-laden punch.

She found a spot among the taciturn inmates and sat. At the table behind her, two women burst out arguing, drawing laughter and attention from surrounding inmates. Jaide kept her eyes on her own tray as she swallowed the gluey meal. She bussed her dishes before returning to her cell to discover Baggy Pants once again sprawled across one entire cot, one dark-skinned arm crooked over her eyes. Yet Jaide had no doubt the woman was fully aware of each person entering the cell. With a small sigh, she resumed her spot on the concrete.

Guards came and went, escorting prisoners in and out of other cells. Lunchtime arrived, and Jaide shuffled to the cafeteria with the others. This time she received a white-bread sandwich and a handful of dry-looking carrot sticks. She lifted the edge of the bread to reveal a pink slab of processed meat.

"Excuse me," she said to the hair-netted woman serving up trays from behind the counter.

"Keep moving," said the server.

"Do you have a vegetarian option?"

The women all around her snickered, including the server. The stocky woman in line behind Jaide brushed past with a hard bump of her shoulder against Jaide's back.

The server shoved a tray across the counter to the next woman in line. "This is jail, honey. Eat it or don't. That's all you get."

Jaide's stomach churned. "I don't eat meat."

The inmate beside Jaide reached across Jaide's tray and

picked up the sandwich. She opened it, retrieved the greasy pink round, then slapped the bread back onto Jaide's tray. Indentations where her fingers had been remained in the white sponge. "There. Now get out of the way so we can eat."

Jaide eyed the bread in horror and decided not to argue. She'd be out of here in a few days. She could handle a little hunger.

Keeping her chin down, she found a seat among the snickering inmates and nibbled on the carrot sticks. As soon as the guards allowed inmates to return to their cells, she bussed her tray and scuttled back down the corridor. None of her cellmates were there yet, so Jaide sat on the far end of Baggy Pants's bed, back against the wall. Short-hair arrived first and chortled as she spotted Jaide. "This'll be fun."

Jaide's insides trembled and her pulse raced. What had she gotten herself into? But she couldn't change her mind now that Short-hair had seen her. She remained silent as she watched the door.

Short-hair took her usual spot at the end of the other bed, drawing one foot onto the mattress and wrapping her arms around her shin. She rested her chin on her knee. "You been in jail before?"

Jaide shook her head.

"Didn't think so. Let me give you a word of advice. Don't piss off the black chicks. Or the Latinas or the Asians. Stick with your own kind." She patted the mattress beside her. "Come sit over here by me."

Throat tight, Jaide swallowed her urge to regurgitate her carrot-stick lunch. Would she rather confront Black-eye or Baggy Pants? Black-eye obviously had no qualms about getting violent. But Baggy Pants's unusual calm sent chills down Jaide's spine every time the woman looked at her.

Jaide rose and swapped to the opposite bed, as far away

from Short-hair as she could manage. She'd seen a documentary once that said to make sure to humanize yourself if you were ever taken hostage. Maybe that advice applied here, too. She forced herself to meet Short-hair's gaze. "My name's Jaide."

"Amy," the woman said.

"I have a daughter. She's thirteen. Do you have kids?"

Amy scrunched up one eye as if she wasn't sure what she was seeing.

Was the kid approach a mistake in prison? Jaide's heartbeat threatened to crack her ribs. The tension broke as a guard spoke at the cell door. "Jaide Acosta?"

Jaide shot to her feet. "Yes?

"Your lawyer's here to see you."

"Oh, thank God." She graced Amy with a smile and strode out of the cell, pleased her trembling legs didn't give out beneath her.

The guard guided her down the corridor and toward the interrogation room where she'd spoken to the FBI yesterday. Inside, a red-faced man with broad shoulders sat at one side of the familiar wood-veneer table. The officer shut the door, leaving them alone. The lawyer rose to thrust out a hand. "Ms. Acosta, I'm Zeb Rankin. I've been assigned to your case."

Jaide shook his hand then sat in the opposite chair. "Are they really charging me with terrorism?"

"Correct." His voice was so succinct and matter-of-fact, she wondered whose side he was on. The FBI couldn't send in a fake lawyer to get her to confess, could they?

"I'm not a terrorist," she insisted.

Zeb opened a file and flipped through a few papers. "The DA's not actually after you. They want this Finkman fellow. He's part of an eco-terrorist cell the FBI's been after for years."

How could Trevor have dragged her into this? Why hadn't she thought things through before joining him? She'd wanted to save the world from being taken over by corporate greed, but she had a daughter to care for. "I don't know anything about a cell."

"Do you know anything about Trevor Finkman's plans? We might be able to cut you a deal if you can lead the FBI to him."

"He showed up at my house a few months ago asking for a place to stay. I told him no. I haven't seen him since."

Zeb looked up from his paperwork and met her gaze. "I want to take a moment here to remind you that as your lawyer, I'm sworn to confidentiality. My job is not to decide if you're guilty or innocent. My job is to give you the best possible defense strategy. You need to tell me the truth. All of it. I can't defend against what I don't know."

Jaide clutched her hands together in her lap, wishing she had something to bargain with. She thought she'd been doing the right thing, sending Trevor off, refusing to get any more involved. But now she regretted not at least asking a few questions. "I don't know anything about his plans. He just said it was something big."

Zeb riffled through his papers again. "Tell me about the greenhouse, then. What happened there?"

Tears pricked Jaide's eyes, and her whole body began to tremble. "I can tell you everything?"

The lawyer nodded.

Jaide related the incident on autopilot while Zeb jotted notes. He did an amazing job of remaining neutral through the entire story, and she grew more and more uncomfortable as she talked. Didn't he have an opinion about these corporate giants trying to ruin the Earth? But he gave no indication of his preference one way or the other.

When she'd finished, he tapped his pen against the pad of paper and took a deep breath. "Okay. Let's talk about how to proceed. The camera images they have are pretty compelling when coupled with your known environmental activities and your association with Finkman. I'm not positive I can beat this if we go to trial."

"I have an alibi. I told them I was home with my daughter that night."

He shook his head. "I can't knowingly lie or allow you to lie in court."

"Why did you make me tell you the truth, then?" Jaide gritted her teeth.

"Believe me, it's better if I know. They'd likely shred your alibi, anyway. I think our best option here is to pursue a plea bargain. Maybe get off light if you agree to help catch Trevor."

Jaide stared at the tabletop. She'd made a pact with Trevor and Cindy. One broken link, and everyone would pay. "Do they have Cindy, too?"

"They do. I'm sure her lawyer is giving her the same advice."

Much as Jaide loved Cindy, she knew her friend's resolve would be weaker than her own. And Cindy didn't have a daughter to consider. "Can we both make a deal?"

"I don't know yet what the prosecution is willing to offer. But it may be a matter of first come, first served."

Jaide cleared her throat. Swallowed. Took a breath. "Find out what I have to do."

"All right. I'll talk to the district attorney." Zeb flipped to a new page in his notebook. "Your detention hearing is tomorrow. I'll try to get you released on bail."

"I don't have money for bail."

"I can contact a bondsman for you. You have a daughter, right? With a family, your flight risk is ranked lower. I'd like to gather some character witnesses, preferably some who are not involved in the Coalition or another activist movement."

Jaide bit her lip, going over everyone she knew. "How about the weed warriors?"

"I'm not familiar with them, but they sound activist. They'd be better than the Coalition but still not ideal. Any co-workers?"

"I work from home." Should she mention Lucas? She didn't want him to see her this way, yet he might be her best option. "I've been dating a man named Lucas Harmon. He's not a member of the Coalition."

"Great." Zeb took down his information. "I'll contact him and see if he'll make a statement on your behalf."

"Can you find out if he has my dog, please? I'm worried about her."

"Certainly." He closed his notebook and gathered his other papers before meeting her gaze again. "The FBI will have more questions. Do not talk to anyone without me present. Is there anything else you need to discuss before I go?"

She sighed. He had asked her to tell him everything, and there was one item she'd yet to bring up. "You should probably know that the GMO weed that's loose is our fault. The greenhouse was growing amaranth. I think we tracked seeds out when we ran."

The paper shuffling stopped. Deep lines furrowed Zeb's brow, the first slip of emotion he'd had this entire time. "Have you said this to anyone else?"

"Cindy and Trevor. I thought we could band together and stop the spread."

Zeb leaned forward to stare more deeply at her. "Do not, I repeat, do not say this or even hint about it to anyone. Not your cellmates. Not your mother. Not over the phone or in person. No one. We want your case to get smaller, not bigger. Do you understand?"

"What about Cindy? She already knows."

"Talk to no one. I'll contact Cindy's lawyer." He slid his papers and file into his briefcase and snapped it shut.

Guilt churned in Jaide's stomach. Her lawyer obviously couldn't see the bigger picture. Much as she wanted all this to go away, she had a responsibility to the world. "TelomerGen shouldn't have been altering nature to begin with. Can we do something about that? People should know what the corporations are doing."

Zeb rose, straightening his suit jacket. "That's a whole different can of worms, Jaide. The media is all over this plant, and people are scared. If word gets out that you might be responsible, I can't guarantee an impartial jury if you go to trial."

He rapped on the door, and a guard opened it. Before departing, he turned to her, his gaze reminding her to hold her tongue. "I'll contact you soon."

People would relish a scapegoat.

Hell, if she were on the jury, she'd condemn herself.

———

Jaide returned to her cell to find Baggy Pants and Black-eye gone. No new inmates joined her and Amy, but although she now had a bed to herself, Jaide hardly slept. Amy snored in the other bed, waking when the guard opened the doors for breakfast. Jaide followed the others to the cafeteria, infinitely glad for the gluey oatmeal, since supper last night had been some sort of pasta bake with chicken. The inmates around her had joked it might be horse meat or dog. She'd had nightmares about Trigger all night.

Her lawyer visited her late in the afternoon, pulling her from her cell to the interrogation room once again.

"I checked on your dog, and she's with your boyfriend. As far as your case goes, I have good news and bad." He set his briefcase on the table but didn't open it. "Which do you want first?"

Jaide shrugged. "Bad news, I guess."

"The judge plans to set bail at five hundred thousand dollars, considering the current charges are terrorism. No bondsman will touch that without collateral."

"No surprise there," Jaide said. She'd had all night to contemplate the fact she was being called a terrorist. She deserved it, if not for breaking and entering, then for letting the amaranth loose.

"The good news is TelomerGen doesn't want a PR mess. They've agreed to lower the charges to felony vandalism if you sign a nondisclosure agreement. But you have to decide before the detention hearing this afternoon."

Jaide tilted her head, trying to understand. Lack of sleep was making her feel woozy. "How's that better than the other charges?"

Zeb nodded slowly. "Believe me, you'd rather be charged as a felon than a terrorist. The jail time will be lower. You won't be relegated to large blocks of solitary confinement and censorship like terrorist convicts often are. And any time you serve will be here, in state, where your family can visit you. "

All she could do was stare at him wide eyed. The reality of prison time was really sinking in. "Can they just up and swap charges like that?"

"The DA has agreed to defer to TelomerGen's lawyers."

Of course they had. Big corporations could do anything they wanted. "So they want me to sign something saying I won't tell anyone they were growing the amaranth?"

"Exactly. You'll serve one to five years. That Lucas fellow gave me an outstanding character reference and said he'd be willing to come to court. Between him, your employer, and your landlord, I'll bet the judge will give two years. Two and a half, tops."

Jaide stared at him, a chill settling into her bones. "But TelomerGen should take responsibility for the weed, don't you think? If I sign, they won't be held accountable for cleanup."

Zeb pressed his lips tight and nodded. "True. All I can tell you is that this is a good deal for you, personally. I'll defend your case no matter what you decide."

She closed her eyes. Zeb was right. This deal would get her back into Flora's life in a reasonable time. She should accept it. But how could she allow TelomerGen to escape retribution for their evil experiments? They needed to step up and hunt that Franken-weed to extinction. Her chin dropped to her chest as she realized TelomerGen's tactics to eradicate the amaranth would most likely be gallons of poison. Thousands of gallons. Was that any better than the weed itself? Would choosing the cause over her daughter actually do any good?

Indecision was making her dizzy. She opened her eyes and focused on the knot of Zeb's tie. "Are they offering Cindy the same deal?"

He nodded. "She's already accepted."

"What about Trevor?"

"I can't speak to that. He's wanted for far more than the greenhouse break-in."

"But he could still talk."

Zeb narrowed one eye. "Yes. But they've stipulated that if he does, new charges—terrorism charges—will be brought against all of you."

Jaide's spine stiffened. "Me, too? What about double jeopardy?"

"Not relevant. These would be new charges. The plaintiff would no longer be TelomerGen but the federal government."

She dropped her head into her hands. Everywhere she

turned, disaster threatened. "So if Trevor reveals this information, I pay the price even if they don't catch him?"

Zeb's voice was soft. "That is correct."

She raised her face to take in his clean-shaven cheeks and Republican haircut. He was just one of the masses, a part of a broken system. And he didn't even realize it. She finally understood why so many Coalition members chose to remain childless: not just for world population issues, but because those connections could compromise the cause. The image of all the amaranth she'd pulled filled her mind. She didn't have the strength to keep fighting, especially when her daughter needed her. Jaide couldn't choose the cause. She had to make the best decision for Flora.

"Just show me where to sign."

Part Two

MAY, Two Years Later

And then the Tox came, and the food stopped.

~ THE HISTORIES

Chapter Twelve

J aide paused in her walk along the prison fence, bending to crush another amaranth seedling that had crept under the barrier. Policing the weeds that dared appear inside was the only thing keeping her from going crazy.

The judge had sentenced Jaide to four and a half years in a state prison almost two hundred miles from home. At least once a month, Lucas made the trip to see her, but she'd not had personal contact with Mother or Flora in more than two years. Her phone calls were refused, letters to Flora were returned unopened, and even Lucas's attempts to contact her daughter had met with threats of a restraining order.

Nine weeks ago, she'd received probate papers seeking to remove her as Flora's guardian. Prison budget cuts wouldn't pay for transport to the hearing, and she'd only been able to attend via phone call. Because Jaide was ineligible for parole until after Flora turned eighteen, the judge had granted Chona full legal and physical custody.

Jaide stared through the chain link to the corn and soybean fields beyond the prison grounds. How would Flora be filling her summer this year? Had she made new friends at school? Was Chona allowing her to pick her own friends? Thoughts of her daughter at Chona's mercy threatened to become a vortex, sucking Jaide into insanity, so she kept walking, casting her gaze down to assess every bit of greenery dotting the prison yard.

Her first summer here, a few distinctive flower spikes had sprouted along the edges of the paved road beyond the prison walls. This spring, the amaranth dotted the lawn mere inches outside the chain link, a startling green against the drought-brown grass. Maintenance had mown the perimeter once a few weeks ago, but the plants came back bushier than ever, clumped ankle high. Stunted spear heads now rose above the leaves, rushing to set seed before another human intervened.

She'd attempted to assemble a group of weed warriors when she'd first arrived at the facility, but the warden refused to provide guards for off-premises community service work. Not that any other inmates wanted to pull weeds anyway. Most of them sat in the shady side of the yard, avoiding another scorching spring day while Jaide patrolled the fence.

"Hey, Tree Hugger!" A voice behind her brought her upright and stiff. A group of inmates had given her the name after she'd accidentally tipped the warden to the marijuana growing in the prison garden. She'd only been trying to show him the invading amaranth but had stumbled upon the illicit plants growing among the tomatoes. The prison no longer had a garden program, and she'd spent nine days in the infirmary with a concussion.

Spinning to face the voice, Jaide relaxed. Teri, the messenger for the prison counselors, stood at the edge of the basketball court about ten yards away, skinny arms crossed over her chest. "Simone wants to see you."

Jaide brushed her dirty palms against her canvas pants and followed Teri toward the building. Inside, the stifling air smelled like mildewed socks, overlaid by the cabbage-y scent of prison stew—a new daily menu item after budget cuts last winter. At least the ingredients were primarily vegetarian, although Jaide had adopted a blind eye when it came to prison food. Unless it was obviously meat, she ate what she got.

Teri pointed toward the turn to the counselor's office and spoke to a nearby guard. "She's got an appointment. I got more messages to deliver."

The guard tilted her head down the hall, approving Jaide's passage, and remained where she was at the corner of the intersection, thumbs hooked in her belt. Up and down the hallways, a scattering of prisoners went about their business. Jaide kept moving until she reached the offices, easing past a wide-hipped woman standing in the corridor so she could knock on Simone's door.

A vise slammed down on her shoulder and hurled her against the opposite wall. The wide-hipped woman stood facing her with feet apart. "Wait your turn, bitch."

Jaide remained pressed against the wall, the back of her skull throbbing where it had hit the concrete. A few feet down, two more women waited in line, watching the interaction with neutral expressions. The wide-hipped woman crossed her arms and sank back into her bored pose, eyes on the door's frosted-glass window. Jaide backed up and took a place behind the farthest woman. "There's a line?"

The short woman in front of Jaide turned, eyes alight. "Word is they're letting more inmates out on early parole."

Last month, the prison board had released a wave of inmates serving misdemeanors. Could this possibly be another round of releases? One Jaide might be eligible for? The door opened, and a scrawny blonde emerged, grinning widely to expose a gap where her front teeth should have been. "I'm going home!"

Simone's crackly voice carried from the office. "Next."

The wide-hipped woman sauntered inside, shutting the door behind her.

Blondie didn't hang around to give details, darting down the hall toward the cell block until the guard yelled at her to slow down.

The woman ahead of Jaide pumped a fist. "I knew it!"

Another inmate took a spot behind Jaide in line. Jaide's heart galloped like a wild horse trapped in a corral. *Going home.* Could she really hope?

Light-headed, she shuffled forward as the next woman took her turn. The frosted glass showed only shadows of the room inside and blocked the voices until a whoop penetrated the heavy door. The woman who'd been in front of Jaide emerged and charged down the hall without a backward glance.

And then it was Jaide's turn. With an unsteady hand she closed the door behind her then took a seat opposite the gray-haired counselor. Simone glanced up, her lacquered fingernails clacking over her keyboard. "Just a moment."

Self-conscious, Jaide smoothed a hand over her lank hair and then folded her hands in her lap. Waiting even four more seconds seemed like an eternity. Finally the counselor met Jaide's eyes. "Name?"

"Jaide Acosta."

Simone jiggled her mouse, clicking on files. "Acosta. Felony vandal—oh..." She leaned forward to take a closer look at the screen, eyes sweeping back and forth as she read.

All the air left Jaide's lungs. What did her file say? Her skin prickled, and she forced her hands to remain clenched in her lap.

Simone blew a breath between her lips and shook her head. "I hadn't realized your sentence was categorized under violent crimes. I'm sorry."

A yawning void opened up, engulfing everything between Jaide and the counselor. "Violent? I never hurt anybody."

"You must've done some serious property damage, then."

Jaide pressed the tears back down her throat, swallowing them whole as she'd learned to do, living among these hardened women. "Does this mean I don't get to go home?"

"The parole board is only looking at nonviolent felons at this point."

"Please, I didn't hurt anyone. I'm only here because TelomerGen can afford better lawyers than I can." Jaide beseeched Simone with her gaze, fighting to keep her emotions in check. The counselors hated hysterics.

Simone looked at her computer screen again. "You do have an exemplary record here." She tapped a fingernail against the desktop. "I could take this to the warden, I suppose."

"Would you?" The chasm seemed to shrink, just a little. It had been a long time since anyone had done anything for her just to be nice, except for Lucas, who mailed her weekly letters with news about Trigger. "I have a daughter I haven't seen in two years."

"I'm supposed to clear at least ten percent of our population, and frankly, I don't want to see most of the women I've screened walking around my neighborhood." She leaned back in her chair. "Tell me, why should I go to bat for you?"

Jaide sat up straight as though she was in a job interview. "I've always held down a job, supported myself and my daughter through the toughest times, and I regularly volunteer for community service activities."

One side of Simone's mouth turned up in a smile. "Well, part of the requirement for your parole will be community service." She picked up a pen and scratched a note onto a sticky pad beside her keyboard. "I'll let you know in a day or two what the warden says."

"Thank you." Jaide rose, reaching out to shake hands. "I promise you won't regret letting me go."

Simone looked from Jaide's outstretched hand to her face, and raised her brows. "I'm not promising anything."

"I appreciate you even trying."

The counselor gave Jaide's hand a perfunctory shake. "You can go, then."

Jaide exited the office, unsure whether to float on air or drag her feet.

Simone proved better than her word, and two days later she told Jaide to gather her belongings. Jaide headed to the phone banks to call her mother. As usual, Mother refused the call, but Jaide spoke over the operator's recording, hoping her mother would at least hear some of what she had to say. "Mother, I'm being released."

The dial tone keened in her ear.

She pressed her finger to the receiver cradle to end the call and then picked it back up.

A short Latino woman tried to grab the receiver from her hand. "You had your turn."

Jaide snatched the phone away. "I'm still on my fifteen minutes."

The woman curled her lip in a snarl, reaching forward again. Normally, Jaide would've backed down, but this was her only chance to let Lucas know she was coming. She leaned forward to glare into the woman's face. "I'm still on my fifteen."

The woman wrinkled her nose and took a single step backward. Jaide returned to the keypad and dialed Lucas's cell. He accepted the charges, as always. "What's up, Jaide?"

"They're letting me out, Lucas." Saying the words out loud made her all fluttery and breathless. "Do you still have my car?"

"Wow, that's abrupt. But great." He sounded like he was smiling. At least, she hoped he was. "I'll take off work to pick you up."

"I can take a bus."

"Nonsense. Are they putting you in a halfway house or something?"

She ran her fingers along the worn metal receiver cord. Her excitement about upcoming freedom had blotted out practical things, such as where she'd live. She'd gone into prison with little money and was coming out with even less. Lucas had rescued her belongings from her apartment, but she'd had him sell off the furniture and other valuables so she could have funds for the commissary. "I just need to keep in contact with my parole officer. I'll live in my car until I find a job."

"You're not living in your car. You can stay at my place. I'm not there half the time, anyway."

Although she and Lucas had been a couple before all this jail time, and he'd kept in contact, she'd never assumed he'd wait for her. Did he want to take up where they'd left off? She couldn't quite tell, and it felt awkward to outright ask. "You've already done so much. I don't want to take advantage of you."

"You're not. I need someone to watch my dog." He chortled at his own joke, but the comment only made Jaide feel more guilty. He sucked in a calming breath. "Seriously, Jaide. I miss you. Plus the economy's gone to shit, so don't expect to land a position any time soon. I can't stand the thought of you homeless."

She swept her gaze over the line of women behind her waiting for a turn at the phone. Many were calling loved ones to announce their upcoming freedom. How many other prisons were releasing inmates? Would there be any jobs left with so many new bodies flooding the workforce? How would she support her daughter? "I'll have Flora."

"She can share Suzanne's room. Suz hardly stays over any more and usually crashes on the couch in front of the TV anyway."

Throat tight, Jaide tried to keep her voice from cracking. "Lucas, I don't know what to say. You've been so good to me."

"Say yes."

Living in her car with Flora sounded terrible. And there was no way she'd live with her mother. She swallowed her pride. "Only until I find a job. Thank you. But I'll be taking a bus, so don't drive all the way down here."

"Fair enough. I'll leave a key with Mrs. Obermeir next door. She can let you in if I'm not there."

"I can't tell you how much I appreciate this." A nudge on her arm drew her attention to the Latino woman, who pointed toward the clock in the wall above the phones. Time was up. "I have to go, Lucas. I'll see you... tomorrow."

Saying the words out loud roused butterflies in her stomach as she handed the phone to the woman behind her.

Chapter Thirteen

J aide loaded onto the prison bus along with fifteen other women, clutching a plastic bag of her belongings and paperwork against her chest. All along the drive into the town, tall amaranth spikes jabbed skyward along the roadside, some fat and ponderous with seed. Surrounding fields of early corn and soybeans stood mangy with the weed, and dry, brown earth spread from patches of amaranth like infected scabs.

At the transit station, the female bus guard handed each inmate a ticket voucher good to take them anywhere in the state. "Check in with your parole officer within the next forty-eight hours. I don't want to see any of your sorry asses back at the prison."

Jaide disembarked, taking a deep breath of hot pavement and bus exhaust. Freedom smelled great. She followed the other women into the station, digging three quarters out of her pocket and searching for a pay phone. She'd been arrested outside her apartment without her cell—not that it mattered, because her contract had expired unpaid years ago. She tried to think positive. Maybe Mother would answer a call from an unfamiliar number. Or better yet, Flora might answer. Jaide ached to hear her daughter's voice.

Passengers sat shoulder to shoulder along the station benches, suitcases and duffel bags at their feet. Jaide stepped around a crying toddler who was leashed to a haggard, nearly catatonic mother. Nearby, a man in a baggy suit broke a candy bar into three pieces and handed portions to a woman and two children before licking crumbs from his palm. Near the phone bank, a man with dark stubble on his face sat in the corner, head back against the wall and mouth open as he snored.

The ambiance reminded her of photos of the Great Depression. Lucas's admonition to not expect a job too soon flicked at her memory again. What would she do if she couldn't get a position? She clenched her jaw. She'd weathered hard times before. She'd find a way to earn money, even if it meant working minimum wage at a fast food joint and growing veggies on the roof of her car.

At the banged-up pay phones, she picked up receiver after receiver until she found one that emitted a dial tone. She plugged money in and waited for it to ring, heart in her throat. After three rings her mother picked up. "Hello?"

"Mother, it's Jaide."

No answer but at least no hang-up.

"I'm out of prison."

"Did you break out?"

"God, no! They're letting low-risk convicts go because of budget cuts. I'm coming to get Flora."

"We have legal custody of her. She's no longer your concern."

Bile rose in Jaide's throat, and her skin prickled. She wished she could reach through the phone and strangle her mother. "I appreciate you taking care of her, but she's my daughter."

"Don't make me bring our lawyer into this, Jaide. You're no good for her. Just stay away."

The phone went dead.

Jaide slammed the receiver back into its cradle. The scruffy man sitting in the corner opened his eyes, but she turned and stalked away before he could engage. How could her mother do this? Jaide couldn't afford a lawyer to fight for custody. Her mother might as well be TelomerGen.

But she wouldn't allow Flora to remain Chona's prisoner. Jaide marched over to the ticket counter and studied the board. The next bus for her mother's town didn't leave for four hours. If she used her ticket to go there instead of Lucas's, she could rescue Flora before the day was through.

She clutched the voucher, palm sweating. She didn't have money for two fares to bring Flora home once she got to Mom's. They'd have to hitchhike or ask Lucas to rescue them. Calling Lucas wouldn't be fair to him, and hitchhiking sounded more dangerous than leaving Flora where she was for the moment. The adrenaline drained out of Jaide, leaving her cold in spite of the sweltering station air. The responsible thing to do was go to Lucas's, start her job search, and then rescue Flora once she had a little money.

Exchanging her voucher for a ticket to Lucas's felt like a betrayal. Flora would have to forgive her for a few more days.

Jaide slept nearly the entire bus ride to the city. Lucas lived far out on the west edge of town in a relatively new neighborhood. She got off the bus a few blocks from Lucas's condo and walked the rest of the way with her eyes on the sidewalk. Her plastic bag of underclothes and shower shoes felt an awful lot like the grocery bags some of the homeless carried around.

She passed a mom-and-pop store, its usual sidewalk displays of produce devoid of stock. A sign on the tables told customers to come inside to shop. Through the window, a yellow price plaque for apples made Jaide's jaw drop. She paused to stare inside at the other tags. If the fresh items on display were any indication, food prices had doubled since she'd been in prison. No wonder the warden was releasing prisoners—he could no longer feed them. She should get a garden going at Lucas's as soon as possible.

In front of Lucas's condo building, a pair of shade oaks sheltered a handful of teenagers lounging against the big trunks. Jaide couldn't help looking at them, trying to guess their ages. What did her daughter look like now? A dirt-smudged girl jumped up and approached her. "Hey, lady, you got a dollar?"

She shook her head and broke eye contact, entering the condo parking lot. If she'd had money, she'd have shared. No child deserved to be on the street. A rush of gratitude swelled within her that Lucas was making sure she and Flora would have a place to stay.

Ahead, the buzz of a weed whacker echoed from the courtyard between the two buildings. Jaide was hit by the damp coppery scent of chopped amaranth as she entered the protected space. Green plant bits spattered along the south wall as the maintenance man swung the head of the device back and forth. Good. The weed wasn't being allowed to set seed here. She continued along the cement path toward the Obermeirs' door.

Their stoop displayed the same welcome mat and surname wood-cutout on the wall that Jaide remembered from before she'd gone away. Had Lucas told the old woman why Jaide had been missing for two years? She ascended the two steps to the front door on stiff legs, forcing herself to move forward instead of searching for a place to hide.

Her first encounter as an ex-con.

She knocked. Footsteps vibrated inside. The door swung open to reveal Mrs. Obermeir's plump face. The gray-haired woman opened her arms and swept Jaide into a hug that smelled of pot roast and potatoes. "Jaide, dear! You're back!"

Jaide hugged her, relief making her knees weak. Either the woman didn't know, or Lucas had invented a story. Either way, Jaide appreciated it. She patted the old woman's rounded shoulder. "I'm happy to be back."

"Come in and have some supper."

Stomach empty after a long day of travel, Jaide's mouth watered at the salty odor of pot roast. She swallowed back her unwelcome reaction; she'd been too long at the mercy of the prison kitchen. "No, thank you, Mrs. Obermeir. I'm going to cook something vegetarian for Lucas."

"Oh, of course. I forgot you don't eat meat." The old lady reached into her apron pocket and produced a key. "Come on over if you need anything."

"I appreciate it." Jaide accepted the key and walked to the next stoop.

As she turned the knob, a familiar whine reached her ears. She pushed, and Trigger's furry nose jimmied the door fully open. The dog danced and reared, licking Jaide's face, wriggling and crying. Jaide dropped to her knees, hands fumbling against fur and paws and wet nose. Trigger rolled against Jaide's lap for a few moments before bolting upright to lick her face again. The familiar doggy scent and rough kisses sent sobs of relief and release through Jaide's entire body. She was home.

"I missed you, too." She wrapped her arms around Trigger's shaggy neck, absorbing the wriggling love until her knees hurt. Keeping her hand on the dog's furry ruff, she rose. "Show me around, girl."

She closed the door and let out a shaky breath before

kicking off her tennis shoes. Inside the condo, little had changed. A sectional sofa faced a huge television attached to the wall. On the breakfast bar that separated the small kitchen from the main living space, she found a note addressed to her in Lucas's blocky handwriting. She set her meager belongings down and picked up the paper. "Jaide, Make yourself at home. My shift ends at midnight. Feel free to use whatever you need. Love, Lucas."

She ran a forefinger over the word "love." She'd thought a lot about that while in prison, when Lucas was her only supporter. Her affection for him ran deep, but she was leery of using such a strong word. Wasn't there a clinical name for falling in love during times of stress? Yet how could she not love him, when he'd been better to her than her own family? He was too good to be true, and that made her nervous. What if she was just another person to be rescued? That was what Lucas did, in his job and his life in general.

She set the note aside and turned to the refrigerator. Now wasn't the time to resolve her feelings about Lucas. He wasn't even here. Whether she was in love with him or not, as long as she was with him, she'd treat him right, starting with having a nice dinner ready when he got home.

The fridge shelves held little more than two grapefruits, a bottle of catsup, and four beers. He obviously never cooked. She found an onion and some baby carrots in the crisper drawer. The small freezer, however, was packed. She freed an oddly shaped package wrapped in white paper labeled "squab" with last year's date. Shuddering, she realized most of the freezer items were pigeons.

Moving on to the cupboards, she found a can of chickpeas and a can of tomatoes, as well as a canister of rice, and decided to make a modified version of her curry. With the onion and a bag of frozen spinach from the freezer, all she'd need were a few simple spices.

As she worked, she sipped beer and crunched on potato chips from a bag on the counter. She'd never known what he saw in the processed, commercial junk, but tonight each chip tasted like a wafer of manna. Soon, the entire bag held nothing but crumbs and salt. Her dad's favorite saying came to mind: never drink a man's last beer. Were potato chips like beer? She hoped not. Maybe the curry would make up for it.

Turning the heat down on the rice while it steamed, she padded into the living room to sit down for a few minutes. After two years of linoleum tiles, the carpet cushioned her bare feet like a cloud. Sunset bathed the small, fenced backyard through the sliding glass patio doors at the other end of the living room, and she considered going outside to enjoy the air, but the beer had gone to her head. Each of her feet seemed to weigh as much as a bowling ball, and the couch cushions enveloped her in what felt like an embrace. Nothing in prison had been this soft. Trigger curled up at her feet, and Jaide put her soles against the dog's side, burying her toes in fur. She closed her eyes for a moment of relaxation.

And woke to the scream of smoke detectors.

The acrid scent of something burning launched her upright, momentarily without bearings. Where was she? Trigger cowered near the patio doors. Outside, only streetlights kept the darkness at bay. Lucas's place. How long had she been asleep? She raced to the kitchen and flipped on the light. Smoke rolled from beneath the lids of both saucepans. She turned off the burners and hit the button on the range fan.

The doorbell rang, and someone pounded on the door. Ignoring it, Jaide grabbed the handle of one pan to move it off the burner and jerked back, scalded. "Damn it!"

Above the wailing alarm, a man's muffled voice carried

through the door panel. "Are you okay in there? Do we need to call the fire department?"

She grabbed the dishtowel and used it to push the pots off the glowing electric coils. Wrapping her burnt hand with the towel, she scrambled to answer the door.

Mr. Obermeir choked as a cloud of smoke enveloped him. "Oh!"

"Do you know how to shut off the alarm?" Jaide shouted over the blaring noise. Across the courtyard, doors stood open as people emerged to see what the fuss was about.

He scowled, deepening the wrinkles in his face, and shoved past her into the house toward the bedrooms. He popped open a breaker box and flipped a switch. The condo fell blessedly silent. "You can turn that back on once you've cleared out the smoke. If you can clear out the smoke." He waved a stout arm in front of him. "What a stench."

The reek of burned curry had tears running down both their faces, but Jaide's tears were from more than smoke. She'd not only ruined supper but also likely just ruined two pans and maybe added smoke damage to her list of mishaps. She glanced at the microwave clock. Eleven fifteen. Lucas would be home soon.

Mrs. Obermeir appeared through the front door wrapped in a frothy pink bathrobe. "Are you all right, dear? What happened?"

Jaide showed her the pans, and Mrs. Obermeir clucked her tongue. "Open all the windows in the front here. If any of the bedroom doors were closed, leave them that way until the smoke clears."

Jaide's chest wanted to explode. She wiped at her burning eyes and nodded.

Mrs. Obermeir put an arm around Jaide's shoulders. "Why don't you come stay at our house while the place airs out?"

"I don't want Lucas to find this mess without me here." The layer of smoke had already thinned considerably with the door open.

The old woman nodded. "I understand. If you change your mind, come on over."

"Thank you."

The Obermeirs retreated, leaving Jaide to stare at the stove with burning eyes. At least she hadn't started an actual fire; other than the ruined pots and the acrid odor, the kitchen was intact. She unwrapped her burned hand. The skin was red and sore but not blistered. She went through the house and opened every window. The bedrooms had all been open, and tendrils of smoke still lingered in corners. Would every item in the house smell like burned curry forever? She put the bathroom fan to work and returned to the kitchen.

Using the dishtowel again, she carried the first pan to the trash bins at the back of the building. Trigger stayed close against her knee, nearly tripping her. She griped under her breath, conscious of the sleeping residents behind nearby windows. In the alley streetlight, she cracked open the pot's lid and peeked at the blackened interior. She could no longer tell if this had been curry or rice. How long had she slept through the alarm? "Trigger, why didn't you wake me?"

The dog's tail twitched, but her ears remained flattened in shared shame.

Jaide tossed the pan into the bin and went back for the other one. Lucas met her at the door, handsome in his paramedic's uniform. All she wanted was to wrap her arms around him and cry, but he was busy fanning the door back and forth to let out more smoke. A blue sling cradled his right arm.

"What happened?" she asked at the exact moment he asked the same thing.

Tears blurred her vision as guilt overwhelmed her. She

launched into an explanation and apology. "I just wanted to make you dinner. I'll buy you new pans," she promised. "And scrub the whole house to get the smell out."

He made a gagging face and let out a few choice words that made Jaide cringe. "It's been one of those days. Let's go out to have a bite to eat." He stepped out of the door frame and snapped his fingers at Trigger. "Come inside, girl. You get to play guard dog while this place airs out."

Trigger complied, tail between her legs. She gave Jaide a reproachful look over her shoulder before disappearing inside. Lucas pulled the door shut and fumbled with putting the key in the deadbolt using his left hand.

"Here, let me." Jaide put a hand over his. "What happened? Are you okay?"

He relinquished the keys. "A gurney collapsed, and I tried to catch it. Wrenched my arm. At least the patient didn't fall off."

She finished locking up and offered the keys back.

He shook his head. "You mind driving?"

"Anything you need. I feel terrible you're being chased out of your own home."

"Burned pans aren't the end of the world."

She waited a heartbeat for him to move off the porch so she could follow him to his car. When he didn't move, she steeled herself. Was he about to ask her to find somewhere else to stay? Instead, he moved closer, wrapped his good arm around her, and buried his face in her hair. "God, it's good to see you in person."

Trembling, she wrapped her arms around his waist. Even with the sling between them, the contact of his chest against hers set a fire in her belly. Two years of relief flooded her all at once. "I love you."

She didn't know where the words came from, but there they were, out in the open, bared and full of raw vulnerability.

He squeezed her tighter, his voice rumbling against her cheek. "I love you, too." He pulled back, nose wrinkled as he cracked a smile. "But you stink."

A bubble of laughter shook her. He chuckled along with her, smoothing a strand of her hair behind her ear. She doubled over, hands on her knees, as the laughter became hysteria. She couldn't catch her breath. The more she attempted to rein in the laughter, the funnier everything seemed. Tears washed her cheeks, and her throat ached with trying to hold back. Soon she had no energy left. She swayed, tripping down the first porch step.

Lucas steadied her with a grunt, good arm painfully tight at her waist as he tried to maintain his own balance. "Sit down before you fall." He eased her to the landing and sat beside her. She continued to giggle, sucking in air as if she were drowning. He rubbed her back. "Put your head between your knees."

She gasped and choked, staring at the concrete step below her feet. There was so much she wanted to tell him. Yet she didn't want to talk about any of it. Now she understood why some mental patients went catatonic.

"I forgot this has been an emotional day for you, too," he said. "You're probably exhausted. I have a pop-up tent Suzanne uses for slumber parties we can set up in the backyard. Let's stay home and order pizza."

His hand continued rubbing little circles over her shoulder blades. The world eased its spinning, and she sucked another slow breath of air. She nodded, hoping he could see her in the dim porch light.

He rose and helped her up. Trigger greeted them at the door as if they'd been gone for hours. While Lucas called for pizza, Jaide washed her grimy, flushed face. A knock on the half-open bathroom door behind her drew her upright. Lucas's reflected gaze met hers in the mirror. His eyes seemed to smolder, and her core ignited as if he'd touched her.

"If you want to shower, you know where the towels are." His husky voice matched her emotions.

"Is that a hint?" Her previous laughter threatened to return despite the desire burning within her.

He cracked a smile. "I could hose you off in the back yard."

She grinned back, imagining a water fight she didn't have the energy for. "I don't know if I have the strength for that."

He eased into the room behind her and placed a hand on her hip, drawing her backward against him. His fingers crept to the gap between her shirt and her jeans, caressing the sensitive skin near her hip bone. "I could help."

Shivers raced outward from his touch, and she spun to face him, raising her face to his kiss. His mouth engulfed hers, his free arm crushing her against his sling. With a frustrated grunt, he ducked out of the strap around his neck and freed his arm, allowing it to hang by his side as he resumed devouring her lips.

The fire he'd kindled inside her spread, strengthening her muscles and fortifying her bones. Giving her the energy to return his caresses...

Chapter Fourteen

The children honored the gift the First Mother offered, and the Tribe became One.
~ THE HISTORIES

Jaide stared at her mother's house from Lucas's Jeep. In the back seat, Trigger lay with her chin on her paws, as if afraid to move. Lucas sat cradling his sling-arm in the passenger seat, giving her a moment to compose herself. He'd insisted they come today, right after Jaide's parole check-in, to retrieve Flora. Once Jaide started working, she might not have time for the long trip to her mother's. But Jaide was nervous, unsure what her daughter might think of her after so long without contact.

"She can't keep Flora from you," Lucas reminded her softly, squeezing her hand. He'd read all the custody paperwork yesterday, picking out nuances and clauses Jaide had been blind to during her stressful incarceration. She still didn't understand all of it, but apparently one clause allowed Flora to request custody reassignment once she turned sixteen, which had been two weeks ago.

Her parents' one-and-a-half-story brick house seemed smaller than she remembered, the covered front porch darker. On the south side, a stump marked the spot where a cherry tree had succumbed to the heart rot it had been fighting since Jaide was a child. A few feet over, a replacement sapling of red maple drooped in the heat, leaves crispy at the edges. The brown, dry lawn sprouted no weeds, but in the vacant lot next door, burgundy amaranth flower spikes poked upward like an army of spears. Shorter plants erupted from cracks in the sidewalk on both sides of the street.

Jaide shuddered and kept her focus on the house. Flora first, then she'd decide if and how she'd join the battle against the weeds.

Easing out of the vehicle, she dragged her feet around the Jeep to the sidewalk. Lucas joined her with a reassuring nod. She headed toward the gravel driveway hugging the foundation to the right of the house then halted at the paved walk to the front entry. Family used the back kitchen door. Guests entered through the front.

Taking a deep breath and holding it, Jaide reversed and strode to the front porch steps. This wasn't a friendly family visit. This was business. After Flora's birth, she'd made a few attempts at reconciliation with her parents, like attending her sister's graduation dinner or Uncle Blue's funeral. But her mother's comments always devolved into not-so-subtle digs about Jaide's morals and responsibilities, and Jaide had stormed out every time, swearing never to return. She hadn't been inside the house in more than ten years.

Jaide took the steps quickly, as if ripping off a bandage, and stopped under the shade of the covered porch. The wooden bench swing to her left had a fresh coat of lacquer, but the coco-fiber doormat was worn and dirty. Mother's flower boxes held only a few heat-weary pansies gone to seed.

Heart fluttering like a bird in a trap, Jaide pressed the doorbell. A classic bing-bong resonated from inside. Footsteps echoed behind the door, then silence. Jaide squared her shoulders and focused on the peephole. "I know you're there, Mother. Answer the door."

The lock clicked, and the door opened a crack to expose a single dark eye. "Flora's not here."

"I can wait. When will she be back?"

Mother shook her head, eye disappearing and reappearing through the crack in the door. "She's exactly like you at sixteen, Jaide. I don't know what to do with her."

Acid worry burned beneath Jaide's ribs. Something was wrong. "Why are you evading the question? Where is she, Mother?"

"She refused to come home," Mother clipped out. "I called the police. She's at a women's shelter."

The acid in Jaide's stomach leapt to her throat. Her little girl had run away? Of course she had. Jaide understood the need to get away from Chona more than anyone. "When? How long has she been there?"

"The day you called. I don't even know if she's still there."

"Did you tell her I was out of prison? That I was coming?"

"I never got the chance. She didn't come home from school that day. She's been hanging out with some boy. Going to get herself into the same situation you did."

Panic and guilt cycled through Jaide so fast, she wavered on her feet. A boy? Mother's version of sex ed was complete avoidance of boys. And while Jaide had covered a few basic "respect your body" talks with Flora before the world blew up —and, of course, instilled in her a respect for the heavy burden humanity put upon the planet by reproducing—Jaide had not yet felt the need to go into the specifics of birth control. She'd assumed she'd be around when the time came. "You should have answered my phone calls. Let her talk to me."

The door swung open with a waft of air-conditioned chill, exposing Jaide's mother with one hand on her hip. "Don't you blame me, Jaide Acosta. She's only acting out because her mother's a felon. Poor little girl never had a chance."

"She was fine before I left. She'll be fine again once she's home with me."

"Do you have a job yet? A place to live?"

Jaide's throat tightened. "I'm staying with my friend Lucas until I'm on my feet again."

From the porch steps, Lucas added, "She and Flora can stay as long as they need to."

Mother's eyes raked Lucas head to toe. "Shacking up. I should have guessed." She sniffed with disdain and shifted her attention back to Jaide. "You'd do best to leave Flora at the shelter until you can provide for her yourself. Your dad pulled a few strings to make sure she had a bed there."

Jaide gritted her teeth. "I'm not leaving her in a shelter."

"Do what you like, then. She's at the one on Church Street. Just don't come crying to me when you can't take care of her again." Mother shut the door.

Jaide spun and nearly bowled right through Lucas in her hurry to get off the porch.

How could a grandmother act like this? Jaide wrenched open the car door and jabbed the key into the ignition. The motor roared to life as Lucas opened his door. For a few heartbeats, Jaide sat there, unable to focus beyond the dash in front of her. She pounded her palms against the steering wheel. The jolting pain running up her arms couldn't calm her.

Lucas got in and shut the door, face turned to watch the

house out his window. His voice seemed lower than usual. "I don't know how you turned out so well with a mother like that."

Jaide closed her eyes and let out a bark of laughter. "Oh, yeah. This ex-con is so well adjusted. God, what am I doing?"

"Your best. Let's get out of here. Drive."

She put the Jeep in gear and pulled away from the curb. Mother lived in the suburbs, a good fifteen or twenty minutes from the downtown shelter, which was fine by Jaide. She needed the time to cool off. She wanted to see Flora on happy terms, to be reunited in joy, not anger or revenge or any other negative emotion Mother always seemed to coax into bloom.

Downtown teemed with scrawny kids hunkered in groups against building fronts and old men with cardboard signs asking for food. The women's shelter had a line of people outside the door, teens and women with young kids and even a few elderly women. She'd never seen a line there, let alone one this long. Dozens of eyes followed the Jeep as Jaide drove five blocks out of her way to find a parking space. She got out and opened the door for Trigger, attaching her leash for the walk.

They dodged beggars, Lucas's purposeful stride deterring all but the most determined. Those he turned away with an empathetic "Not today, buddy," and kept moving.

As they reached the door to the Church Street shelter, Jaide flinched under the glare of the young woman at the front of the line. The stranger crossed her arms, half blocking the entry. "You taking out or putting in?"

"Pardon me?"

"There's no room for more," she said. "I've been here two days waiting for a spot."

"Oh." Jaide turned to look down the line at the rest of the applicants. There had to be at least thirty people waiting. How many beds did this facility even have? She'd never been inside, but she doubted they could accommodate everyone in line.

"We'll be taking my daughter home, so that should open up one more bed."

The woman's scowl melted, making her appear younger than she had at first.

Lucas pulled his billfold out of his pocket. "Hey, would you mind watching our dog while we step inside? We shouldn't be long, and I'll give you a couple of bucks."

The girl's face brightened, and she nodded, accepting the leash and the bill Lucas produced from his wallet.

"I'll give you another when we come back out," Lucas added.

Jaide pulled open the poster-filled glass door and stepped inside. The mildewy stink of an ancient air conditioner barely held back the heat from outside. A thin woman in faded jeans sat on a folding chair, clipboard on her lap. The small waiting room's other chairs had been stacked awkwardly in one corner to make room for two cots. A teller window in the opposite wall had the blind drawn to reveal the words No Vacancy. Beside it, a pamphlet display held only a few tattered guides on quitting smoking, and several inspirational posters around the room had been redecorated with black marker graffiti.

The woman rose as Jaide entered. "No room today."

"I'm looking for my daughter. Flora Acosta."

"I'm sorry, the names of our residents are confidential."

"Can you just tell her I'm here, please?"

"I'll tell her you stopped by if she's here, which I can't confirm."

"I already know she's here. I just want her to know I'm here."

The woman smiled tightly. "We pass out messages at dinner. I'm sorry."

The woman didn't look sorry. She looked like one of the prison guards Jaide had dealt with for the last two years. Jaide's pulse thundered in her ears. This wasn't prison; the woman could be reasoned with. Taking a deep breath, Jaide calmed herself before speaking. "Flora didn't run away from me. She ran away from her grandmother's house. She knows she's safe with me. All I ask is that you tell her I'm here."

"If she is here, it's because we determined that she's in immediate danger, from you or elsewhere. Our job is to protect these women. I'm going to have to ask you to leave the premises."

"You can't keep me from her!" Jaide's temper won out, and she stepped around the woman to the door. The handle refused to budge. Locked. She leaned close to the glass window and shouted, "Flora! Flora Acosta!"

"I'm calling the police."

Jaide pounded on the glass. "Flora, it's Mom! I'm out of prison, love! You can come home."

A hand wrapped around Jaide's biceps. She shrugged it off, violently, then realized it was Lucas—his mouth was a thin line of pain. She'd bumped his wounded shoulder. Remorse swept her, and she ceased her pounding.

"Jaide." He reached for her other hand where the palm rested flat against the glass. "We can leave her a message. She'll call us, and we'll come back for her."

"She said they won't tell her!" Jaide struggled half-heartedly against his one-handed grip.

"You're not helping your case here." He kept his voice low, boring into her with his eyes.

Jaide slumped in defeat. He was right. She shot a glance to the woman, who held a cell phone to her ear.

Lucas let go and pulled a card from his wallet. He offered it to the woman. "I work for Lafayette Grace Hospital. Please tell Flora Acosta that her mother is free and looking for her. She can call this number any time."

The woman took the card but kept her eyes on Jaide. "Take her out of here."

Lucas placed a hand in the small of Jaide's back and pushed her to the door. "Come on, before the police get involved."

Jaide relented, breathing hard. How could she have come this far—be this close—only to be turned back? In a daze, she accepted Trigger's leash from the girl. Lucas took her hand and guided her half a block before her feet suddenly refused to move. "I can't leave."

Lucas pointed to a cafe across the intersection. "Why don't we wait there? See if she calls right away."

Body numb with emotional overload, Jaide followed Lucas down the sidewalk. Lucas headed toward an outdoor table that hadn't been bussed yet. She sat, Trigger taking a spot beneath the table, out of the sun. Lucas disappeared inside, carrying the dirty cup, and returned with a steaming mug of tea for her. Then he headed back inside. Reality slowly crept back into her head that he was doing everything one-handed. Before she could rise to help him, he'd returned with his own coffee.

"I'm sorry, Lucas. I should've helped." She looped Trigger's leash over the handle of her chair.

"Don't worry about it." He grimaced. "I'm more hurt by the prices here. This is worse than Lafayette."

"I should've known Mother wouldn't give in so easily. She probably knew they'd never release Flora to me, but she sent me here anyway." Jaide's scowled into her tea, forehead aching.

"They're just doing their job. Some women really do need protection, and they don't know you from Adam."

"I didn't mean to embarrass you back there."

He quirked an eyebrow and shrugged. "Just try to keep it under control, or you might make things worse."

Jaide nodded, heat flooding her cheeks, and took a sip of scalding tea. Her time in prison had changed her, made her more volatile. Had taken away her rose-colored glasses. Could she ever return to the peaceful life she'd had before?

Lucas's phone beeped, and he fumbled to retrieve it from his back pocket. Jaide's heart filled her throat. He glanced at the number before answering. "This is Lucas." A short pause then a grin. "She's right here."

He handed the phone to Jaide, eyes twinkling with triumph. "Flora?"

"Mom! Where are you?"

"Oh, love, I'm just down the street. We'll come back and get you right now."

Crying erupted on the other end of the line.

Jaide's throat tightened painfully as she struggled against her own tears. "Flora, it's going to be okay. Everything will be better now."

Through the sobbing, Flora said, "Why didn't you ever call or write?"

"I did. I called every chance I could, and I wrote every week. Your gran—" Jaide choked back the word. "Chona rejected my calls and returned my letters. I have a stack of them at home to prove it."

"Come get me, Mom. Now. I'm ready now."

"We'll be right there."

Thrusting the phone back toward Lucas, she rose from her chair so quickly it toppled over backward. She tripped over Trigger's leash before she remembered the dog. Lucas said, "I've got Trigger. Go."

Shooting him a grateful smile, she sprinted toward the door. The two blocks to the shelter felt like the final bend in a marathon. Ahead, a solitary female figure stood apart from the line outside. Flora.

The dark-haired figure spotted her and closed the distance, throwing herself into Jaide's arms. "Mom!"

"Flora!" Jaide squeezed her back, sucking in lungfuls of air that smelled like Flora, unfamiliar hair products, and cheap perfume.

Trying to get her sobbing under control, Jaide pulled back to look the sixteen-year-old over. Her little girl stood eye to eye with her now, her once-long hair now short. She wore an off-shoulder slouch shirt, short shorts, and leather sandals. No longer that scrawny kid who wanted salted caramel from the food co-op. More tears rose to Jaide's eyes. She'd missed so much in two years.

A horn's beep drew her attention to the street. Lucas sat there in the Jeep, engine idling, Trigger's nose shoved out the gap in the back window. "Come on. Let's blow this Popsicle stand."

Jaide took Flora's hand and pulled her toward the street.

"Wait, Mom." Flora held back, resisting Jaide's grip.

Jaide turned to meet her daughter's gaze.

"There's one thing." Flora gnawed her bottom lip as a teenage boy Jaide hadn't noticed stepped to Flora's side and took her other hand. His black hair reminded Jaide of a mushroom, cut to stand up in a slight pouf all over his head. "We need to bring Shayne with us."

"Love, I don't have a job yet." She avoided the young man's gaze. "We're living with Lucas as it is. I can't support another person."

Flora lifted her chin, her shoulders rising as she took a deep breath. "Well, you have to. I'm pregnant.

Chapter Fifteen

J aide stood on the sidewalk, one hand outstretched toward her daughter. Pregnant? But Flora was just a baby herself. Chona's words came unbidden: *She's just like you were.*

Shayne's voice interrupted her shock, the timbre deeper than Jaide expected for one so young. "It won't be for long. We just need a fresh start. Somewhere I can find a job."

She couldn't take her eyes off Flora's midsection. "Why?"

"I love him, Mom. We want to be a family."

Dragging her gaze upward, she locked onto Flora's face. "But you haven't finished school."

"She can get her GED before the baby's born. Flora's smart."

Jaide snapped her attention toward the boy. The knot inside her chest felt ready to explode. "How old are you? Do you have a diploma? You should have a job before you have a baby, don't you think?"

Shayne's face drained of color, but he drew himself taller. "I might not be good at school, but I can fix things. I'll find work."

Flora stuck out her lower lip and scowled at Jaide. "You're just like Grandma."

An angry honk came from behind her, followed by the roar of an engine. Out of the corner of her eye, she saw a sedan whip around Lucas's double-parked Jeep. He called from the window again, his voice sounding a million miles away. "Can't sit here much longer!"

The hard knot in Jaide's chest turned into a boulder and dropped to the pit of her stomach. She ground her teeth. "Get in. Both of you. We'll discuss this on the way."

She spun toward the Jeep. Lucas opened the driver's door and climbed out, stroking his wounded arm with his free hand. "I wish I could drive and let you two chat, but shifting gears one-handed probably isn't a good idea. Sorry."

In what she hoped passed for appreciation, she smiled weakly at him and climbed in while he walked around the front to get in the other side. Having a deep discussion with her child would be more difficult if she drove, but she probably should let herself simmer a bit first, anyway. In the back seat, Trigger's high-pitched whine grated like nails on a chalkboard. Flora's baby-talk voice was just as bad. "Trigger! Oh my God, Trigger!"

Flora continued her crooning, encouraging the dog into the cargo area behind the back seats so she and Shayne could get in. Lucas shot a raised-eyebrow look toward Jaide.

She shook her head and sighed. "I don't even know where to begin."

All she wanted was to take her daughter home and be a family again. She shifted the Jeep into gear. Trigger continued to whine, tail sweeping the rear window like a berserk wiper blade as she crept over the seat back to lick Flora's face.

"Trigger, lay down." Jaide's voice came out harder than she intended, but she didn't have the fortitude to apologize.

Trigger sat but kept her chin propped on top of the back seats near Flora's head, whining sporadically.

Jaide pulled forward to join traffic, revving through a yellow light before slowing to a crawl behind a box truck. In the rearview mirror, she caught a glimpse of Flora clutching hands with her boyfriend, eyes wide with determination. Jaide knew that look. She knew that feeling. Memories of her own youthful pregnancy pounded at her; Chona's insistence she get an abortion, Jaide's undying love for the boy who'd skip out only a few months later, her obstinate refusal to consider adoption. She could raise a child on her own. Be a better parent.

And here was history repeating itself.

"Not if I don't let it," Jaide muttered to herself. Lucas shot her a quizzical look but stayed silent. First things first—verify that Flora really was pregnant. Then they could discuss options.

She threaded her way through downtown. The enormity of the situation called for a better venue than a crowded Jeep. What if they decided not to let the boy stay? He'd be far away from his hometown. She'd feel responsible for him. She had to take control of the situation before it was too late. Wrenching the steering wheel, she made a turn into an amarantox-peppered parking lot and ground to a stop across two overgrown parking spaces.

For several breathless moments, everyone sat in silence. Finally, Lucas broke the spell. "Someone want to tell me what's up?"

Gritting her teeth, Jaide said, "She's pregnant."

Lucas made a sour face and peeked toward the back seat. "I suppose he's the father?"

"That's what they say."

"So she's having it?"

Jaide bent forward to rest her head on the steering wheel. "We haven't gotten that far."

"Don't talk about us like we're not here," Flora said.

"We both want this baby," Shayne added.

How could she argue against a father wanting to be part of his kid's life? What she would have given for Flora's father to have stuck around. But this was bigger than Flora's child having a father. Jaide couldn't support herself, let alone a daughter, a grandbaby, and a baby daddy. Even Lucas, with all his generosity, would balk at that. Keeping her cheek against the steering wheel, Jaide turned her face to look at him. "My baggage has baggage. You should kick us all out right now."

One side of his mouth turned up slightly. "Probably. But I like your cooking too much." He unbuckled his seatbelt and swiveled so he could better face the kids in the back. "I'm Lucas, by the way. Good to see you again, Flora."

"Hi," Flora said. "Thanks for picking us up. This is Shayne."

"Shayne." Lucas nodded a greeting. "I wish we'd met under better circumstances."

"Me too, sir."

"I appreciate your desire to take responsibility in this situation, but you don't know what you're getting into. Neither of you do."

"You're one to talk." Flora's voice was a sneer. "You abandoned your daughter to your parents."

Jaide jerked upright. Had Flora really just said that?

Lucas sat very still, but his free hand had curled into a fist in his lap.

Shoving open the door, Jaide flung herself outside and grappled open the back door. Shayne cringed away, but Jaide barely saw him, her eyes glued on Flora. "Get out."

Shayne's hand slowly released his seatbelt, and he climbed from the vehicle. Flora shouted, "Mom! What are you doing?"

Jaide's gaze didn't waver from her daughter. "I meant you."

Flora sat there a moment, mouth hanging open. Then she fumbled behind her for the door handle and slid from the Jeep.

Jaide stalked past Shayne and around the back of the Jeep until she stood face to face with her daughter. "Lucas opened his home not only to us, but he's cared for Trigger these past few years. He kept me sane while I was in prison—the only one who kept me sane after your grandmother kept you from me. You have no right to talk to him that way."

To Jaide's gratification, Flora flushed and nodded, eyes downcast.

"I've always supported your choices, whether I agree with them or not. But I'm not in a position to feed and clothe us. Lucas has no obligation to either of us, let alone your boyfriend."

Lucas got out of the Jeep and shut the door.

Shayne eased around to stand at Flora's side, looking back and forth between Jaide and Lucas. "I don't want to owe anyone anything."

"Then you shouldn't have gotten my daughter pregnant," shouted Jaide. "But you have, and you'll owe a heck of a lot more people before you're done. Take my word for it."

Shayne flushed, slumping until his shoulders seemed to meet his ears.

Flora wrapped one arm around her middle. "Are you saying you want me to have an abortion?"

Jaide slammed a palm against the side of the Jeep and pressed her forehead to the glass. Trigger peered through the window at her, tail twitching hesitantly. What could Jaide say? Yes, she wanted Flora to end the pregnancy, for many reasons that were more than personal. But given Jaide's own life choices, she had no right to demand that course of action. She sucked in a breath of amaranth-tainted air and let it out. "I can't tell you what to do. I know what I did in your situation. My life would be different if I'd taken another path."

"You mean your life would be better."

"That's not what I said."

An arm slid around Jaide's shoulders. "I think your mom means that she wishes she'd had you under better circumstances," Lucas said. "That she'd been able to give you a better life."

Jaide leaned gratefully against him, nodding. She took a deep breath and straightened to face everyone again. "I never regretted having you. But I'm asking you to consider all the options. And yes, abortion is one of them. If you insist on bringing another life into this overgrown world, there's also adoption. Lots of families out there want babies. You and Shayne don't have to shackle your futures."

"But we want to be together," Flora whined, taking her boyfriend's hand.

Shayne nodded. "We want to be a family."

"Life's not about getting what you want," Jaide said, her chest tight. "You're lucky to get what you need."

Lucas squeezed her shoulder and then dropped his arm. "Shayne, may I have a word with you in private?"

The young man's eyes grew round, but he nodded. Lucas led him across the parking lot toward a yellowing maple tree surrounded by waist-high green amaranth.

Flora clenched her fists at her sides, watching them go. "What's he saying to him?"

Jaide shrugged and leaned back against the Jeep. She couldn't begin to imagine what Lucas was saying. Probably something brilliant. That was Lucas. She studied her daughter's slender figure. Baby fat rounded her cheeks, and the legs poking from her shorts had the effortless tone of youth. The air smelled of crushed amaranth, the scent of futility. "How far along are you?"

Flora dropped her chin to her chest, hugging her arms around herself. "I peed on a stick last week."

"But how long since your last period?"

"I don't know. A couple of months?"

Jaide was too exhausted to pry for more.

"I tried to get birth control, Mom. I did. But Grandma checked my room." Flora stared at her a few moments then moved to lean next to her against the Jeep. "You're really skinny, Mom. Not good skinny, just skinny."

Looking down to her bony knees, Jaide nodded. "Not a lot of vegetarian options in jail."

"Oh." Flora drummed her fingertips against the Jeep's side. "Did you really break into a greenhouse?"

Jaide nodded.

"Why?"

Jaide exhaled and raised her face to the sun. The heat coming down met the heat rising from the concrete, clamping down on her like a trap. She wanted to justify why she'd been away. She'd been trying to do the world a favor, trying to rid it of corporate ruination. Could Flora possibly understand her motives? Even more important—could she understand the consequences? "I can't tell you."

Flora launched forward off the Jeep and stalked a few paces toward where Lucas and Shayne stood talking. "Of course not."

"I signed papers saying I wouldn't talk. Otherwise, I'd still be in prison."

"But I'm your daughter."

"It doesn't matter." The escaped amaranth paled in comparison to the more immediate issue of Flora's pregnancy. "Anyway, telling you won't change anything. Just believe I had the best intentions."

"One of your protests." Flora crossed her arms.

Jaide nodded again before realizing Flora had her back to her. "Yes."

Lucas and Shayne started back toward the Jeep. Flora rushed to her boyfriend's side, taking his hand and leaning close to whisper in his ear. He gave her a quick kiss. They all stopped in front of Jaide.

Lucas hooked his thumb into his belt loop and took a deep breath. "So we've come to an understanding. Shayne will be coming with us, and he can sleep in the tent in the backyard. He'll look for work while Flora goes back to school—"

Flora began, "I'm not go—"

"You will go back to school, Flora. My house, my rules."

Shayne shushed her when she opened her mouth again. She crossed her arms and glared at all of them.

"As soon as he starts earning money, he'll contribute to the household expenses plus start saving for a place of his own. In the meantime, a decision must be made about the pregnancy." Lucas focused on Flora. "Shayne has agreed to leave that up to you, Flora. If you choose to have the baby and keep it, he'll do his part to support and raise it. But if you decide to abort or to give it up for adoption, he will abide by that decision, as well. You don't have to keep the baby to stay together."

Jaide's heart raced, trying to keep pace with her thoughts. "Lucas, I can't ask you to do this."

"You're not asking. I'm offering. He says he loves Flora no matter what and wishes to remain with her in any scenario." He took Jaide's hand. "I know the feeling."

"But Lucas—"

"Where else are you going to go? Shayne was sleeping in the alley while Flora was in the shelter. It's like that all over."

"What about Suzanne?" Jaide asked. "We shouldn't take over her space without asking her."

She didn't miss the quick flicker in his eye—Flora's earlier comment had cut him. "Suzanne's busy with her own life and happy at my parents' house. I'll call her to be sure, but between school and all her activities, she hasn't slept over in months. I don't think she'll mind."

Flora stared at her feet. "Thank you, Lucas."

Shayne repeated the thanks.

All Jaide could do was kiss Lucas on the cheek. He continued to be the best thing in her life while the world went to shit around her. He deserved better, but for whatever reason, he wanted her. She climbed into the Jeep and swore to herself that tomorrow she'd find a job. She'd pull her own weight if it killed her.

Chapter Sixteen

Slowing the Jeep to a stop at the library's front doors, Jaide frowned at the line of people extending around the building. "What's going on?"

Flora had insisted on trying to get a job until classes resumed in the fall, which meant a trip to the library's public computers while Jaide drove Lucas to his follow-up appointment. Jaide was both proud and sad that Flora was old enough to pitch in.

"In Bloomington, they gave us a thirty-minute limit at the computers." Shayne opened his door. "Then we had to get back in line."

He slammed the door and raced to catch up with Flora, who already had a spot behind an overweight woman holding an umbrella for shade.

"I told you things were bad." Lucas was digging in the glovebox. He found a fast food napkin and blew his nose. "Someone must be field burning outside of town. Wish they'd wait until the wind shifted."

Jaide had been ignoring the tickle in her nose. "Trying to keep the amaranth under control, you think?"

"Probably." He stuffed the napkin in a used plastic grocery bag at his feet.

She pulled away from the library and wove the Jeep through the city, dodging peddlers and beggars, until they reached the hospital's medical center. Lucas went straight to an exam room, and Jaide took a seat on a waiting-area chair away from the other patients. She hunched over his smart phone, swishing through ads for a data-entry specialist. Without a computer to work at from home, she'd have to secure an office position. The idea daunted her. She hadn't worked in an office since Flora's preschool days. A government office position was accepting applications and sounded perfect for her. Government jobs had benefits, including medical for Flora.

Using the phone to fill out the application was awkward, but she proceeded through the initial questionnaire, only to be brought up short by the inquiry about criminal records. The position wouldn't accept an ex-con.

Her stomach roiled like a ball of baby snakes. She searched several job sites for more options. There were no other office jobs. If she couldn't do data entry, what else could she do? So many jobs required previous experience—even janitorial or food service jobs. By the time Lucas emerged, she was ready to throw the phone across the room.

A vein pulsed in his flushed forehead, and she bit back her complaints. He must have been given bad news. As he finalized his next appointment, she rose and waited near the door, shifting his phone from hand to hand. He crumpled his paperwork in one fist and stalked past her as if he wanted to bomb the building.

She rushed to keep up with him. "What'd they say?"

The muscle in Lucas's jaw bulged. "Apparently this injury is a pre-existing condition. I don't qualify for workman's comp. Plus, I'm going to need surgery."

"But you got hurt on the job."

Lucas heaved an angry breath. "The doctor insists it's a flare-up of an old injury. I need to talk to my union rep."

The snakes in her gut constricted. Without workman's comp, Lucas would have to pay for the surgery himself. "Can you see another doctor?"

"Only at this office. My insurance is sticky about preferred providers." They reached the Jeep, and he opened the driver's-side door for her. "How'd your job search go?"

Putting the key in the ignition, she avoided looking at him. "There's a few more places I need to look."

He shut the door and went around to climb in the passenger side. "Well, I don't mind keeping you around to chauffeur me a while longer, now that I know this shoulder's going to need surgery."

She forced a smile and pulled out of the parking lot. He always tried to find the best in a situation. And he always seemed to come out okay. Maybe things would be all right.

Lucas tuned the radio to one of his favorite talk shows.

A man's voice was saying, "...Herbicides touted as the solution two years ago are now useless. Farmers are losing crops so fast, they've turned to field burning in hope of eradicating dormant seeds."

A different male voice responded, "If that's true, field burning sounds like it might be our quickest option to wipe out the problem."

"All that does is expose the soil to erosion. With the current drought, we're already seeing signs of another Dust Bowl..."

Lucas turned up the volume. "You were right about the burning."

Jaide blinked, the haze seeming thicker suddenly. More ominous.

"...Traditional large-scale farming practices are no longer valid. We've got to band together to manually keep this weed at bay. Feet on the ground, hands in the dirt. That's the motto of our organization, Field Hands. Our goal is to preserve agrarian development through hand planting, watering, and harvesting. That's the only way we're going to keep this weed at bay."

"Forgive me, but that sounds rather medieval."

"Broad-spectrum methods aren't working. This weed's so aggressive, it poisons the soil around it so no other plants can grow. It regenerates from any bit of root left in the ground. If allowed to mature, it makes millions of seeds per plant. The sheer volume of seeds that have already spread along roadways and riverbeds will be impossible to overcome entirely. We're looking at a floral cataclysm to rival the extinction of the dinosaurs. And with no food, humanity will follow..."

Jaide's head felt as if it might explode, and her hands gripped the wheel like letting go would drop her off a cliff. Extinction? The Franken-weed was worse than even her most terrifying nightmares. And she'd released it. The end of the world was her fault. A Smart Car pulled out of the intersection in front of her, and she stomped the brake, nearly rear-ending it.

"If this is bothering you, we can turn it off," Lucas said, switching off the radio.

"No!" Jaide reached out and turned it back on. "I need to hear this."

The host continued, "...Approval of another herbicide for corn and grass crops that should only affect amaranth and other broad-leafed weeds."

"Herbicides have a shelf life," the guest speaker said. "Superweeds always emerge, and palmer amarantox has always had a knack at overcoming chemical measures. That will be a short-term solution, at best. We need eyes and hands on the fields."

Lucas pointed to an abandoned parking lot. "Why don't you pull over to listen?"

Pulse thundering in her ears, Jaide pulled over.

The guest speaker said, "Both natural and agrarian habitats have been overrun with amarantox—"

"Amarantox," the host interrupted. "I haven't heard it called that before. That's great."

Jaide leaned forward and spoke to the radio. "Just because you give it a cutesy name doesn't make it any less dangerous."

"So what can people do on their own? Obviously pull and burn the weed, but are there other measures you'd recommend? What about something along the lines of victory gardening?"

"Home gardens could take a large burden off commercial producers, but it takes over half an acre to support one human being, depending on soil and climate conditions. Most people don't own enough land to feed themselves, let alone a family."

Lucas added, "Plus people like me can't tell the weeds from the crops."

A light bulb went on in Jaide's head. "I can teach people." She turned to Lucas with a grin. "Maybe this guy'll hire me! I should contact him."

Lucas's good shoulder sagged. "Not another activist group, Jaide. Please."

The announcer was thanking his guest. "That was Nolan Schmidt, spokesman for Field Hands, a grassroots organization promoting hands-on farming. To learn more about Field Hands, or to order a transcript of this show, log onto..."

"Jobs are scarce, and I'm well qualified for this one. Give me your phone, Lucas. Quick."

He shook his head but handed it over. She logged on and scrolled through the website. If she could land a job pulling weeds, teaching others how to fight the invasion, maybe she could not only make some money, but also atone for what she'd done. Maybe.

Chapter Seventeen

JUNE

Take and eat...

~ THE HISTORIES

Jaide slipped quickly through Lucas's patio doors into the backyard to keep the air conditioning from escaping. The morning heat hit her like a concrete wall, and a yellow haze smudged the sky, blotting out the sun. Smoke had drifted thick over the city all week, and the radio issued daily air-quality warnings, advising people to stay inside. She tried not to breathe too deeply while she checked her seedlings. In this weather, she had to water them several times a day, but she wanted to do something useful until she could secure a job.

A month had passed since Field Hands had rejected her inquiry. Apparently a simple Googling of her name revealed her crime, and no one would touch her with a ten-foot pole.

She poured a measured amount of used dishwater around the base of a tiny tomato plant, careful not to spill any onto the dead lawn. The city was under a water-rationing program until the drought ended. Cardboard over the top of each pot's soil conserved moisture, but even so, the seedlings drooped with exhaustion. An assortment of potted vegetables took up most of the backyard. The first lettuce might be ready in a week or two, assuming she could keep up on the watering.

After watering came weed patrol. The fence between the backyard and the alley kept intruders out, but the amarantox knew no bounds. Scouting the property line on both sides of the fence, she crushed a few green bits poking up from the dry earth and eyed the surrounding lots. Homeowners might mow or spray or pull, but the weed snuck up in places no one seemed to want responsibility for: beneath the dumpsters, down the center of the dirt alley, at the base of the stop sign. The seeds' ability to not only spread but also sprout during dry weather made her blood run cold.

She was still enamored with the idea of working on a larger scale to eradicate the amarantox, or at least control it. But every job opening—agricultural or otherwise—filled before she could even apply. At least Shayne had managed to get a part-time position crushing boxes at a small warehouse. Lucas's unemployment benefits barely covered his condo payments and utilities, and his savings had been sapped by the cost of his surgery.

A siren's wail started up nearby, and Jaide watched the neighbor's police cruiser zip down the alley. More and more trouble filled the city every day, from looting to murders. Thank God Lucas lived in a good part of town. Having a police officer for a neighbor helped deter crime as well.

She cleaned up Trigger's latest mess and then went back inside to wash up. The house smelled delightfully of fresh coffee.

On the sofa reading his phone, Lucas sprawled with his feet

propped on the coffee table, wearing nothing but his boxer briefs and arm sling. With the cost of air conditioning so high, they all managed the heat by being half naked most of the time. His surgery had gone well, but recovery would be slow. The therapeutic ice machine he'd borrowed from a friend hummed on the floor next to him. Trigger lay with her back against the box as if she could soak up some of the coolness.

Lucas set his phone aside and lifted a coffee mug from its precarious perch on the sofa's arm. "There's more, if you'd like. Half and half's in the fridge."

"How's the shoulder?"

He raised his mug in a salute. "Coffee with Bailey's helps. There's more on the counter, if you're so inclined."

She rolled her eyes. "You're not supposed to be drinking with your pain meds."

"Who's the paramedic here?" He thrust his chin out in mock defiance.

"It's your liver." Following the delicious aroma, she went to the kitchen and poured herself a modest cup of the expensive, free-trade Kona. She wished he'd take his budget a little more seriously and buy generic, especially since he'd spent so much of his savings on hospital bills.

Adding a generous dollop of cream, she brought her mug out to join him on the sofa. "Kids still sleeping?"

She'd relented and allowed Shayne to bunk with Flora after her daughter pointed out she was pregnant already, what more could happen? Much as Jaide wanted to hate him, he was a decent kid. He'd come home with groceries after his first paycheck, which was good, because he had a teenage boy's never-ending appetite.

Pounding footsteps rattled the nearby shelves, followed by the slam of the bathroom door and the sound of retching.

"Not anymore," Lucas replied. "Poor girl."

Jaide clenched her teeth and said nothing. On one hand, she felt sorry for her daughter, but she wished the child would listen to reason. How many years had Jaide pointed out how the overpopulation of the Earth was destroying the planet? Flora couldn't even feed herself, and she wanted to bring another life into the world. She refused to consider an abortion, and talk of contacting an adoption agency resulted in distraught tears.

Shayne emerged from the hallway, his mushroom of hair smashed flat on one side. "Morning," he mumbled and headed for the kitchen. Trigger jumped up to follow him, ever hopeful.

"Shayne, do you work today?" Jaide called.

He joined them with a slice of bread in one hand and a mug of coffee in the other. "No. I heard of a place where people hang out for field work. Flora and I thought we'd check it out."

Lucas frowned. "Hang out?"

"Farmers who need help come pick people." Shayne spoke around a bite of bread. "Guys willing to work under the table."

Waiting on a street corner for work seemed dangerous to Jaide, especially for a sixteen-year-old girl. She shook her head. "Sounds too risky. Especially for Flora."

Shayne shrugged. "If we stick together, we should be fine. Wanna come?"

She considered a moment. Together they'd be safe, and perhaps they could all earn a little cash. This might be her best opportunity, considering her recent job search results. "Um, yeah, actually."

Lucas sat forward. "What if someone only wants one of you?"

"We come as a package," Jaide said. "Will you be okay alone today?"

"I can manage. But maybe Flora should stay here. She's pretty sick."

The retching from the bathroom had been replaced by

running water. With morning sickness hitting her all times of the day, Flora would be useless. "I suppose that works."

"Take my Jeep. Your rattle-trap car'll leave you stranded somewhere."

"What if you need to go somewhere?"

"I don't. Besides, there's a condo association meeting today I need to stay here for."

Flora trudged out of the bathroom looking wan. "When does this end?"

"Some women have it the entire pregnancy," Jaide said, aware of her attempt at manipulation yet unable to stop herself.

Lucas laughed. "Most women only have it the first couple of months. Go to the clinic. They'll give you a due date."

"The lines are so long, I can never get in," Flora said.

Jaide had attempted to take her to the free clinic several times. A nurse had roamed a line of patients that stretched around the building, triaging and pulling the most serious cases first. Suspected pregnancy was low on the list. They'd waited in line for hours only to be shooed away at closing.

Face sobering, Lucas sat forward, pulling the hoses of his ice machine free of the cushions. "I'd feel better if a doctor saw you. Plus then you can get on W.I.C."

Flora took a big breath and let her head fall back in childish resignation. "All right. I'll go today."

Jaide shook her head. "You're staying here to take care of Lucas today. Besides, that line will already be too long this late in the morning. I'll take you tomorrow before it opens."

"Where are you going?" Flora scowled.

Shayne draped an arm around her shoulder. "The field worker place we talked about. Remember?"

She shied away from him, hand over her nose, and sprinted toward the bathroom. "You smell like coffee."

Shayne followed behind. "Um, I need to use the toilet."

Jaide raised an eyebrow at Lucas. "Who's going to be looking after who, here?"

Lucas squeezed his eyes shut in a pained smile, settling back against his cushions. "We'll be mutually supportive."

"Softie." She leaned sideways and kissed his cheek. "I'll fill your ice machine before I go."

After making sure Lucas and Flora were as prepared as she could make them, Jaide gathered her sun hat and Lucas's work gloves. She and Shayne drove to the outskirts of the university, where a crowd waited at a bus transit station. A chain-link fence separated the campus from the swath of pavement and scattered benches filled with people.

So much competition, most of them wiry, sun-beaten men. A particularly short man in a soiled white T-shirt cast her a lascivious grin as she joined the crowd. Giving him a wide berth, she selected a spot near a ginger-haired teenager along the university's fence where the narrow strip of brown grass had been trampled to bare dirt. She leaned against the chain link to watch the street, doubly glad she had Shayne along.

A black pickup pulled into the lot. Like a single organism, the crowd swarmed the passenger side. Three men climbed into the pickup's bed before Jaide or Shayne could even get close enough to hear about the job. She retreated to the curb. "This is going to be tough."

Shane only nodded and took a seat on the edge of the cement.

Eight more trucks came and left while the sun finished its ascent and began to drop. Jaide managed to hear the jobs on the last three—two requests for lugging hundred-pound bags of fertilizer and one guy who wanted someone to man a cattle chute.

Jaide shuddered, picturing the poor, frightened animals about to be slaughtered. How could anyone stand there, look into their eyes, and send them to be killed, one after another?

The crowd thinned as people either took jobs or gave up and went home. In the distance, the university bell tower chimed three o'clock, and the remaining people gathered their things to leave. "Is that all?" Jaide asked no one in particular. "The jobs are over?"

"Unless you want to come home with me, precious," said a guy wearing faded overalls and a lewd grin.

Shayne glared at him. "Hey, man. Back off."

"No thanks." Jaide kept her eye on the man as he departed.

"Should we go, then?" Shayne looked around at the handful of people remaining. "This was harder than I thought."

Jaide sighed and moved off the curb toward the Jeep. Today was going to be a bust. "We can try again tomorrow."

A blue minivan pulled into the station, stopping mere feet from where she stood. Several people who'd been leaving scrambled back toward the vehicle. Jaide took two more steps and reached the open window. A young guy with a beard down his neck leaned over from the driver's seat to yell through the open window. "I'm offering futures, not money."

Most of the group wheeled around, resuming their departure. A middle-aged man with a huge bald spot asked, "What're you growing, and when's the harvest?"

"Community Supported Agriculture—mixed crops," the bearded man said.

The middle-aged man flapped a hand at the truck and left. All that remained were Jaide and Shayne, plus four others. Jaide bent to look inside the minivan. The man appeared clean in spite of the scruffy beard. A crucifix hung from his rearview mirror. He met her gaze and nodded once. "Interested?"

"Futures means crop shares, right?"

The man nodded.

Payment in food would leave Lucas's income to pay other bills. "What are the terms?"

"We're keeping ahead of the amarantox the old-fashioned way. Fourteen acres that need to be weeded, watered, and harvested. Plus keep the varmints and deer out. That's the hard part this year. I need two people on shift twenty-four hours."

"You expect us to stay overnight?" asked a woman with a baby tied on her back. "For just shares?"

His gaze flicked to the baby. "Times are tough for me, too. 'Coons already dug up my rows of corn twice. This is a CSA farm. I got no capital to pay wages. The work you put in will be what you get out of it."

"How much is a share?" Jaide asked.

"'Bout a five-gallon bucket a week. I need four people ready to go now."

Based on the general response to his offer, she thought she ought to dicker a little. "I've got experience with weed identification and disposal. Can I get more?"

The guy threw back his head and laughed. "Everyone working the fields has experience. One share's fair. I already paid for seed and planting."

The woman with the baby retorted, "You want us full time, you need to make it worth our while. I'm feeding more than myself, and I have bills."

He rested a forearm on his steering wheel and sized up the remaining people outside his truck. Jaide and Shayne stood closest, but behind them stood another kid about Shayne's age and a lanky man with pasty skin, plus the woman. "Two shares, then. But only to the four who get in right now."

"Three shares," said the pasty guy.

The woman nodded.

The driver's shoulders lifted in a sigh. "Two and a half."

The pasty guy opened the minivan's sliding door. "I'm in. The name's Ian."

Jaide shouldered in behind him before the other slots were taken. Between her and Shayne, they could earn five whole buckets of food. If it wasn't all lettuce, that would be plenty to feed the family. Maybe even enough to contribute to those poor kids hanging out near the oak trees in front of Lucas's condo. She held out a hand to Shayne. "We're in. Me and him."

Shayne screwed up one eye. "You sure? I'm making money at the warehouse."

The woman with the infant and the red-headed kid were jockeying for the final seat.

"Shayne, get in."

"I don't think shares are a good deal," he said.

"We can eat shares. We can't eat money."

The mother and kid squeezed into the back seat together. The driver looked at Shayne. "That's four. Sorry, kid."

"Wait," said Jaide, putting one foot on the pavement but keeping her hip on the middle seat.

"In or out," said the driver. "If you're not coming, I have one more stop to check for a worker."

"You should go," said Shayne.

She clenched her fists, torn between opportunity and responsibility. "Can you follow in the Jeep?"

His face flushed. "I don't have my license. Plus, I can't drive a stick."

"Shit." She got out of the van.

Ian started to slide the door closed. Shayne thrust out an arm to stop it and climbed inside. He spoke to the glowering driver. "What if I hold her place so she can follow us?"

Jaide met the bearded man's eyes across the seats. "Is that okay? Please?"

He shrugged. "Hurry up."

Without wasting another breath, she sprinted for the Jeep. Maybe her luck was turning at last.

———

The CSA farm stood in the middle of amarantox-ridden soybean fields. A long dirt lane extended between the fenced fields, soybeans on the left, vegetable rows on the right, ending at a boxy brick farmhouse and a barn in need of a new coat of red paint. Jaide followed the dust kicked up by the minivan ahead of her and parked next to it near the house. The others had already disembarked and were walking toward the barn.

Shayne leaned close to her. "Farmer's name is Ray. I think the woman's Chia. Can't recall the other names."

"Thanks."

"Since I'm not working, is it okay if I take a nap?" He cracked a big yawn that made her throat ache with the desire to join him.

"Take one for both of us, okay?"

He climbed into the Jeep and rolled down all the windows. Jaide trotted to catch up to the moving group. Ray was saying, "Let me introduce you all to Bones." He headed toward a big black dog chained near the barn at the end of the lane. "He'll accompany the foot patrol each night."

Possibility sparked in Jaide's chest. "I have a border collie who'd be great on patrols. Can I bring her?"

Ray tilted his head. "Long as she and Bones get along. And I ain't responsible if she gets hurt on the job."

Jaide beamed at him and squatted low near the dog to let

him sniff her hand. After introductions, Ray waved them forward around the corner of the barn. A patchy field of alfalfa spread out before them, spots of bare dirt here and there where amarantox had seeped its poison into the soil before being pulled.

Ian faced Ray with his arms crossed. "You didn't tell us the CSA included hay fields. You expect us to keep this weeded?"

Chia nodded. "Yeah. When and how do we get our share from this?"

Ray turned and looked them all over. "I'll be making the first cutting some time this week. But you ain't worked for that, so those shares are all mine. Next cutting will be in July. But if that damned poisonous weed infests the crop, it's worthless as animal feed. That's why I need you. I have a regular buyer, so when he pays, I'll divvy up the proceeds. The farm gets half. The rest in equal portions among us."

Jaide gauged the reactions of the other workers. She had no idea whether this was a good deal or not, but it was at least hope for some actual money. The others made angry faces but didn't argue.

"Deer are into the alfalfa this year, probably because that damn weed's taken over so much of their usual forage, and Big-Ag farms are burning everything instead of hiring people like you. Daytime ain't much of a problem yet, but at night the deer'll move in by the hundreds. I've set up a stand in the middle there where you can keep watch with a rifle." He pointed to a rickety-looking scaffold across the field. "You all have experience with a gun?"

Chia and Ian nodded, while Jaide shook her head. It hadn't occurred to her she'd be using a gun. The ginger-haired kid said, "Do video games count?"

Ray scowled. "No." He showed them the gun's safety and how to aim and pull the trigger. "Killing deer ain't important.

Not shooting me is. Keep the muzzle pointed down until you're ready to fire. Me or my wife'll pair off with each of you this first week to show you the ropes." He looked at Jaide and the boy. "And we'll get you some target practice. Any venison you take becomes part of the CSA shares. 'Coons and 'possum or birds go to Bones and the cats."

Jaide gulped. She prayed shooting the gun would be enough to scare the creatures off without actually hitting and killing one.

"I'll cover tonight, but I need volunteers for tomorrow night."

They all looked at each other, and then Ian raised a hand. "I will."

Relief flooded Jaide. She needed some time to adjust to the idea of holding a gun, let alone hunting animals under the moonlight. Apparently farming wasn't as much like gardening as she thought.

"Everyone good?" asked Ray. Without waiting for a reply, he turned toward the house. "Okay. Let me take you to meet the family. We all take turns and earn shares same as you. I got two regular hands you'll meet tomorrow." A stout woman and two teen boys with messy hair waited on the screened porch to meet them. "This here's Martha and my sons, Roger and Eddie."

The woman looked as though she was about to cry, her square face drawn into tense lines, her body rigid. She thrust an arm out to point toward two cherry trees in the yard. "Fruit trees ain't part of the co-op."

"I was gettin' to that, Martha." Ray swept a hand toward a fenced area between the house and the barn. "The henhouse there along with these fruit trees are the family's. The rest of the crops get divided up into equal parts, including the ones that go out to my customers. Everyone here earns the same as everyone else. No arguing when time comes each week for what's fair." Ray made eye contact with each person to be sure they understood. "Main harvest's coming on now, so I expect you'll each have something to take home and feed the family every night."

"What about tonight?" Chia asked, her voice quiet. "I haven't eaten today."

The farmer's gaze softened, and he looked at his wife. "We have anything left over from sales today?"

Martha's lips tightened, but she nodded. "I was gonna make jam out of the bruised strawberries. But they can have a few, I suppose."

Jaide's mouth watered. Fresh fruit. Prices at the market had become outlandish, and she'd been denying herself to make sure Flora had enough to stay healthy.

Martha returned from the house with a plastic container of berries and held it out. Chia moved quickly, grabbing a dripping handful and thrusting it into her mouth. The sweet fragrance of strawberries wafted through the afternoon air as the red-headed boy scurried forward to take some. Jaide eased in next to them, carefully choosing a slightly squished red fruit. She placed it on her tongue and savored the juice sliding down her parched throat.

Behind her, the pasty man coughed, and she moved aside to allow him room.

He remained where he was, his gaze on Chia. "I'll give my share to the baby tonight."

Jaide paused with her next berry halfway to her mouth. She looked sideways at the mother and realized how gaunt the woman's cheeks were. Likely every ounce of nutrition she ate was going toward nursing her baby. Cheeks burning, Jaide lowered the fruit back to the bin. "Have mine, too."

The red-haired teenager shoved another gooey handful into

his red-stained mouth. He looked about as hungry as Chia did. Jaide realized just how lucky she was to have Lucas. Real hunger had yet to strike her little family.

She followed Ray to the vegetable patch to pull weeds, stomach empty but heart full.

Chapter Eighteen

JULY

The Tox can eat itself.

~ Mother's Proverb

J aide waded through the alfalfa, the light from her wind-
up flashlight frosting across the moonlit foliage. Ian
had lucked out and won the coin toss to get platform
duty while she walked the property. Her arms ached
from carrying both the rifle and the light. The owner of the
infested soybeans on the other side of the fence had incinerated
his field the day before, and the scent of burned greenery
cloyed the early night air. Cicadas and crickets lamented the
destruction with vibrating songs, while over the horizon, the
sky glowed orange from more fires. Ray's land felt like a last
bastion amid a wasteland of blackened fields.

She checked the alfalfa behind her where the orange light
blinking on Trigger's collar bounced through the foliage. As
usual, her dog was tailing Bones like a lovesick puppy. Trigger
might be enamored of the big lab, but for Jaide, Bones had

taken some getting used to. At least his tail was up at the moment. When it went down, that meant he'd found something, and when he found something, he caught it.

She shuddered at the memory of her first night on patrol three weeks ago. After getting the dog to release his prey, she'd barely been able to force herself to pick up the limp gray corpse of the rabbit. Trigger had lain next to her and whined while she lowered it into the burlap sack, trying not to throw up. Neither she nor her dog was a killer. She supposed she ought to be grateful Bones was willing to do the job, but she hated having to pick up after him.

Reaching the low wood fence separating Ray's alfalfa from the neighbor's property, she pivoted to begin her walk along the north lot line. Her jeans clung against her legs in the heat, but she'd learned the hard way that to patrol in shorts left her exposed to not only grass cuts but also the insects that seemed to multiply once the sun set.

To ease the boredom of patrol, she pretended the fireflies were will-o'-wisps who'd lead her to a treasure. She'd choose a light and try to follow it, most often losing it as soon as it blinked off. A few yards away, a pair of lights stayed on longer than a firefly ought to, and she slowed. The lights blinked off then reappeared, joined by another pair. Her heartbeat thundered in her ears. Eyes. She lifted the faltering beam of her flashlight higher. More eyes appeared. *Deer.*

She'd only seen deer from a distance on previous nights. Holding her breath, she set the butt of her rifle on the ground and propped the tip against her hip. Slowly, she cranked the rechargeable flashlight to strengthen its beam, hoping the movement didn't scare them off. She wanted to see them up close before scaring them off.

Picking up her gun again, she crept forward, holding the base of her flashlight against her shoulder. What felt like hundreds of eyes glinted back at her. A concentrated group of glowing circles hovered low at one spot only a few paces away. Several lifted their faces to look at her, dark muzzles opening and closing as they chewed.

She advanced another step, awed by their lack of fear. The poor things must be truly hungry. A voice in her head reminded her they were eating the alfalfa she was supposed to protect. She should shoo them away, but the moment felt magical, as if those fairy lights truly had brought her to a treasure.

A strange, zippery whistle followed by a rattle broke the air. Bones's deep bark started up somewhere to her right, followed by Trigger's higher voice. The deer sprang into the air, tawny backs limned silver with moonlight. The ground rumbled, and the air vibrated with a weird, wheezing sound.

Like a wave, the herd shifted to her left, circling away from the dogs. Keeping an eye on them, Jaide shuffled right, toward the spot they'd vacated, and fumbled for a grip on her rifle. Would it be too much to hope the dogs would do her work for her? Lifting the rifle to her shoulder, she stumbled against something on the ground and had to take a few steps to regain her balance. She turned her flashlight to the spot, revealing a mangled, bloody deer splayed against the crushed alfalfa, patches of fur hanging in shreds from its flanks.

She raised her light again, watching the herd sway in a wave along the fence. Had the deer been standing here grieving? She'd heard elephants did that, but not deer. Something sinister churned at the base of her stomach as she re-envisioned those chewing mouths.

Trigger's orange beacon trailed in the herd's wake. The wave swirled like a whirlpool then broke to head her direction again. The collar's light disappeared behind a tsunami of leaping bodies. Jaide swung the flashlight's beam up in a wild arc, ducking as knobby legs and sharp hooves and flashing white tails swept over her head and against her shoulders. For the first time, she wondered if she was in danger.

A dog yelped.

She shuffled back a few steps, arms tight against her sides, but there was nowhere to escape. A musky smell commingled with the green scent of crushed alfalfa and soybean ash. A pair of antlers flashed by, almost close enough to put out her eye. She recoiled, tripping over the dead deer and landing painfully on one hip. The rifle flipped out of her grasp, and the flashlight buried itself in the alfalfa a few feet from her head and went out.

Bones continued barking, voice a higher pitch than she'd heard before. Frantic. But she couldn't hear Trigger.

The walkie-talkie that should have been at her belt crackled, Ian's voice coming from somewhere in the foliage nearby. "You okay? Your light disappeared, and there's a lot of action your direction right now."

She rolled to her knees and thrust a hand through the hay toward where her light had fallen. The earth shuddered around her, and she flattened as a scrawny deer sailed over her head, sharp hooves inches from her scalp. Her fingertips connected with the flashlight's smooth plastic casing, and she yanked it toward her. The on-off button did nothing, nor did cranking the charger handle. She slapped it, hoping to rattle a connection back into place. Nothing.

Standing, she searched the moonlit foliage to find the gun or the walkie. She needed help. Why weren't the dogs chasing the deer away? Instead of running off, the herd seemed to be multiplying. Deer bleated and cried and wheezed around her. Bodies surged too close for comfort, making her flinch and recoil.

"Trigger!" she screamed.

The deer nearest her veered away. Trigger didn't come.

She blinked, trying to orient herself toward the scaffolding where Ian kept watch three hundred feet away. She raised her hands and waved them in the air. "Help!"

Her toes kicked against something metallic. Her rifle. She bent and wrapped her fingers around the smooth barrel.

The alfalfa around her had been beaten flat, the crushed green scent enough to make her eyes water. Deer bleated and cried, louder than she'd imagined deer could be.

She screamed for Trigger again. The herd swayed left then split, revealing a deer rearing up on its hind legs, backlit by the moon's glow. Directly below it an orange light blinked. The deer's feet pedaled the air and came down hard. Then it hunched up and jumped again with all four feet, smashing the light into the ground.

"No!" Jaide screamed, raising the rifle's butt to her shoulder. She squinted down its length, trying to decide how to aim. The deer reared again. Her hand clenched, finger on the trigger, and the shot went off, leaving her ears ringing and her shoulder aching. The deer slammed sideways.

She dodged through the herd to kneel next to Trigger's limp form. How badly was she hurt? Running her hands along Trigger's sides, Jaide checked for blood. Trigger lay with paws outstretched as if to crawl, whining but not moving. Her eyes rolled wildly, the whites at the edges glinting in the moonlight. Had the deer broken her back? A sob wrenched from Jaide's throat. She had to get Trigger out of here, but they were surrounded. "It's okay, girl. It's gonna be okay. Stay still."

Farther off, Bones continued yapping. A gun's blast came from behind her, and a deer went down only a few yards in front of her. She ducked, keeping her body over Trigger's. What the hell? Could Ian even see her? Another shot echoed across the field.

She jumped to her feet, waving her arms. "Ian, stop firing! I'm in the middle of this. Stop firing!"

"Jaide?" A flashlight beam danced off the ground near her, drawing closer until she could see Ian's face. In the light, a wounded deer scrabbled its front hooves against the ground, unable to rise. Ian pointed his rifle at the thing and fired. The creature jerked and went slack. He lowered the gun. "You okay?"

"I... I think so."

"Good. Help me take out as many as you can." He aimed at the retreating mass of deer.

"My dog's hurt. We need to get her help."

His rifle tip leapt upward as he squeezed off a round and chambered another. "We can't leave the herd roaming free, or the entire harvest will be ruined. A few more shots should do it."

Her stomach churned, but she lifted her gun and peered down the scope. "I don't want to hit Bones."

"Aim left. He's harrying them over the fence."

She closed her eyes and squeezed her finger. The recoil against her bruised shoulder brought tears to her eyes. Ian banged out two more before he lowered his gun. "I think we got a few."

He turned and knelt by Trigger's side, pointing his flashlight along her body. There didn't appear to be any blood, but the poor dog only lay there and whined.

Jaide squatted, hands hovering over Trigger's fur. She wished Lucas were here to tell her what to do. "What if her back's broken? We need a stretcher, don't you think?"

Ian pulled his walkie-talkie from his belt and dialed the house channel. "Ray, this is Ian. We downed a few deer out here, but one of the dogs is hurt. Bring the truck to the north fence."

Ray's voice burst over the line. "I heard the shots. Already got the engine running. Be there in a few."

Jaide put a gentle hand on Trigger's cheek and smoothed the fur back. The tip of Trigger's tail tapped the ground. Hope flooded Jaide. If Trigger's tail worked, maybe her back would be okay. "Good girl. Hang in there."

Ian whistled for Bones and walked several yards toward the fence. He squatted down and poked at something. "Did the dogs do this?"

Jaide remembered the mangled carcass. Her throat felt too dry to speak, but she managed to reply. "I'm not sure."

"Hmm. This wasn't dogs. Looks like it was caught in the neighbor's field fire yesterday. I'd say the deer were at it." He stood and whistled again, shining his flashlight over the fence in search of Bones.

"A-at it?"

"Eating. They'll do that when they're starving. Saw one catch and eat a baby bird once. I imagine we're going to be seeing a lot more stuff like this."

Her worst fears hardened like cement in her gut. This was not what nature intended. Deer were supposed to be gentle, timid creatures that ran away at the slightest scare. If desperation could turn them into cannibalistic monsters, what would the rest of the world be like if the amarantox took over?

The truck arrived in a wash of headlights, and Ray climbed out, rifle in hand. Stopping next to Trigger, he crouched and ran a hand over the dog. "She won't get up?"

Jaide shook her head, silent tears scalding her cheeks. This was her fault. Trigger was too kind to hold her own against carnivorous deer.

"Looks bad." He rose. "Probably internal damage."

"Help me get her out of here and find a vet."

"Poor thing's suffering." Ray wrapped both hands around his rifle. "I'll put her out of her misery."

Jaide lurched forward and covered the dog's body with her arms. "No!"

"Ain't no vet gonna treat her for free, and I know you ain't got the money," Ray said.

"I'll set up a payment plan." Jaide gritted her teeth. So many people didn't take pet ownership seriously. "Trigger's a member of my family."

A huge sigh sounded behind her then Ray's boots scuffing the broken alfalfa as he walked away. "Suit yourself. She's in pain and'll probably die before the vets open tomorrow. Ian, how many deer'd you get?"

Jaide pressed her forehead to Trigger's, breathing in the sour smell of the dog's terror and pain. Trigger's tongue snaked out and caressed Jaide's cheek. Kissing her muzzle, Jaide whispered, "I won't let you die."

While the men picked up deer carcasses, Jaide slid Trigger onto a tarp from the truck, trying to keep her body as stable as possible. Trigger cried and twitched her front paws. Jaide put a calming hand over the dog's forehead. "Can you guys help me put her into the truck?"

Ray tossed a lanky deer into the truck bed alongside the four others already there. "Ian, give me a hand."

They carefully used the tarp to lift Trigger into the back end. After reaching the barn, Ray opened the tailgate beneath the sick, orange glow of the farm's pole light. He scrubbed one hand through his hair, face hidden by his bushy beard. "You sure you don't want me to take care of her? I'll do it out back so you don't have to watch."

"No." Jaide could hardly find enough oxygen. Trigger seemed to have passed out during the ride back. But she was still breathing. "Just help me put her into my car, please."

They carried Trigger on her tarp to Jaide's Jeep. Ian had to lift the dog like a baby to put her into the back seat. Ray put a hand on Jaide's shoulder. "I still say you're making a mistake. But do what you need to do. I'll handle the rest of your shift. Be back to work tomorrow night, or I'll have to replace you."

The hollow chasm within Jaide grew. "Thank you."

He set off to the barn, and she climbed into the driver's seat, pulling the prepaid, emergencies-only phone Lucas had insisted on buying her from the glove compartment. After two rings, he picked up.

"Jaide? What's going on?"

"Trigger's hurt. She needs a vet."

"What happened?"

"She was trampled by deer. I can't tell if her back's broken."

"Oh, shit." His voice suddenly sounded more alert. "Hold on, let me look up an emergency vet."

"I can't pay for an emergency visit. I don't know how I'm going to afford a regular visit." Jaide's voice hitched, and the lump in her throat threatened to choke her. Her car's dash clock read 10:57. Would Trigger hang on until regular business hours in the morning?

Lucas sighed into the receiver. "Good point. My credit card's maxed out with medical bills."

Guilt and worry commingled in Jaide's veins. She hadn't been asking him to pay, but it was so like him to want to. "I know. But someone might take her pro bono. Or take payments."

"I'll look it up. Let me call you back."

She hung up and pressed her forehead to the steering wheel with a moan. After a few deep breaths, she started the engine and headed for town. Still no word from Lucas by the time she reached the condo parking lot. She checked that Trigger was still breathing then dashed toward Lucas's door. Inside, he sat on the sofa with his phone to his ear, recharger cord stretched to the wall. He met her eyes and pointed to the phone. "On hold. How is she?"

"Breathing. But I think she's unconscious."

His face tightened. "I'll have a look at her if you want to take over here. This is the last emergency vet within a fifty-mile radius."

She took the phone and checked the charge. The bar was down to six percent. She'd have to stay and babysit it instead of going with Lucas. She put the phone on speaker, allowing the crackly Muzak into the room, and set it beside her on the sofa's arm. Exhaustion pulled at her limbs like a magnet in the floor.

Lucas returned before someone answered, his mouth grim. "She woke up for me, but I'm pretty sure she's got broken ribs. Probably a concussion, too. No way to tell about internal bleeding without X-rays, but her abdomen's not distended, so that's good news."

"Is she going to die?" Ray's offer haunted her.

Lucas came to the sofa and sat beside her. "I honestly don't know, Jaide."

She wanted to lean against his shoulder, but his wounded arm faced her. Instead, she folded over and put her head into his lap. He brushed his fingers through her hair. "I wish I could do more."

A woman's voice broke the Muzak's drone. "Mr. Harmon?"

Jaide bolted upright and grabbed the phone. "This is Jaide Acosta. I'm the dog's owner."

"Ma'am, I'm afraid we can't take your dog at this time. I'm truly sorry."

"What do you suggest we do, then?" Jaide's jaw tightened around the next words, Ray's exact words. "She's suffering."

"I'm sorry. I wish I knew. We've been swamped with requests for pro bono work, and we're no longer accepting credit. Too many pet owners are out of jobs. Perhaps the Humane Society can help you. Good luck." The line went dead.

Jaide stared at the phone, her entire body going icy. How could a doctor refuse to help someone who was injured? But then, Trigger wasn't a someone. To most people, she was a something.

That thought sparked some heat in her chest. *No.* Trigger was part of the family. She ground her teeth and turned to Lucas. "What would you do if she were human?"

Lucas straightened, nodding thoughtfully. "I've still got friends at the hospital. Let me make some calls and see what I can do. I doubt we can get X-rays, but we can at least get her an IV and a second opinion."

Tears making her vision blurry, Jaide offered him the phone. Trigger was going to survive. She had to.

Chapter Nineteen

J aide roused to the gentle music of Lucas's phone alarm. The floor pressed uncomfortably against her hip and shoulder; she could've slept on the sofa, but she wanted to be as near Trigger as possible. Twilight from the patio doors painted the living room in black and white. Rolling over, she stared into the dog's sleeping face. Last night, one of Lucas's paramedic friends had stopped by with a "borrowed" bag of saline fluid and a few other supplies. Lucas had found a YouTube video on how to use an IV with a dog, then they'd refitted Lucas's ice machine from his surgery to help Trigger's probably busted ribs.

Now all they could do was wait.

She used a bit of nearby paper towel to clean a crusty bit of sleep dust from the corner of Trigger's eyelid. The dog opened her eyes, but only one met Jaide's—the other roamed off to the left. The scent of urine reached Jaide. A lump swelled up in her throat, and tears clouded her vision. Lucas said it was good the dog was passing fluid, and Jaide had no problem cleaning up after her. But the roaming eye was almost too much. Was Trigger even in there?

Jaide sat up and twisted side to side to relieve her sore back. Trigger's ice needed replacing, and the IV bag was nearly empty, which meant they'd soon need to resort to feeding her water with a turkey baster every half hour. Jaide looked at the phone, irrationally hoping she could sleep a little longer. Ray expected her at the farm this morning, but caring for Trigger would be a full-time endeavor. Wasn't the life of a family member more important than a day of work? Ray would surely understand. And she'd work extra hard tomorrow to make up for it.

Soft footsteps, then Flora knelt on the floor beside her wearing a long T-shirt and sleep shorts. The girl put her fingertips on Trigger's forehead and gently brushed the fur, as if afraid to hurt her. "How is she?"

"No change." Jaide looked over the dog again, hoping maybe she was lying. But Trigger hadn't moved on her own since the trampling.

Flora leaned over and put her head on Jaide's shoulder. "Is it wrong that I'm hungry?"

Jaide wrapped both arms around her daughter. She'd forgotten to collect her share bucket from the farm last night. In her mind, she recalled Lucas's empty fridge and cupboards. The W.I.C. program had been shut down before Flora could even sign up. "Better than being sick. Are there any peas ready in the pots outside?"

Flora shook her head. "We ate them all yesterday. And Shayne doesn't get paid until Friday."

Hunger burned below Jaide's ribcage. How long had it been since she'd eaten? Over the past few weeks, much of what they ate came from the CSA, with minuscule additions from the backyard "garden" Flora and Lucas now cared for. Jaide kissed the top of Flora's head then pushed her gently upright. "I left my lunch in the Jeep. Go get it while I get ready for work. I'll bring home more food today."

"What will you eat?"

"Don't worry about me. There's plenty of food at the farm," Jaide lied. Snacking while harvesting wasn't allowed. Ray had fired the red-headed kid after catching him slurping down strawberries.

Rising on stiff legs, Jaide stretched the kinks out of her back. Since skipping work wasn't an option, she filled her belly with a glass of water, splashed her face, and headed to the Jeep.

Flora met her part way, chewing a bit of cheese. "Thanks, Mom."

Jaide smiled tightly. "Keep a close eye on Trigger while I'm gone. I'll have my phone on if you need to call."

"Of course."

"Tell Shayne and Lucas I'll have food tonight."

Flora looked at the fragment of stale cheese she held and stopped chewing.

Jaide's chest tightened. "You're eating for two. Finish it."

Brows knit, Flora nodded and turned toward the condo, carrying the cheese between two fingers like a rare gemstone.

Jaide sighed. Flora would probably give the morsel to Shayne. The girl needed to learn to be a little more selfish when it came to her baby.

In the parking lot, the Jeep's stuffy interior promised another hot day. She turned the key. The gas tank was nearly empty. She hoped there was enough to get her to the farm—she had nothing to trade for fuel at the moment, and the clock on the dash told her she was already late for work.

At least the streets were fairly empty—with gas prices at record highs, people who still had jobs in the city used mass transit or walked. Jaide reached the exit to the interstate in record time and shot down the county road toward the farm.

Ropes of greasy smoke boiled upward from a field burning in the south as she pulled off the pavement toward the farmhouse.

In the vegetable patch, Ray's boys raced through the rows as though they were playing tag. Jaide parked in her usual spot near the minivan and got out. As she closed the Jeep's door, a gunshot echoed from the garden. The boys must be varmint hunting. She'd be free to pull weeds or harvest.

At the cherry tree near the house, Martha teetered on a three-legged ladder among the branches. Her hands moved quickly between the barely pink fruit, yanking clusters free and dropping them into a pouch slung over one shoulder.

"Are those ripe?" Jaide asked.

Martha shook her head and kept working. "Critters from the burned fields seem to have gathered here. If I don't take the cherries now, we'll have none left."

Jaide glanced at the second tree around the corner of the house. The branches rustled with birds.

"The boys are out shooting rabbits in the vegetables now. I'd be obliged if you'd start on that other tree."

Jaide eyed the pale fruit, recalling Martha's insistence that the cherries weren't part of the shares. Normally, she'd have pitched in and helped without a qualm. But Flora's gaunt face still haunted her. "We getting cherries in our buckets today?"

Martha halted picking long enough to scowl down at her. "Ray's in the barn butchering those deer if you'd rather join him."

The chore evoked a surprising lack of emotion for Jaide. She hadn't exactly forgotten the deer, but she hadn't really pieced together that dead deer meant meat. Until now. A small part of her wanted those creatures to pay for what they'd done to Trigger. And Flora ate meat. Those deer's lives ought not be wasted. She'd do this for Flora.

Turning around, she marched toward the barn. Leggy

carcasses hung from the rafters by their hind feet, body cavities empty of entrails. A makeshift table stood nearby— plywood and sawhorses draped in plastic sheeting—a dull metal hand-crank machine clamped at one end. Flies buzzed over a bloody tarp piled with what Jaide could only assume were guts.

Ray looked up from skinning the first deer. "Glad you're here. I worried I might have to drive into town for a replacement. How's your dog?"

She pressed her lips together and shrugged, knowing her voice would break if she spoke.

"Sorry to hear that." He handed her a knife. "You ever done a deer before?"

Her gorge rose in the barn's stuffy air. She should've stuck to picking cherries. "I'm a vegetarian." Her voice sounded husky.

He laughed. "I might've guessed. All right. I'll skin them. Important to keep the fur off the meat. Think you can chop them up?"

She swallowed. "I can try."

The back legs of the deer he'd been working on were already skinned. Using both hands, he ripped the rest of the skin free like a sweater. Empathetic tingles raced down Jaide's arms. Naked of fur, the carcass appeared even more pitiful and scrawny than before.

Ray tossed the skin onto the bloody tarp and moved to the next deer. "There's a bone saw on the table."

Jaide moved close to the skinned deer, trying to be clinical, to remove herself from the revulsion welling in her gut. She poked a tentative finger against the tacky white-and-red exterior. There was surprisingly little blood, but the contact against her skin made her shudder. She pulled back, heart squeezing painfully. She needed more distance. "Do you have any gloves?"

He pointed to a counter mounted against the barn wall. "Martha's got a box of latex ones on the shelf over there."

She snapped the gloves over her hands and again approached the dead animal. The only thing she knew about meat was from commercials about fried chicken—wings and breasts and legs. With a tentative hand, she grasped a hind leg to keep the body from swinging. Wasn't this essentially a drumstick? She hadn't touched a dead animal since the frog she'd dissected in high school biology. Placing her knife against the round part of the hip, she started sawing. The flesh gave under her blade like an overripe tomato, making her gag.

Partway through, she paused, realizing if she severed this leg first, the thing might fall. "I don't know what I'm doing."

Ray glanced up from the second deer he'd nearly finished skinning. "Wrong leg. Take the shoulder blade off first, then use the saw on the ribs. And be careful of that back strap."

"How do I do that?"

Heaving a sigh, he let go of the skin he'd been pulling and thrust a finger toward the deer's armpit. "Start there. Slide your knife along under the bone until it comes free."

She poked the tip of the blade into the crease and cut. Ray returned to his skinning. Bloody meat stuck against her shirt, and she fought back the need to retch. Eventually the front leg gave way with a sickening rip, muscle and tendon still clinging to the joint in long, stringy tendrils. Her face felt hot and her eyes weepy, but she refused to cry. "Where do I put it?"

Ray looked up from the third deer and pointed to the sawhorse table. His beard twitched as he assessed her work. "You really made a mess of that meat, didn't you? Good thing most of it's only fit for burger. Slice it off the bone, and I'll show you how to use the grinder."

Jaide's stomach rolled over. She reminded herself that she was doing this for Flora. And for Trigger. Dog food was as expensive as regular food, and Trigger'd been eating what the family ate for weeks. Meat would help her heal, right?

Hacking off uneven hunks of flesh, she deposited them in a pile to one side. By the time she had bone showing, Ray had finished skinning all five deer and taken the remaining front leg off hers. "I ought to pay you by the pound, rate you're going. Here. Start feeding the grinder."

He showed her how to drop meat chunks into the hopper on the metal contraption on the table and crank the handle. Chewed-up meat emerged from the thing's mouth to dribble into a big bowl. She was glad her stomach was empty.

Ray flayed meat from bones faster than she could operate the hand crank. She swapped arms, but soon both her shoulders burned with exertion. When the bowl was full, Ray gave her a break in the form of filling plastic zipper bags with even portions of meat. She packed the burger in, breathing shallowly of the scent of death.

Although she'd hoped to be sent home early, the butchering took her entire shift to finish. Ray helped bag the last meat and handed her a couple of packages. "Close to ten pounds here. You want to trade for vegetables? Lot of shareholders would be glad for meat, since the amarantox has killed off so many cattle."

The idea tempted her. She looked at the darkly filled bags and grimaced. Everyone at her house was a carnivore except her. "No, I'll take the meat."

Ray handed her the heavy bags, and she dropped them into the Jeep's cargo area before going back to wash up and retrieve her vegetable shares. The sight of pea pods and lettuce eased her stomach; she hadn't eaten all day. Guiltily, she took the entire container of strawberries with her to eat on the way home. The odor of dead flesh cloyed the hot interior of the Jeep before she reached the end of the gravel lane, but the smell couldn't deter her appetite. She stuffed another strawberry into her mouth, sucking every juicy morsel off the green crown before tossing it out the window.

She turned onto the narrow country road toward the interstate, yearning to call and check on Trigger. The prepaid plan only allowed sixty minutes, though, and she'd be home soon enough. Checking to reassure herself the phone was at least on to receive calls, she set it on the seat beside her. No news was good news, right?

When she reached the interstate, the Jeep's low-fuel light came on. On the road ahead, a convoy of military vehicles chugged along, dominating the highway. With her exit coming up, she didn't try to pass, only gripped the wheel tightly, anticipating the turn. The vehicles took the off-ramp in front of her, and she groaned. God, what was going on now? At the end of the ramp, the camouflage trucks pulled to either side of the pavement, and she passed through the gauntlet, wondering why they'd stopped. She lost sight of them in the rearview mirror as she turned toward the gas station.

Three cars waited at the pumps in front of her. Fighting impatience, Jaide guiltily finished the strawberries, eyeing the amarantox entrenched along the gas station's foundation. When her turn at the pump arrived, she loaded the empty strawberry container with pea pods and carried it into the station. She had no cash, but she'd been able to barter for gas here before.

The female attendant sat near the counter with a shotgun in clear view on the counter. The gray roots of her red hair were a full inch wide down either side of her part.

Jaide placed the container on the counter. "How much gas can I buy with this?"

The woman raised an eyebrow. "How fresh?"

"Picked them yesterday. They should be worth at least five gallons, don't you think?"

Reaching for the peas, the attendant nodded. "Which pump you at?"

Jaide told her, wishing she'd asked for more. She'd expected to be haggled down to a gallon, maybe two. Behind her, a woman touched her arm then pulled a wallet from her purse. "Do you have more of those to sell? I can pay cash."

Looking at the money the woman held out, Jaide hesitated. Money for produce—how could she resist? But then, Flora could eat the peas. Cash was just paper. She didn't meet the woman's eyes, brushing past toward the pumps. "Sorry."

She'd never imagined this job working for shares would turn out to be the main breadwinner for the household. A new thought flashed in her head; maybe she could get Trigger in for an X-ray with the right produce. She looked in the rear window at her shares as she pumped gas. With the meat, she had enough food to feed everyone comfortably for two or three days. Once, three days of food would have seemed like plenty. Now all she could see was days between them and starvation.

An X-ray wouldn't save Trigger, only confirm a need for surgery, which she couldn't afford, even with the produce.

She drove away, wondering how long before modern medicine wouldn't only be out of reach for pets.

Chapter Twenty

As Jaide slowed to make the turn into the condo parking lot, a man and a woman holding a dirt-smudged baby approached the Jeep, blocking the entrance. The man came to her window, holding his palms up. "Ma'am." His voice came muffled through the glass. "We're starving and been evicted from our house. If you have anything to spare, we'd truly appreciate it."

Jaide's chest tightened. Her share bucket was in plain view in her cargo area. She shook her head. "Sorry."

The woman joined the man, her baby clutching the filthy collar of her shirt. "Please. If not for us, for the baby."

The thought of Flora and Shayne in the same situation threatened to crack Jaide's resolve. Wouldn't she want someone to help if this was her daughter and grandchild? Yet giving to these people now would be taking food out of Flora's mouth.

"I'm sorry. I have my own daughter to feed," Jaide replied, snapping her gaze forward and driving past the family.

Fortunately, the couple didn't follow her into the lot itself. She parked and walked round to the Jeep's back end, alert for more beggars. People were panhandling all over the city, but Lucas's neighborhood had been relatively quiet until now. How much longer until the sidewalk outside his building became dotted with tents and blankets like downtown? Or until she and her family were begging on someone's doorstep?

Arms tired from grinding meat all day, Jaide pulled the heavy vegetable bucket from the back of the Jeep and set it on the pavement, eyeing the bags of meat. Carrying everything at once seemed overwhelming, yet leaving any food unattended seemed unwise to her. She gathered the two bags in her free hand before shutting the cargo door and locking up.

Picking up the bucket, she lumbered toward the courtyard and Lucas's front door. Her arms burned, and she had to pause twice to swap her grip. As she passed the Obermeirs' stoop, the door opened, and Mrs. Obermeir poked her head out. "Flora said your dog's hurt. I found the leftover pain medicine from when our dog had surgery. We don't need it now that he's gone." She held out a white pill bottle. "Here."

Jaide grimaced in what she hoped passed for a smile and checked over her shoulder before setting the bucket and bags down. Accepting the half-full bottle, she glanced at the label. Not a medication she recognized. She wasn't sure how she'd get Trigger to eat pills, but maybe Lucas could figure something out. "How much do I give her?"

"Gifford only weighed fourteen pounds, and the doctor had us cut these in quarters for him. Twice a day. That's all I can tell you."

"Thank you." Jaide shoved the bottle awkwardly into her front jeans pocket. She hated to owe anyone, even if the Obermeirs no longer needed the pills. "I'd hug you, but I smell like a dead animal. Can I send some venison over later?"

Mrs. Obermeir's face brightened, and for the first time,

Jaide noticed that her usually plump cheeks sagged. "That would be delightful."

Nodding, Jaide resumed her trek toward home. She stepped inside and shut the door behind her. From the living room, Flora called out, "Mom?"

"How is she?" Jaide kicked off her tennis shoes.

Flora appeared and grabbed her hand to drag her to where Trigger lay on her dog bed. "She tried to stand up this afternoon."

Lucas sat on the sofa, his daughter next to him. "Hi, Jaide," Suzanne said. "Sorry about Trigger."

Jaide nodded, gaze on Trigger's shallow but even chest movements.

Leaning forward from his seat, Lucas said, "I've been researching dogs and injuries. They're a little harder to assess than humans because they can't talk, but I think Trigger's making progress."

Jaide let out a breath she felt she'd been holding all day and fell to her knees. The dog rolled her gaze upward and twitched her tail. One eye still drifted, but there was no doubt she was present and aware. Jaide folded over to rub her cheek against the furry forehead.

Something dug into her hip, reminding her of the pills. Sitting up, she pulled the bottle free and handed it to Lucas. "Mrs. Obermeir gave me these. Should we use them?"

"Let me look them up."

While he tapped out a search on his phone, Jaide gave in to exhaustion and collapsed on her side, facing Trigger. "Flora, can you put the food in the fridge, please?"

Suzanne rose. "I'll help."

Jaide still felt bad about displacing Lucas's only daughter, but Suzanne seemed to actually enjoy the extra people in the house on the rare occasions she came to visit. While the girls took care of groceries, Jaide rubbed Trigger's ears. From the kitchen, Flora squealed. "Meat? She brought home meat!"

Jaide rolled over onto her back and shouted toward Flora. "I promised some to the Obermeir's. Will you run some over?"

Lucas popped open the medicine bottle and rattled the pills. "Would you say Trigger weighs about thirty pounds?"

"Thirty-five last time I took her to a vet. But that was three years ago."

"I think she's gotten leaner working at the farm." He held up a pill about the size of a nickel. "Let's say thirty. That's one pill per day."

"How can we get her to eat them?"

Lucas sighed and dropped the medication back into the bottle. "She's swallowing water reluctantly. Maybe we can dissolve one. I'm worried about giving these to her on an empty stomach, though."

The front door opened and shut as the girls took some meat next door. Jaide said, "Maybe she'll eat some venison."

"I could go for some venison." He stood up, and Jaide noticed for the first time he wasn't wearing his sling.

"How's your arm?"

He rolled his shoulder slightly. "Hurts. But the doctor said it's time to start weaning myself off the sling."

"Did you see the doctor today?" He hadn't mentioned an appointment when she'd taken the Jeep.

"I called in to the nurse line. Less expensive that way." He disappeared into the kitchen. "Oh, and Suzanne's staying for a while. Hope that's okay."

"Okay? She's your daughter, Lucas. Of course she can stay. Is everything all right?"

"Mom and Dad always take a honeymoon mid-July."

The words felt so normal and yet surreal at the same time. She felt as though her family was living on the brink of starvation, and Lucas's parents were taking a honeymoon? "How can they afford that?"

"Actually, they're taking a stay-cation. I try not to think about them swinging from the chandelier."

Jaide smiled at the ceiling. She loved the way his parents continued to be a romantic couple, even when times were tough. Would she and Lucas ever be able to be like his folks? Someday, she told herself, unable to summon any true conviction. Necessity had forced her relationship with Lucas to whirlwind into practicality without ever pausing for wooing and romance.

The girls returned from next door chattering and joined Lucas in the kitchen. Soon the scent of food filled the house, and Jaide's stomach grumbled. She whispered at Trigger, "Will you eat for me? Just a bite? Then we can give you medicine."

Trigger blinked at her.

Lucas approached carrying the turkey baster and a small bowl. "I dissolved a pill in some water. Sort of. It wants to stay grainy. Plus here's a little food for her." He set a dish of gray-and-green-flecked paste beside Jaide. "Looks gross, I know, but I tried to make it like baby food."

"Thanks." She sat up and smeared a tired finger through the paste. Forcing the fingers of her other hand between Trigger's teeth, she wiped the food on the dog's tongue. Trigger seemed to swallow—or at least smacked her lips and didn't spit all of it out. Jaide repeated the action several times before moving in with the turkey baster. She squeezed a few drops into Trigger's mouth. Fluid spilled down the dog's chin. "C'mon, Baby Girl, you can swallow this."

She put a hand under Trigger's muzzle and lifted it so the water would better slide down her throat. This time most of it seemed to disappear. "Good girl."

Alternating meat and fluid, Jaide managed to get Trigger to

swallow the medicine. By then, the sky outside had burned to rust with the setting sun. She ate the bowl of potato and peas Lucas brought out for her and fell asleep on the carpet.

The next morning, Trigger managed to rock to her feet and wobble through the patio doors to relieve herself before giving up and lying down next to the building. Jaide joined her outside and crouched to pet her head, trying to get her to move inside. The dog only responded with a tail wag. Jaide could carry her inside, but perhaps it was better to let the dog rest a little and do it herself. Even Trigger had her pride.

Rising, Jaide stretched, pulling a deep lungful of air in through her nose. A small breeze thinned the acrid smoke that had hung over the city for days. Far-off sirens serenaded the otherwise-quiet morning. A flock of pigeons swept ponderously over a building a few blocks away, wings loud in the dawn air. Too bad Lucas had divested himself of his coop while she'd been in prison. A breakfast of eggs would've been nice. She turned in a lazy circle toward the vegetable planters.

And all the air left her body.

The assortment of planters that should have been burgeoning with vegetables were empty. The pieces of cardboard covering the tops were either missing or sprinkled with dirt from plants yanked out by the roots.

She took a trembling step toward the middle of the yard. Flora had been in charge of watering, weeding, and harvesting. She'd never have ripped everything up like this. The gate in the low fence along the alley stood ajar.

A deep ache radiated from her core through her bones. *Robbed.* Someone had come in and stolen everything.

Moving to the gate, Jaide stepped out and looked along the

alley's other small yards and parking areas, hoping for a clue. But there were no signs of people. Amarantox either bloomed rampant or had left behind spots of dead soil that was poisoned to other plant life by the weed's chemicals. The house directly across the street had the noxious plant growing along the foundation, so entrenched that it touched the lower sills of the second-story windows.

She turned back to face their yard again. Her eyes still imagined the pots like she had when she'd seeded them, overflowing with mature crops. Yesterday the little green tomatoes would have hardly been worth eating, the carrots no more than tops this early in the season. Yet they were gone. Every part of every plant, gone.

Burying her face in her hands, she breathed until she could move without crying.

Eventually, she dragged herself toward the patio and Trigger and lowered herself to the dead grass along the fence between them and the Obermeirs'. Whoever'd done it must've been starving. Maybe those homeless kids from the oak trees out front? Or the family that had stopped her yesterday? The thought didn't make her feel any better. Maybe she was just exhausted and overwrought about Trigger, but the loss of her backyard garden sapped any hope she'd held in reserve. Closing her eyes, she leaned her head back against the fence and settled a hand on Trigger's front paw, seeking strength, although she knew the dog had none to give.

The patio door rumbled open, rousing her. Lucas slid it shut behind him, gaze settling on Trigger. "She came out herself?"

Jaide nodded.

"Good girl! Yes, you are!" He bent and rubbed the dog's ears with his good hand before turning to Jaide. He did a small double take as he noticed the yard. "What the...? Did you do this?"

She could barely choke out the word. "Thieves."

He stood gaping, attention drifting from planter to planter. "They took everything?"

"Roots and all." Her voice sounded dead in her own ears.

"Damn." He squeezed his eyes shut and rubbed his fingertips along his forehead. "I worried about something like this."

"Do you think it might be one of the kids from out front?"

He shrugged. "Could be anyone. Albertson's closed another store yesterday. News said the Red Cross and the National Guard are going to oversee a rationing program at the city center."

Jaide perked up a bit. Rationing could be a good thing. "So they're handing out food?"

"Limiting the amount each person can buy."

"Oh." She slumped back against the fence.

He lowered himself next to her along the fence and took her free hand in both of his. "We're going to need to be vigilant for thieves. Hopefully Trigger will improve quickly so she can be a guard dog—unless you planned on taking her back to work?"

"Oh, God, no!" Jaide blurted out. The trampling remained fresh in her mind, and she doubted she'd ever be free of the horrible, helpless feeling of that moment. "I'm not putting her in danger again. Trigger's not cut out for farm work."

"But you're safe, right?" He squeezed her hand and stared intently at her. "I have nightmares about you being trampled by deer."

Her mind reeled back to that night. Could those animals really have been eating one another? Here, in the light of day, she doubted what she'd seen. "Lucas, have you ever heard of deer eating each other?"

His lip curled in disgust. "They're browsers, so they do have a wide diet, but I didn't think meat was part of it."

"Ian said the herd was eating one that had been killed by the neighbor's fire." Paired pinpricks of light blinked in and out of her memory.

"Meat's concentrated calories." He rubbed a thumb along his jawline, thinking. "I wonder if they're that starving."

Those chewing muzzles grew fangs in her imagination. "It was really weird, especially since they were surrounded by alfalfa. Surely deer would rather starve than consume flesh?"

"There are documented cases of herbivores eating their young, but that's almost always in artificial, caged settings. I'll have to Google it."

"So it's a fluke? Like Ripley's Believe It Or Not?"

Lucas shrugged. "This amarantox is changing the world and forcing the world to change along with it. What was a fluke yesterday may be a survival tactic today. Maybe even the mechanics of evolution." He frowned at the fence. "I think we need to have a family meeting about protecting ourselves."

"The garden's gone. What else do we have worth stealing?"

"You bring home food every day, Jaide. And even if you didn't, some people wouldn't hesitate to force their way in to check. Hunger is a powerful motivator."

"You want us to get a gun?" The idea repulsed her. Carrying a gun on the farm was bad enough. Keeping one at the house, one intended for people was... unthinkable.

"I already have one."

She stared at him. "Since when?"

"I've always had one. Dad gave it to me for hunting deer when I was a boy."

Her chest tightened. Old mantras about the danger of personal-use firearms crowded her mind. "Why didn't you tell me there was a gun in the house?"

He shrugged. "I knew you'd react like this. But now I think we should train the kids to use it."

"We have a police officer living two doors down." That presence had made her feel safe in spite of her previous interactions with prison guards.

"You can't count on the police. Besides, you use a gun at the farm."

"Only if I have to. And only on invading animals." The rising sun broke over the clouds on the horizon, forcing her to shade her eyes with one hand.

"So you'd rather Flora got hurt than defend herself?"

"If someone breaks in, we'll give them what they want, and they'll leave." Even as she said it, she knew how stupid she was being.

"And what if they want more than our food? I know you don't read the news much these days, but society is breaking down. Not-so-nice people are becoming bolder. Flora and Suz are pretty girls. So are you."

Rising, she dusted off the seat of her pants. She'd been avoiding the radio because it depressed her: people hurting one another, basic government services going down, foreign trade cut off as the amarantox spread. All because she'd broken into a greenhouse. Lucas couldn't understand the guilt behind her desire for peace.

He stood, too, hand on the patio door. "I'm not saying we initiate anything. But we have to protect ourselves."

Instead of responding, she crouched by Trigger and prodded the dog to get up. "Come on, girl. It's getting hot out here. Let's go back inside."

The dog rose and limped into the house. Inside, Suzanne slept on the sofa, one arm thrown over her eyes.

Picking up Trigger's water dish, Jaide headed toward the kitchen. Lucas followed, speaking low. "I want to protect you, Jaide. If I'm not here, I want to know you can protect yourself. That you can protect Flora and Suzanne and, eventually, the new baby."

She turned on the tap only long enough to fill the dish halfway then shut it off and dropped her chin to her chest. Why was he always so pragmatic? And why did her ideals suddenly seem so very wrong?

His hand settled against the back of her neck and squeezed gently, pulling her sideways against his chest. "What if those thieves hadn't stopped with the garden? What if they'd come inside? I can't bear the thought of you hurt. Or dead. People are killing for food, Jaide."

Turning, she wrapped her arms around him, pressing her cheek above his beating heart. She inhaled his clove scent and nodded against him. "All right. Just because we learn to shoot doesn't mean we have to kill anyone, right?"

He squeezed her, good arm tighter than his injured one. "You do need to be willing to actually fire, or knowledge gets you squat."

"I'll cross that bridge when I come to it." She couldn't think that far ahead. She'd fired at deer. Maybe in an adrenaline rush, she could shoot a person, too. She hoped she'd never have to find out.

Chapter Twenty-One

AUGUST

The Brothers saw that blood must be shed. They accepted the Knife, and left the Tribe.

~ THE HISTORIES

After a back-breaking afternoon yanking amarantox from the alfalfa field and burning it, Jaide sat in the barn to eat a meal of lettuce drizzled with the last of their salad dressing. Her hair and clothes stank of sap, but that in no way diminished her appetite. She wiped her bowl clean with a slice of bread from the Red Cross ration truck then set the bowl down to allow Ray's new dog, Alba, to lick what she could from it. The dog liked the barn more than hunting with Bones, and Ray tolerated it because she was expecting puppies in a few weeks. Jaide appreciated the dog's gentle nature.

She left Alba to her cleaning and gathered her dusk-patrol gear. Tonight she had a turn sitting in the deer stand to guard the alfalfa until Chia arrived to relieve her at nine. A lone cricket chirped somewhere in the surrounding field as she approached the platform.

Before she'd even climbed the ladder, she spotted movement in the northwest corner of the lot. Deer again, swarming the field, at least sixty. She lifted the rifle and took aim, dropping one before the rest of the herd knew what had hit them. Ray's insistence on target practice had paid off.

As a mass, the creatures flowed up and over the fence, but not before Jaide squeezed off another round. A second deer stumbled, limping in a tight circle just inside the fence while the rest of the herd retreated. She pumped another round into the chamber. Finish it off, she thought, and set aside her pain. There'd be fresh meat tomorrow.

As she watched the herd fade into the horizon, she spoke the prayer Chia had taught her when the woman had caught Jaide sniffling over another of Bones's kills. "Blessed deer, thank you for your life, which you gave that my family may live. Pass swiftly and without pain. I thank you for your body, for your meat, and ask Mother Earth to guide your soul to the other side."

The prayer always brought tears to her eyes once the adrenaline of killing was over, and she allowed a moment of reverent silence to pass before lifting the radio from her belt. She'd never been religious, preferring instead to think of herself as a part of nature. But that was back when she believed nature was kind and harmonious. Now she knew that nature didn't discriminate against good and evil. Nature was about survival. Or death.

She informed Ray of the kills so he could come with the truck to pick up the carcasses, then she sat down to wait and watch.

Dusk faded to darkness, and Chia arrived late, baby crying loudly from her back carrier. Chia's head popped through the hole in the slatted floor as she reached the top of the ladder. "Sorry I'm late. Esmerelda's sick."

"She okay?"

"Small fever and diarrhea. She'll be fine. I brought extra diapers."

"If you're sure," Jaide said, reluctant to offer to stay. Her family was waiting for today's share bucket. She pointed toward the corner where she'd shot the deer. "I downed two deer over there at sunset. They may be back, so keep a close eye."

"You better go. The military set up roadblocks into the city. Curfew starts at ten."

Jaide's stomach flip-flopped. "Curfew?"

"They announced it today. Ten at night to six in the morning, no one's allowed on the streets."

"Shit."

Jaide lowered herself down the ladder and hurried back to the house. By the time she put her gear away, picked up her half-full bucket of produce, and started down the lane to the road, the Jeep's dash clock read 9:50. She accelerated down the narrow road, heedless of the speed limit, and barreled onto the interstate. Her phone rang from her back pocket, making her jump. Slowing only enough to dig it out, she pushed the speaker button.

"Jaide, are you okay? Where are you?" Lucas said. "The governor's announced a curfew. No one's supposed to be outside after ten."

"I heard. I'm hurrying."

"You've got a criminal record, Jaide. You can't risk getting caught out that late."

"What do you suggest I do? Wave a magic wand? I'm driving as fast as I can."

"Turn around and go back to the farm. Ask Ray to let you stay the night."

"I'm almost to the exit now. Oh shit. Gotta go."

She flung the phone onto the passenger seat and stepped on the brake. Taillights lit the exit ahead of her, three cars waiting in line as military personnel with guns questioned them. To either side of the exit, camouflage vehicles crouched like hulking guard dogs ready to chase down rabbits. She pulled up behind a Ford Taurus, deja vu filling her senses. This felt like prison all over again, armed guards at every corner.

The lead car rolled away, apparently passing muster, and the khaki-clad man doing most of the talking moved to the next vehicle with his tablet computer. She looked in the rearview mirror. A pickup had pulled up close behind her, blocking any hope of retreat.

Ahead, the officer tapped on his tablet, speaking and nodding. Jaide couldn't hear, but he passed that car through and moved on to the Taurus. Her clock now read 10:01. In prison, it didn't matter why you were late. Late was late. Sweat prickled under her arms and down her back.

The Taurus got waved through, and she let her foot off the brake, easing forward. She knew she should smile, be cute and friendly, but she couldn't. She lowered the window.

The man met her eyes. "You live in the city?"

"Yes, sir."

"License and registration, please."

Fingers numb, she scrabbled in the visor for the Jeep's registration then dug her driver's license from her purse. "I only just heard about the curfew. I was at work. I won't be late again."

The man accepted them, comparing the photo on her license with her face, then checked his computer. He paused, hand over the screen, then looked up to scan the Jeep. "Who's the owner of this vehicle?"

Air refused to fill her lungs. "My boyfriend. Lucas Harmon."

"He know you have the car?"

"Yes." Her voice wobbled, and the officer peered at her face for a few moments. Her eyes burned. "We live together. You can call him. He's waiting for me."

In the side mirror, she caught sight of an armed man looking into the back window where she'd covered the share bucket with a quilt to keep passersby from seeing it. He strolled toward them and stopped beside the questioning officer. "I'm going to have to ask you to pull off to the side for a minute."

All hope she had of skating through the checkpoint slithered into the weeds. "What for?"

"Please pull over and turn off your engine." He pointed toward a spot near a looming military truck.

Throat tightening, Jaide did as he instructed. She kept her hands on the steering wheel and tried to breathe normally. A new guard approached her window and asked her to get out of the Jeep. The muscle in her jaw twitched as she complied. Behind her, two men opened the other doors to the Jeep and began searching.

The guard facing her asked, "Why were you away from home, Ms. Acosta?"

"Work. I work at a farm."

"Awful late for farm work."

Sweat dripped down her back. "Guard duty. Several of us trade shifts to scare away animals."

"And people?"

What felt like a lead weight settled inside her chest. "No."

"Been a lot of reports of crop theft lately."

One of the men at the Jeep approached, carrying the bucket with her crop shares. He dropped it on the pavement next to the interrogator. "Did you steal these vegetables?"

"Those are my wages." Jaide shifted her gaze from man to man. "He pays us in crop shares."

The first man bent and dug through the bucket, removing the head of broccoli before looking up at her again. "You have a receipt?"

"Why would he give me a receipt? Listen, you can call him and confirm. Ray Townsend." She reached into her back pocket for her phone then remembered she'd left it on the seat. "His number's on my phone."

The guard dropped the broccoli back into the bucket then used his foot to slide the whole thing behind him. "Tell you what. We'll let you go this time. But next time, have proof of purchase." He looked at a bulky watch on his wrist. "And make sure you're not out after curfew. With your record, not every cop's going to be as understanding."

Jaide stood there for a moment. She didn't want to create more trouble for herself, but she had to ask. "Can I have my bucket, please?"

"Consider it impounded," the second guard said, flat faced.

Her empty stomach burned. "I worked for that."

His eyes narrowed.

She decided to approach from a different angle. "That food's for my pregnant daughter."

The first guard looked pointedly at his watch. "You want to argue?"

Swallowing, she took a step back. She'd been on the wrong end of these bullying tactics before, by both inmates and guards. He had the law. He had backup. He had a gun. She was powerless.

Climbing into the Jeep, she pulled away from the exit and headed home, blood boiling. How dare he? These men were supposed to be protecting people like her, not stealing from her. She scrolled her mind for people she could contact to report him. He wasn't local police; she'd have to take this to a higher level. The governor? A senator? Who did this man report to?

The more she thought, about it the lower she sank. Would a government official even care? Once upon a time she'd believed in society—in humanity. People shouldn't need to protect themselves from the law. But ideals seldom matched up with reality.

When she reached the house, Lucas's relief she was home safe quickly turned to fury. He grabbed the Jeep keys from their hook. "He had no right. I'm not going to stand for this."

She raced to the door and stood in front of it. "They'll just lock you up. Or worse. Please stay here."

A vein on his forehead pulsed. "How has our government come to this? Stealing from helpless women. You'd think we were in Somalia or something."

"I'll have Ray issue me a receipt for my pay from now on. At least they didn't hurt me or arrest me."

"But that's next. Dammit, I hate feeling so helpless." He paced two steps away before spinning toward the door again. "I need to buy more bullets. We used most of what I had during target practice."

His talk was making her sick to her stomach. "You can go tomorrow. Nothing's open tonight. Curfew, remember?"

"I'm getting a second gun, too." He ran a hand through his hair and winced at the shoulder movement.

A knock came from the door behind her. She jumped and spun, knocking into Lucas. Who'd be out after curfew? Had the police followed her? Her heartbeat thundered in her ears.

Lucas eased her aside and put his eye to the peephole, then opened the door. "Mrs. Obermeir? Is everything all right?"

The old woman stood with her hands clasped in front of her. Her gaze shifted between Jaide and Lucas. "I heard Jaide come home. I hate to ask, but do you have any food you could spare? The Red Cross ran out of rations, and we've had nothing to eat all day. We'll take anything."

Jaide lowered her gaze. Was there anything left in the house to eat? There'd been little this morning, and the police had stolen tomorrow's groceries. The flavor of her meager lunch seemed like a million years ago, and her insides felt as if someone had taken a carving knife to them, leaving her hollow as a Halloween pumpkin. She clenched her fists, looking at the tough sinews of her sun-browned forearms.

"I'm sorry," Lucas answered, his voice thick. "The curfew police stopped Jaide on the way home and confiscated her crop share."

"Oh, you poor dear," Mrs. Obermeir said. "They didn't hurt you, did they?"

Jaide furrowed her brows and shook her head, throat too tight to speak.

Mrs. Obermeir smoothed her hands over her apron. "Don't tell Ralph I asked, okay?"

Lucas sighed. "Will you be okay?"

"Oh, these old bodies will be fine. I just hoped a little snack might still the noise. We'll try the Red Cross again tomorrow." She gave them a pained smile and turned to go.

Lucas shut the door then took Jaide's hand and led her into the kitchen. "The kids saved you dinner."

Jaide's stomach turned over with guilt.

Opening the fridge, he pulled out a plate with another plate upside down over the top of it. He uncovered it to show her a small mound of sautéed spinach and potatoes. "Not much here, but we knew you'd be hungry after working today."

"Did Flora get enough to eat?"

"Flora's fine. Everyone here is fine."

"I feel like I should share with the Obermeirs." Exhaustion from work plus emotional overload made her want to collapse right there and sleep. Maybe she should send the dish over and just go to bed.

Lucas slid the food into the microwave and pushed start. "If we had any to spare, we would. But you're our only breadwinner, now. You need to keep your strength up."

She frowned. "Shayne makes money, too."

He shook his head. "They closed the box company today. He said he'd be surprised if they even give him a final paycheck."

"What?" She stepped back. "They can't do that."

Lines creased the edges of Lucas's mouth. Frown lines. When had those appeared? "All bets are off, Jaide. That's what I'm trying to say."

"How can they do that?" Jaide asked again, feeling stupid. What would her family do without the little bit of money Shayne provided?

"I think this is better anyway. Now he can stand in line with us at the Red Cross truck."

"Unless they run out of rations again."

"Four people have more chance of getting food than three. And he'll provide more protection for those of us who manage to get food. I've been worried about being the only one there to guard the girls, especially with my gimpy arm." He pulled Jaide's dinner from the microwave. The smell of sautéed spinach and new potatoes wafted through the kitchen.

"Will things ever be normal again?"

Lucas sighed and handed her a fork. "Prepare for the worst, hope for the best."

"How can I prepare when I can't even fathom what might come next?" She took the plate and inhaled the savory aroma before taking a big bite. The sensation of warm food on her empty stomach flooded her with pleasure, even in these dire circumstances.

"Just eat and be grateful that we're together to watch each other's backs."

After a few more bites, the plate was empty. Staring at the streaks of juice remaining, she considered licking it. "I miss quinoa and beans."

"I want chocolate-covered almonds."

"Cashews." She smacked her lips, remembering the salty, satisfying crunch of dry-roasted nuts.

"Avocado," Lucas added. "A big bowl of guacamole and tortilla chips."

"Oh, you're killing me."

Lucas put an arm around her and pressed a kiss against the side of her forehead. "I wonder if we'll ever taste those again."

"I hope so." She raised her plate to her face and followed through with licking it clean.

Chapter Twenty-Two

The smell of coffee brought Jaide out of a deep sleep, and it took her a few moments to place why that bothered her; they'd drunk the last of their supply two days ago. She rose from bed and slipped down the hall to the kitchen. If Lucas had spent precious cash on coffee, she'd skin him alive.

He stood alone in the kitchen, wearing only his boxers, mug in hand. Holding it out to her, he half grinned. "Not too bad for two-day-old beans."

She accepted the cup, anger deflating. The aroma rising from the hot liquid revived her, but after taking a sip, she grimaced. Definitely two-day-old beans. "You must have scalded your taste buds off. This is terrible."

One eyebrow raised, he reached for her cup. "Fine, then, don't drink it."

She held it away from him, smiling. "I didn't say I wouldn't drink it. Thank you."

"Haha." He pulled a second mug from the rack and poured

himself a cup. "Is there gas in the Jeep? My benefits should be deposited today. I'm going to buy ammo."

"Don't we need that money for the house payment?" She thought of all the homeless people roaming the streets, all the foreclosure signs dotting lawns around the city.

"Home protection is just as important as keeping the bank happy right now."

Suzanne entered the kitchen, rubbing her eyes, Trigger following stiffly behind her. "Morning."

"Hey, Suz." Lucas put his good arm around his daughter in a brief hug.

"Morning," Jaide said but refused to be distracted. "We can't risk getting kicked out."

Suzanne poured herself a glass of water. "We could go live at Grandpa and Grandma's."

Lucas shook his head. "I'm thinking of inviting them here. They shouldn't be at their place alone."

Jaide stared into her coffee mug. Two more mouths taking food away from Flora. But these were Lucas's parents. A brief flash of guilt burned her gut. How were her own parents right now? She hadn't had contact since the day she'd picked up Flora. Maybe this changing world had changed Chona, too. "I could call my mother. They have more bedrooms and a big yard to garden in."

"Not an option. Your mother's a bitch."

"Dad!" Suzanne shied away from her father.

Jaide laughed, imagining her mother's face if her daughter showed up on her doorstep with all these people. "No, he's right, she's a bitch. She'd probably shoot us the second we set foot on her property."

Lucas drained the rest of his coffee. "Anyway, they all live too far away from Ray's farm. We need Jaide to keep working."

She inhaled the scent of coffee, reveling in the validation.

Providing for Flora had seemed impossible after prison, yet now she was an integral part of not one but four other lives. Five counting Trigger.

"Think Ray would mind us all coming out for target practice today?" Lucas rinsed his coffee mug and set it on the drainboard to dry.

"He'd love it. More people in the fields means less vermin eating his crop."

"If we get evicted, we can go live in his barn," Lucas joked.

Jaide met his gaze with a serious one. "I don't want my grandchild born in a barn."

She'd already reconciled herself to the fact that the child would be born without the aid of a midwife or the fallback of modern technology. Between Lucas's medical knowledge and the comforts of home, Flora could at least deliver comfortably.

"I'm joking." Lucas winked. "Sort of. We do need to consider worst-case scenarios."

"Bug-out bags," Suzanne added. "Flora and I have been putting together duffels in case we have to leave here fast."

As if to pound home the idea, the overhead light flickered, and the microwave beeped. Everyone stared at each other in silence for a moment.

Jaide cleared her throat. "I'm glad to hear you're thinking ahead."

Suzanne downed the rest of her water. "I'm off to the library."

Lucas frowned. "Is your phone Internet not working?"

"I've been checking out books. Learning about homesteading and survival."

Jaide eyed the girl with new appreciation. In her mind, Suzanne was the perpetual child, coddled by grandparents and father alike. Seeing her take initiative made Jaide realize how much the world had changed.

Lucas grinned and gave Suzanne a thumbs-up. "Guess I raised you right."

"Grandma raised me," Suzanne replied but pecked him on the cheek to soften the rebuke.

Lucas seemed unfazed. "Well, she did an excellent job."

After his daughter left, he sidled up to Jaide and put an arm around her waist, leaning his cheek against her hair. "Are you okay with me bringing my parents here?"

Jaide imagined two more people crammed into the condo. His parents lived in a gated community in the suburbs about twenty-five miles away. "If we moved to their place, we could start over on the vegetable garden."

"Too late to get much out of a garden now." Lucas shook his head. "Staying here, near your job, really is our best option. Your crop shares are worth more in a month than Dad or I make put together now."

"Assuming I can get the vegetables home." She regretted saying it the moment it was out of her mouth.

He straightened and pulled his arm free of her waist. "Bullets. I hope the Mega-Mart has stock left."

She downed the rest of her coffee. Seeing him this angry made her nervous. "I'll come with you." Maybe she could help keep him calm on this expedition. "Give me a minute to let Trigger out."

The dog was much improved since the accident, although she'd lost some of her previous energy and spent a lot of time on her bed. She sat at the patio door, waiting for someone to let her out. Watching the dog sniff around the yard, Jaide felt safe. The dog's presence put a barrier between Jaide and the world— even though Trigger would probably only lick an intruder to death. But strangers didn't know that, and the buffer gave Jaide comfort.

She let Flora know where they were going then headed to

the Jeep. Lucas drove; his arm was almost as good as new. They had to thread through the foot traffic downtown to reach the only Mega-Mart still in business. Jaide lost count of the storefronts with boarded-up windows or liquidation banners on the way.

Amarantox grew thick along the bases of buildings, even creeping up through the pavement to feather against cars that had obviously been parked too long. Almost every vehicle had a "for sale" sign plastered to the window, and several times Lucas had to maneuver around double-parked cars, most of them vandalized. Fear gnawed her gut, and she leaned over to check the Jeep's gas gauge. So far she'd been able to keep enough in the tank to make the trip to and from work. Barely. This side trip for bullets would probably cost them a meal.

The Mega-Mart was also the distribution point for the Red Cross rations, and the once-grassy buffers around the huge parking lot overflowed with tents and tarps. Any amarantox that might have taken hold had been crushed into the dry, packed pathways. Children chased each other between residences, and the smell of burning charcoal and garbage permeated the air. Lucas drove a narrow path between the building and the tents until the pavement cleared near the main doors. Three military trucks sat parked on the sidewalk along the storefront, an armed guard stationed at the nose of each one.

Pulling in next to a dusty Lexus, Lucas pocketed the keys and climbed out. Nerves jangling, Jaide joined him to pass between the military trucks into the front doors. Everything reminded her of prison lately. Inside, more armed guards stood among the checkout counters and half-stocked shelves.

"Holy shit," Jaide muttered.

Taking her hand, Lucas walked purposefully toward the sporting goods at the rear corner of the store. A kiosk of glass cases encircled two employees, and three men in military garb stood armed with automatic rifles nearby.

"I want to go home," Jaide whispered.

Lucas squeezed her hand. "I didn't expect this. We'll be all right."

Jaide stared at the scratched glass countertop as they passed between the guards. Knives, guns, and boxes of ammunition dotted the inside of the cases. Handwritten cards in front of each item announced the price. She hissed at Lucas, "One box is almost as much as we pay for your mortgage!"

"Can I help you?" the nearest clerk asked.

Lucas released her hand and pulled out his wallet. "I need bullets for a twenty-two rifle."

The clerk stepped sideways and pointed to several yellow-and-white boxes. "Which kind?"

Lucas pointed to one with blue letters. The clerk nodded but didn't remove the ammunition. "You have money?"

"Debit card."

"Okay. I'll need your IDs."

Jaide's heart thundered against her ribs. The moment the clerk learned she had a record, he'd probably refuse to sell them bullets. Why hadn't she considered that before? Lucas didn't miss a beat, pulling out his debit card. "Jaide, go pick up what you needed and I'll meet you up front."

One of the military men spoke from his position at the corner of the counter. "New regs require background checks for any person attempting to purchase firearms or ammunition. We'll need you both to remain and fill out the requisition."

"That's bullshit." Lucas slapped his debit card on the counter. "She's just my ride."

Jaide backed away, trying to be casual, to keep Lucas calm. He was already fuming about her encounter last night. She didn't want to see him blow up in front of these guards. "I don't even like guns."

"Stop right there, ma'am."

She halted, entire body tense. "I don't have my ID," she lied.

The guard narrowed his eyes. "I thought you were his ride."

Her tongue thickened.

Lucas frowned. "Are you traffic cops or here to watch the merchandise?"

The armed man swept a cold gaze over Jaide then Lucas. "Sir, I'm going to have to ask you to move on."

Ramrod-straight, Lucas turned to the clerk. "Customers provide your paycheck. You want my money or not?"

The clerk shrugged. "Nothing I can do about it. Sorry."

Glaring at the well-armed men around the kiosk, Lucas spun on his heel and guided Jaide away. "The government spends money to regulate guns but can't keep people fed. Typical."

She had to jog to match his furious pace. "I shouldn't have come with you. I didn't even think. I'm sorry."

He frowned. "You're not trying to buy anything. They shouldn't need your ID."

"It's like a liquor store." She shrugged, trying to remain calm for his sake, even though her insides quaked. "They can't sell to someone obviously intending to provide to a minor—or in this case, a terrorist."

"You're not a terrorist."

"But I am." Dizziness swept over her, and her shoes scuffed against the tile. He stopped walking and put a hand around her waist to support her. She looked up into his concerned face, palms flat against his chest. "It's all my fault."

Lucas shook his head. "I'll come back tomorrow. They won't even remember me."

"No, I mean the amarantox. It's my fault. That greenhouse I broke into was growing it."

Lucas's grip relaxed. "What're you saying?"

"I tracked out seeds or something." Her voice broke, and she buried her face in her hands. She shouldn't be telling him. But what did it matter now? "The world's gone to shit because of me."

"The greenhouse was growing a toxic weed?" He stepped backward, away from her. His voice was thick. "Why?"

She dropped her chin to her chest, afraid to see the recrimination on his face. She'd held her secret so close for so long. Would the corporation really hunt her down and lock her up? Was it even still in business in this economy? "I don't think they intended it to be a weed. But it bred with wild amaranth, and now it's unstoppable."

She felt his stare on her, the silence building until she couldn't resist peeking up at him.

He shook his head. "Why didn't you tell me?"

"At first, I didn't want to drag you into anything. Then, after I was arrested, TelomerGen offered me a plea bargain. I'm not supposed to tell anyone." She sagged as if a gale force had suddenly ceased keeping her inflated. What could their lawyers do to her now? Put her in prison again, with three square meals a day? Perhaps she should shout the news to the world. "They'll send me back to jail."

Lucas seemed not to hear. "Growing a toxic weed's as bad as anthrax or smallpox or any of those diseases the CDC keeps locked behind multiple layers of security. What would TelomerGen have done if the greenhouse had been leveled in a tornado? Struck by lightning? Split by an earthquake, for God's sake?"

"But none of that did happen. I happened."

He stepped close and gripped her shoulders. "Did you genetically manipulate a plant's genome?"

She stiffened and shook her head.

"Did you fail to place test plants in a secure facility?"

"No. But—"

"You committed a crime, but you didn't create the amarantox. In fact, you tried to fix things, while TelomerGen tried to cover it up and shirk responsibility. I watched you fight that weed at every turn. You tried to warn us. No one would listen. This isn't your fault. This is the hubris of mankind."

Tingles of relief rippled across Jaide's skin. Absolution. But it didn't feel sweet. She felt as she had after she'd gone boating on Lake Michigan; hours and hours of adjusting to waves rocking the deck made her legs wobbly on dry land. She met Lucas's eyes and put her hands on his elbows to steady herself. "We're a part of mankind."

His nostrils flared. "Indeed we are. And if we want to survive, we have to be willing to pay. Now, let's go check out camping gear. Maybe by the time we're finished looking, they'll have swapped out the guards."

"What about the clerk?"

"The store wants to make money. If he can pretend I'm a new person, he will." He slid his hands down her arms and laced the fingers of one hand with hers. "I just hope they don't hike prices again between now and then."

Jaide followed him toward a row of fishing poles, thinking the cost of living had an entirely new meaning.

Chapter Twenty-Three

*The Hunters scoured the land, taking from the Tribes
without measure.*
~ THE HISTORIES

J aide drove slowly home from work, watching the
pavement ahead through the tunnel created by her
headlights. The end of August had brought increasing
power outages, as well as steeper water rationing. She
was out later than usual tonight because Ray had increased
everyone's hours. He'd chased a stranger from the rows, and
Bones roamed the property freely, no longer on a tether during
daytime hours. The alfalfa field had been abandoned altogether
because the vegetable crop was worth more.

Not that Jaide would argue about her increased duties—
anyone would jump at the chance to take over. The entire city
was desperate for food, water, relief.

Lucas called his parents every day, fretting and fighting.
They refused to leave home, refused to become a burden.
Suzanne added to his pressure by insisting she should return

there and take care of them. But Lucas wanted her close where he could protect her. Jaide hated to see him distraught, but she was secretly relieved to have fewer people to provide for.

Slowing to allow a stray dog to get out of the way, Jaide scanned an apartment window flickering with candlelight. The darkness of a city without lights felt suffocating. Piles of trash, abandoned vehicles, and empty food cans dotted the deserted street.

Ahead on the left, the pavement narrowed next to a set of double-parked vehicles. A jumble of garbage flowed into the street. She slowed and drove through the gap, bumping over a chunk of broken plywood. Within a block, the steering wheel pulled hard to her left. She wobbled to a stop. A flat. "Shit."

She was only a mile or so from home and had forty minutes until curfew. Outside the Jeep's windows, the darkness pressed close. The streets seemed empty, but there were so many shadows, she couldn't be sure. She leaned over and opened the glove box. Her cell phone lay inside, next to the nine-millimeter pistol Lucas insisted she carry. Looking out the windows again, she reached for the cell phone.

Lucas answered on the first ring. "Jaide?"

"I've got a flat tire. I wanted you to know I'd be late."

"Where are you?"

She didn't want to be reliant on him, but it wouldn't hurt for him to know where she was in case something happened. "On Sutherland. I'll let you know if I need help."

"I'm biking over now."

"Lu—"

"Don't argue." He hung up.

Jaide tossed the phone back into the glove box. Lucas was on his way, but she hated to sit here doing nothing. She could at least start changing the tire. Her headlights seemed to create a box of light ahead, with darkness pressing close on all sides—

darker still behind the Jeep where the spare was kept. Tingles raced up her spine. She refused to be afraid. If anyone was watching, seeing her with a gun should be enough to scare them off. Yet her stomach still twisted into knots.

Hand itching, she wrapped her fingers around the pistol's cool handle. Holding it out, she opened the Jeep's door. The humid night air smelled of smoke and the wet copper stink of amarantox.

A clatter made her stiffen, and she aimed the pistol, hand trembling. She squinted to see beyond the small puddle of light cast by the Jeep's interior light. A dog slunk near a pile of bulging trash bags piled against a two-story apartment building across from her. The stray nosed the garbage again, rattling a metal can against the pavement.

Letting out a breath, she proceeded to the back of the Jeep and opened the cargo door.

From the blackness behind her came a man's voice. "Don't move."

All the breath left Jaide's body. Knees locked, she rolled her eyes left and right. Where'd he come from? Had he been waiting for her? Should she scream? What if he had a gun? Would he blast her the moment she moved? She stared straight ahead, hoping to see Lucas arriving like a white knight. But it would be too early for him to have reached her. Still, maybe knowing someone was coming would give the mugger second thoughts. "My boyfriend will be here any second."

"Whatever. Put down your gun."

She didn't want to shoot anyone. And if he had a gun on her, she'd be dead before she could aim. She laid the pistol on the ground. "I have food under the blanket here. Take it and go."

"Move aside."

She stepped sideways, turning slightly to face him. In the wan yellow light, a short man stood facing her, dark stubble of a not-quite-beard over his cheeks. He held a shotgun pointed in her direction and used it to gesture sideways. "Keep going."

Swallowing, she inched away from the Jeep's interior light. What would happen if Lucas arrived now? She didn't want to consider the consequences. "Take it, before my boyfriend arrives. I don't want anyone to get hurt."

The man stepped closer and bent to pick up her pistol.

She hadn't even considered he'd take the gun. The food she could part with. The pistol had cost Lucas every penny of his benefit check, and prices had soared since then. Without thinking, she reached toward the man. "Please, no."

He jerked upright. An explosion rocked her backward, spun her to the right. She flung out a hand for support and slammed against a parked car. Pain blazed through her right side. She doubled over. Her fingers groped her abdomen. Came away hot and sticky. She held one palm out in the weak light, amazed at the crimson shine coating her skin. "You shot me?"

Her voice sounded like a stranger's.

The man grabbed the bucket from the Jeep and ran. The dark street swallowed him in shadow.

Jaide slid to her knees. The light from the headlights swirled bright and dark nearby. From far away, she heard her name. "Jaide! Jaide!"

She rolled onto her side, both hands against her wound. Stop the bleeding. That's what she needed to do. But she couldn't seem to catch her breath. She wrapped herself around the searing pain. Stars danced in and out of her vision.

Someone knelt beside her, pushed her onto her back. Lucas. He pried her hands away from the wound. "Oh God, Jaide. Stay still. Don't... Just stay still."

Ripping his shirt over his head, he thrust it against her. Her side exploded in mind-numbing pain. Then darkness grabbed hold and pulled her under.

She woke to the scream of a siren. Her mouth felt full of cotton. A bed rattled and swayed beneath her, jarring her spine and hip bones and radiating agony through her core. Something stung her arm, and she cracked her eyes open. Walls, draped with tubes and wires, pressed in close. An ambulance. Everything came back. "I've been shot."

Lucas's face slid into view above her, and he smiled tightly. "You lost a lot of blood. But you're stable now."

An unknown voice said, "Good thing Lucas had my cell number."

Her throat felt like someone was sitting on it. "He took the gun."

"Don't worry about that now." Lucas smoothed a palm over her hair.

She licked her lips. "I'm so thirsty."

"We'll get you water as soon as the doc checks you out. Hang in there."

Her head spun like she'd had too much wine, and the coppery scent of her own blood made her feel sick. "Blood smells like amarantox."

A Hispanic man in uniform leaned over her other side. He seemed familiar. She squinted at him. "I know you."

His lips parted in a gentle smile. "I helped with your dog. Stay calm."

The ambulance came to a stop, and both men disappeared from her view. Next thing she knew, the gurney jolted out of the back of the vehicle and into the bright lights of the hospital emergency room. Pain exploded in her side from the movement, and she squeezed her eyes shut. Everyone talked around her as though she wasn't there, greeting Lucas by name.

When she was again able to open her eyes, she was still

moving, lights flashing past overhead. Directly above her head bobbed a man's chin, his chest covered in standard green scrubs.

"Where's Lucas?"

He glanced downward. "Your husband's filling out paperwork. You can see him once you're finished in radiology."

Jaide stared at the ceiling, the enormity of being in a hospital too much for her to handle right now. She drifted into a pain-filled stupor while faceless technicians maneuvered her for imaging. Next thing she knew, she was lying in a narrow bed with a curtain drawn around her, the noise of a busy emergency room all around.

A nurse in a ponytail, loose hairs drifting over her forehead and cheeks, shushed the curtain aside and approached the bed, pushing a wheeled tray. "Ready to be stitched up? The doctor says the bullet passed through your abdominal obliques without hitting any organs. You're a lucky lady."

Relief washed through Jaide. "No surgery?"

"Nope. Just antibiotics and bed rest."

Behind the curtain, a man's voice approached then receded as he walked past. Somewhere, a child screamed. The nurse snapped surgical gloves over her hands and lifted Jaide's paper gown. When had they undressed her? "Where are my clothes? Do you know where Lucas is?"

The nurse shook her head. "Billing, most likely." She raised a threaded needle and assessed it before meeting Jaide's gaze. "We're out of staples, so we have to do this the old-fashioned way, I'm afraid. And I don't have anything for the pain unless you can pay up front."

How was Lucas paying for the services she was getting now? Jaide gulped. "No."

"Okay, then. I need you to hold very, very still, and keep

your hands out of the way, or I'll have to call someone to hold you down. I'll try to be quick."

Jaide gritted her teeth as the first stitch jabbed her skin. Her torso wanted to curl like a cooked shrimp, and she dug her nails into the mattress to keep from batting the nurse away. The thread grating through her flesh sent violent shivers across every inch of her skin.

The nurse pulled the first stitch tight and dove in for another. Jaide lost count of the number of tugs, eyes screwed shut.

"Can I come in?"

Her eyes popped open, shifting in and out of focus on Lucas's mop of curly hair. "Lucas!"

"Glad you're conscious. You're one lucky woman." He moved to the opposite side of the bed from the nurse. Jaide stretched out a hand to take his, struck by the warmth of his skin.

The nurse had her turn onto her side and started all over again on the exit wound. More agony at Jaide's waistline, bearable only because she clung to Lucas's hand like a drowning woman. Then the clatter of tools. "That's it." The nurse peeled her surgical gloves off and tossed them into the trash. "I know times are tough, but if you can get any red meat, eat it. After losing so much blood, you need iron and protein. I'll be back with your antibiotic shot, and you'll be good to go."

"You're sending me home?"

The nurse paused at the curtain with a pained expression. "I'm sorry. Unless you can pay up front, we send almost everyone home now. Most of the staff here are working pro bono as it is. You'll need to follow up with your own doctor in a few days."

Lucas squeezed Jaide's hand. "You'll be fine." After the nurse left, he whispered, "Manny's going to slip us a few painkillers for your recovery."

Tears pushed through the pain. "Thank him for me."

Lucas's paramedic friend offered them a ride back to the condo. When her wheelchair reached the ambulance bay, Lucas offered her two pills. "Here, take these."

She shook her head. "Save them for Flora's birth. I can endure the pain."

"I wouldn't give these to Flora during delivery." He pressed them into her mouth and held up a paper cup of water. "Oxy can affect the baby's breathing."

Guilty but grateful, she swallowed the pills. She transferred to the ambulance gurney and closed her eyes, praying for the medication to put her to sleep while the vehicle rumbled to life.

Chapter Twenty-Four

She opened her eyes again to sunlight hitting her in the face from a crack in the curtains. A glass of water with a straw was thrust before her. Jaide adjusted her focus. *Flora*. She tried to smile.

The girl burst into tears. "Mom, I was so worried."

"I'm okay, baby."

Flora set the untouched glass on the nightstand and leaned in to hug her. Jaide endured the pain of the embrace as long as she could then gently pushed her away. "What time is it?"

"Three."

Jaide shifted upright and immediately wanted to vomit from pain. "I was supposed to work today."

"Yesterday, actually. Lucas and Shayne went for you. You're on bed rest for at least a week. Probably two."

Jaide furrowed her brow. "What about his shoulder?"

Flora shrugged. "Lucas said Ray'd be glad to have two workers instead of one, even if one only had one working arm."

That was likely true. She might not have a job after this. But at least it had passed to someone in the family. Easing herself back against the pillows, she closed her eyes and sighed. Each breath felt as if her spine was being ripped in half. "Can I have another painkiller?"

"You took them all. Lucas said he could only get a few."

All? She didn't remember taking any after the ambulance ride. A growl erupted from Flora's stomach, and Jaide's eyes drifted open. The sharp bump of her daughter's abdomen pressed against Flora's stretchy T-shirt. The morning sickness had subsided, and now Flora was always hungry. By their best guess, the baby would deliver sometime in late winter. "How are you? Have you eaten?"

"There was venison left in the Jeep after the attack. Do you want some? Lucas said you're supposed to eat meat."

In truth, Jaide's pain overrode any hunger she might have felt. "I'll be okay. What happened to the Jeep?"

"Shayne and Suzanne went and fixed the tire while Lucas took you to the hospital."

The terror of the armed man at her back replayed in Jaide's mind. "They left you alone?"

"I had Trigger."

Tears filmed Jaide's vision. "Trigger's better than any gun. No one can take her away."

"Lucas said the guy stole your gun. That must have been scary."

"I should've been more alert."

"We're using the buddy system from now on. Always in pairs, Lucas says."

"Who has the rifle?" At least they had that left.

Flora rolled her eyes. "There was some serious melodrama about that this morning. Lucas wanted to leave it here, but Suzanne insisted they take it since we have Trigger. I'm surprised you didn't hear the argument."

Jaide breathed a sigh of relief. She hated to think of Lucas and Shayne on the road without protection. "Will you wake me when they get home?"

"Yes. Here." Flora picked up the glass and eased the straw between Jaide's lips. "Lucas said you need to drink lots of water to replace your blood."

After taking several obligatory pulls from the straw, Jaide relaxed against the pillow. "Thank you."

She fell back into a fitful sleep, dreaming of men with guns.

Jaide stared at the bowl on her lap, stomach growling yet rebelling at the same time. Small brown bits floated in a sauce of tomatoes and corn. Bits of a once-living creature, likely killed while searching for food of its own. She turned a beseeching look to the doorway, where Flora leaned against the jamb. Her daughter pressed her lips together and said nothing.

Lucas stood at the side of the bed with his arms crossed. "No picking it out today. You need iron and protein."

Jaide glowered at him. Yesterday he'd brought thinly sliced bites of venison, expecting her to choke them down. She'd eaten the side of potatoes, even though they'd touched the meat, and given the rest to Trigger, who currently lay at Lucas's feet, waiting for the rejects.

Looking out the bedroom window at the amarantox jungle in the alley, Jaide knew she was being childish. But it was hard to be grown up when she hurt so bad. "I need comfort food. You should be babying me."

Lucas chuckled and sat on the edge of the bed. The mattress sagged beneath his weight, and she sucked in a sharp breath at the change in her posture, hands flying out as if to catch her balance. He jerked back to standing. "Sorry."

He picked up the spoon, scooping a small bite onto the end.

"I'd advise you to eat it while it's hot. The power's been on and off all day, so no guarantee we can reheat it."

A single brown fleck mocked her between the kernels of corn. "I'll probably just throw it up."

"I worked hard for this food." He gestured over his shoulder to the doorway. "And Flora slaved over cooking it into something you might eat. Give it a try."

"Close your eyes and eat it, Mom. The bites are so small, you won't even know they're there."

Jaide frowned and closed her eyes, recalling her days in prison and how she'd forced herself to eat what she was given. Was this so different? She opened her mouth. The spoon hit her tongue, savory warmness flooding her senses. It's just corn and tomatoes, she thought. Trembling, she closed her lips over it and swallowed. Meat or not, her mouth rewarded her with a wash of saliva. The pinch in her stomach demanded more.

She kept her eyes closed while Lucas fed her, until she heard the spoon scraping the bowl. Cracking her lids, she found the dish nearly empty. A wash of euphoria rocked her. The food in her stomach must have made her giddy—or maybe it was the agony of her stitches. She couldn't tell. She took the spoon from him and licked it clean, then cocked an eyebrow. "There. I ate it all. Proud of me?"

To her surprise, Flora swept into the room and held out a palm with two red strawberries, grinning. "Lucas found them at the farm today."

He winked at her. "Ray said I could bring them to you. How's that for babying?"

"Oh," Jaide gasped and gingerly picked up one of the berries. They were small, but she'd never tasted anything sweeter as she bit into it, savoring the juice washing away the flavor of the stew. "There are only two?"

Flora nodded and held out the other one.

"You eat it," Jaide said.

"All for you, Mom." Flora's face glowed as she opened Jaide's palm and placed the berry on it.

Jaide's throat swelled again, this time with tears instead of revulsion. Flora would make a fantastic mother. "Lucas? You want it?"

He shook his head.

"You really are too good to me. All of you." She ate the berry in one small bite. "Thank you."

"Now lie back and rest." Lucas handed the empty bowl to Flora and helped Jaide adjust her pillows. "We're fattening you up to put you back to work on the farm."

Her head relaxed against the sheets, and her eyes drifted shut before she could even laugh.

Jaide lay on her back on the sofa, face turned to the big-screen TV. With steady power unreliable of late, everyone had gathered in the living room to enjoy the television while they could.

The scabs around Jaide's stitches ached and burned, fighting off a minor infection, and a new dose of antibiotic pills Lucas had managed to scrounge up roiled her stomach. Or maybe it was the images on the television making her sick.

Enormous bonfires burned across the screen. The news-copter camera panned over blazing houses and condos and shops, orange light turning night into day. Cars blocked the maze of surrounding streets, while the flashing lights of service vehicles at the outskirts of the burn prodded the edges like flies on a window screen.

The view zoomed in on a fleeing family, father carrying a limp toddler, blood dripping from the man's scalp. Across the screen's bottom, a banner of words repeated themselves. Rioting in West Lafayette after Red Cross rations run low. Fire raging out of control. Authorities warn residents to evacuate.

She swallowed bile for what felt like the hundredth time, refusing to give in to her nausea. The food in her stomach was too precious, not to mention the further pain vomiting would inflict.

Lucas paced near the door, cell phone in hand as he dialed his parents again. They lived in the affected area, but he hadn't been able to reach them.

"Maybe they're on their way here." Suzanne huddled on the floor, holding her knees to her chest. Flora sat close with an arm draped around her friend. Trigger lay curled close to the girls' legs, brown eyes following Lucas's pacing.

He smiled tightly at his daughter. "I hope so." He aimed the remote at the television and turned up the volume. "I should have insisted they move here earlier."

The female reporter's voice was remarkably collected in light of the destruction. "...The blaze. The mayor has requested air support from state wildfire units to contain the spread..."

"Look! That's their street!" Suzanne thrust a finger toward the screen. Jaide caught sight of dark rooftops as the camera panned over. Fires shot through the windows of the houses one street beyond and crept across dry lawns and shrubbery. The camera angle caught the front of the quaint, gingerbread-shuttered windows of the Harmon home. A car stood in front of their garage.

"They haven't left yet? Why haven't they evacuated?" Shaking, Lucas pushed send on his phone again.

From her spot on the sofa, Jaide could hear the recorded voice declaring all circuits busy. Lucas's face screwed up into frustrated lines. He bellowed, pulling his arm back to hurl his phone, then thought better of it. After a second, he threw the television remote instead. Bits of plastic flew in several directions as it shattered against the wall. "God! It's just like him to think he can wait this out!"

Trigger jumped up and slunk toward the open patio doors.

Shayne poked his head in as Trigger exited, rifle gripped in both hands. Although the fires were a long way off, he'd been outside, alert to potential rioters moving their direction. "Everyone okay?"

"We're fine," Jaide answered, feeling like a liar. Everything outside remained eerily silent, as though all the energy had been sucked to the other side of the city to fuel the riots.

Lucas shoved his phone into his pocket and turned toward the door. "I'm going to get them."

"Me, too." Suzanne launched to her feet.

"No, you stay here." He put both hands on her shoulders and pushed her firmly but gently back toward the others. "I don't want you out after curfew."

"Wait!" Jaide struggled to sit up. He couldn't leave. But how could she ask him to stay? He loved his parents. Just because she'd barely given her own a thought didn't mean he should abandon his.

Shayne stepped all the way into the house, leaving the door open behind him. "We shouldn't split up. We only have one gun."

"I'm a paramedic. I'll be fine."

Jaide panted through gritted teeth. Sitting up had drained her strength. "And how will anyone know you're a paramedic? You're not in an ambulance or even a uniform. And what about curfew?"

The power flickered off then on again, the television taking a moment to reorient on the news report. Lucas clenched his hands at his sides. "Screw curfew. I can't stand here and do nothing."

The eerie stillness outside cracked with the sound of a gunshot. Shayne spun to face the yard, gun at the ready. Shouting and another shot farther away. Then the night fell back to tomb-like silence.

No one said a word for what felt like forever as they listened. Jaide turned her attention from the door to Lucas, but he refused to meet her eyes. The muscles of his jaw twitched, and his chest heaved.

Flora's mouth curled down in that look she used to get when she got in trouble. "Please take the gun. I don't want you to get shot, too."

Lucas raked his fingers through his curly hair. "I'm not leaving you all without a gun."

Planting her feet firmly on the carpet, Jaide steeled herself to rise. Lucas needed her to be strong. To help save his parents. Her head spun from the agony in her side. "Then we all go. It's safest to stay together."

"You can't travel."

She wobbled to her feet. "Sitting in the Jeep won't hurt me. I'll guard it while you look for them."

Screwing his eyes shut, he seemed to consider.

"Let's do it." Shayne nodded. He called Trigger back inside. She curled up in her bed while he locked the patio door.

Suzanne grabbed her father's hunting knife from the kitchen drawer, and Flora took up the baseball bat they stored near the hallway. Jaide followed along behind, glad she could at least carry herself to the Jeep without falling. Lucas kept a hand at her elbow, and she tried to be brave. To keep him from worrying. But the lines on his face deepened with every step she took.

Passing the sickly yellow glow from a handful of porch lights, they reached the Jeep to find the kids already inside.

Lucas opened the rear door. "Let Jaide sit in the middle. Suzanne, you can keep watch up front."

Jaide leaned against the rear window as the kids rearranged. Of course she'd be no good up front. Her stomach felt sick for letting Lucas down. She climbed into the middle and latched her seatbelt. Exhaustion pulled at her eyelids in spite of the adrenaline running through her. She'd be useless if anything happened. But at least she was here, and Lucas could rescue his family.

"Where're Grandma and Grandpa going to sit?" Suzanne asked as she rolled down the window.

Lucas settled into the driver's seat and started the engine. "Two of you will have to sit in the cargo area on the way home."

He backed out of the parking spot, headlights sweeping rows of dusty, unused cars. The streetlights were out, and the darkness made Jaide's gut churn. At the exit to the street, Lucas slammed on the brake, throwing Jaide against her seatbelt. She let out a whoosh of air, trying not to vomit. What was he doing?

He sat there a few seconds, motor running, as if waiting for nonexistent traffic to pass. Jaide panted, squinting into the darkness on either side. She saw nothing.

Suzanne cleared her throat. "Dad?"

Lucas put the Jeep into reverse again and retreated slowly to their parking spot. He cut the engine. "We can't go."

"Why?" It seemed everyone spoke at once.

"Not enough gas."

Shayne leaned forward. "We just put almost two gallons in this afternoon."

"That'd get us there. But not back."

"So we trade for more gas." Suzanne twisted in her seat to look square at her father.

"The only place I know for sure's still selling gas is in the opposite direction." Lucas gripped the steering wheel in both hands, as if unwilling to give up. But his voice cracked as he continued. "And we've already eaten everything I brought home today. We have nothing to trade."

"Then we get as far as we can and walk back! We have to save Grandma."

"Jaide barely made it to the Jeep." Lucas jerked the keys from the ignition.

Tears rose in Jaide's throat, filling her vision. She was more than letting him down. She was hindering him. He couldn't abandon his parents because of her. She wouldn't allow it. "Leave me here with Trigger." The thought of being alone terrified her, but she was proud her voice remained steady. "She and I will be fine together."

"Trigger's about as fearsome as a teddy bear these days." Lucas thrust open the driver's-side door. "We all go together, or no one goes. Not with a riot going on."

Flora and Shayne opened their doors and climbed out. Jaide remained in her seat, partly because she was too tired to move and partly because she didn't want to give up so easily. "Only ten minutes ago, you were ready to head out by yourself."

"I wasn't thinking straight." He leaned into the back seat and offered her a helping hand.

Still in the front seat, Suzanne shook her head violently. "We can't leave them out there! What if they're hurt?"

"I don't want to take a chance on losing you all in the hope of rescuing people who may already be dead." Lucas pulled Jaide's hand until her body followed.

"Dad!" Suzanne's face creased into pain-filled lines. She flung open the door.

"You should go," Jaide breathed, even as she willed her legs to support her weight. "Take Suzanne and the gun and find them."

"They're adults. They can find their way here." In the faint glow from nearby condo windows, his face remained pale in spite of his firm words.

Somewhere not too far away, a woman's high-pitched scream rent the night. Jaide felt like screaming herself. But she moved toward the condo, Flora supporting her on one side and Lucas on the other.

Suzanne followed last, sobbing.

Chapter Twenty-Five

SEPTEMBER

The Hunger will chase you, so you'd better run fast.
—Mother's Proverb

Outside the windows of the farm's clapboard sorting shed, the sun had painted the early September landscape bronze. Jaide added the last zucchini to the reusable share bag and placed it into the cooler with the others. Between the drought and the varmint damages, the shareholder portions seemed to have grown smaller rather than larger as the season progressed. But Ray always made sure his workers got what he considered a "fair" portion, filling the buckets before divvying up the rest among his buyers.

Her stomach growled, telling her it was break time, and she leaned sideways to stretch, the scar from her bullet wound aching as though she'd been running a marathon. Lucas had just removed the stitches yesterday, apologizing that she'd scar because he'd left them in so long. Without them, though, she imagined her flesh might rip open at any moment. She ran her fingertips over the dry scabs to reassure herself then closed up the shareholder cooler and retrieved her lunch from the refrigerator in the corner. Stepping outside, she headed for the barn to find Lucas.

He'd continued to accompany her to the farm and then stayed to work, claiming he had nothing better to do. He'd been morose after the riots, and with no word from his parents, the silent consensus was that they must be among the many fatalities. Poor Suzanne, the only one who refused to accept the obvious, attempted to call her grandparents' cell numbers every day. Her hope only made Lucas sadder and probably contributed to his desire to work away from home.

Jaide was glad he was here. She wasn't sure she could make the commute alone without having a panic attack. Every night, her dreams were filled with gunshots and blood.

Entering the barn quietly, she paused to pet Alba, Bones's mate. The dog lay in a pile of straw at the door, her belly round with puppies due any day now. Her tail wagged, shushing dry straw back and forth.

Lucas turned from sharpening knives at the workbench, and although he didn't smile, Jaide felt he was happy to see her. He wiped the blade he was working on and set it down among several others. His usually trim beard had grown scruffy of late, and she reached up to scratch it. "You're starting to look like Ray."

He jiggled his knee at her touch, pretending to be a dog in bliss. "You give so much attention to all the dogs around here, it's the only way I can compete."

She patted his cheek. "I'll more than pet you if you trim that beard."

"In that case, I'm shaving the moment I get home." He reached for the rifles hanging on the wall over the workbench and handed her one. "You want to take a break before patrol?"

"Let's sit on the porch swing and eat while it's still light."

Leading the way, she exited the barn and ascended the concrete steps to the porch off Ray's living room. Martha hated it when workers sat here, but Ray'd cajoled her into allowing it so he maintained constant eyes on the garden rows. Alba had followed them, lying down near the swing with one eye on the food dish, one eye on the garden where Bones trotted through the rows.

Jaide handed Lucas a fork and took a seat on the slatted-wood porch swing. When she opened the food container, her mouth filled with saliva at the wonderful scent of zucchini sautéed with fresh tomatoes, onions, and corn. Taking a bite, she studied the heat-beaten vegetable rows. Lucas stabbed a forkful and leaned back to rock the swing with his long legs. For a brief moment, Jaide could imagine they were an old farming couple, living the idyllic life she'd once dreamed for herself.

They finished eating, and Jaide held the dish down for Alba to clean. The dog licked the plastic spotless, gave Jaide a baleful glance that there wasn't more, and trundled down the porch steps. By now, the sun had set and the sky faded to murky twilight.

Lucas clicked on his flashlight and followed the dog down the steps. "Let's get a drink and wash up before we hit the garden."

Jaide picked up her rifle. Her feet ached from standing at the sorting table all day, and she rolled each ankle before moving forward to join him. The water from the pump tasted fresh and clear, and she drank until her belly ached. "Ray's so lucky to have this."

The past week, the city had posted notices advising people to boil tap water before drinking it, but Ray's well was so far withstanding the drought. Jaide had hauled drinking water home along with their crop shares the past four shifts.

"Speaking of water, have you thought any more about moving onto the farm?" Lucas shook water from his hands and headed toward the garden. Ray'd offered to set up bedrooms for his workers in the barn loft, and Chia and Ian had already moved in.

Jaide knew she was being irrational, but she wasn't ready to start living like a medieval serf. "I'm not ready to start using an outhouse and a hose. At least at home we can shower and flush."

"There's probably more than concentrated bacteria in the city water, you know." Lucas paused and pointed his flashlight across a swath of onions. Whatever had been there scurried off before Jaide could take aim. He kept moving. "The low reservoir is probably a slurry of heavy metals and pesticides. And who knows how long the electricity will stay on?"

She kicked a clod of dirt back against the nearby potato hill. "If we leave the condo, squatters will move in. What happens come winter? Ray won't need farm workers then."

"We need to buy another gun."

Jaide's insides tightened. She still felt enormous guilt over losing the pistol. They walked in silence for a while, paused once to pry a dead raccoon from Bones's mouth, then took a break behind the rows of corn for a kiss. At least she had this, the warmth and love of a good man.

He was probably right about moving to the farm. Every shift, she worried about leaving the kids behind at the condo, even with the rifle. The drive to and from work left her jittery. Come winter, the commute would end, but so would the food. They hadn't been able to save or preserve any. The Red Cross handouts supplemented her supply of vegetables and venison but wouldn't be enough to feed them all. Across the city, people had resorted to eating amarantox, in spite of emergency broadcast warnings. Government trucks toured the streets every morning, collecting blue-lipped corpses—usually children or the elderly—left on street corners for pickup.

Ian arrived for the night shift to relieve them, and Lucas filled a five-gallon water container while Jaide loaded their share bucket into the back of the Jeep. They drove the pitch-black county road to the equally dark highway; the state had shut off power to the streetlights a week ago. Lucas drove slowly, watching for obstacles or blockades. The trip home now took three times what it used to. They stopped at the brightly lit exit into the city for mandatory ID checks. When Jaide showed the guard her share receipt, he curled his lip, seemed to assess Lucas and herself, then waved them on.

Jaide hardly breathed until they reached the condo parking lot, and even then her heart continued to race while they walked to the courtyard, alert for muggers. In the distance, the drone of increasing downtown riots and sirens sounded like wind through tree branches. The air no longer stunk of burned weeds but the acidic taint of blazing tires and plastic. Looting and burning hadn't reached their neighborhood yet, and she prayed the military could get things under control before then.

Flora greeted them at the door with a tear-streaked face, clutching her little mound of a belly. "Mom, Trigger's missing."

Jaide's heart skipped. "What do you mean?"

"I let her out for a potty break, and when I came back, she wasn't in the yard. I called and called, but she hasn't come back. Shayne's out looking for her now."

Jaide darted to the patio doors and flung them open. "Triiiiiiggerrrrrrr!"

Lucas's voice was sharp behind her. "Shayne went out alone?"

Flora spoke through tears. "Suzanne's with him. We didn't know what to do. Why would Trigger run off? She's always stayed in the yard."

Lucas slid past Jaide into the night. "How long ago?"

"Just after dark." Flora stood wringing her hands at the threshold while Jaide followed Lucas to the back fence. "I'm sorry, Mom. I only left her outside a few minutes."

Jaide barely heard her daughter as she stepped out into the dark alley. She called for Trigger again.

Suzanne's voice came from the far end of the lane near the dumpsters. "We can't find her."

"Thank God you're all right." Lucas hurried toward her voice. "Don't go running off like that, especially at night."

Jaide dashed after him, scouring the darkness for her dog. Shayne appeared from behind the overflowing trash bins. He held the rifle cradled in one elbow. "We thought she might have chased a raccoon or something."

Suzanne twisted to look again at the dumpsters. "We scared two out of the trash while we were looking, but there's no sign of Trigger."

Jaide led the way back to the gate. "She didn't bark?"

"She's been really timid since the accident," Flora answered from the other side of the fence. "She hardly makes any noise at all anymore."

Lucas shooed them back into the yard. "Leave the gate open. Maybe she'll find her way back."

"We have to find her," Jaide insisted. "Some of those raccoons are almost as big as she is. What if she's hurt?"

Quietly, Suzanne said, "I think someone took her."

Stillness settled over the small group. The distant roar of the rioting seemed to magnify in the darkness. Jaide spoke past tight vocal cords. "Why would someone take her?"

Lucas's arm settled around her shoulder, but she shrugged it off, craning her head around as if she might find Trigger at any moment. "She has to be nearby."

Flora began sobbing. Jaide belted out Trigger's name again,

eyes wide as she scanned the darkness. Her daughter continued to cry.

"Flora, be quiet!" Jaide said. "I need to hear."

The girls' sobbing muffled but didn't stop. Shayne shambled her off toward the condo. Jaide took several steps down the alley away from the dumpsters. "Did you guys look in this direction?"

Lucas's hand grasped hers, holding her back. "Jaide, wait."

"I have to find her." Jaide tried to pull away, but his grip tightened until it became painful.

"Stop."

"Lucas!" She gritted her teeth at him, still trying to free her hand.

"Jaide, I can't let you go. It's too dangerous. We'll look in the morning. And she may come back before then."

"I can't just leave her out there, all alone." Tears overflowed her eyes, her intuition telling her Trigger wasn't alone. Trigger—her other child—who loved people and couldn't kill a raccoon and had only just come back to her from a near-death experience. Jaide began sobbing. "I want my dog."

"I know," Lucas wrapped both arms around her and pulled her head against his chest.

She stood stiff in his grasp but only for a heartbeat. Then she slumped against him and moaned.

He held her, rocking gently back and forth, his own breathing ragged and shaking. After she'd worn herself out, he pulled her toward the gate. He left it ajar and passed through the patio doors. When he went to close them, she asked, "Can we leave that open?"

He nodded and cupped her cheek. Turning, he took up the rifle, sat on the sofa, and laid the weapon across his lap.

Jaide stood staring into blackness beyond the doors, calling for Trigger in her mind, if not out loud.

Chapter Twenty-Six

In the dirty morning light, smudged gray by riot fires, Jaide scoured the alley, calling for Trigger. Thick stands of amarantox created a wall down either side of the narrow road, forcing her to part the foliage to examine the neighbors' equally overgrown yards. Lucas followed close beside her with the rifle. They found no clues about the dog's disappearance. At the end of the dirt lane where it intersected the main street, a young woman poked her head out of a lower-level window shrouded by amarantox.

"Would you shut up? My kid's been awake all night, and you just woke her up again."

"Have you seen a black-and-white border collie?" Jaide approached the window.

A gun appeared in the woman's hand. "Stay back."

Jaide raised her palms outward. "My dog's missing. Please, have you seen her?"

"Lady, your dog's the least of my worries. Go find another one. There're plenty of strays if you can get close enough." She slammed the window.

Jaide's chest felt like it might implode. She turned to Lucas, afraid of the answer but needing to hear it out loud. "What do you think happened to her?"

He looked at his feet, mouth turned down. "She was still weak from the accident. Easily hurt."

Suzanne approached, dark circles under her eyes. No one had slept much last night. "There's food in the kitchen. We thought you guys should eat before work."

Jaide straightened, reality jolting her like an electric current. Her farm shift started at eight. How could she leave when Trigger was missing? She turned her gaze toward Lucas.

He put a hand on his daughter's shoulder. "Thank you, Suz. Come on, Jaide."

Jaide's stomach wrenched inward, hunger mixed with worry and regret and fear and so many other emotions, she didn't know how to fill it. She followed Lucas on autopilot. He held open the gate for her to enter. Little sprouts of amarantox had crept under the fence on either side of the once-clean yard like a carpet of doom smothering her and everything she loved.

Inside, Shayne handed her a plate mounded high with vegetable succotash. Still moving as if by remote control, she stabbed zucchini rounds and slid them past her teeth. Chewed as if part of her knew she needed to eat even as the rest of her yearned to search without stopping.

Once the dish was clean, she handed it back. "Thank you."

Gunfire echoed from somewhere close by. Everyone stiffened and looked through the patio glass, collective breath held for a few heartbeats. Shuddering with nerves, Jaide moved to the door and peered out. The alley felt like a ghost town, nothing but tall amarantox swaying in the breeze. She turned back into the room. "We should search the next street over."

"It's after seven, Jaide." Lucas rubbed his healing shoulder, his face a map of worry. "We have to get you to work."

Suzanne's eyes glinted with tears. "Shayne and I will keep looking after you go."

Lucas shook his head and pointed to the rifle he'd stood near the patio door. "No. You have to stay and guard our food and supplies. No splitting up. If someone took Trigger, they may be watching us."

The girl's eyes went wide. "Watching us?"

"These are desperate times. People see us bringing food home every day when so many have none. No one's to be trusted." He turned to Jaide. "We need to seriously consider moving to the farm—"

Jaide clenched her fists at her sides. "Don't you dare suggest we leave. Not with Trigger still—"

"Calm down. I was going to say we should give Trigger a day or two to come home. But after that... I don't think we're safe here anymore."

Shoulders shaking, Jaide fought the urge to collapse to her knees. She couldn't see anything through the tears flooding her eyes. "I'm not leaving Trigger behind. You can go if you want, but I'm staying until she comes home."

"Would you put Flora at further risk to find her?"

"Trigger's part of my family." Jaide nearly spat the words. "I won't abandon my family."

Turning, she flung open the patio door.

"What about work?" Anger tinged his voice for the first time. "Do you plan to lose your job over this?"

Her hand tightened around the sliding door's handle. Losing her job meant starvation for all of them. Frustration threatened to tear her in two. She stared hopelessly over the invading amarantox. "Of course not."

The front door banged open, jarring Jaide into relinquishing her gaze on the empty yard.

Flora stood across the living room, her face pale. In front of her, she held a strip of red nylon.

Trigger's collar.

Jaide's legs wanted to give way. "Where did you find that?"

"Mrs. Obermeir," Flora's voice broke.

"Where... where's Trigger?"

Flora shook her head. "She kept apologizing. She said he didn't mean it. She said..." Flora doubled over and vomited on the floor.

Jaide rushed forward, pushed Flora's hair back from her face, moved her away from the mess.

"What's wrong? Is she okay?" Suzanne slid into view beside her.

"Flora, what did she say?" Jaide ducked to look into Flora's peaked face. "Who didn't mean what?"

"Oh, God, Mom." Flora raised her chin, brown eyes wild and dilated. "They ate her. The Obermeirs ate Trigger."

The succotash rose into Jaide's throat. She gulped for breath, fighting to keep everything down. Her gaze fell on the red collar still clutched in her daughter's fist. *No.* Lovely, gentle Mrs. Obermeir wouldn't do such a thing. There had to be a mistake. "You heard wrong. They wouldn't eat our dog."

She staggered toward the front door. Outside, the Obermeirs' stoop wavered in and out of focus. If she hurried, she might stop them. Her feet stumbled forward.

Lucas lifted her arm over his shoulder and continued walking. He led her to the neighbors' door. His strong knuckles rapped against the panel. Inside, arguing voices grew louder.

Reaching forward, she pummeled the surface with both hands. "Give me back my dog!"

Lucas pressed a thumb against the doorbell over and over. With one hand, he pushed Jaide away and tried the handle, but it was locked. He kicked at the door. "Open this goddamn door!"

Inside, a man shouted, a woman cried.

"I'm getting the gun." Lucas dashed away.

Jaide couldn't breathe. She leaned forward, forehead against the door.

The pressure against her head disappeared, and she tumbled forward, falling into Mrs. Obermeir's arms. The old woman sagged to her knees under Jaide's weight.

Jaide gasped, looking into the gray, crepe-papery face of a woman she barely recognized. The once-plump grandmother looked like death warmed over. Jaide asked, "My dog?"

The old lady's voice spilled out, crackling and brittle. "I'm so sorry. Hunger's made him irrational."

In the main living area, Mr. Obermeir paced the Oriental rug in the middle of the room, waving a long knife. His knobby knees and gaunt cheeks made him barely pass for a skeleton. "You crazy old woman! They didn't need to know!"

Jaide's hands trembled as she pulled them from Mrs. Obermeir's grip. "Please tell me she's okay."

"We'll share the meat with you if you want," Mrs. Obermeir replied.

"Meat?" Jaide choked.

The woman's fingers flew to her mouth. "You're a vegetarian. I forgot."

From the doorway, Lucas gritted out. "Tell us what happened."

Mr. Obermeir squared off, knife at waist level. "A man's got to feed his family. You know that."

The word "meat" bounced around inside Jaide's skull like a Ping-Pong ball. With each echoing, silent impact, her blood grew hotter. She exploded upright and lunged toward the old man. Lucas's arm caught her from behind and jerked her to a stop. She strained against his grip.

"He has a knife." Lucas said in her ear. "Calm down."

"Trigger's part of our family!" She flailed to free herself from his arm.

"It was just an animal!" Mr. Obermeir shouted. "Stop acting like I'm a murderer."

Mrs. Obermeir crawled backward. "Please forgive us."

"Let me go!" Jaide screamed. "Trigger trusted them. How could they do this?"

The old woman covered her face with shaking, skeletal hands. Weak sobs filled the room.

The boiling rage clawing through Jaide's veins flash-froze. How long had the Obermeirs been without food?

Jaide sagged. She should've shared food with them. Trigger had been a dog to them. An animal. And people ate animals. If deer could become cannibals, then certainly sweet Mrs. Obermeir could eat a dog.

But that didn't mean Jaide had to forgive them. "You're monsters."

Lucas was breathing hard. "Even if you don't think you're a murderer, you're a thief. Trigger didn't belong to you."

The old man brandished his knife. "Get out of my house! I did what I had to do. Go, before I do it to you, too!"

Grabbing her shoulder, Lucas spun Jaide behind him. He leveled the rifle at the old man. "You going to eat me too? I think you might find I put up more of a fight than a friendly neighbor dog."

Mr. Obermeir bared his teeth. He looked crazy. Beyond reason. Dying. Lucas didn't need to make that happen any faster. She put both hands around his flexed arm. "Come on. We can't do anything now."

Lucas resisted her pull. "If you come near our property again, or even look at anyone in my family, you'll regret it."

Without turning his back on the couple, Lucas shuffled out the door, pushing Jaide behind him.

Jaide retreated on stiff legs back to Lucas's place. Just inside the front door, she stopped, staring at the place she'd called home for months. Flora and Suzanne knelt on the floor, cleaning up vomit and sniffling. Shayne stood a few feet away, fists tight at his sides, tendons standing out on his neck. "They just told me."

Jaide could barely focus. The condo felt hollow. No longer a haven. As usual, Lucas was right. The city was dangerous. They had no reason to stay.

"Go pack your things," she said in a monotone. "We're moving."

Part Three

When the first Hunger Times drew a knife across the land,
our Mother saw that life must not be wasted.
~ THE HISTORIES

Chapter Twenty-Seven

J aide stood in the living room, staring at Trigger's empty bed, her half-full duffel bag heavy in her hand. As she'd packed, her anger had burned to a pinprick of heat inside her chest. She wondered if this was what death felt like. Numb.

Around her, the girls scurried to pack clothes, dishes, and bedding. Lucas and Shayne man-handled one of the mattresses out to the Jeep. Jaide was already late for her shift at the farm, but Lucas worried about getting two trips out of the little gas left in the Jeep. They were trying desperately to gather everything they'd need.

Except for Jaide. Even though she'd been the one to give the order to pack, she couldn't force her limbs to move. Her bullet scar pinched her side, making it hard to breathe. How was she to get through work today after a night looking for—she couldn't even think the name. If she did, it might topple her.

The weight of her duffel disappeared, and from the corner of her eye, she caught Lucas taking it from her hand. He put a palm between her shoulder blades and guided her toward the door. "Come on." His voice flowed over her like a shroud.

She followed him to the Jeep. The kids already sat in the back seat, shoulder to shoulder. Cargo filled the space behind them to the ceiling, and Suzanne ducked aside to allow Lucas to add Jaide's bag to the top over the back seat. Two queen-sized mattresses sagged over the roof, cinched down with nylon rope.

Lucas held the door for Jaide, bending to kiss her temple before closing her in. Everyone remained silent. The lack of Trigger in her usual spot in the cargo area felt like a knife in Jaide's spine, twisting another scar alongside her bullet wound. They pulled from the lot and rolled down the street, past mounds of picked-over garbage. On one corner, a dark-skinned woman wearing a pistol at her hip turned to watch the Jeep's movement with a hostile glare. Jaide's skin prickled. Lucas had been right; the city wasn't safe. Would the farm be any safer?

On the highway on-ramp, they passed a couple pulling a little red wagon laden with household goods. Then two hitchhikers and a man trying to fix a broken-down minivan while his family sat inside. Lucas drove by without turning his head, but the muscles in his jaw bulged.

They reached the quiet stretch of the interstate and picked up speed, passing stalled cars at what felt like every hundred feet. Ahead, the taillights of a vehicle flared as it swerved around something in the road. Lucas did the same when he reached the broken sofa spread across one lane. Remembering the night she'd been shot, Jaide searched for an ambush, refusing to relax until they were well past the mess.

Lucas turned onto the winding county road. The open fields appeared less hostile than the cluttered highway but still hopeless. Flocks of buzzards circled the sky in numbers Jaide had never seen before. At a sharp bend, the well-tended gardens of Ray's farm rose out of the burned and barren fields like a desert island.

While Lucas and the kids unloaded at the barn, Jaide walked out to the gardens. Ray met her with a scowl. "Everything okay? Ain't like you to show up late."

Her throat ached, and she found she couldn't meet his eyes. She wasn't ready to talk about Trigger. "We're moving into the barn, if that's still okay?"

He stretched to look past her toward the parking area and raised a brow. "Sure. Tell your kids not to go leaving the hose on or nothing. Well's been a little persnickety lately. I'll leave it to you to work out your living space with Chia and Ian."

She nodded. "Sorry I'm late."

"Just glad you ain't hurt. Go hook up the irrigation lines to the pole beans then take a hoe to the late cabbages. Martha'll join you in a bit."

She did as told and unscrewed the irrigation hoses from the block of corn and reconnected them to the lines along the row of beans. Among the cabbage, amarantox seedlings peeked from beneath the broad leaves. She hadn't thought it possible, but her hopelessness deepened; she'd just weeded the cabbage last week. Squatting, she lifted each leaf, using a hand hoe to cut off the encroaching growth. Her movements felt like a zombie was controlling her, but she kept working.

She'd nearly finished weeding the row by the time Martha joined her. "Sorry to hear about your dog." Martha's weathered face creased with concern.

Jaide quickly returned her attention to her work. She didn't want to cry in front of this woman.

Martha continued, "Ray's calling a meeting over lunch. Deer burger barbecue, on us. Whole family's invited."

Jaide's hands stopped working. "Is something wrong?"

Martha sighed and held out a hand to help her up. "I'll let Ray tell everyone at once. Go have your people wash up."

Jaide couldn't recall a time in her life when she'd actually been so tired that she couldn't rise on her own, but today she didn't think she'd have been able to without Martha's strong pull. She shuffled the long distance to the barn and up the stairs inside.

Dust motes swirled in the sunlight streaming through chinks in the siding. Ian and Chia had already taken up the spacious end of the loft near the hay hood, where they could look out over the gardens and catch a stray breeze from the open loading door. Jaide's family gathered over the stuffy partition at the back where stacks of moldering hay stood in tiers five deep. At least there was no livestock living in the stalls below to add to the smell.

Lucas and Shayne had carried the queen-sized mattresses up the stairs, setting them one atop the other while they debated on placement. Bits of straw clung to the fabric. Everything would probably be infested with bugs by the time they had to move for winter.

Flora was saying, "We can use the bales to make dividing walls."

"We should lay the mattresses on top of them," Shayne argued. "More cushion."

"But if Ray needs a bale or two, he'll have to uproot our whole bed if we're sleeping on top of them."

Suzanne glowered at her father. "I want to sleep downstairs in a stall."

"Out of the question." Lucas said. "We need to stick together."

"Hey," Jaide moved in to get their attention, throat thick. "Ray's called a meeting. He wants all of us there."

"He say why?" Lucas's brow creased.

Shayne's eyes lit up. "Maybe he's offering us all jobs!"

Jaide smiled tremulously. The kid didn't mind hard work, and his positive attitude refreshed her. "At the very least, he's feeding us. Venison barbecue."

"Woo hoo!" Shayne pumped a fist. "Let's go."

The kids thundered down the stairs, and Lucas put an arm around her. "How're you holding up?"

She turned into him and squeezed him tight. "I'm glad you're all here and safe."

"I think we have everything unloaded." He kissed the top of her head. "Let's go see what Ray wants."

Two long wooden tables normally used for sorting produce shares were set up out on the driveway near the house. Ian sat in a lawn chair close to Chia while she nursed her baby; they'd obviously become more than friends since taking up residence in the barn. Ray stood in front of his half-barrel grill, tending thick patties. Jaide was glad to see long spears of zucchini and corn cobs roasting in their husks alongside the meat.

The farmer gestured to the table with his spatula. "Take a seat. I already fed my boys. They'll patrol varmints while we pow-wow."

"Thanks, Ray." Jaide led her family to the nearby produce sink to wash up.

Once everyone had a plate and a seat around the tables, Ray stood for attention.

"Times have gotten tough all around. There's rioting in the city." He met Lucas's eyes. Lucas nodded affirmation. Ray's brows tightened. "The money our shareholders paid at the beginning of the season ain't going to cover expenses. I hate to do it, but the CSA's got to declare bankruptcy."

Jaide clenched her fork and stared at her plate. So this was it. A barbecue lunch for severance pay. But why would Ray have agreed to allow them to move in just this morning if he meant to sack everyone? She turned toward the farmer, refusing to relinquish hope just yet.

Ian asked, "Are you saying we're out of a job?"

Ray shook his head. "Far as I'm concerned, you're the only shareholders that matter anymore." A gunshot echoed from the gardens. Ray didn't even flinch. "Martha and I have a proposal I think you'll all be good with, but we want you to understand there may be risks.

"You been good employees, but the time for employees is over. We need more than shareholders, we need stakeholders. From talking to most of you, it sounds like everyone's worried about surviving the winter. I'm proposing a communal cache. Save what we have for winter to feed those who live on the property."

Lucas's hand crept along the edge of the table and took Jaide's. She glanced at him, and he shot her a hopeful half-smile before returning his attention to Ray. She did the same. Could their luck be turning, finally?

"Meaning us?" Chia sat up straight, looking at the assembled group and then back at Ray. "All of us?"

Ray nodded. "Everyone living here. But I need you to understand—people from the city will come this way, looking for food. Hell, our own disgruntled shareholders may come seeking retribution. At some point, we'll have to defend those stores."

The hope in Jaide's heart tempered itself, and the air regained some of the heaviness she'd been feeling since Trigger's death. More killing would be inevitable. She looked across the table at her daughter. Flora chewed while she listened. Her cheeks were thin but not hollow like so many Jaide saw on the city streets. Her hair still held a healthy gloss. She would continue to have food with this plan. If providing meant becoming a soldier, Jaide would do it.

"We got to think about ourselves, now," Ray said. "To create a fortress. The more eyes we have on the property, the better. So I propose all of us, kids included, start taking on patrols. Pulling our weight to protect the crop. We do this right, and no one needs to go hungry this winter."

Ian and Chia chimed in without hesitation, "I'm in."

Jaide met the eyes of her three teenagers. They were waiting on her. Lucas squeezed her hand, and she nodded.

"We're in," Lucas said.

"Yes," Jaide added. The kids all bobbed their heads in agreement.

Ray's teeth showed between his mustache and beard. "Thought that's what you'd say. I'll set up the new schedule this afternoon."

"One more thing," Martha rose from her seat, shooting a long glance at her husband. "You all agree that this here land's still our property. You do right by us, and we'll do right by you. But if there's ever disagreement, what we say goes. Got it?"

Jaide felt her jaw muscles tighten. Martha'd always been protective of her ownership, so the pronouncement shouldn't have surprised anyone, but it sounded as if the woman was setting up a dictatorship. Chia asked, "You mean we'll be slaves?"

"Not at all." Ray put a hand on his wife's shoulder. "There's bound to be arguments. Hell, sometimes I think my own kids might murder each other. Most the time, everything'll be done by vote. Think of us as moderators rather than rulers."

"And if you disagree strongly enough, you can always leave," Martha added.

Ray looked to the heavens, as though he'd had this conversation with her already. "No one's gonna leave. We need them as much as they need us." He looked over the table again.

"I'm proposing partnership here. But all things being equal, Martha and I are the tie-breakers. Got it?"

Chia nodded grudgingly, and Jaide sighed in agreement as well. They truly were becoming feudal serfs under the leadership of the local property lords. But compared to city dwellers, they were living like kings.

Chapter Twenty-Eight

Ashes to ashes, dust to dust, Amen.
~ MOTHER'S PRAYER

Clouds scudded overhead, filling the horizon with a purple-gray promise of rain, and the scent of ozone accompanying the humidity reminded Jaide of a swimming pool. She reached up for another handful of pole beans, still ultra-conscious of the pull on her scar. The sharp sounds of shovels cutting dirt made an irregular drumbeat through the late-afternoon air. With the immediate threat overhead, Ray'd put all able bodies to work on last-minute fortifications.

Jaide's healing wound, only six weeks old, made carrying or lifting impossible. Lucas had exercised his medical expertise to declare her unfit for ditch duty. She'd tried to argue the same for his shoulder, but he'd brushed off her concerns, saying he was past his required allotment for physical therapy.

Ray hadn't let her off easy just because she couldn't dig, though. The beans were coming on strong, and the pods required picking every day. She lifted her half-full harvest bucket and tried to gauge whether she should pick more or take it to the wagon and empty it before it got too heavy.

A rustle of foliage to her right drew her attention. Probably Bones checking in or bringing her a carcass. The varmint population had decreased dramatically over the last few weeks, but he still took out at least one a day. She peered over her shoulder to where she'd left the varmint bag. The dead creatures no longer bothered her except for the annoyance of keeping track of her carrying sack and making sure it didn't get too heavy to handle.

The stalks crackled again. She whistled. "Bones, bring it here."

The rustling stopped.

She cocked her head to listen. Surely it wasn't Alba—she'd just delivered her puppies a couple days ago. "Alba?"

Bones's deep barking echoed from the opposite quadrant of the garden. *Damn it.* That meant this was probably a varmint. Killing animals still bothered her, but she never hesitated anymore. All meat, varmint or otherwise, went into the cache. Or into the nightly meal. She choked down whatever anyone cooked in the communal kitchen. Prison had taught her how to suck it up or go hungry, at least.

Jaw tight, she pulled a pistol from the holster at her belt and stepped toward the noise. Rabbits would be at the base of the stalks, but raccoons or opossums might be in the ears. She eased between the first few plants.

Between the sharp leaves, a pair of blue eyes met hers. A blink of long blonde lashes. The eyes vanished.

For a heartbeat, Jaide froze. The varmint was... a person. A person in the corn. The gun trembled in her hand. Ian had reported scaring off thieves, but so far no one had drawn blood.

Extending one stiff arm to push the stalks aside, she peered deeper into the thick, leafy rows. A few feet away, shredded husks and a gnawed cob littered the ground. Something lime green skulked between the stalks, setting the tops swaying.

After her close call with the flat tire, she had no hesitation to defend herself. Jaide leveled her gun, ready to fire. A flash of denim appeared next to the green, and then a child's voice came through the stalks. "Run."

Her weapon suddenly weighed fifty pounds. *Kids?* In her mind, she'd always pictured invaders to be like the man who'd shot her, scruffy and wielding weapons. Or maybe like gangsters she'd seen on TV: colored bandanas and pants sagging to their knees. She could shoot them if she felt threatened. But children?

She didn't want to fire at them.

Her lungs burned, and she grew light-headed. She had to chase kids out of the garden. Gulping air, she reminded herself that she couldn't allow them to stay and steal. She had her own kids to feed. But that didn't mean she had to shoot them. "Get out of here," she yelled. "Go on, scat!"

Bones must've heard her shouting, because his barking drew near then passed as he caught the scent.

She pressed through the foliage behind him and burst from the block of corn near the road. Small sneaker prints dotted the freshly turned dirt from where Ray'd had the ditch crew tie the trench into the roadside drainage. Bones paced up and down the fence, barking and spitting. Across the burned field on the other side of the road, two small figures, one in green, one in blue, sprinted toward the windbreak of trees at the far end. Jaide watched until they disappeared among the gray trunks.

Ray arrived a few moments later, rifle in his hands. "What was that?"

Nauseated at the prospect of shooting at children, she said, "Kids."

His brows lowered. "Don't go soft, Jaide. Our own'll go hungry this winter if we let a bunch of strays steal our crop."

"I know, Ray," she snapped back. "I chased them off."

"All right, then. You see which way they went?"

She raised an arm to point toward the windbreak, still holding her pistol in a death grip. "Tree line."

Bones let out a final, dismissive woof then came over to sniff Ray's boot. Ray patted the dog on the head. "I got a roll of barbed wire in the barn. We'll look to beefing up this fence a notch or two after the rain. Tonight we better step up our guard. Those trees could hide a lot of people." He turned away from the fence. "Since you can't dig, why don't you go rest up? You can join Flora on guard duty tonight."

Swallowing, she holstered her weapon, fingers of her right hand tingling as circulation returned to her palm. Guard duty was technically light duty, walking and watching. Bones did most of the work. She'd lobbied to give Flora the job as often as possible, and no one wanted to argue against a pregnant girl. But tonight the work might be harder than any other job on the farm.

Ray headed down the row of beans and picked up her bucket, carrying it for her.

"Thanks."

They approached the house where the ditch diggers were deepening the drainage around the garden. Lucas glanced up and smiled at her, but his face pinched with pain.

"Don't re-injure yourself, Lucas." She placed her hands on her hips and tried to be playful, even though she was serious in her chastising. "We can't afford more medical bills."

Ray snorted. "Be lucky to even find a doctor. Lucas is the closest thing in these parts to a medical professional."

Lucas stood upright and arched his back. "Hey, I am a medical professional."

"You look like a ditch digger to me," Jaide ribbed him.

A fat drop of rain hit Jaide's forearm. She turned her face to the sky. "You sure you don't want me to help dig? Even if I'm only moving a quarter of what the others do, it's something."

Ray shook his head. "Better you're awake for guard duty tonight. Martha, why don't you take care of the beans while Jaide sleeps."

"Is there a problem?" his wife asked.

"Couple of kids were in the corn. Took off into the tree line."

She leaned on her shovel, her sweaty face smudged with dirt. "You think they'll be back?"

"We're the only viable farm left for a mile in every direction. If not them kids, then others. Rain ain't the only flood about to hit us."

Martha tossed her shovel aside and took the bean bucket from her husband. "I'll get some supper going."

She and Jaide walked side by side toward the house. On the other side of the property, over the alfalfa field, two buzzards drifted in lazy circles. With each step, Jaide's pistol bumped against her hip, reminding her of her coming patrol. What if those kids came back? She wasn't the right person for this job. But then, who was?

When they reached the back porch, Jaide blurted, "I don't want to shoot kids."

Martha stopped with her foot hovering over the first step. Slowly she turned to Jaide, her mouth a thin, pale line. "None of us do. But think of your own kids first."

Jaide's gaze connected with Martha's in a way only mothers could understand. The drive to protect offspring was biological. She had to allow that drive to take over. She took a deep breath. "I'll do anything for my daughter."

Martha nodded once and turned to go then seemed to think

better. She looked over her shoulder one last time. "If it helps, don't think of 'em as kids. They're varmints."

The porch door clattered shut behind her, and Jaide was left standing under the bruised-purple sky.

Jaide and Flora stood next to each other on the house's front porch and peered uselessly into the night. The rain had begun at dusk, spewing from the sky like someone had opened an artery. Beneath their feet, the wooden planks vibrated from the rain's impact against the structure's roof, and their flashlights reflected a river of falling water. Bones lay at the edge of the steps, chin on his front paws, looking dolefully out over his domain.

"Think we'll drown if we go out?" Flora joked.

A distant, throaty rumble of thunder answered her. *Great*. Jaide plopped down on the porch swing and rested her rifle across her knees. "Let's see how close the lightning is. If it's moving our way, we'll wait."

Flora settled back against the swing's worn bench slats, her rain slicker crackling, and leaned into Jaide like she had as a child.

Jaide lifted an arm and put it around her daughter's shoulders. "Remember watching storms together from our balcony when you were little?"

Flora nodded against her. "You used to tell me the angels were bowling."

The phrase brought back such warm memories, Jaide could almost forget the circumstances that brought them to the porch tonight. Almost. "I bet we won't have to scare anyone off tonight. The rain'll keep them away for us."

A mild flicker turned the eastern sky lavender, and Flora

started counting out loud. "One Mississippi, two Mississippi..." She reached twelve before the thunder rolled. Then she sat up and looked at her mom. "I'll shoot someone if I have to."

Jaide nodded. Flora had always been stronger than herself. Pragmatic. And more stubborn, if that were possible. "I'm sorry you've inherited this world."

"We have each other. And soon Shayne and I will have our own baby to love."

"You don't worry about feeding a child? I worry about feeding you every day."

Flora sighed. "You've always worried about feeding me, even before the amarantox came. Somehow you did. Life goes on, right?"

Another strobe of lightning. Flora counted to twelve again.

"Life's been kind to us," Jaide said. "It may not always be so. We don't even have access to a hospital for you. What if you have complications?" Pressure rose through her ribcage and settled in her throat.

"Women have been having babies forever." Flora waved her off with the immortality of youth. "Plus, we have Lucas. I'll be fine." She rose from the bench. "Do you think the storm's far enough out?"

Jaide stood, taking a huge breath, mind returning to the task before them. Worrying about the birth wouldn't matter if they lost the crops and Flora starved to death beforehand. Settling her rain hat firmly against her head, she moved toward the porch steps. "Keep counting while you're out there. If it gets to five, head for the house until it passes."

Flora patted her thigh, palm loud against her rain slicker. "C'mon, Bones."

Bones stayed put, lifting his head and tilting it to one side as if telling them they were crazy.

Bracing herself, Jaide stepped into the deluge. The force of the rain threatened to drive her to her knees, beating the brim of her hat flat and sending rivulets of water down the back of her neck. "Holy shit! It's like it's going to make up for a summer of drought all at once!"

Next to her, Flora adjusted the hood of her slicker to hide her face.

Wishing they had more one-piece raingear, Jaide pulled her own collar up higher, trying to keep her neck dry under her hat's brim. "I'll take the right. Meet you at the other end."

Flora nodded and slapped her thigh again. "Bones, come."

The dog reluctantly rose and skulked down the steps into the rain. Tail between his legs, he plodded out into the garden ahead of them. Jaide wondered whether he'd stay on patrol or sneak back to the dry porch once they were gone.

Training her flashlight on the ground near her feet, she moved toward the fence, a sheet of water welling over the toes of her black rubber boots. The water pouring off the brim of her hat forced her to keep her head down. How was she supposed to watch the field when she couldn't even look up?

She followed the fence, pausing every few feet to squint toward the rain-beaten crops. How much damage was the storm doing to the plants? She hoped Ray's ditches and sandbags were enough to divert water from the surrounding fields, or the crops would be washed out by their roots.

Every time the sky lit up, she counted. The storm was drawing closer, now only a count of nine between flash and boom. The wind had also increased, molding her slicker against her torso and arms. She picked up her pace, splashing muddy water up around her legs. Maybe she could finish one round before being forced back to the house.

She slogged along the fence line until she reached the corner and turned to follow the next border. One of her boots had a slow leak, and her sock squished every time she stepped down. The water cresting over her toes at this end of the garden was muddy and brown, exuding a swampy scent that reminded her of raw shrimp.

A faint light reflected through the sheeting rain ahead, probably Flora's flashlight. Jaide pressed forward. Better tell Flora to head back to the house. The light bobbed and disappeared. Her foot slipped, forcing her to watch her footing. The top layer of packed soil was becoming slick.

A sharp crack brought her head up. That wasn't thunder. That was the report from a firearm. She squinted toward where she'd last seen the light. "Flora?"

In spite of the treacherous surface, she started to jog. She hoped her daughter had only brought down a varmint; the memory of those kids sprinting across the fields remained fresh in Jaide's mind. Please don't let Flora have to shoot a child.

Another gunshot was swallowed by a bellow of thunder, closely followed by a second lightning strike. In the strobe of light, Jaide spotted three figures kicking something on the ground.

"Flora!" Jaide dropped her flashlight, mud immediately swallowing the glow. She aimed her rifle at the cluster of people. Or where she thought the people were. How could she aim in the dark? What if she accidentally hit Flora instead of the intruders?

The report of a gun and a flash of light from directly ahead dropped her to her knees. Were they shooting at her? Her mostly healed wound throbbed with the memory of the bullet. Every atom in her body screamed at her to crawl away. Yet they'd been kicking someone. And the only other person out here was Flora. Jaide had to stop them.

Letting out a slow breath, she rose and fired. The rifle bucked. She pumped another round into the chamber. Men's voices swore in the darkness.

She shouted, "Get off our property, or I'll shoot again!"

"Fucking bitch!" *Crack!* Someone was definitely firing at her.

She kept her rifle pointed their direction. Lightning flickered again, directly behind the men. Jaide's rifle happened to be targeted directly at the middle man's chest. *Definitely a man.* She pulled the trigger.

Her gunshot coincided with an explosion of thunder. Screams and cursing.

From somewhere to her left, Flora yelled, "Mom!"

A weird sense of relief flooded Jaide. Who'd they been kicking? She cocked her rifle again, heart racing. Hoping Flora's voice made the men think they were outnumbered, she called out, "We're done giving you chances. Next time you all go down."

From over the fence, a gun fired again. A man's voice said, "Stop wasting bullets and run!"

Lightning flashed. Two lumpy figures remained on the ground where the men had previously stood.

Flora called again, closer. "Mom?"

"I'm here. Are you okay?" Jaide rose, swinging her rifle around to aim toward where the men had disappeared. The wind drove the rain at an angle into her face, and she blinked away water. She inched toward the figures. Flora's light met her at the site, catching on a stranger sprawled in a crimson stream of his own blood. A smaller black shape nearby turned out to be Bones, also swimming in blood.

Jaide lowered her weapon. She stared from man to dog and back again. Bones's tongue hung loosely out of his mouth, his unblinking eyes washed in muddy water. The man had one hand over his chest, fingers pink with watery blood. His eyes stared at the clouds above.

Flora squatted next to the man, creating a waterfall over him from her rain hood. "Dead."

Jaide couldn't see her daughter's face in the dark. She returned her gaze to the body spotlighted by Flora's flashlight. This was no deer. No opossum to feed to Bones. She'd just killed a man. What should she do now? Call Ray to pick him up? What were they going to do with the body? "I killed him. I killed a human being."

"He killed Bones." Flora shouted over a peal of thunder. "He would've killed you."

Jaide's gaze slid from the man to the dog. She hadn't even heard Bones barking. Those men had killed him. She wasn't sure what she was most upset about at the moment, her action or theirs. Shuddering sobs rose from her chest, and she squeezed her eyes shut, gritting her teeth.

"I better call Ray." Flora used her walkie and told Ray what had happened.

Jaide struggled to breathe, shoulders heaving in panic. A ringing in her ears muted the rolling thunder. Flora grabbed hold of her wrist. "The lightning's getting closer. Ray says come back."

On weak legs, Jaide followed her across the field, ankle-deep mud sucking against her boots. Indigo light filled the sky, illuminating the thrashing blades of nearby corn, tassels bent sideways beneath the onslaught. One of her boots sucked straight off her foot, and she sprawled forward into the mud. She blinked gritty water from her eyes as lightning crackled again, followed immediately by the peal of thunder. The scent of ozone filled her nose.

"It's right on top of us!" Flora screamed, pulling at Jaide's slicker.

"Go!" Jaide shouted, struggling to rise.

Flora ignored her and helped her back to her feet.

Leaving the missing boot, Jaide raced toward the porch,

Flora at her side. Ray stood under the roof, beckoning them with a flashlight. "Thank God. You all right?"

She limped up the steps, and Ray pried the rifle from her clawed grip. The night felt like a nightmare.

"Mom?"

She turned to her daughter, blinking away rain. Or was that tears? Her lungs heaved and her head spun. She stumbled and nearly fell.

Ray caught her under the arms and eased her onto the bench swing. "You're not hit, are you?"

She shook her head and lowered her face between her knees, sure she was about to pass out.

"I think she's in shock." Ray's voice floated above her. "Go find Lucas."

Footsteps squelched across the porch, then the screen door squeaked open and banged shut. The murmur of voices rose from inside.

Flora was safe. At least there was that. And Lucas was coming.

The door squeaked again, and Lucas's warmth filled the seat next to her. He draped an arm around her hunched shoulders and bent to put his cheek near her ear. "Are you hurt?"

"I can't breathe."

"You're hyperventilating. Keep your head down." He sat back up and gently rubbed her back.

Jaide's heart rate slowed, and her breathing steadied. She sat up. Lucas moved his palm from behind her and reached out to hold her hand instead. "Better?"

"I killed a man."

"Flora told me."

A double bolt of lightning lit the horizon, and she started counting. "...Ten Mississippi." Thunder growled like a satiated beast. "It's moving away."

"Yes."

She squeezed his hand tight. Muted light from inside the house backlit his profile.

"Flora said they shot at you?" His voice was thick.

"I think so." Flashes of lightning and explosive bursts of gunfire jumbled her brain. "They killed Bones."

Lucas freed his hand from hers and wrapped both arms around her shoulders, pulling her close. "I can't bear the thought of losing you." His voice rumbled against her ear. "But I don't know how to protect you. The world's fucked up, and I feel like we're cripples limping through it together."

His voice centered her, and a moment of clarity washed over her. She lifted her head enough to glimpse the figures moving around behind the screen door. She'd lost Trigger, but Flora was safe. Lucas was safe. So far, everyone on the farm was safe. When push came to shove, all they had was each other. Flora had basically said the same thing earlier that night.

"Together's all I need." Jaide pushed a wet strand of hair from her eyes and laid her cheek against Lucas's chest. His heartbeat thrummed with the heat of life. "As long as I have one person left to love, I'll keep fighting."

She stared out into the darkness, the weight of her sins suddenly becoming her strength. She'd killed a man. And without regret, she'd do it again.

Chapter Twenty-Nine

The floodwater took two days to subside, forcing them to postpone burying the corpse. When they finally could, the flies swarmed thickly over the bloating body, wafting upward at their approach in a wave of stinking air. As they carried him out past the alfalfa and into the barren neighboring field, Jaide turned her head to take shallow breaths, but the stink of death couldn't be so easily escaped.

She stood stiffly near the shallow hole, Martha on one side and Flora on the other, as Lucas and Ray lowered the body and began shoveling wet dirt back over the corpse.

"Should we say a prayer?" Jaide's voice trembled, her hands fidgeting with each other.

Ray paused to wipe his sleeve across his brow. The heat had returned, even though the sun remained hidden as if ashamed of the havoc below. "That's a good idea."

Lucas stopped shoveling and looked at her expectantly.

Put on the spot, Jaide felt suddenly tongue-tied. This wasn't thanking a deer for meat. This man had tried to kill her—he had killed Bones—and only through luck or fate or whatever had she been the one to survive.

Bones. Yesterday she'd walked into the barn to find an ashen-faced Ray skinning his pet, tears running into his beard.

"What are you doing?" Jaide had gasped.

Ray wouldn't meet her gaze. He kept working. "Alba and her brood'll need to eat."

Her throat closed up. Bones's mate lay on her straw bed, sightless gray pups in a lumpy pile along her abdomen.

Jaide turned back to the farmer. "But that's cannibalism."

"Would you rather eat him?"

She physically recoiled at the suggestion. Venison was bad enough—she'd only been eating it because Lucas insisted she needed the iron and protein. But to eat a dog, especially one she knew...

Her answer must have shown on her face, because Ray returned to his work. "Varmints've become scarce. We can't afford to waste. I figured us humans'll eat the opossum that's left, since Alba don't know the difference."

At that moment, some sort of cold and pragmatic spirit had possessed Jaide, and she'd backed out of the barn without another word.

Now, standing here over the grave of a man she'd killed, the same spirit took hold of her, and she knew exactly the prayer to be said. "Thank you, Mother Earth, for allowing me to live while this man perished. Good or evil, may you guide him to the other side."

Martha made a little noise in the back of her throat and stepped forward, giving Jaide a reproachful glance. She folded her hands and dropped her head. "In sure and certain hope of the resurrection and eternal life through our Lord Jesus Christ, we commend to God this stranger's body, earth to earth, ashes to ashes, dust to dust. The Lord bless him and keep him, the

Lord make his face to shine upon him and be gracious to him and give him peace. Amen."

Ray muttered "amen" and began heaving dirt back into the hole. Lucas met Jaide's gaze again and gave a little shrug. She shrugged back. Let Martha have her rituals.

Dirt-streaked and sweating, they all returned to the farmhouse for lunch. The power had been out since the storm, and they had to use the hand pump outside to wash up. Luckily, the kitchen stove ran on propane, and Ray's place had two huge tanks.

Martha called everyone to lunch, except Ian and Shayne, who continued to keep watch. The two men would take their break later. The scent of cabbage and potato soup flavored with some sort of meat filled the kitchen as Jaide took her seat. Martha and Flora did the cooking, and Jaide never asked any more about ingredients. Her stomach accepted what she gave it and was grateful. Being a vegetarian was no longer a choice she could make.

Toward the end of the meal, Ray cleared his throat and rose from his spot at the head of the table to face everyone. "I been thinking. Burying that man today took us away from the field. Divided our forces and used up time we should've spent on the crop."

Jaide noticed Flora licking her spoon clean and slid her own bowl over, offering her daughter the last two chunks of potato. She returned her attention to Ray before Flora could protest.

He stood ramrod straight in front of his chair. "From now on, we ain't burying strangers."

A collective gasp rose from the table. Jaide blinked at him, trying to understand what he was saying. Images of Bones's skinned corpse blocked her vision.

Martha set her spoon down with a clunk. "It's bad enough

we have to kill people, Ray. Don't suggest we leave their bodies out to rot, too."

Ray's throat bobbed and he seemed unwilling to meet anyone's gaze. "I guess we ought to vote on this. My thinking was to make no-trespassing signs and place them along the property. Bodies could be left by the signs to prove we mean business."

"Ew, Dad!" Ray's boys made gagging sounds.

"That's disgusting," Flora said.

"Not to mention a health hazard," Lucas added.

The soup roiled in Jaide's stomach. Yet she had to admit Ray had a point. The world they lived in no longer had a place for civilities like funerals for strangers. She cleared her throat. "What if we place the signs well away from the farm? Extend our borders, if you will. Proving we mean business will mean fewer trespassers we have to shoot."

Lucas shook his head. "Posting signs will just tell people we have something worth protecting. Better to keep a low profile."

Ray gestured through the living area to the windows facing the garden. "People already find us. More will come. Shouldn't we give them fair warning? If we can veer them off before we have to shoot them, ain't that better?"

"Fine. Warn them." Lucas pushed his bowl away, as if he couldn't bear to think of food while having this discussion. "But we bury the dead. You thought the corpse today smelled bad? Wait until the abdomen ruptures from built-up gasses. I've encountered a few bodies like that, locked in apartments for days before they were found. We don't want to go there."

"Oh, God," Flora gagged.

Chia sighed loudly. "Animals would eat them before they rot. Centuries ago, my tribe would intentionally leave their dead exposed in sacred areas. Burying the dead is a Western tradition."

A flush deepened Lucas's face. "Disease aside, you want to attract buzzards, coyotes... feral dogs and cats? What happens when they've eaten the body and come searching for more food? We have one baby with us and another on the way."

"We shoot them like any other varmint." Ray remained standing, arms crossed.

Jaide thought again of Bones, skinned and quartered in the barn. "We've had fewer and fewer critters in the garden to feed Alba. And her puppies will need meat before we know it. This plan could serve a dual purpose."

Lucas looked at her as though he was seeing a stranger. She felt like a stranger to herself. Prison hadn't toughened her half as much as the world afterward.

Martha buried her face in her hands. "It's un-Christian."

Her youngest son rose and wrapped his arms around her.

Lucas blew a breath between tight lips and slumped back against his chair. "I don't like it."

Ray scrubbed his fingers through his unruly mop of hair. "We should include Ian and Shayne in this. Out of curiosity, what's the vote right now? Who's in favor?"

Jaide raised her hand, along with Chia, Ray, and Ray's oldest boy, Roger. To Jaide's surprise, Suzanne raised a tremulous hand as well.

"Opposed?"

Lucas's hand shot up, and Flora looked apologetically at Jaide as she joined him. Martha shook her head, one hand leaving her face to indicate affirmation. Edward continued clinging to her neck without venturing a vote.

"All right, then," Ray said. "I'll take it up with the other two, but it looks like we have a plan."

Lucas rose quickly, knocking his chair back with a clatter, and stalked from the kitchen.

Jaide picked up his chair then headed outside with Suzanne.

Chia settled in to nurse her baby, and Flora stayed to take care of the dishes. Martha remained seated at the table, sobbing softly.

From the house, the devastation to the garden looked horrible. Up close, the damage was worse than Jaide had imagined. The straw they'd used to mulch the rows had floated into haphazard drifts, snaking around cornstalks or compacting over smaller plants as the water receded. Tomato plants, once thick with fruit, now hung ragged and bare. Suzanne joined Ray's boys as they scouted the mud and straw, salvaging any fruit that hadn't floated away in the deluge.

Farther out, half the corn stalks leaned haphazardly against their neighbors, and she wondered if the plants would recover to ripen their ears. The pole beans straggled in a tangled blanket over the neighboring aisle of winter squash. Past the fence, water continued to gush through the ditch along the country road, carrying debris like cargo on a freight train to parts unknown.

Near the block of corn, Ray, Ian, and Shayne listened as Lucas talked animatedly. She headed their direction. The muddy aisles sucked against her rubber boots. She'd reclaimed the missing footwear from the garden earlier this morning, and the inside felt clammy against her foot. A car edged down the road, slowing as it passed the farm. Ray waved his rifle at it, and the vehicle sped up, spraying mud in a plume behind it.

Jaide reached the men in time to hear Ian say, "Hard to tell hungry kids to keep moving."

"No one's a kid anymore. It's us or them." Shayne's eyes had a bleakness about them that made Jaide's heart ache. Not too long ago, he'd been a kid on the street himself.

Ray hitched his jeans higher onto his scrawny hips. "It's settled, then. We show people we mean business."

Lucas met Jaide's eyes in silent sorrow. She felt strange, as though they'd switched sides and she had to be the voice of reason for him.

Within a week after the rain, the neighboring fields, once stubbled with ash, sprouted a carpet of amarantox in a false green promise of life. The weed rose like magical beanstalks, smothering the competition. Inside the fence's boundaries, the crew battled the incursion with hoes, and the storm-battered crops recovered some semblance of productivity. But they'd lost most of the remaining tomato harvest, and the cabbage heads had split from the influx of water.

"We got to talk about rationing," Martha said one night over a paltry dinner of cubed squash and sweet corn. The power had never returned after the storm, and an antique kerosene lamp cast flickering shadows. The faces around the table reminded Jaide of hollow-eyed zombies.

"We still have the late potatoes and sugar pumpkins to bring in." Ian held Chia's daughter while the woman fed her tiny spoonfuls of mashed squash.

The child wasn't fully on solid food yet. Could Chia maintain nursing on restricted calories? Jaide cast a sidelong look toward Flora. At around six months pregnant, the mound beneath her daughter's shirt loomed all the larger because of Flora's sinewy limbs.

"Don't count your chickens before they're hatched." Martha drew a small notebook from her shirt pocket and flipped through the pages. "I've divided our stores into portions to last us into May. We can add the other items to the list as we harvest."

Lucas cleared his throat. "Those of us in the barn will need more calories than those in the house once winter weather comes in."

Ray set down his fork. "I been thinking about that. I'm moving everyone into the house."

Martha sputtered, drawing up straight in her chair. "Ray—"

"Martha, I know you don't want to, but it's gonna get cold, and there's a baby out there." His gaze fell on Flora. "Soon two."

Jaide's chest swelled with gratitude.

"That wasn't the deal when we took them in." Martha slapped her notebook onto the table beside her plate. "We agreed. And we're already sharing our food."

"They worked for that food, too. Some've killed for it."

Jaide felt every eye around the table fall on her. Over the last three weeks, only Shayne had been forced to shoot someone. The wounded man had fled into the amarantox across the road, leaving only a blood trail no one wanted to follow.

Martha pushed back her chair, wooden legs grating against the floor. "My daddy grew up in this house, Ray." Her voice hitched with repressed sobs. "You've all but given away the farm. It's all I got left of him."

Ray seemed to shrink. His gaze dropped to his plate, and he scrubbed his hands through his hair. The room joined him in awkward silence while Martha continued crying. Jaide glanced at Lucas, who bit his lip and shrugged. Why were men so flustered by a crying woman?

Closing her eyes, Jaide centered herself then opened them and rose. She walked around the table and squatted next to Martha's chair. Slowly, she extended a hand and rested it on Martha's shoulder. "None of us have much left of our old life. Those days are gone." Her throat thickened around the words, and her eyes burned with tears. "I killed a man to protect our crops. To protect you, and your family, and my family. Our family. Because that's what we are now. Family. I can only hope you'd do the same."

Martha sucked in a breath. She turned her teary gaze to meet Jaide's. "You're right," she choked out and visibly swallowed before continuing. "Of course you're right. The boys can move into a room together."

Ray shot Jaide a grateful look. "And we can partition the family room for the rest of you."

Jaide rose, keeping a gentle hand on Martha's shoulder. "Thank you."

Martha nodded. As Jaide passed Ray to return to her seat, he squeezed her hand. They finished the meal, and Jaide found herself smiling across the table at Chia's baby. The little girl kept grabbing Chia's spoon, until eventually Chia gave up and let her have it. The baby banged Ian's plate and chortled, making the whole table laugh.

Ray's oldest boy, Roger, held up a hand for attention. "Here's a good one. What's the difference between cabbage and snot?"

"Roger, not at the table," Martha chided, but without any conviction.

Edward giggled. "I know! Kids don't eat cabbage!"

Everyone laughed again then took turns telling jokes until even Martha laughed herself to tears.

A dozen odd strangers truly had become a family.

Chapter Thirty

OCTOBER

*The Sisters called a meeting and sent the choking smoke
into the air to call the Hunters. This is how the First Peace
was made.*

~ THE HISTORIES

Jaide jabbed the trowel into the sod and pried up a woody amarantox stem until it released in a clump of dirt and roots. While everyone's attention had been on the garden, the weed had crept into the lawn near the abandoned chicken coop, and brown patches of dead grass had begun to merge into a mosaic of death, creeping toward the cherry tree. She shook the clod, raining dirt, and tossed the roots into the wheelbarrow. The soil had returned to its hard, dry state after the rain three weeks ago.

Taking a half step to her left, she squatted and jabbed the trowel again.

A gunshot cracked the air. Ducking, she looked around for

the source. A woman's wail rose from the direction of the garden.

Jaide dropped her trowel and leaped to her feet, teeth gritted against the residual pain of the scar in her side.

The scream grew more intense. Flora was in the garden, gleaning what she could from the late bean harvest. Jaide checked her pistol holster and hurried around the corner of the house. As she hurdled the row of fall broccoli, another shot cracked the air.

The screaming ceased.

Trembling, Jaide rounded the yellowing tomato plants and spotted Flora standing in the pumpkin patch, pistol gripped in both hands. Chia stood a few feet away, shotgun pointed downward to a spot hidden by sprawling vines. Jaide's steps slowed as she approached. A woman in yellow capri pants and a striped tank top spattered with blood lay face up among the pumpkins, clutching a basketball-sized gourd against her middle with one hand. Her face had been nearly obliterated by a shotgun blast.

Jaide looked Flora over, then Chia. "Are you both okay?"

"She wouldn't drop the pumpkin." Flora's voice shook. She turned her eyes to her mother. "She tried to run away."

Chia relaxed the shotgun. "You did right. But we need to work on your aim. You hit the pumpkin."

Jaide looked again, seeing the small, perfect hole penetrating the front of the orange globe. A crimson stain spread over the woman's tank top behind it. Flora's gun hand shook.

All because of a pumpkin.

Shayne arrived, breathing hard. He placed his palms against his knees and bent over to catch his breath. "Everything okay?"

The others nodded. Jaide forced herself to remember that one pumpkin could give them an edge to survive the winter.

There was no room for sympathy when it came to survival. Reaching over, she guided Flora's gun back into its holster. "Shayne, let's take this body out to the road."

About a week ago, they'd deposited a trespasser's body at the sign near the interstate—a man who'd shot at and missed Alba before Ian took him down. Buzzards had circled the farm for days. No one had the stomach to go check on the body.

Jaide eyed the gory pumpkin. The side against the woman's belly glistened crimson. The bloody squash would have to be relegated to Alba and her pups. Clenching her teeth, Jaide nudged the pumpkin away with her toe and wrapped her fingers around the woman's blood-slick arm. "Let's get this over with."

Shayne took both ankles, and Chia grasped the woman's other hand. Together they lifted her from the vines and toward the path. Jaide glanced at Flora's ashen face. The girl needed something to take her mind off what had just happened. "Flora, go back and tell everyone what's going on. Then see what Ray wants you to do."

Flora nodded sharply and spun toward the house.

At the fence, Chia held down the line of barbed wire, and Jaide and Shayne heaved the body over the top rail. They took turns climbing over into the lush amarantox on the other side.

Jaide wiped her sweaty forearm across her equally sweaty brow and scanned the wood fence. The line of barbed wire around most of the property was obviously still too easy to get past. Every ten feet, hand-painted signs read, INTRUDERS WILL BE SHOT ON SIGHT. Ray had posted larger signs a hundred yards down the road in each direction.

"We need another line or two of wire," she said to no one in particular. "That'll keep people out."

Chia and Shayne only grunted in return, already dragging the body through the weeds toward the pavement. The stink of blood was lost in the odor of crushed leaves.

The road happened to be clear at the moment, but traffic had increased since the flooding, two or three groups every day, some in cars but many on foot. Usually, the sight of a rifle kept them moving.

Jaide trudged down the pavement behind Shayne. The body grew heavier with every step, and she glanced at the sky, expecting buzzards to set in at any moment. What would they find when they reached the sign? The previous corpse had been there almost a week, picked at by buzzards and infested with flies. Would it be nothing but skeleton by now? Or the bloated horror Lucas had described? She steeled herself as they approached.

But when they reached the marker—a pound-in fence post Ray had forced into a crack in the pavement—there was no carnage. The body was gone. Only a dark spot remained where the man had once sat propped against the post.

They dropped the woman, and Jaide shaded her eyes with one hand, looking for the other body. "What happened to it?"

Chia shook her head. "Coyotes, probably. I've heard them calling all night."

A shiver ran down Jaide's spine. She rubbed her bloody hand on the front of her jeans. "So we're just feeding coyotes with these people?"

Chia's face scrunched into a grimace.

Shayne looked the fence post up and down. "Maybe we can tie the body to the post?"

"The coyotes will just rip it free unless we suspend it out of reach." Chia bent to search the woman's pockets. Jaide cringed at her practicality.

Shayne scuffed the crack in the pavement with his toe. "Maybe a couple of tripods or something?"

"Have to be high." Chia rose, empty handed. "Coyotes can jump. Or knock it down."

Jaide peered back toward the farm. "What if we park the tractor here? We could raise the bucket and use that."

Chia clapped her hands. "Good! That would also block the road to other cars. Make them turn around."

Shayne raised his shoulders, a pained expression on his face. "What if people wreck the tractor?"

Jaide sighed. "Unless we can come up with more gas, the tractor's useless anyway."

Nodding, Chia said, "Let's go ask Ray."

"What about her?" Shayne pointed to the dead woman. "She might be gone by the time we come back."

A single buzzard scouted a lazy circle overhead. Jaide started walking home. "We'll hurry."

They strode back to the farm and told Ray their thoughts. He took a big breath, face long. "I worked hard to buy that tractor. But you're right, it's about useless now. Should be enough fuel left to get it to the road."

"Can I drive it?" Shayne's eyes were bright with excitement. A part of Jaide wept for a boy who'd never earned his driver's license and might never have the opportunity.

Ray smiled softly. "Sure."

The farmer showed Shayne how to operate the levers and the gas then hopped onto the sideboard to ride along. Chia had retreated to the house to nurse the baby, so Jaide grabbed a coil of rope and took a spot on the other sideboard. With a jerk forward, they chugged down the amarantox-infested lane to the road. Shayne swerved onto the pavement from the lane and nearly toppled them. The grin on the boy's face made Jaide bite back her reprimand. Let him have this last taste of speed before his world slowed into technological winter.

They approached the signpost. Several buzzards circled high overhead. Why hadn't they landed? Had the coyotes already moved in and scared the birds away? Jaide put a hand on the butt of her pistol, ready for anything. The body came into view, and Shayne let off the gas. No coyotes in sight. But a small, dark-haired figure sat on the pavement at the woman's side, navy T-shirt emblazoned with a cartoon fire truck.

The tractor slowed then stopped, engine chugging rhythmically. No one said a word. Finally, Shayne spoke. "What do we do?"

The blood flowing through Jaide's veins felt like ice water. They'd turned away children before. Chased them from the fields. Spoken of the need to protect themselves, no matter the age, sex, or race of a thief. But none this small. She stepped down off the sideboard. "Pull closer to the sign."

Focusing on the pavement next to the dead woman's out-flung hand, Jaide tried to pretend the child wasn't there. She had to become steel. To become stone. Stepping forward, she felt as if her bones might collapse under a crushing weight. The coil of rope burned her hand from the intensity of her grip.

Behind her, the tractor growled like an angry, impatient beast.

When she reached the body, Shayne raised the tractor bucket as high as it would go, casting a shadow over the pavement. The engine ceased. In the silence, the child asked, "Can you hewp my mommy?"

"Oh, God," Jaide choked. Don't look at him, she thought, and bent to wrap the rope around the dead woman's hands. Tears blinded her as she fumbled to knot the rope. Another set of hands joined her.

Ray's bearded cheeks glistened with moisture as his red-rimmed gaze met hers. The child whimpered, stroking his mother's shotgun-ravaged cheek. "Mommy, wake up."

Shayne remained on the tractor seat, face pale as ash. "Maybe we should bury her."

"What good would that do?" Ray's voice cracked. He threw

the other end of the rope over the raised bucket and pulled, hands trembling as he pulled the body upright.

The child clutched his mother's bloody shirt. "Mommy!"

All steel left Jaide's body. She sank to her knees. The mother's death-glazed eyes condemned the very air Jaide breathed. There'd been a chance—slim, but a chance—the little one could survive with his mother. That chance had died with her.

Another horror filled Jaide's mind. "The coyotes will eat him alive."

Ray released the rope. The woman's body slumped back to the pavement with a thud, rope slithering free of the tractor arm. He stalked to the other side of the road, both hands pulling at his hair as he raised his face to the sky. "No, no no!"

Shayne's voice came from her left. When had he gotten off the tractor? "Hey, little guy."

Jaide twisted to look at the toddler. Shayne held the child against his chest, a foreshadowing of the father he would soon become. "He's so little." Shayne said. "I don't think he'd eat much."

Her heart melted. Hope remained in the innocence of a child, even in a world ruled by survival. The strength returned to her limbs, and she rose. "I'll feed him from my plate."

The corners of Shayne's mouth lifted. "And mine."

Ray flung his hands in the air then clenched them at his sides. "We can't take in every child. Even if we kill its parents."

Jaide nodded, knowing this was true. "But we can save this one. And perhaps a bit of our humanity, as well."

Jaw bulging, Ray pointed toward the house. "Take him away, then."

As soon as Shayne was out of sight, Ray hoisted the dead mother into the air and tied her off.

Chapter Thirty-One

NOVEMBER

The unmarked stranger must be shown the Knife.

~ MOTHER'S PROVERB

Jaide hunkered near the picked-over rows of potatoes, fingertips stinging as she gleaned the last thumbnail-sized tubers from clods of freezing soil. Winter had blown in on a windstorm the prior week, skipping autumn's usual cool-down and plunging nighttime temperatures into the teens. The skies hung thick with clouds yet released no snow. Amarantox in the surrounding fields had shriveled and blackened, leaves tumbling to the ground in a loose blanket below barren stalks.

Days before the wind, billowing smoke had filled the horizon in the direction of the city. Traffic along the road had surged, convoys of cadaverous people with hollow eyes. Repeated attempts to jump the fence had forced Jaide and the others to cease all garden work and maintain an armed presence. For about a week, there had been daily gunfire. Edward had lost an ear to an enemy bullet.

Rising, Jaide moved down a few feet to keep sifting dirt, clenching and unclenching her fingers in an attempt to warm them.

With the arrival of the cold, the traffic had trickled down to almost nothing. Swarms of buzzards dotted the sky. The farm had resumed a frenzy of work to button things up before the snow arrived.

Two rows over, Little Orphan Andrew, as the boy had come to be called, chased two of Alba's puppies. He'd proven remarkably resilient to change and earned his keep by making everyone around him smile. Even Ray had bounced him on a knee once or twice after dinner, eliciting the child's chortling laughter. The innocent joy warmed the house better than the wood-burning furnace in the basement.

She reached the end of the potato row, joints stiff with cold. Normally tubers as small as these would've been ignored, but they couldn't afford to waste a single ounce, especially with an extra mouth to feed. "Andrew, come help me carry potatoes."

Shayne pushed a wheelbarrow mounded with dead squash vines toward the compost heap. "I just saw him over by Martha at the clothesline."

"Thanks." She lifted the lumpy burlap sack over her shoulder. "Does Ray need help with the garlic?"

"No, but Chia might want a hand. I heard Esmerelda crying a few minutes ago."

"Right." Jaide left the garden for the sorting shed. The baby's snuffling whimpers echoed from inside.

At the door, the sulfurous stink of boiled broccoli leaves hit her. Two big pots simmered atop portable propane burners, filling the room with steam. Chia ladled green glop into jars at the sideboard, nose red from a head cold everyone had been fighting.

Jaide stepped inside. "Why don't you and Esmerelda go inside and rest. I can take over here."

"That's all right. She's just fussy." The woman finished the jar and wiped the rim. "The steam in here is good for her. You go finish the garden."

"You sure?"

Chia waved a hand without looking up from her ladle. "Go."

"All right." Jaide held out the burlap sack. "Want the last potatoes for the soup?"

"Sure."

Leaving the potatoes, Jaide exited the shed. She waved at Ian where he leaned on his ax in a break from splitting wood. Through the half-open barn door, she spotted Alba on her pile of straw. Unlike Bones, the dog didn't take initiative patrolling the property, and Jaide sometimes wondered why they were still feeding her. For the sake of the puppies, she supposed.

She continued around the far side of the house toward the garden, keeping an eye on the property's perimeter. Martha and Flora stood hanging laundry near the house, the basket of wet clothes on the ground wisping steam. Flora's belly strained against her jacket, and she pressed a hand to it after hanging each item of clothing, as if to comfort the baby. Andrew was nowhere in sight.

Rounding the second corner of the house, Jaide scanned the mostly bare garden. Nine acres looked a lot bigger when mature plants didn't block her view. Ray bent over the small garlic patch, shoving seed cloves into the bed. At the far end of the acreage, Lucas smoothed soil in preparation for planting spinach, while Ian gathered up the last of the crispy brown pumpkin vines.

A gleeful squeal came from the desiccated corn stalks. Half

hidden, Andrew and the puppies tumbled over one another near the farthest corner of the fence. The boy looked up sharply, attention drawn by something in the amarantox.

Jaide's spine stiffened.

The patch of bare stalks beyond the fence swayed and parted as something—someone—approached the fence.

At this distance, her pistol was nearly useless. Yanking the gun from her belt, Jaide sprinted forward. "Andrew!"

A man's face appeared through the amarantox. Hands reached for the barbed wire. The strands of fencing sprang into loose coils, dangling like ringlets down the fence posts to either side.

She hurdled over a soft mound of earth where tomatoes had once grown.

Andrew pushed a puppy off his lap and stood. Facing the man, the second puppy barked in adolescent imitation of its mother. *Where was Alba?*

Jaide tripped over an irrigation hose and crashed to a knee, pistol flying from her hand. "Andrew, come here!"

Behind her, Lucas yelled, "What is it?"

"Stranger! The corn!" Lurching upright, she searched for the gun but couldn't see it. She abandoned the pistol and kept running.

Andrew gestured as though he was having a conversation. The puppy's barking continued, little feet dancing back and forth along the fence border. The second puppy cowered close against Andrew's legs.

The man leaned over the top rail and beckoned the child closer.

"No! Andrew!" Jaide screamed so loud, her chest and throat burned.

The child turned to stare at her. A gunshot deafened her,

causing her to duck as she reached the first cornstalks. The man disappeared back into the amarantox.

"Andrew, come here!" She panted. "Now!"

Andrew looked over his shoulder at where the man had disappeared and then ran toward Jaide, eyes wide with confusion.

The puppy at the fence put its front paws onto the lower plank, continuing to bark.

From between the stalks, long, thin arms snaked out over a wooden rail. The puppy gave a surprised yelp and was gone.

Jaide swooped down and grabbed Andrew into a tight embrace. "Never talk to strangers! Never!"

Another gunshot split the air. Through the dead amarantox stalks, a figure zigzagged across the road. Drawing up beside her, Lucas paused and fired again. The man flew forward, stumbled upright three steps, then collapsed.

Lucas breathed heavy beside her. "Got him. But he took the puppy."

Andrew sucked back shuddering tears, clutching the fabric of her jacket with both hands. Jaide trembled deep in her core and crushed him against her. "He was after Andrew."

Ray and the others arrived, guns in hand. "What happened?"

Lucas explained, and Ian stalked the last few feet to the fence. He used the length of his rifle to push the dead stalks aside. "Think there's more of them?"

"If not, there will be," Ray said.

Alba barreled by, skidding to a stop near the spot the man had leaned over the fence. She circled the area, sniffing the ground and growling. Her remaining puppy skulked toward her with its tail between its legs. Alba barked once, as if asking what was going on.

Lucas knelt and put an arm around Jaide, leaning close. She

pried the boy's fingers loose, thrusting him at Lucas. "Take him."

Lucas accepted the weight. "What are you doing?"

"Getting that puppy."

"It's probably dead, Jaide."

"Either way, it's ours." She stepped over the fence, hyperaware of the open space all around. No way was she letting scavengers steal the farm's dog, alive or dead. She'd eat it before she'd let them have it.

Chapter Thirty-Two

JANUARY

Reclaim, reuse, recycle.

~ MOTHER'S PROVERB

J aide sat on a kitchen chair, a half-unraveled sweater on her lap. Beside her, Lucas raised a fishing hook he'd been whittling out of bone close to his face, squinting at it in the dim kerosene light. She reached over and squeezed his knee. He smiled at her and resumed his knife work.

Across the table, Martha's knitting needles clacked rhythmically, while next to her, Suzanne fumbled with her own knitting attempt. Jaide had tried to learn but kept losing count and dropping stitches. She'd been relegated to the destruction side of the process, unweaving old garments or tattered afghans for others to create new items. She flexed her hands. Her fingertips ached from working wool fibers loose without breaking the yarn.

Outside, wind whistled under the house's eaves. Gusts sent

bursts of snow against the siding like sandpaper. The only reason to go out now was to fetch water from the pump, feed the dogs, or keep guard.

Hunched over a book at the end of the table, Roger read aloud from Les Miserables, face close to the pages. Night pressed in on them like a void. The kerosene would run out before spring, but no one suggested giving up the two hours of light they allowed themselves every evening.

Jaide only half listened to the story, lost in her own thoughts about amarantox and corporate greed. Would anyone ever tell the story of the fall of mankind? Were there corporate fat cats still out there, sitting in well-stocked bunkers and creating a revisionist history of what had happened? How could she make sure the right story was told?

Roger's voice rose in melodramatic tension; Jean Valjean was protecting his adopted daughter Cosette with every ounce of his being, protecting the person Cosette loved for the simple sake of her loving him.

Jaide's gaze strayed to the seat next to her, where her daughter sat. Flora's huge belly served as a ledge while she stitched a tear in the knee of someone's jeans. The birth could happen any day now, and everyone seemed to be holding their breath in anticipation of the moment.

The old wind-up grandfather clock in the living room chimed the first stroke of eight o'clock. One more hour of wakeful light. Then it would be wakeful darkness.

This baby would grow up in a world far different from any mankind had ever imagined. The hand-crank radio had emitted a last repeat from the emergency broadcast system two weeks ago, warning people to remain calm and watch for Red Cross workers in the area. Then it had gone to static. The child's legacy would be struggle and starvation and hardship.

Jaide wanted her grandchild to know, to remember, the

consequences of irresponsibility. She wanted the world to remember.

"I have a story I want to tell." Jaide interrupted Roger's reading. "About the Tox." The shortened name for amarantox had somehow come to mean everywhere and everything outside the farm.

Everyone looked up from their projects, eyes alight with the prospect of something new. Roger slid his bookmark into place and closed the cover. "Good. My voice is tired."

Jaide licked her lips and looked around. Lucas raised his eyebrows at her. Did it matter if the others knew she'd released the amarantox? The true story of the Tox began before that. It began with an idea. An idea that mankind could control and overcome nature. An idea even she had bought into, just in a different way.

"This is as much confession as story," she began. "I think all of you know I spent some time in jail."

The faces at the table grew even more eager. While she'd never hidden her past, she hadn't talked about it, either. Flora paused her stitching to give Jaide her full attention.

"I once believed nature would grant us what we need. That nature was pure and benevolent. If only I could homogenize people's thinking, to see what I saw, the world would exist in harmony." She took a breath, formulating how she wanted to relate what had happened. To give it some context. "Scientists with ideals as strong as mine wanted to feed the world, or cure cancer, or stop climate change. But the corporations that funded the scientists wanted to make money, of course. That's where idealism and nature diverged."

She smiled at Lucas, recalling those early days when all they'd done was debate ideals. "One day, altering people's minds wasn't enough for me. I had to do something concrete. Something to truly change the course humanity had set for itself. I broke into a TelomerGen greenhouse where they were growing genetically modified test crops. Where they were growing amarantox."

Across the table, Martha gasped, lowering her knitting into her lap.

"Oh, God." Flora covered her mouth with one hand.

Jaide swallowed, finding she could no longer meet the gazes around her. Why had she initiated this conversation? "I don't know what they intended to do with that experiment, other than to eventually make money. I wanted to stop what I called Frankenstein plants. What I saw as disruption of the balance in nature. If I could corrupt their data and set their experiment back, I could give the government—humanity—a chance to change its mind. So a group of us broke in, uploaded a virus to their computers, and ran away just as the police arrived."

That night flared black and vivid in her memory, the frigid winter air biting her sweat-soaked skin as she fled. The beginning and the end of everything. "I was among the first to see the weeds and recognize them for what they were outside the greenhouse."

Flora's voice trembled. "That's why you were out with the weed warriors all the time."

"Yes. I thought I could stop the spread near the source."

Roger piped up, "Is that why you went to jail? How'd they catch you?"

Ian added, "Why didn't you tell someone about the weed?"

Her heartbeat thundered through her ears. Now that she'd started, she had to finish. "I wasn't one hundred percent sure the weed was from the greenhouse until the news announced it. And by then, the FBI had arrested me. TelomerGen wanted to prosecute me for domestic terrorism and send me to prison for twenty-five years. But because I knew where the weed had originated, they cut me a deal."

Lucas took Jaide's closest hand and squeezed it. Her jittery nerves calmed a bit at his show of solidarity. He said, "They made her keep silent."

Ray hit a palm against the table, his dark brows drawn together in a single line. "Those bastards! I bet they knew early on and didn't want to admit fault."

"Yes." Tears prickled Jaide's eyes. "I feel guilty for a lot of things. Taking the deal, for one. I don't know if holding TelomerGen publicly accountable would have changed the spread of the Tox or not, but we can't go back and change history. All we can do is move forward and make our own history. I want us to remember where we came from and what we lost, what we gave up."

Ian picked up the boot he'd been mending and gestured with the awl in his other hand. "In order to pass history on, we have to survive."

Martha picked up her knitting. "Jaide has a point, Ian. Survival isn't enough. We should keep records."

"Like a historian!" Roger looked at his father. "Some old dude who knows everything and passes on knowledge and stuff."

Ray snorted and waved the boy back. "Don't look at me. I can barely remember what I had for breakfast."

"Carrot soup," both Roger and Suzanne said together, wrinkling their noses. They exchanged a laugh.

"Jaide, you're passionate about this." Lucas squeezed her hand again. "I nominate you as our official historian."

"Yeah, Mom." Flora agreed. "And you can tell us bedtime stories every night."

A flush rose up Jaide's neck. "Me?"

"You started it with your greenhouse story."

The clock's gears wound loudly and began to chime lights

out. Ray scooted his chair back and reached for the lamp. "Good enough for me."

Lucas pulled Jaide to her feet and guided her to bed. As the house went dark, his kisses coaxed all thoughts of history from her mind.

Chapter Thirty-Three

They found other Tribes on the land, and the Brothers became Hunters.
~ The Histories

Gunfire startled Jaide awake, followed by incoherent shouting from outside. She rolled off the mattress, hit the floor of the dark living room, and scrambled on her knees toward the window. The floorboards creaked and popped as Lucas rolled to the other window. In the corner, Andrew whimpered on his pallet.

Flora's voice floated from the kitchen. "Stay put, Andrew."

The voices outside cut off as suddenly as they'd started. Peeking over the edge of the windowsill, Jaide used one finger to lift the heavy curtain. Moonlight glinted off the snow-covered gardens. The deer stand cast a deep purple shadow across the field. Everything was so still, the view could've been a painting.

Another gunshot shattered the night.

She ducked. The curtain fell back into place. Who was

outside on patrol this shift? Her sleep-addled brain called up tonight's roster: Suzanne, Ian, and Shayne.

Heart pumping, Jaide felt around on the floor for the pistol she kept near the bed.

More gunshots. Silence. Overhead, the floorboards squeaked. Chia's baby wailed.

Jaide's fingers found the cold metal of her gun barrel. She dragged the weapon to her and curled her fingers around the grip. Had the invaders killed Alba? She was too groggy to recall barking. What about the patrol? Nausea roiled through her. So many shots had been exchanged. Someone was bound to be hurt.

Andrew whined again. "Jaide?"

"Lay down, little one," she whispered. "Just keep quiet."

Lucas rasped, "Jaide, go help Flora protect the kitchen. I've got this room."

"Okay." Jaide crawled over the mattress. Two of the farmhouse's three exterior doors accessed the kitchen, part of a long-ago remodel to add the garage. She moved slowly, one hand in front of her. Her shoulder bumped a wooden chair, squeaking it across the linoleum.

"Mom?" A sliver of moonlight arcing through the sink window cut a line across Flora's pale face. She stood with her back against the interior wall, watching the door to the garage.

"It's me, baby. Hold tight." Jaide veered toward the long, narrow window next to the porch door. She passed the door panels and froze.

Crunching feet on snow outside.

Jaide trembled. Someone was right there on the other side of the door. If she showed her face in the window, they'd shoot.

A man's gravelly voice cut through the glass. "We've got your people. Let us in and no one gets hurt!"

Ray's voice was muffled by the floorboards. "How do we know you ain't killed them already?"

More crunching footsteps and whispered voices. Jaide inched closer to the glass. The man shouted again. "The pretty girl here says her name's Suzanne."

Lucas's voice boiled out of the living room. "Give her back!"

Did these men have everyone, or just Suzanne? Jaide's throat constricted. She eased around to peer sidelong out the window. This side of the house was in deep shadow, the cherry tree a dark skeleton against the snow. A filmy hedge blocked the view of the lane. But the man's voice had sounded close. They couldn't be far away. Probably hunkered down next to the foundation, using the porch for cover. Swallowing past the lump in her throat, she eased closer, hoping for a glimpse of the attackers.

"We been watching you a while," the gravelly voice continued. "We know you've got kids in there. Don't make us take this to the next level."

The stairs squeaked, someone coming down. A hissed whisper, "Psst."

She ducked back around to face the room. Was that Roger or Edward? She couldn't tell. "Here."

"Dad says we got to use the storm tunnel and try to ambush them." The old farmhouse had a narrow underground passage in the basement leading to the barn. The original builder had excavated it to access the livestock during the winter, a quaint historical addition Jaide had never imagined using. It could work.

Lucas hissed from the living room. "I'll go. Jaide, come watch the front."

Jaide knew better than to argue. His daughter was out there. She drew back from the window so her whisper couldn't be heard outside. "There's one guy near the door here, against the foundation, I think. Go."

She hurried back to the front windows, moving around the mattresses on the floor by memory.

Upstairs, Ray shouted again. "I won't sacrifice my whole house for one girl. Get off my property."

Jaide pushed the edge of the curtain aside and peeked one eye into the gap. How many people were they facing?

An anguished scream outside chilled Jaide to the bone. The stranger's voice cut over the top of it. "We have your men, too. The girl's just the most entertaining."

Andrew sniffled in the darkness. "Jaide, I wanna sleep in your bed."

"Lay down and be quiet." She didn't have time to be gentle. Those men were torturing Suzanne and doing who knew what to Shayne and Ian. She itched to follow Lucas, but someone had to keep the invaders out of the house.

"Three people ain't worth sacrificing the rest of us." Ray bluffed. At least she hoped he bluffed. "They knew that when they signed on."

Gunshots split the darkness. Shouting. Feet scuffling against dry snow. "Mother fucker! I thought you said we had all three?"

"Where'd he come from?"

Jaide raised her pistol between the curtains, frantic for a target.

Another shot. Breaking glass. "I got him."

"No!" Jaide shouted pulling the curtain wider. Had Lucas been shot? She had to help him. The window in front of her spider-webbed, a bullet hole appearing just above her forehead. She dropped the drapery and stumbled backward.

More breaking glass and the stinging scent of alcohol. Flora screamed, "They're throwing bottles!"

A man's laughter through the windows. "Next one will be lit."

Molotov cocktails? Why would they do that? Setting the house on fire would destroy anything worth stealing.

The upstairs floorboards creaked and thumped, people changing positions. "You can't bluff us that easily," Ray called.

"Roast pork," a new voice crowed.

Jaide's stomach lurched. *Roast pork?* The possibilities around that statement made the air hard to breathe. Or maybe it was the alcohol fumes.

The stranger shouted, "We'll give you to the count of twenty to think about it."

Martha's low-pitched voice rose in argument upstairs. Ray's reply came louder. "Do as I say!"

The stairs groaned, and the shush of moving limbs entered the kitchen.

Ray started cussing from the upper level, words she'd never heard the kindly farmer use before. He shouted out the window. "Give us a few minutes to talk it over."

Jaide stumbled across the bedding toward the kitchen. She stopped at the partition when a voice hissed, "Through the tunnel."

Of course. They could escape through the storm tunnel before these crazy people cooked them alive. But what about their supplies? All the food they'd stored?

Small hands locked onto the fabric of her pajama leg. Andrew's frightened voice was a whisper. "Jaide?"

More glass shattered from somewhere on the upper level. The food stores meant nothing if everyone died in a fire. She grabbed the child's arm and pushed him forward. Keeping her voice low, she said, "Flora, take Andrew with the others."

"What about you?"

"I'm coming. But we need coats and shoes, or we'll end up freezing to death. Move!"

She shoved the little boy at her daughter's shadow and darted through the kitchen. With so many people living in the house, they'd moved everyone's outdoor gear to the garage. She could grab some clothes, even if she had to leave the food.

Gunshots outside.

She peered into the garage. The window in the top half of the side door cast a rectangle of moonlight onto the concrete floor. Shoving her pistol into her waistband, she leaped down the step. A tub of summer shoes sat under a bench. That would be the fastest option, if not the warmest. She could pile coats on top of it and carry the whole thing at once. She wrapped her arms around as many hanging coats as she could.

A shadow blotted out the rectangle of moonlight from the exterior door. The nose of a double-barrel shotgun pressed against the glass.

Jaide dropped the coats, jerked her pistol free, and pulled the trigger. The glass disintegrated, and shadow arms cartwheeled, dark blurs against lavender snow. The figure fell away from the door.

Heart pounding, she scooped up the coats and threw them on top of the tub. She hoisted the load, gun hand awkwardly double-gripping the tub handle. Clothing slid over the sides, tangling around her feet. She kicked free and dashed back into the house.

The night was alive with gunfire. Ray shouted upstairs. More crashing glass. A whoosh sucked all the air from the room.

Blindness and heat.

Jaide beelined for the tiny door beneath the stairs. Broken glass bit into her heel, but she kept going. She sucked in a stinging breath of smoke and screamed, "Ray!"

Footsteps thundered on the stairs above her head, pounding like a heartbeat through the roar of flames. She limped down the steps into the cellar while the house overhead roared like a moving freight train. The red-brick cellar walls glowed from the open grate in the furnace. The plywood door over the tunnel hung loose on one hinge.

Ray plunged down the stairs behind her, one side of his hair singed short, face blistered and gleaming with sweat. "Move!"

Jaide ducked under the tunnel's first tar-blackened support beam and plunged into darkness, knees bumping awkwardly against the tub. An explosion rocked the earth, raining grit down around her. Her forehead collided with a low beam, and she stumbled, stars shooting through her vision. Behind her, she could hear Ray's feet scuffing the dirt floor.

A warm trickle ran into her eyebrow. She blinked it away and took a wobbly step forward. Forced the other foot to repeat the motion. Her head throbbed. Her lungs felt like they were choking on pure darkness. *How long was the tunnel?* She'd only seen the entrances at both ends, never the inside. The barn was at least a hundred feet away up top.

The tub bumped something solid, rebounding her two steps back. She landed hard on the heel with the glass in it and cried out. Her awkward double-grip on the gun and tub handle slipped. The weapon clunked to her feet among a pile of shoes and coats. Ray collided against her backside, knocking her forward, feet tangling in the clothing. She caught her balance on a ladder rung.

"Up," Ray said.

"I dropped everything." She squatted to scoop clothing into the tub. She could sort her gun out of the mess later.

Ray's hands bumped hers as he helped then shoved her toward the ladder. "Enough. I'll hand it up."

She climbed the ladder, emerging ten feet up into the frigid, straw-scented barn. Outside, an orgy of noise—hoots and laughter and gunfire—filled the night.

She paused at the top, allowing her eyes to adjust. A dim orange glow permeated the cracks in the barn's siding. The house must be engulfed in flame. Their entire winter supply of food gone in a single night. Not by people but by fire.

Dropping to her belly, she reached down and grabbed the tub, straining to bring it up over the lip of the hole. Ray pushed from below as he climbed. He cleared the top, rifle poking up behind his back.

Jaide stood, feet burning with cold through her socks. She could no longer distinguish the sharpness of the glass embedded in her heel from the bite of the frozen ground. Taking a moment, she scavenged a mismatched pair of rubber boots from the tub and slid them on. Her wounded foot throbbed in protest, but at least she might avoid frostbite.

Ray took the tub, and she sighed gratefully. Her arms and back cramped from hunching through the tunnel, and they had a way yet to go. Ages ago, they'd agreed that if a catastrophe ever happened, they'd meet at a copse of trees where Ray harvested firewood. She prayed everyone remembered.

Limping toward the stall door, she was relieved to see the bay doors closed; no one could spot them from outside. The side door stood ajar, a lavender slit of moonlit snow beyond.

Laughter, then a drawn-out scream permeated the night. "Mom!"

She stiffened, heart refusing to beat. "Oh, God, they have Flora!"

Eyes straining in the darkness, Jaide moved out of the stall, groping for a gun no longer in her waistband.

Then something hit her from behind and drove her to the floor.

Chapter Thirty-Four

Palms grating against the dirt floor, Jaide attempted to buck herself free of the weight on her back. She got one knee under her, but a hand grabbed her hair and pounded her face into the ground.

Somewhere behind her, she could hear Ray grunting and scuffling.

A nasal voice spoke close to her ear, "I'd be just as happy to slit your throat as keep you, so I suggest you play nice."

Jaide flexed her spine, continuing to struggle until a knife's point prodded below her ear. She let her limbs fall still but kept her core tight, waiting for a chance.

Strangling noises and more struggling, then Ray landed face down on the floor next to her. The strap of his rifle was looped tight around his neck. Ray's eyes bulged as a booted foot between his shoulder blades increased tension on the leash.

"Think that's all of them, Gator?" The man with the knife at Jaide's throat leaned his knee harder against her kidneys.

"Tell me, little lady." Gator's voice sounded full of gravel, the same man who'd been shouting outside the house. "Is this all of you?"

Jaide squirmed again, the knife scraping her skin. "We're the last. I promise. Please, you're killing him."

Ray's face thumped to the dirt close to her. The loop jerked free. He took a gargling breath.

"Ray?"

Nasal Guy yanked her hands behind her, cinching her wrists together with the rasp of a zip tie. His fist returned to her hair, jerking her upright. In the filtered orange light, she faced the man called Gator. His ragged white beard brushed the collar of a camouflage parka, and a gray wool cap slouched low over his eyebrows. He reached out, and she flinched, expecting him to grope a breast. Instead, he fingered her ribcage. "So skinny." He motioned to the side door. "Put her with the others."

The hand in her hair yanked her around and propelled her forward, the knife against her ribs surely drawing blood. She limped as fast as she could, her wounded foot driving pain up her leg at every step.

Once they were outside, Jaide could discern the sound of crying hovering below the roar of fire. The house came into view, every window spewing flames. Even at this distance, waves of heat blew outward through the chill air. Like a hungry wolf pack, three people in parkas like Gator's circled a line of figures huddled on the driveway.

At the near end of the line, a figure in the dark-and-light checked flannel shirt Flora had worn to bed last night lay in a fetal position, knees drawn to her chest as far as her enormous belly would allow.

"Flora!" Jaide surged against the man's grip. Hair ripped free, and hot blood trickled down the back of her neck, but she barely noticed. She dropped to her knees beside her daughter.

"Mom," Flora moaned, groping for Jaide. Unlike the other prisoners, her hands remained free. "They killed him, Mom."

"Who?" Jaide's gaze shot up again, taking count. Eleven? The adult residents at the farmhouse only numbered eleven counting herself. And as far as she knew, Ray was still in the barn. These marauders must have gathered prisoners from elsewhere.

Rough hands yanked her sideways, and another zip tie connected her on a chain next to Chia. The small woman sat on her knees, bouncing slightly to calm the crying baby tied against her chest. Past Chia, Martha rocked back and forth, murmuring the Lord's Prayer. Andrew cowered against her hip. Relief flooded Jaide at the sight of Lucas's profile in the flickering light.

At the far end of the line, Gator dragged a body she assumed to be Ray's and dropped it. One of the revelers dodged forward and connected the farmer's bound hands to the chain at that end. Several paces past them, two figures lay still on the snow.

"Mom," Flora sobbed, curling tighter around herself. "I can't... Ohhh. They killed Shayne."

Jaide gasped, squinting harder at the figures on the ground. One wore a bloodstained camouflage parka, but in the flickering light, Jaide couldn't mistake the vibrant orange scarf Flora had knit for Shayne. The sinking feeling in her gut made it hard to breathe. "Maybe he's just hurt."

Flora shivered.

The heat from the burning house made the winter air tolerable, but the earth remained locked in a frigid grip, sucking the life from Jaide's knees. Flora must be near hypothermia. "Flora, sit up. You can't lie there and freeze."

Gator turned from where he'd been admiring the fire. "This

fire's too damn hot. I saw firewood in the barn." He pointed toward the bay doors. "Set up over there."

One of the captors—a woman, her black braid hanging long over one shoulder—nudged two people from the line to their feet. "Tania, Eve, get to it."

The strange captives each wore dirty blue parkas and knee-high boots. Gaunt faces, so skeletal Jaide couldn't know age or sex, passed by toward the barn. The young women's hands were bound in front of them loosely enough to allow them to work.

While they carried wood to the new blaze, two of the captors picked up Shayne by his arms and legs. They carried him toward the barn and dropped him near the new fire. Jaide leaned forward, waiting to see some hint of movement, a sign of life. She refused to believe Shayne was dead.

The captive women began stripping Shayne of his clothing. His boots, his mittens and parka, his flannel shirt. He was down to a blood-soaked T-shirt and underwear when the female marauder took off her gloves and held them out to one of the women. The other prisoner yanked up Shayne's tee shirt, exposing his pale brown belly.

Unsheathing a big buck knife from her belt, the woman with the braid plunged it into Shayne's gut.

"No!" Jaide screamed. Even as the women had undressed him, she'd told herself he might wake up any minute. But the body didn't even quiver.

The woman scooped looping handfuls of intestines from him as if he were a deer.

Jaide retched into the snow, but her empty stomach had nothing to offer. Flora lay on the earth beside her, curled in on herself, but her eyes stared at the scene with a dead glaze.

"Flora, don't," Jaide gagged out. "Look away."

Her daughter's frame shivered. Jaide knee-walked forward

until the chain stopped her. Her knee sank into slush near Flora's hip. Urine? A rippling contraction curled Flora inward like a dying insect then relaxed, but the girl seemed to barely notice it. "Oh, God, no." Jaide turned and sought Chia's eye. "She's in labor."

Chia hung her head and shrugged. Her baby had quieted, but Jaide wasn't sure that was a good thing.

"Woe unto them with children..." Martha continued her prayer.

Nasal Guy held Ray's rifle now, pacing the line of prisoners. When he drew near, Jaide pleaded with him. "My daughter's in labor. Free my hands so I can help her. Please."

He stared coldly at her, orange firelight dancing across his features. One side of his lip curled upward in a sneer and he stretched out the rifle toward Flora's gut, poking her hard. Flora contracted again in response.

The one called Gator hollered from the fire. "No sense losing good meat to frostbite. Take them into the barn."

Nasal Guy cackled. "You heard him. Up."

Jaide struggled to her feet, her brain swimming at being called meat. Her wounded foot had gone numb with pain. "Flora, get up."

Flora didn't move.

"Maybe I should just put her down now." The rifle slid up Flora's ribcage to rest against her temple.

"Tom!" Gator barked out again.

The rifle withdrew. The rest of the group had risen, except for Ray at the opposite end of the line. He wobbled halfway up then toppled sideways, dragging Ian down with him.

Jaide called to Andrew, who still clung against Martha's leg. "Andrew! Go help Flora stand up."

The boy clutched Martha's pant leg tighter.

Trying to smile, Jaide nodded at him. "She needs a big strong boy to help her. Can you be strong?"

His little body trembled, but his fingers released Martha's pant leg. Keeping an eye on the men with guns, he scuttled over to Flora and stroked a palm down her cheek. "You need hewp?"

The touch seemed to wake her from a dream. Her gaze shifted to the child's face.

"C'mon." He tugged at her arm, and somehow, magically, got her to her feet. Chia and Jaide moved in close, allowing her to use them for support as they trudged to the barn. Jaide tried to keep herself between the fire and her daughter, but Flora paused anyway, staring at the woman with the knife slicing wide strips of muscle from bone.

Jaide pressed her shoulder against her daughter's back to move her while Andrew tugged on Flora's hand. Closing her eyes against a contraction, Flora allowed it to pass and kept moving.

"Baby stew by breakfast time," Nasal Guy sang.

The line of prisoners slowed, those closest to Flora bunching around her even as they shot hunched looks toward the man.

"You wouldn't," Martha said.

The man cackled.

Lucas eased in next to Flora. The whole line had stopped moving now. "Hang in there, Flora," he muttered. "We'll get you through this."

Ian stepped slightly away from the group, shoulders thrust back in challenge. "You're sick. You know that?"

"The whole world's sick." Nasal Guy wove the rifle back and forth in front of Ian's face, taunting him. "Only the sick survive!"

"Jesus Christ." Gator stomped over to the line. He punched Ian in the gut, doubling him over. Then he turned to his man. "Stop teasing them, Tom, and do what I tell you, or I'll throw you on the fire next."

Tom leered, his hungry eyes roving over Ian. "Right, Gator."

The group continued forward, entering the dusky barn through the side door. The walls flickered with orange light from the bonfire outside, but the far corners remained in the night's black grip. Tom pointed to the pile of hay Alba used as a bed. "Sit there, and no talking."

Jaide settled into the hay near Flora, wiggling down into the bedding for warmth. Where was the dog? Why wouldn't these people choose to eat a dog before butchering Shayne? The image of his stripped body seemed burned into her retinas.

Flora breathed raggedly. How far apart were the contractions coming now? Jaide looked to the two female prisoners who came and went carrying split wood from the stack inside the barn. Perhaps one of them could help Flora. "Hey! Tania? Eve? Hey!"

The girl looked at her, then Tom, and scurried outside. Tom smirked.

Flora groaned. "I'm so cold."

Jaide's insides quivered with adrenaline that kept her warm, but her fingers and toes were numb. Flora's pajamas would do little against the winter air, especially now that her water had broken and soaked her pant legs. What would they do for the baby when it came? Lucas's birthing kit was burning along with everything else in the house.

Peering around the dim barn, Jaide spotted an old horse blanket lying on the workbench. "Can we have that blanket from the workbench? Please?"

"Sure, whatever." Tom shrugged. He made no move to get it.

Throat tight, Jaide flicked her gaze between Tom, the blanket, and the rest of the group. Besides Flora, Andrew was the only one not tethered to the chain. "Andrew, there's a blanket on the workbench. Do you see it? Bring it for Flora, please."

Andrew nodded and ran in a wide arc to avoid Tom. Tom pivoted to watch the boy, his face an impassive mask of evil. Pausing with the blanket clutched to his chest, Andrew seemed to sense ill intent. He edged sideways, away from the man.

"Where do you think you're going?" Tom said.

Andrew froze.

"Your mom said bring her the blanket. Do you want to be punished?"

Andrew shook his head vehemently and bolted for the hay pile.

Jaide let out a slow breath. "Good job, Andrew. Tuck it around her, okay?"

His little arms flapped the heavy gray wool over Flora, feet sinking into the hay as he stepped to her other side to pull the fabric even. Lucas sat cross-legged at Flora's head. "This part of labor takes a while, so just try to rest, okay?"

Flora didn't answer. Jaide met his worried gaze. His eyes glittered dark in the dim barn.

"How could this be happening?" she whispered.

"Maybe they'll let one of the girls help her," Lucas said. "I can talk them through it."

"I want my bed," Andrew whispered, settling next to Jaide and leaning his head against her side.

"Why don't you snuggle in with Flora? You can keep each other warm."

One of the blue-parka girls who'd been moving firewood arrived and offered Tom a skewer of meat. Every nerve in Jaide's body cried out in denial. Shayne had become meat. Tom's gaze connected with hers, and he grinned as he tore off a big bite.

Jaide shifted her back to the man. She couldn't watch him eat.

He smacked his lips in what seemed like an exaggerated

manner. "Too bad you haven't earned a share. This is mighty tasty barbecue."

Bile rose into her throat. She stared helplessly at the orange light flickering across the back wall.

One by one, the other attackers entered the barn, spreading camouflage sleeping bags on mats across the floor. Between the high-end parkas and expensive camping gear, Jaide wondered if they were ex-military. She hoped the blanket was keeping Flora warm enough.

Pale dawn light filled the half-open doorway when Tom held the rifle out to one of the other attackers. "I'm taking a break."

The man nodded and accepted the gun. Tom eyed the group on the hay and then moved forward like a hyena stalking prey. He pulled a knife from his pocket and flipped it open. "Now where's that pretty girl?"

Chapter Thirty-Five

Everyone sitting in the hay stiffened. Tom shoved Ian aside and yanked Suzanne's arm, knife sawing at her bonds.

Lucas surged to his knees, unstable on the soft hay. "Don't touch her!"

Tom swung out with the knife, slashing Lucas's cheek from his eye to his chin.

Lucas shied back, blood gushing from the wound.

"Lucas!" Jaide cried, tugging against the zip ties on her wrists.

The attacker pounced forward, Suzanne forgotten as he drove a knee into Lucas's chest. Lucas tipped backward, knees still bent beneath him.

"I'm going to carve you up." Tom's nasal voice rose with excitement. The knife hand flashed again, slicing a matching cut on Lucas's other cheekbone.

"Tom!" A gravel-deep voice froze Tom's next swipe mid-air. "Take the girl and leave the rest alone."

Tom lowered the weapon slowly, tip down toward Lucas's eye. "Next time."

Then he lurched upright, upper lip curled in a half grin of victory and disdain. He once again grabbed Suzanne.

"No! Stop!" She struggled in his grip, breath heaving in ragged terror.

"Don't scar her," Gator said in an offhand manner. "You're not the only one who wants some."

Tom's shoulders fell a fraction as he glanced toward his leader. "If she doesn't struggle, I won't have to."

Gator leveled an emotionless gaze the man's way.

"Fine." Tom dragged Suzanne off the hay. Lucas blinked blood from his eyes and rolled to his side. Jaide shuffled forward on her knees. "Did he get your eye? Lucas?"

He shook his head, torso hunched over the bloody hay. His shoulders shook with repressed sobbing.

From the other end of the barn, Suzanne cried out, whimpered, silenced.

Jaide raised her head enough to see Tom cutting the clothing from Suzanne's trembling limbs. Her arms remained bound behind her. Every time she tried to turn or avoid his blade, he poked her hard enough to draw blood. The other men watched or slept on their mats.

Gasping for air that seemed too thin, Jaide searched the barn walls. There had to be something here to help them. This was their space. They should be able to defend it.

The workbench held a few tools, but she couldn't wield them with her hands bound. Nor the rake or shovels leaning against one wall. Her gaze shifted to the dark recesses of the stalls. The tub of clothing Ray had carried was back there. Had Gator searched it and found her gun? She shifted her attention to Flora, who seemed to be sleeping. Her contractions had eased, and Jaide wasn't sure whether that was a good thing or bad. Could she wield a gun? She was the only one with free hands.

Andrew's small frame shifted beneath the blanket. He'd dug out a hollow in the hay, and she'd almost forgotten he was there. She leaned down close, an eye on their captors. Their attention remained on Tom's torture. She whispered, "Andrew, wake up."

"I'm 'wake, Jaide." He moved his head enough to peek over the edge of the blanket at her.

"Shh. I need you to do something very important, and you have to be very quiet. Like when you play hide and seek with..." She choked on the name. "Shayne."

Andrew's head bobbed beneath the blanket.

"In the stalls over there Ray dropped a tub of clothes and shoes. My gun was inside. I need you to bring me my gun."

Andrew sat up, his eyes flicking to the others, who were lying on the hay. He whispered loudly. "You said I never to touch guns."

Glancing at the invaders to be sure no one had heard, Jaide leaned close to the boy's ear. "I know, Andrew. I don't want you to shoot it, just to bring it here. Are you big enough to do that?"

He nodded slowly.

Jaide scanned the attackers. Tom was lying atop Suzanne and rutting noisily while another of the men did the same with one of the blue-parka girls. Gator had gone outside to the bonfire. The fourth man and the braided woman each appeared to be asleep in their bags. "One more thing, Andrew. These mean people mustn't see you. And they especially can't see the gun. Wrap it in a coat when you bring it to me, okay? And try to sneak so they don't see you at all. If someone stops you, you tell them you're cold, and you wanted a coat."

Andrew's lower lip trembled.

"You're good at hide and seek, remember? You can do it."

"Okay, Jaide." He slithered from beneath the blanket and

crawled over the hay until he slipped down the side near the wall. Jaide forced herself to look away, to not watch his progress in case anyone was watching her. What if he got there and the weapon was gone? Or what if the men caught him? She gritted her teeth and reminded herself that these men would feed on Andrew along with the rest of her friends unless she could defeat them. The gun might be their only hope.

She eased to her side, spooning Flora's body. "Love, how're you doing?"

After a pause, Flora's shoulders moved in a shrug beneath the blanket.

"Have the contractions stopped?"

"I guess." Flora's voice sounded weak.

"Did you hear what I told Andrew?"

"No."

Jaide exhaled slowly. "He's going to get a gun. But you're going to have to use it."

Flora rolled onto her back. Her dull eyes had a spark deep inside. "Gladly."

Gator returned to the barn, his gaze skimming the prisoners. Seeming content, he strode to the sleeping man as if to wake him, then paused. Slowly, he looked back over his shoulder. Equally slowly, he turned to face them. His hand drew a huge pistol from his belt.

Just then, Andrew emerged from the corridor between the stalls. He wore a long-sleeved fleece jacket that reached below his knees. When he saw Gator looking at him, he froze.

In what seemed like two strides, Gator was on him, free hand jerking the collar of the jacket. He shook the child, making Andrew's head flop back and forth. "Where did you go?"

Andrew started crying.

"Maybe we'll have veal for breakfast after all." Gator raised the pistol to the boy's head.

"He was cold!" Jaide shouted, leaning on one elbow in an attempt to bring herself upright. "He went looking for a coat! That's all! We're all cold!"

Gator dropped the child in a heap. "Give me the coat."

Andrew slipped free of the big jacket. Sniffling, he held it out to the man. Jaide held her breath. They were all dead. Gator would find the gun in a pocket and execute the boy on the spot. Or worse, torture him in front of her as punishment.

But Gator's search of the pockets bore nothing. He shifted his attention to the huddled prisoners and tossed the coat back at the boy. "Don't let him wander off again."

Jaide nodded furiously, swallowing hard. Andrew pulled the coat over his shoulders once more before running back to her side. He dropped to his knees and pressed his face into her lap, crying.

"It's okay, Andrew." The lack of a gun felt like a punch in the gut. Might it still be lying at the bottom of the tunnel? She doubted Gator would forgive a second trip. At least the little boy had something to keep him warm now. "You did good."

Andrew sniffled again and moved his hands inside the voluminous jacket. The shiny cylinder of a gun barrel slid up through the collar and onto her lap.

With a gasp, Jaide twisted so he tumbled to the hay, hidden from the attackers by her legs.

"I hided it in my pants like you do."

Jaide wanted to cry. To hug him. She whispered, "Give it to Flora."

Andrew crawled up Flora's side and slid the gun beneath the blanket.

Sitting up, Jaide looked at the faces of her friends. She needed a distraction. Something to allow Flora time to set up and aim. But without being able to talk, arranging something was going to be difficult.

Before Jaide could form a plan, Flora flipped the blanket off and rolled over onto her knees. "It's coming."

Jaide's heart cramped. Now? She remained frozen, unsure what to do. If she called for help, someone would find the gun. If she didn't, could Flora deliver on her own? None of the attackers seemed inclined to come over and lend aid.

Flora rocked back onto her heels and met Jaide's eye with a wink. Then she pushed to her knees, swiveled, and raised the gun.

The girl's aim had improved. The first blast hit Gator square in the chest, releasing a spray of blood. He jerked backward off his feet and collapsed onto the woman in the sleeping bag. Flora's second shot took out the woman. The other three men scrambled for weapons. Flora swung her aim and blasted a hole square in one's forehead. The girl who'd been beneath him curled into a ball with her hands over her head.

The sleeping man's bag zipper was stuck, and he flailed to get free of the cocoon. "Don't kill me. Please. I only joined them because they threatened to kill me."

Flora seemed not to hear. She fired, and the man bucked. Inch-worming up onto his knees, he crawled for the door. Her next shot rammed through the side of his neck and he collapsed, gurgling, onto his belly.

Tom was on his feet, pants around his ankles. He held Suzanne in front of him, knife to her throat. "I'll kill her."

"You murdered Shayne!" Flora's voice screeched like metal against metal. Her abdomen tightened in a contraction.

Kicking free of his pants, he dragged Suzanne backward to the door.

"Just shoot him!" Suzanne screamed, "Shoot us both!"

Lucas had risen to his knees. "No!"

Flora fired anyway, splintering a hole in the wood above Tom's head. Tom flinched but continued shouldering backward through the door. In a moment, he'd be outside and out of sight.

Flora rocked awkwardly to her feet. Taking a deep breath, she squeezed the trigger again.

Click.

Tom stopped moving, an evil grin taking over his entire face. Flinging Suzanne aside, he advanced back into the barn. He waved the knife sinuously in front of his face. "I'm going to cut that brat right out of your belly, and you can watch while I eat it."

Another contraction doubled Flora over. The gun slid from her grip. Jaide tried to stand. To put herself between Tom and her daughter. She got her feet under her, but the chain kept her from rising. She shouted, "All of you, get up! Together we can take him!"

Tom narrowed his eyes. His gaze flicked to the ground where Gator had dropped his pistol. Cocking his head, he languidly picked up the weapon, his eyes locked on Jaide.

Beside her, the others were attempting to rise, struggling and falling in the cushion of hay, jerking those who had gained their feet back down.

Near the exit, Suzanne stood with her clothes in tatters around her limbs. Blood scored her skin from Tom's knife marks, ran in trails down her thighs. In the half light of dawn, her face was an unrecognizable mask of bruised blood and righteous fury. A strangled cry rose from her lips.

She lowered her head and charged.

The impact to Tom's kidneys sent him flying forward. He flung both hands out to break his fall. The knife in his left hand pointed upright like a lance, and Jaide watched in mute fascination as he fell in slow motion toward it. As he hit the ground, the tip of the knife drove itself into his eye.

His body twitched once and then lay still.

For a moment, no one moved. It seemed no one breathed. Flora supported herself with her hands on her knees, panting loudly. Then, like a falling tree, she toppled over. The legs of her pajamas were stained crimson.

"Flora!" Jaide jerked her wrists against her bindings.

"The knife." Chia waded forward on her knees toward the fallen Tom. Her baby cried and thrashed against the fabric binding her to her mother.

Suzanne lay on the floor where she'd fallen after tackling Tom, her knees drawn to her chest in a fetal position.

Chia wriggled the knife loose, and soon Jaide was free. She knelt by Flora's side, pulling the drawstring of her daughter's pajama bottoms loose. "Lucas, help."

Lucas stood frozen, knee deep in hay as he looked at his daughter. The cuts on his cheeks gaped, exposing raw muscle. Dried blood caked his chin and beard and clumped in his eyelashes.

Flora cried out, her limbs bunching and shuddering like a dying insect.

"Lucas!" Jaide screeched. She felt bad for Suzanne, but Flora was dying right now.

He shuddered and came to kneel at Flora's opposite side.

Flora's stomach rippled. She moaned, "Nooo."

"Flora, I think it's time to push." Lucas gripped her arm. "Do you want to squat?"

Flora lay there shaking her head, tears streaming from the corners of her eyes. "No. Take it back."

Jaide gripped her daughter's other arm and tried to pull her up. "Be strong for your baby."

"I don't want it anymore," Flora slurred. "I only want Shayne."

Jaide's chest and throat clamped tight against her own grief. "Flora, Shayne would want you to fight for this baby, don't you think? He wouldn't want everything you've gone through to be wasted. Now get up and push."

After a second, Flora forced herself to roll over onto her knees. She moaned with a contraction, bearing down.

"That's fine. If that feels best, do that." Lucas slid the gray blanket over the hay below her. Blood dribbled in looping strands over the gray fabric.

"I'll get some water," Martha said.

"Clean that knife, too," Lucas called.

"What about them?" Roger asked. Jaide vaguely saw him point to one of the blue-parka women.

"Please don't hurt us," she said. "We were prisoners like you."

Jaide didn't have time for logistics. Didn't care what happened to those women. She had little attention to spare for anything but Flora.

In numbness, she watched her grandchild emerge into a world of death and blood.

Chapter Thirty-Six

FEBRUARY

The Knife shall come to the Knowing last, for without them,
there is no past.

~ MOTHER'S PROVERB

As soon as Flora could walk, they headed south in search of both warmer weather and food. Suzanne had stashed two bug-out bags in the barn loft earlier that fall, but rodents had gotten into the food, leaving nothing but droppings behind. That left them with a few knives, the attackers' guns and the ammo in them, and whatever clothing they salvaged from Jaide's fallen tub. Ray had decided the two female prisoners could join them, and no one argued; with nothing to share, there was nothing to lose.

Flora walked with zombie footsteps, clutching her newborn son to her breast. Her milk refused to come in, and the baby barely left the nipple. The child had wailed like an emergency siren the first two days but now remained silent. Jaide stayed close and looked with anguish at a grandson surely too small to survive these harsh conditions.

After a shootout and flight from the main street at a no-name town, they decided to avoid humans of any kind. Anyone holding a territory wanted one of two things; to drive off intruders by any means necessary, much as Jaide and the others had done at the farm, or to lure travelers closer for more nefarious purposes.

Following the waterways, Jaide dug cattail roots until her fingers bled. They stopped at every abandoned house along the way, shucking summer shoes for warmer footwear as they found it. They layered coats and other clothing over their own. Anything remotely edible they boiled, from leather shoes to seashell displays.

In one attic, Jaide discovered a box of Christmas decorations full of rock-hard ornament cookies. She carried the box down to where they'd set up a camp in the living room. Mattresses and upholstered furniture created a shelter that felt a lot like the blanket tents she'd created while growing up, but the faces around the smoky lamplight didn't look like childhood friends. Scabs and scars and the sallow creep of starvation lined these faces.

Jaide pulled an ornament out of the box. "Anyone want cookie stew?"

A chorus of excitement greeted her. Her gaze found Flora, slumped on a sofa. Her daughter hadn't even looked up. The baby rooted against her breast.

"Flora, we should name your baby tonight." Flora had refused to pick a name. Had barely spoken since the attack. "We can have a celebration."

"Why? It's just going to die. We all are."

The celebratory mood in the room evaporated. Heaviness in Jaide's heart threatened to pull her into the earth. Every night she told stories, trying to keep spirits alive along with bodies. But hope was getting harder and harder to muster. "We don't know what lies over the hill. Tomorrow something could save us all."

"You're deluded, Mom. Just like always, your ideals are empty promises."

Jaide straightened her spine. She lowered the box to the coffee table. "Many times in my life I've had nothing but hope, Flora. When you give up hope, then you're surely doomed."

"We can't eat hope."

Swallowing, Jaide scrounged her mind for a saying or story to lift the mood. Her eyes met Lucas's. He pointed to the box. "But we can eat those, right?"

The scabs on his cheeks were dark lines, scars he'd bear forever no matter what lay ahead. They all bore scars, both inside and out. Those scars created a web of survival. A web of hope. "Yes." She smiled at him. "Christmas in... February? Is it February?"

Ray nodded. "Think so." His voice had been hoarse since the attack, a rasping whisper no matter how loud he tried to yell. Lucas said his vocal cords had probably been damaged.

Suzanne slid forward on the carpet and looked inside the box. One at a time, she removed the cookies, plopping them into the small pan over the flame. "One, two, three..." She reached seven and stopped. "There are three more. We should save them for tomorrow. Seven is a lucky number, and so is three."

The rape seemed to have strengthened her spirit rather than weakened it. She found a mysticism in everything around her, counting lucky and unlucky omens at least once a day.

Jaide's stomach wanted to take control of her mind. The thought of keeping back food for tomorrow when they were so hungry today went against every cell in her body. But keeping food back meant they had hope for tomorrow, and that was what Flora needed to see. Opening the small pack Ray carried, she said, "Good idea. Ray can carry them, don't you think?"

Chia leaned forward, pointing to her own pack. "Three cookies, three packs. Losing one mustn't mean losing all."

"Even better," Jaide acknowledged. "One in Ray's, one in Chia's, and one in Lucas's."

The scent of cinnamon from the softening cookies permeated the room. She settled onto the sofa near Flora. "Tonight I want to tell a story about hope. About a group of people who became a family as the world crumbled to chaos around them..."

Chapter Thirty-Seven

The wasted body is dishonored among the Tribe, fit only for the spirits of the Tox.
—THE HISTORIES

Ten days into their exodus—or was it eleven? Jaide had lost count—the hope she'd painted froze, shattered, and blew away on a winter storm. They fought blindly through the blowing snow to reach a solitary farmhouse Ray had spotted before the weather had turned from bad to terrible.

The house was frigid, not much warmer than outside, but at least shielded from the wind. The group pulled plush furniture and clothing into a nest-like circle in the living room and slid a window open a crack for ventilation against the sooty, used-motor-oil lamp. The small flame worked for light as well as cooking, but today they had nothing to cook, not even a scrap of a leather belt.

Ray lit the wick anyway, sending a dark spiral of smoke toward the ceiling. A circle of emaciated faces stared listlessly at the flame, shoulders hunched beneath layers of blankets. The gnawing root of hunger in Jaide's gut had reached into her bones and wrapped tight around her soul until she no longer felt it as sensation, only awareness. They'd been rationing before the attack, but now starvation loomed in stark reality.

Keeping Flora and the baby alive was all that drove her. She leaned over to peer into the space inside Flora's blanket. The baby hadn't made a sound all day that Jaide was aware of. Chia's child wasn't much better, and Andrew maintained a round-eyed silence like something out of a horror film.

Remembering the Christmas cookies, Jaide rose. There had to be some small thing in this house that might provide nourishment. Or hope. "I'm going to search."

The only reply anyone could muster was Lucas shrugging his shoulders slightly beneath his mountain of blankets.

She dragged herself to her feet, taking her blanket-shroud with her. Summoning all her energy, she lifted first one leg then the other over the barrier around their interior camp. After the first step to the second level, she paused and rested a shoulder against the wall. The next step was no easier. Her heartbeat thudded like a bass drum in her ears.

By the time she reached the top, she was panting, her lips dry and cracked in the winter air. The landing split two directions, left and right. She turned right, entering an attic bedroom, dusky with cloud-filtered daylight. Posters of rock stars and celebrities plastered the walls, and near the single dormer window, a long, low dresser held an assortment of makeup and perfume. A ruffled double bed sat with its headboard against the sloped wall.

Jaide shuffled to the dresser to fumble through the bottles. The powder blush and eye shadow boxes were nothing but empty circles of plastic, and the perfume had been drained. Opening one drawer after another, Jaide dug through underwear and fashion T-shirts.

She dropped to her knees, resting her forehead against the cold dresser surface. Her insides trembled with exhaustion and cold. Turning to sit with her back against the drawers, she eyed the bed. The blankets were lumpy, as if the girl who'd lived here still slumbered beneath them.

Drawing on what meager reserves she could, Jaide dragged herself forward and pulled herself up onto the mattress. Sleep sounded so good right now, the comfort of a warm bed. She clawed at the covers, exposing a mop of red-gold hair upon the pillow.

Her breath caught. She pulled the covers away, exposing the sleeping face of a teenage girl, lips blue with cold. Heart thudding, Jaide reached out to shake her.

The girl was frozen like a slab of meat.

In spite of the hollow cheeks and skinny arms, the girl looked peaceful. Rucking up the blanket, Jaide's fingers wrapped around the curve of a calf. Traveled up the leg, past the thigh, to the roundness of a buttocks. There was still some muscle on this body. Still some meat.

She jerked her hand away at the thought, blinking rapidly as if waking from a daze. How could she entertain such thoughts? And yet saliva filled her mouth at the idea of meat cooking over Ray's little lamp.

Would eating this child be so wrong?

She backed up a step and sank to a squat, her back against the dresser once more, unable to look away from the bed. What little flesh existed on this carcass would feed the group for several days. Would the group even consider such an idea? Would Flora? How far would she go to save the newborn baby who grew weaker every day?

The light from the window softened and deepened as Jaide warred within herself.

A voice calling her name drew her from her thoughts.

"Here," she whispered, hesitant to draw another into her crazy idea.

Lucas appeared in the doorway. "There you are. Are you okay?"

She nodded, then shook her head and covered her face with one gloved hand. His shuffling footsteps entered the room and paused by the bed. After a few minutes, she looked up to see him staring at the corpse.

"I thought about it," she said. He would know what she meant. Anyone as hungry as she was would know what she meant.

He licked his lips and backed away a step. His eyes were huge below his deep-set brows. Slow as a wilting leaf, his chin dropped to his chest then rose again in a nod, the movement becoming more vigorous as his resolve solidified. "We should."

"Will the others...?" She didn't want to say the words. Eat. Meat. Food. Human.

He squeezed his eyes shut, opened them, took a big breath. "Let's take the body downstairs."

Together, they rolled the body into a blanket sling and half dragged, half carried it down the hall. The carcass bumped the stairs all the way down, thumping with irregular beats as Jaide attempted to keep her balance under the heavy load. They left the burden at the bottom and returned to the living room camp.

"We found a body." Jaide spoke from outside the furniture circle. "Frozen solid in one of the beds."

Martha shook her head. "So many dead."

Jaide swallowed, seeking her daughter's huddled form. "It's meat."

Several people gasped. Jaide kept her gaze on Flora, who continued to stare down into the dark place between her breasts.

Lucas stepped over the sofa and bent to retrieve the daypack he'd been carrying while they walked. "We'll share with those who want. No pressure for those who don't."

"That's cannibalism!" Edward said, scooting backward against the floor until his way was stopped by a recliner.

Jaide sucked in a huge breath. This was cannibalism. There was no denying it. But to survive, they had to embrace the change in thinking. "If we don't use her, she'll just become food for bacteria and animals. I didn't kill this person. But there's no soul left in that body. It's just meat now, for me or for some other creature. So I'm going to use it before something or someone else does."

Martha pulled her blankets tight around her face and began crying softly. Ray put an arm around her. Chia rose. The baby she kept strapped to her chest whimpered weakly. "I will help. I hope to see a brighter future someday, and I can't do that if I don't survive today."

Chapter Thirty-Eight

MARCH

Each person in their time, as they give the Knife, so shall they take the Knife. The living shall take the Knife as quietly as the dead, that none shall be wasted.
—THE HISTORIES

Through the remaining days of winter, Jaide watched for the first green shoots of spring, imagining a time of celebration. Slowly, the snow melted. Warmer weather allowed them to shed their heavy clothes. Brown earth gave way to tiny seedlings.

Amarantox seedlings.

The houses and farms they scoured became sparser in their offerings as other scavengers reached the leavings before them. Cattail beds along the rivers diminished, Jaide assumed picked clean by fellow survivors. And the few bands of people they saw fired upon them without asking questions.

Early one spring morning, in the unnatural stillness of a world devoid of wildlife, Martha refused to rise. Ray lifted her in his arms, insisting he could carry her. But beneath her weight, he couldn't take more than three or four steps before collapsing. He lowered her skeletal frame to the damp spring earth.

Kneeling beside her, he rasped, "Don't leave me."

Jaide stood with the others around their friend.

Martha's eyes were dull beneath the springtime sun. "I want my boys to survive."

Roger dropped beside her and took her hand. "We are, Mom."

Edward lowered his forehead to his mother's shoulder, weeping openly.

"No, you're not." Martha stroked her younger son's shaggy head. "The cattails here are exhausted. And there's smoke on the horizon. You have to move on."

"We'll find something, Martha," Jaide assured her, but her voice was papery and thin. She'd been giving portions of her food to Flora for the sake of the baby and thought it a miracle she'd been able to rise herself this morning.

Martha closed her eyes, her lids flaky with dry skin. "You have to eat me."

A collective gasp rolled over the group.

"We're not going to eat you," Ray choked out.

Lucas turned away, facing the sunrise.

"I'm dying. Don't waste me." Martha had refused to eat the first body of the girl they'd found. She'd drunk broth from a soup of the second body, a man they'd found dead of a gunshot wound. By the time they'd butchered a third, her survival instinct had altered her morals. She'd become the most adamant among them about not wasting a scrap of the gifts they were given.

To offer the sacrifice of one's own body was more than even Jaide had considered. Yet it made sense.

Ray wobbled to his feet. "I'm not killing my wife!"

Martha lifted a hand into the air. "Give me a knife. I'll do it myself."

"No!" Ray stumbled backward, both hands over his mouth.

Edward sat up, his sobbing cut off, his shoulders stiff. Jaide wondered if he remembered to breathe.

Suzanne pulled her knife from the sheath at her belt and flipped it around to hold it by the blade. With a bow that would have seemed mocking in another life but here held nothing but the greatest respect, she offered the knife to Martha.

"Don't you dare," Ray sputtered. "Don't..."

Jaide's mouth grew dry, her words a breathless, hollow sound. "Martha can't go on. We can leave her here for the buzzards." She forced herself to stand straighter and face the others in the group. "Or we can honor her death by adding it to our lives."

Chia took the knife from Suzanne. "Martha, you're not strong enough to do it yourself."

Martha's gaze met hers, a feverish intensity only another mother might understand. "Then help me. Make it fast. My body for your life."

Lucas spun, his scars livid against his pallid cheeks. "Wait. We need to honor this moment. To remember her sacrifice."

Suzanne nodded agreement. All eyes turned to Jaide.

She took a breath, thinking about how to put this moment into history. Their history. The rising sun warmed her face, while her back remained chilled from the night just past. With slow precision, she met the gaze of each person around her, seeing in them the sorrowful acceptance of what must be done. Chia said, "When it's my time, I want you to honor my death the same way."

"Agreed," several others in the circle muttered.

Remembering the prayer Martha had said over the first man

killed at the farm, Jaide clasped her hands in prayer and dropped her chin. She couldn't remember the exact words, but she wanted to gift Martha by trying. "Hoping for eternal life through Jesus Christ, we ask God to bless Martha's body, and bless her sacrifice for the sake of her loved ones. The Lord bless her and keep her, the Lord make his face shine on her and be gracious to her and give her peace. Ashes to ashes, dust to dust. Amen."

A breathy repetition all around her spoke, "Amen."

Martha's gaze had become feverish with the prayer. Now she nodded, wrapping her hand around Chia's over the knife.

Then Chia drove the blade home.

Epilogue

I'll pass swiftly, without pain.
That my tribe may live again.
—K<small>NIFE</small> S<small>ONG</small>

J aide sat on the rock next to the water, watching Flora's second son splash in the shallows and listening to the Tox rustle languidly on the other side of the river. Lucas and Flora stood calf deep in the water nearby, harvesting fat cattail heads. The brown cylinders reminded Jaide of long-ago sausages, redolent of spices and salt—a life so far in the past, it seemed like a dream. After eight years and more violent encounters than reconciliations with fellow survivors, Jaide's group had swelled to a couple dozen members. Finding food was harder but keeping watch easier as they followed the river to the next harvest grounds.

She looked down at the half-woven mat of reeds in her hands and twined a few more rows, still undecided whether it would become a sleeping mat or carrying sack. The fibers were tough but became soiled easily, and the group was always in need of new items. Her calloused palms were rough from contact with the sharp fronds. Years of hard work had hardened almost everything about her.

Checking on her grandson again, she frowned. He wasn't where he'd been moments ago. A splash to her right drew her eye, and she saw a small, dark head bob above water and go under again. She lurched to her feet. "Paulie!"

Cattail grass tumbling about her feet, she plunged off the bank into the water. A white-hot bolt of pain shot up her leg as she hit bottom, but she kicked out into the current, reaching for the little boy. Her fingers found hair, wrapped tightly, and pulled him close. Half stroking, half hopping toward the bank, she dragged the tiny body with her.

At the muddy shore, she crawled forward, hauling him out of the water. He sputtered and choked.

Flora rushed over. "Oh, thank God. He was there one second and gone the next."

Paulie coughed and cried at the same time, clutching Flora's shirt.

Lucas bent to help Jaide to her feet. "Good catch, Grandma."

She smiled at him and tried to stand. Putting weight on her leg nearly made her black out. She looked down to see a white spire of bone poking from her shin, blood and muck mixing together and furling away in the flowing water.

After a moment to catch her breath, she turned back to her family. Lucas's face had gone ashen. Flora's mouth hung open, her head twisting back and forth in silent negation.

Beyond them, Suzanne arrived carrying empty baskets from camp, her toddler on her back. Flora's older boy, Little Shayne, walked by her side, chattering about the beetle he'd found. Suzanne slowed as she approached, and the chatter fell silent.

Jaide squeezed Lucas's hand, and he bent, scooping her in

his arms to carry her to dry ground. He lowered her gently among the reeds she'd been weaving. "I can set it. You might be okay."

She shook her head, fighting waves of nausea from the pain. Ray had fallen two summers ago and broken his arm the same way. They'd waited until infection set in. Then Lucas amputated. They'd scoured every house or town they came to for drugs, but nothing remained of the old world. Ray had died when the blood poisoning reached his heart.

"It's my time," Jaide said.

"We can't," Flora said firmly. "No."

Jaide sucked in a big breath of coppery-scented air. Was that her blood? Or the ever-present scent of amarantox? She blew out a slow breath, fighting waves of nausea. "Love, I can't walk on a broken leg. And we've been here three days already."

"You can ride the travois," Lucas said, stroking wet strands of hair off her face. "I'll pull you."

"Who will help me watch the boys if you're gone?" Flora pried Paulie from her shoulder so she could clutch Jaide's hand with both of hers.

"Don't wait until I'm spoiled by infection." Jaide wrapped her fingers around Flora's and brought her daughter's palm to her lips. She reached out her other hand to stroke the back of Paulie's head. Her leg throbbed, the pain a spiral she would follow into death. Her life was done, and she was okay with that. "I'm ready for the Knife."

Flora was openly sobbing now, and Jaide blinked back a film of tears in her own eyes.

Lucas again scooped her into his arms. "I'm not ready to lose you."

She hugged him back, relishing the scent of him. "We've had an amazing journey together. Thank you for always believing in me."

His breathing hitched ragged where she cuddled against his heart.

Over his shoulder, she met her daughter's tear-stained gaze. Flora tried to smile, her lips trembling. "I'll tell your stories, Mom. We'll all tell your stories, forever and ever."

"That's how I'll be with you. Always." Jaide's foot and leg felt hot and cold in cycling intervals, like the ever-slowing beating of a heart. Letting her head fall back, she peered into Lucas's face. She wanted to engrave it into her last moments. "Lucas, look at me."

He lowered his face to hers and kissed her before pulling back to stare into her eyes. Tears rolled down his cheeks, mimicking the scars left there so many years ago.

"I love you, Lucas." A light-headedness had come over her, perhaps from blood loss. Or perhaps she was just letting go. "Take me to the others. To say goodbye to the tribe."

His voice was rough when he spoke. "Anything you ask. I love you, too."

Joined by her family, he carried her down the trail in reverent silence.

THE END

Dear Reader,

Thank you so much for reading this series! I'm always honored when people read my books. Amarantox hit a little close to home as I wrote it while raising my kids and watching them make choices beyond my control. Have you ever felt helpless in the face of major changes?

This book was a prequel, and if you have not read

Botanicaust, Book One yet, you can jump to it by tapping here.

If you've read them all, be sure you're signed up for my newsletter to get your free novella plus the latest information about upcoming releases.

Until next time, best of luck in the apocalypse!
Tam Linsey

P.S. If you like sci-fi with a lot of steamy romance (be warned, mature audiences only!) my other pen name has an alien pirate series you might enjoy. Check it out here.

His kiss sends pleasure through her beyond all imagining. But when she discovers just how dangerous his touch can be, will she risk life as she knows it for a chance of forever by his side?

Books by Tam Linsey

Botanicaust

The Reaping Room

Doomseeds

Amarantox

About the Author

Tam Linsey is a lifelong Alaskan who is obsessed with self-sufficiency. In spite of the rigors of living in the High North, she grows, hunts, or fishes for much of her family's food needs. She believes that we should have the right to choose what we eat, and therefore is also a GMO labeling advocate (not to be confused with a GMO opponent.) When she is not writing, she'd probably in the garden or the kitchen, exploring Alaska with her husband, or preparing for the zombie apocalypse. She also loves wine and hard apple cider, is mediocre at crochet, and has an adorable 12-pound bunny named Abigail.

Join the Botanicaust Tribe and get a free book by signing up for the newsletter at http://geni.us/tam-linsey